The Winged Horse

A FIVE DIRECTIONS PRESS BOOK

The Winged Horse

A NOVEL

C. P. LESLEY

LEGENDS OF THE FIVE DIRECTIONS 2: EAST

ISBN-13 978-0615980218
ISBN-10 061598021X

Published in the United States of America.

A Five Directions Press book

Cover photographs: Horse in silhouette © andreiuc/Shutterstock; Kazakh jurt © Konstantin Kikvidze/Photos.com. Map on page ii adapted from "Map of the Volga River System," © Karl Musser (reused under Creative Commons Attribution-Share Alike 2.5 Generic license). Pegasus on half-title page © Cattallina/ Shutterstock.

Book and cover design by Five Directions Press
Five Directions Press logo designed by Colleen Kelley

FIVE DIRECTIONS PRESS

CONTENTS

The Journey of Ogodai's Horde

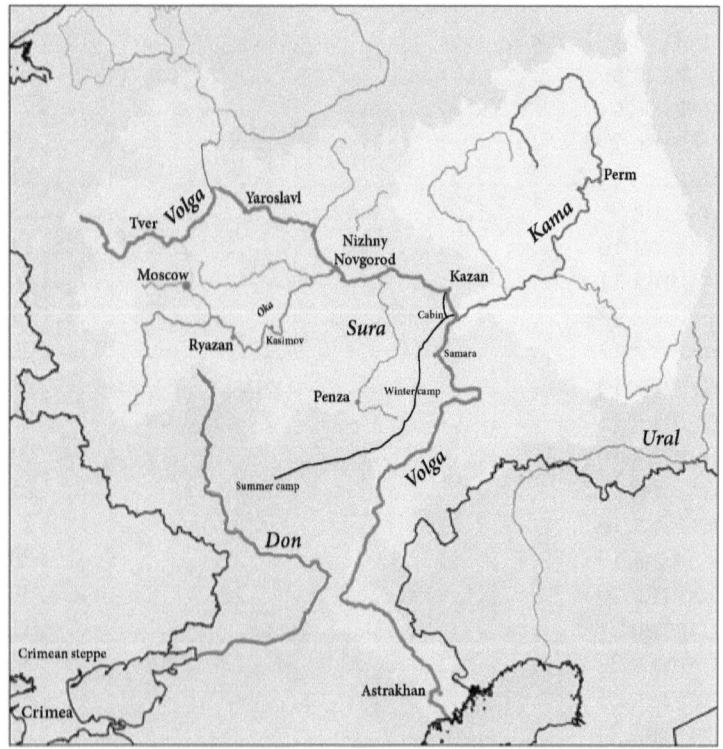

Includes the migration of Bahadur's horde from its summer
grazing lands east of the Don.

Chapter 1

THE RUSTLING OUTSIDE THE FELT TENT STILLED AS THE SUN set over the grasslands. Even the lambs hushed. An owl hooted; a wolf howled in the distance. The guard dogs barked in response, but the high, keening wail drifted away on the wind. Bahadur Bey, head of a nomadic Tatar horde, relaxed against the embroidered cushions that placed him north and center relative to the other diners and reached for the quail leg he had dropped when he heard the howl. One wolf, far away, could not threaten a community of forty or fifty households—nor even its sheep and goats, penned for the night.

The quail leg disappeared in a bite or two. Bahadur licked his lips and savored the lingering richness on his tongue— molten fat flecked with salt, gaminess mixed with herbs.

A few too many herbs, in fact. That tinge of bitterness, although not unpleasant in itself, could easily be overdone. A point to bring up with the cooks tomorrow morning.

Platters of food, stripped almost bare, dotted the felt mats laid over the rugs that protected the diners from the thin grass of the steppe. Elaborately decorated, many of the felts bore the stylized form of the winged horse, Bahadur's banner. His camp, his home: here among family and friends, even a bey could lay down the burdens of leadership at the end of a long day.

In addition to the quail, always a favorite, the platters held braised venison and flat bread, hard and soft cheeses, pomegranates and nuts. Bahadur had drunk deep from pitchers filled with frothy mare's milk and shared cups from a cask of wine, warm with the sunshine of the Crimean hills. One good thing left behind by that scoundrel Tulpar. Its taste lingered on the tongue in happy marriage with the quail.

He considered eating more, but his sash already felt tight to the point of discomfort, and the light slanting through the smoke hole reinforced the message delivered by the quieting of the herds. In the steppe, the midsummer sun hid itself for so short a time that if he did not retire to his private tent to sleep as soon as night fell, he would find himself on horseback again before his muscles ceased to ache. Once he had caroused the night away, as his son Jahangir did, but no more. The counsel of age and wisdom told him he had eaten enough, drunk enough. Time to rest.

Outside, the wind was picking up. "Hear that?" he said to his chief herdsman, seated not far from the door. "Better get the lambs and the weaker animals under cover. It will storm before morning. Check the pens, too."

The herdsman bowed in acknowledgment and ducked from the tent without more ado. A good man, knew his business. Always placed the needs of the animals first, aware that the tribe depended on the herds.

Time for Bahadur, too, to go before the weather changed.

With a sigh, he pushed himself upright. His right knee gave way under his weight, and he staggered. The reception tent rocked as he grabbed at the trellised frame for support. Woven hangings released puffs of dust as they shushed from side to side, setting off a flurry of coughs.

"We must change them," Diliara, his chief wife, said from the women's side of the tent. She pointed at the hangings. "I will order it done tomorrow. After six weeks in place, they have picked up a lot of dirt."

"Yes, do." Bahadur smiled at her. "We have at least another month here before we need to move the herds." Against the fading light, the rich reds and golds of the cloth softened her features, recalling the beauty he had known in their youth. Diliara had once been the jewel of his harem, her physical gifts enhanced by a sweet and generous spirit. These days, she hid the signs of aging with a plethora of veils, but graying hair and a thickening body could not conceal the loveliness of the soul within. Of his many wives, Diliara occupied a special place in his heart. She had raised his twins after his first wife's death and never complained, even when her body failed to produce children of its own.

A silvery gurgle drew his attention in another direction. Roxelana, his concubine of the moment, wrestled playfully with his eldest son, Jahangir, seated on the cushion next to her. Her long brown legs thrashed in their flimsy rose-colored trousers, narrowly missing Jahangir's goblet. A servant dashed forward and wrenched an endangered pitcher off the table, earning a kick from an embroidered royal-blue slipper for his pains.

"Stop tickling her, Jahangir," Bahadur said. His knee gave way again, adding to his irritation. "What are you, an infant?"

Jahangir sputtered half-concealed laughter into his goblet as the four clan leaders who together constituted Bahadur's council stood to bid the bey goodnight. The leaders frowned. Roxelana rallied enough to deliver a smart slap to her tormentor. Jahangir subsided, although an occasional snort escaped him.

A strong young arm caught Bahadur's elbow. "Here, *Ata*," his daughter Firuza said. "Let me help you."

She had noticed the problem with his leg and come to his aid. Bahadur patted her hair to show his gratitude. She blushed, eyes on his boots, ignoring the byplay between her brother and Roxelana.

Out of innocence, perhaps. Or an awareness of her own shortcomings. Although eighteen, only a year younger than the concubine, Firuza could not match Roxelana for allure. No slinky elegance or sultry mystery here. Firuza was nothing if not straightforward—open, generous, and competent, with an air of untouched purity appropriate for a maiden destined to become a khan's chief wife. Slender, tall for a woman, with the dark hair and eyes of her Mongol ancestors, Firuza had a mind like a general, a face that spoke of intelligence and character, and a trim, compact body. He had never known her to shirk a burden, even one posed by a well-fed, somewhat inebriated father with a gimpy knee.

Indeed, the girl needed to stand up for herself more. Stop protecting that worthless brother of hers. Look at him—drunk and flirting with his father's woman!

Bahadur flexed and straightened the knee and found only a lingering weakness and a slight, persistent ache. "Send for the shaman," he said. "Tell her I need her potion—and make it strong. Not that namby-pamby pap she offered me the last time. What's the point of a medicine too weak to do any good?"

"But, *Ata*," his daughter protested. "She said you must not take too much."

He reacted without thinking. "Ah, what does she know, the old fuss-budget? Tulpar brought the recipe from Crimea. It's not even her potion. Fetch her to my tent, girl, and accept no nonsense."

Silenced, she lowered her eyes and retreated, hands tucked in her sleeves. Diliara cast a reproachful glance in his direction.

She was right. He had over-reacted. The girl was only expressing concern for his welfare. Whereas her brother...

Bahadur turned his head at a sound he could scarce believe. Jahangir, chuckling into his wine, so lost to propriety that he found his father's debility amusing.

"Really, Prince," a disapproving voice said before Bahadur could muster the words. "A son should respect his father."

The voice belonged to Kazbek Argyn, the second most powerful man on Bahadur's council—an aging warrior who still swung a sword and shot a bow with a skill equal to Bahadur's own. They had been younger than Jahangir when Kazbek swore his oath of fealty, and Argyn had never wavered in the years that followed.

Nor had he lost an ounce of his military style. The silk caftan and velvet sash he wore for tonight's dinner looked out of place on that massive frame. The shaved head under his skullcap scorned the frivolous side locks and short braids that distinguished most of the men present; his mustache and beard were trimmed short. In peace as in war, Kazbek carried himself as if he sported leather armor and a sword.

"Oh, leave the boy alone," Ildar Shirin, the council leader, responded. "Can't you see that he would find anything funny at this moment?"

Bahadur shook his head, unsurprised. Name any topic, and if Kazbek said yes, Ildar would vote no, and vice versa. Yet they were friends, comrades—his right and left hands. Ildar was older than the other clan leaders, and in his weakening limbs and graying hair Bahadur saw his own future. These days, Ildar favored satin robes and tall, embroidered felt hats that hid his snowy fringe of hair. Tonight's version was gold. His beard straggled, despite his servants' efforts to keep it neat.

"Not laughing at *Ata*. At my sister." Jahangir sniggered. "Did you see her face?"

Bahadur staggered again as he moved to chastise his unruly heir. A heavy hand on his son's shoulder kept him from falling. "Insolent pup!" he told the boy. "Ildar gives you too much credit. Your sister tried to help. Why not you?"

The empty bowl of Jahangir's goblet answered that question. Another young man, brown-haired and brown-eyed, rose smoothly from the cushions and stepped around his drunken prince. "Allow me, Bey."

Rafik Argyn, son of Kazbek. A more satisfactory offspring than his own. Bahadur, tempted to refuse the young man's offer, sensed tremors in his legs. Where were the shaman and her potion?

Heading for his tent, no doubt, as he had ordered. Pride had become a luxury he could not afford. He took Rafik's outstretched arm.

"It's the weather," he said. "My knees ache at the approach of rain." Rafik murmured a courteous assent.

Sore knees were nothing. A momentary discomfort, which a night's sleep would cure. While he argued with his children, the light had faded. Stars showed through the smoke hole in the center of the tent.

Yet he had enjoyed the dinner—echoes of the past, the fellowship of family and old friends, more often apart than together these days. The sound of Roxelana's glorious voice, the sight of her lissome body dancing to the strumming of the *rebab* she had brought from her home among the Sarts of Chorasan and taught her servant to play. He had hoped to follow up on that dance when he had her alone.

Instead, he felt weak. Tired. His belly ached as well as his knees. He had become an old man without noticing.

Rafik waited—his face polite, deferential. Bahadur took one cautious step, then another. "My tent," he said. Bowing to the inevitable, he added, "Roxelana, you need not attend me tonight. I plan to rest."

She raised a sweetmeat in acknowledgment. The council members repeated their goodnights. Jahangir lounged amid the silken cushions. A wave of his goblet signaled his farewell. Bahadur tried not to groan as he inched toward the door, supported by Rafik.

Grandmothers, grant me many years. His people were doomed if they had to depend on Jahangir to lead them. Why, Firuza would make a better ruler, had she not been born a girl!

Inside his tent, Firuza greeted him with a small bow—hands clasped, eyes lowered. He patted her head in unspoken apology. Next to her stood the shaman in full regalia: painted drum, beaded cape, feathered cap rimmed with fur, cloth bag holding equipment she might need. Thin plaits hung down over her face, obscuring her features. As he entered, she knelt. The silver cup between her outstretched hands glowed dark within.

The short walk had tired Bahadur further. He permitted Rafik to ease him onto his sleeping felts. A nod to Firuza brought the cup to his hands. Another dismissed Rafik. The healer smudged the room with beneficial herbs, banged her drum, and prayed until Bahadur lost patience with her and shouted at her to stop.

Startled, she dropped the drum. It reverberated against the ground. She snatched it up and stilled it against her robes.

He downed the potion, grimacing. Honey could not offset the bitterness of the brew; the liquid numbed his tongue to fuzz as it slid down his throat. The flames of the small oil lamps that lit the tent set the air to shimmering. He handed the cup to Firuza and touched his forehead. Too much wine, too much koumiss. His temples throbbed.

"Are you unwell, *Ata*?" she asked.

"No." He blinked. Everything before his eyes had acquired colored edges. The tightness in his stomach intensified into discomfort, hinting at pain. "I need rest, that's all. Give this to the shaman and go. Both of you."

Firuza passed the cup to its owner. "Should I send your servant? Who will help you prepare for bed?"

Another person who would make noise, demand attention—unbearable. Bahadur stuck out a foot. "Remove my boots, daughter, and I will handle the rest myself. Let no one interrupt me."

"Yes, *Ata*." Firuza did as he asked, took the turban from his head, and—blessedly silent—undid the fastenings on his coat. Then she headed for the door.

As her body crossed the light, a flash of metal caught his eye. "Firuza," he called.

She turned, instantly responsive to his voice. "Behind you," he said. "What is that?"

Firuza stopped and investigated. "A medallion, *Ata*, carved with a winged horse."

Medallion? Winged horse? Truly? Excitement chased the trembling from his gut. "Give it to me, then, before you go."

Firuza dropped her find into his waiting hand, then left. The shaman—drumming, praying, mumbling soothing phrases—followed her.

Bahadur, alone at last, tossed his outer robe to one side and lay among the felts. Awe touched his heart. It was indeed his lost medallion. Where had it lain for so long?

He cradled the emblem in his palm, marveling at its beauty. The pewter talisman weighed heavy in his hand. He twisted it this way and that, watching the metal catch the light. A stylized horse pranced among the clouds against a sky formed from drops of turquoise. The animal's mane and tail flew in the breeze created by its passing; graceful wings held it aloft. Not an abstract pattern like those on the felts and hangings but a recognizable steed, a replica of the emblem gold-embroidered on his tribe's banners.

A gift from his *qarïndash*—sworn brother—Bulat. The father of Firuza's betrothed. Not that Bulat and Bahadur had ever been true equals—as a descendant of Genghis, Bulat had always stood apart and above. But when Bahadur had taken the arrow aimed at Bulat Khan, the khan had declared them *qarïndashlar* and offered to join their children in marriage. A great opportunity, not to be scorned.

Bahadur's heart warmed at the memory. Although when Bulat failed to complete the contract, Bahadur had hesitated to prod him, lest the boon he had earned vanish like the dew at dawn.

The talisman had disappeared not long after Bulat left the camp. Odd that it should surface now.

A sign, Bahadur decided, that he should settle his daughter's future. Why, he had not seen Bulat's son since the boy turned twelve!

How old must he be, Bulat's son Ogodai? Bahadur counted on his fingers, then recalled that he had no need. A moon or so older than the twins, Firuza and Jahangir.

Eighteen. High time for a wedding. Remiss of him to let things slide for so long.

He would have a letter sent to Bulat tomorrow.

The sound of women keening woke him. Bahadur frowned. Had he not told them to leave him alone? No servants, no interruptions. Surely he'd made his wants clear.

A nightmare. To ground himself, Bahadur reached sight unseen for the talisman he had regained just before he slept. His fingers tangled in the covers. No medallion.

Here? No. Not there, either.

The keening strengthened. Not a nightmare, then. Real women, mourning. His search became more urgent. One of his unwanted visitors might have removed his winged horse from the felts.

Unless the talisman, its purpose fulfilled, had fled again into the mists whence it came.

No. The spirits often spoke in ways difficult for mere humans to comprehend. But for an object to appear and disappear at will—that was too much.

These wretched women had woken him before he'd slept enough. Every muscle ached. Cramps wracked his abdomen. He had no sensation in his toes. The felts could not offset the chill that wracked his bones.

Chill? In midsummer? From the approaching storm, perhaps.

His eyes opened. Above his head, the smoke hole that connected the hearth below to the heavens above showed the ashen sky of early dawn. The rain had not yet started.

Good. He needed light. The flickering lamps made it difficult to see.

But he could hear. The closest voice belonged to Firuza, who clasped his hand and crouched beside his bed. Beyond her knelt the ring of keening women, led by Diliara. Roxelana's wail dwarfed the rest. His head throbbed in rhythm with the women's sobbing breaths. Wives, concubines, daughters, *children.* Infants, toddlers, youngsters old enough to ride but young enough to squabble—the tent needed only a few lambs and kids to make the cacophony complete.

He scowled at the smoke hole. He was not dying. What demon possessed these women to invade his tent and yowl over his sleeping body? Diliara and Firuza, even. They usually had more sense, however little one could expect of the others.

As if privy to his thoughts, Diliara dismissed the mourners with a sharp command. They filed out, their wailing muffled by the layers of tent coverings. Roxelana, last in line, protested, but Diliara did not yield. Only Firuza received permission to remain.

"Go," Bahadur told Roxelana. "I need no concubine this morning." Especially one howling fit to wake the dead. He shivered. "And send someone to light the fire."

"Fire?" Firuza asked. "*Ata*, you are cold?"

She did not wait for his response. He heard the swish of her skirts as she ran to call the command after the retreating women, then returned to spread an extra coverlet over him. Diliara pressed a damp cloth against his forehead.

A ladle of pomegranate juice touched his lips. He tried to push himself upright enough to drink it, but the pain in his elbows pinned him to the bed. His servant raced in, torch in hand, and lit the pile of dried dung that even in midsummer lay ever-ready on the hearth.

"Help me," Firuza said. The servant left the fire and raised Bahadur so he could drink. The juice dribbled down his chin, and Firuza wiped it away with the damp cloth. But enough trickled into his throat to bring relief.

"No need to fuss," he said. "I'll be fine. Let me sleep."

"Yes, *Ata*." She gestured to the servant, who lowered him to the felts and backed away. They departed together, his daughter in the lead, leaving him with Diliara.

He squeezed his chief wife's hand. "I will recover, dear heart. Do not fear."

Tears spotted her silk sleeves. "Of course you will, husband." Her voice sounded choked.

He sought words to convince her, but like skittish falcons, they refused the lure. In truth, all words rang hollow. He felt worse with every passing moment. Worse than he would have imagined possible. Why, only yesterday he had brought down the deer that had given its haunch to last night's dinner. Yet today he struggled to move.

The thought gave him pause. Suppose what ailed him *was* more than a hangover or a gimpy knee? People died on the steppe without warning, struck by witchcraft, plague, mysterious diseases that originated in marshy soil or bad air. Many perished in wars, but the ill intent of men did not account for every death.

Nonsense. Weaklings submitted to this ailment or that. Not Bahadur. Thus had it always been. Thus would it ever be.

But if he did die, what then? Jahangir could not rule.

Bahadur again reached for the talisman, seeking the reassurance it offered. Bulat's gift, a reminder of their long friendship. He must push the marriage through as soon as possible, then order his people to raise Firuza's husband on the white felt rug and proclaim him khan. Jahangir could not resent such treatment. Only descendants of Genghis could bear the title of khan. Bey marked the limit of Bahadur's ambitions—and his son's.

Jahangir would benefit from following Ogodai's lead. They had been friends as children. Bulat's boy had always had a good head on his shoulders, and his father would back him as needed. Together, they could offset Jahangir's flaws and rein in his vices.

It would work, if the ancestors granted him enough time to set Ogodai and Jahangir on the right road. Then his people would flourish, as they had during Bahadur's own partnership with

Bulat Khan. He foresaw flocks of sheep and goats stretching to the horizon. Mares that foaled in season, their milk supplying every tent. Strong, healthy children to carry the life of the clans forward. Every horde needed a bey, but a khan brought luster. The spirits smiled on a camp with a khan. So the shamans said.

His council might argue the decision. Many nomadic Tatars had lost their respect for Genghis's kin. But Bahadur would persuade them. The old ways reflected the will of the grandmothers, the clan spirits. His camp needed a khan. Indeed, why had he and Bulat ever agreed to travel along separate trails?

Air filled his lungs, and he sank into the felts. With most of the women gone, his temples had stopped pounding. Rest would restore his strength. This illness had shown him what he had to do.

He pressed Diliara's hand once more. "Send for Firuza, dear one. Ask her to summon the council."

Time passed. A lot? A little? He couldn't tell. But after a while, perfumed smoke filled the air as Firuza entered, the shaman in her wake. The swishing of robes and the tromp of booted feet signaled the council's arrival. Pride swelled Bahadur's chest. They understood. They served him, their internal squabbles not withstanding. Loyal unto death, they would obey his commands, as they had since he first united them as a fighting force.

Jahangir slumped near the door, if the aroma of wine that wafted from that direction meant anything. What was wrong with the boy?

The shaman circled the room, the scent of sage wafting from her smudge stick. Milk and fat tossed from her cup sizzled in the flames.

Bahadur's roiling stomach rejected the smell of food. Firuza, squatting next to him, caught the vomit in a bowl. "Feel his pulse," she said, her voice small and scared, as he hadn't heard it since she was a child driven to her mother's bed by monsters lurking in the night. "It's too fast. And hear how he labors to breathe. Did you give him too much of that medicine?"

Medicine. Firuza had warned him to be careful, and he had overruled her. Had he made himself sick?

"Medicine?" Ildar Shirin growled. "Has this witch poisoned our bey?"

"Certainly not." The shaman lifted Bahadur's wrist, feeling for the pulse. "I gave him the same dose I have administered twice a day for the last three months. But Lady Firuza is right. His heart beats too fast."

"I asked for more," Bahadur said. "Firuza, did you not tell her?"

"She did." The shaman's voice was firm. "I refused. I don't kill my patients, even if they command it."

"But what else would affect him so quickly?" Firuza asked. "He ate what we did. No one else fell ill."

"Then it's not poison," the shaman said. "Men sicken, Lady. Sometimes they die. Your father is not young."

"I am not old," Bahadur grumbled, but the three women moved away, murmuring. The drumming changed its rhythm, and the shaman's chanting indicated she was entering a healing trance. In the distance, beyond the tent walls, he heard his women moaning. Again Roxelana's voice rose above the rest. The sound pierced his skull.

"Ildar," he said, desperate to conquer the onrushing sickness.

"Here, Bey." Compassion laced the chief elder's voice.

"Bulat Khan." His throat seized up, breaking the sentences into pieces. "His son. Marry Firuza."

"Of course, Bey. Bulat Khan's son will marry your daughter."

Bahadur couldn't speak. The air flowing through his lungs hit a wall, recoiled, crawled forward again. His breath caught; his heart strained to pump. His feet felt like lumps of snow. Icy tentacles reached up his legs. His thoughts fractured under an onslaught of fear. Perhaps he *was* dying.

No! I'm not ready.

He forced what he needed to say through stiffening lips. "Him khan. Jahangir bey. Promise me."

Kazbek Argyn answered this time. "Fear not, Bey. We will send for Bulat. We will marry your daughter to his son Ogodai and install the boy as khan. With Jahangir as bey. We will honor your memory and your commands."

A murmur of assent rose from the council. Ildar Shirin confirmed it. "Bulat's son will wed your daughter and rule as khan."

Bahadur, hearing an odd note in the council leader's voice, frowned. Ildar sounded ... what? As if he'd chosen his words carefully. But why? The means to probe more deeply eluded him. "Son," he said. "Bring."

The cloud of wine-sodden breath roiled his gorge once more, but he managed to choke it back. In the crowded, smoky tent, he could barely see his son's features. He couldn't raise a hand to touch the blurry brown rectangle that probably marked Jahangir's brow. "Blessing," he croaked. "Be strong, son. Listen. Council. Khan."

For an instant, he felt calloused fingers brush his cheek. A slurred voice spoke. "Farewell, *Ata*. I'm sorry I've been such a disappointment to you." The wine-soaked cloud dissipated once more.

The sensation of a throttling hand tightened steadily around Bahadur's neck. "Go," he told the council. "Begin."

The individual members of the council blurred into a single collective animal that bowed its heads and left. They must have taken Jahangir with them, for the odor of wine faded. Firuza and Diliara remained—and the shaman, crooning to her drum.

Ildar Shirin. He was cunning, always had been. And he disliked Bulat. Would Ildar keep his promises without Bahadur to enforce compliance?

If he had no other option, yes. Which meant that Firuza must warn Bulat—and for that, she needed the talisman. Fear pushed his fingers through the felt as he searched. Medallion, Firuza, Bulat. His *qarïndash*. Sworn to help, no matter what.

"Leave, Diliara," he said. He wanted to convey so much more, but every word stuck in his throat like a precious gem. "Firuza, stay."

Diliara's tears splashed on his cheek as she kissed him, but she didn't protest. "Farewell, husband," she said. "I will seek you among the spirits when my time comes."

"Love," he said. It touched him when she responded in kind. Indeed, she had been a good wife. An excellent wife.

Yet he didn't hear her go. His fingers scrabbled in the blankets, searching.

Nothing. Still nothing.

Someone had taken it. Some thoughtless person had picked up the medallion and put it somewhere else. Stored it for safekeeping, say.

Around his head, the spirits circled. He had missed their arrival, but now even the dim light couldn't conceal their presence. Their chill breath froze his legs and iced his torso, banishing even the memory of midsummer. The ancestral hunting grounds shimmered in the distance.

Wait, he told the grandmothers. *My daughter. I must tell her. Give me that small comfort, and I will follow you without protest.*

But the divine forces refused to bargain. Bahadur sensed his soul separating from his body. Above him, the smoke hole lured it toward the heavens. Only the shaman's spirit, perched on the crossbars, kept him in the tent.

Too soon. Too soon. Stay, he told his soul.

Instead, it freed itself a little more. He would die without finding the talisman. His fumbling fingers resumed their desperate hunt among the piles of quilt.

"Firuza."

She reached across him, plucked the emblem from the covers, and held it inches from his face. "Is this what you seek, *Ata*?"

Bahadur closed his eyes in silent prayer. She had found it. *Mashallah,* he had his chance. If he could only form the words.

Firuza held the talisman right above his nose, her painted nails blotches of color around the pewter frame. The etched lines had smoothed to a circle flecked with red-gold light. He no longer saw the prancing stallion, clouds, or sky. Although the sun must be strengthening outside as dawn progressed, his soul had chosen to cast its eyes on other realms.

Realms where the winged horse waited. Tulpar, guardian of the nomadic Tatars. *Watch over them, Tulpar, as I begin this journey I have no desire to undertake.*

Firuza turned the emblem in her hand and studied it. "Where did it come from, *Ata*? I never saw it before this day."

"Tulpar," he gasped.

"I know it's Tulpar," she said. "Or do you mean he gave it to you?"

Bahadur shook his head, then winced as the pounding transformed into stabbing pains behind his eyes. His abdomen felt as if it might burst open. Death. Release.

"Should we send for him, then?" she asked.

"No." Frustration burned his gullet, bitter as the shaman's potion. He did not want *that* Tulpar, who would only cause more trouble.

"Bulat." His throat closed, forcing him to push each stuttering phrase past paralyzing muscles. "Send it. With note. Danger. Tell no one else."

His breath rasped, harsh in his ears as he fought for air. Firuza dropped the emblem on his chest and caught his hand, as if a daughter's love could forestall the end.

With a flash of brilliance, the skies above the smoke hole cleared. A brisk breeze blew the shaman's spirit off its perch. A surge of strength propelled Bahadur upright as his soul spied its opportunity. Sentences sprang from his throat as if driven from above.

"Bulat," he repeated. "Send him the talisman." Urgency filled his voice. The shaman crooned in a corner. Like him, she had not seen the threat in time. "Marry Ogodai. Advise your brother. You rise and fall together. Don't let him forget."

"Of course," she said. "But, *Ata*, you will get well. You must."

"No." He heard the regret in his own voice, but his soul, poised to spring free, rejected such transitory grief.

"Go," he told Firuza. "Go now."

"But *Ata*—"

"Go!"

He fell back. His daughter sniffed his cheek, grabbed the emblem from his chest, and ran, tripping in her haste, her silhouette distorted against the tent walls. He willed her to stay upright, lest his death pollute her. She could not spend months in isolation, for she bore the camp's future in her hand.

Firuza stumbled across the threshold, missing the sacred plank by the width of a hand. Another disaster averted. Bahadur sank onto the bedding, his exhalation a sigh. The grandmothers had not abandoned him after all.

His rasping breath swelled to a torrent, sputtered, stalled. As the wails of the bereaved filled his ears, his soul tore free from his dying body, leaving only his animal essence, and raced toward the smoke hole. Bahadur rose with it. From a distance, the shaman's spirit swept toward him. When she realized she could no longer intervene, she bowed and raised her horn to summon the celestial steed. Tulpar, whom the Greeks called Pegasus.

The name catapulted Bahadur to another place and time: Kherson on the shores of the Black Sea, a few months after his marriage. The shock he'd felt, discovering that people who lived in houses knew Tulpar, too.

He would see the mother of his twins again when he reached the ancestral hunting grounds. He had loved her once. Before Roxelana, before Diliara. So long ago.

Grandmothers, protect my children. Their fate now lay with the clan spirits. He had done what he could.

In the distance, Tulpar beat his mighty wings. Bahadur's pain had vanished, as in a dream. His legs again stood firm upon the grassy steppe; his right arm could swing a saber, as before. He had not expected death so to resemble life.

A winged stallion appeared amid the clouds. As Bahadur watched, Tulpar descended until he knelt before the bey's waiting soul, offering to carry him to the hunting grounds below. Through the spirit's translucent coat, the stars formed a pattern that shone clear in his dark eyes. But when Bahadur, awed, reached to touch the bony ridge—not so much a horn as the suggestion of one—below the ghostly mane, horsehair tickled his palm.

Bahadur, former bey of his own Tatar horde, mounted. The stallion's flanks felt solid between his thighs. The great bones that propelled the wings pressed against his hamstrings, more supportive than a saddle. He entwined his fingers in Tulpar's mane. The horse tensed, preparing for flight.

Bahadur allowed himself one last, long survey of the camp he had called home. He would miss this place, his friends and family. Round white tents, each identifiable by its embroidered strips binding the felt; spirit banners waving before carved door frames facing south; his own standard flying free, its emblem a pale reflection of his current mount's glory; the herds penned within the corrals that guarded them against predators and thieves—and his people, grieving the loss of their protector, their bey. Kettle drums pounded an unceasing dirge. Bonfires sent flames shooting into the summer heat, ridding the air of contagion. The boundaries of his world—no more.

The storm he had sensed gathering throughout the evening broke. The middle lands of earth and water rallied, staging a farewell appropriate to a hero. Lightning struck sparks amid the feather grass. Thunder rolled across the land, silencing the kettle drums. Wind amplified the mourners' sobs. Rain doused the purifying bonfires. As Bahadur prepared to join his ancestors, the glimpse of one bent figure caught his spirit eye.

His beloved daughter. Amid the storm, Firuza wept. He bent to brush her hair as he flew past.

Chapter 2

THE ATTACK CAME WITHOUT WARNING. AS OGODAI DUCKED amid a hail of arrows to pull his bow from its case, he cursed the scouts he had dispatched this morning to survey the birch woods and flat, rye-waving fields within a stone's throw of Smolensk. How had his men missed this ragtag excuse for an opposing force?

Not that the presence of hostiles in itself surprised him. Here on the border with the Grand Duchy of Lithuania, enemies were everywhere. A wise troop commander anticipated trouble. Too many mixed loyalties, too many dissatisfied warriors eager to switch sides, too many high-strung noblemen poised to shoot first and ask questions later, if ever.

Ogodai snapped his bowstring into place and shot arrows as fast as he could pull them from his quiver. On either side, mounted warriors whooped as they spread into a rough circle. Some added their shots to his. Others waved curved sabers as they urged their ponies toward the enemy. The first ululating howl, with its deliberate echoes of the wolf, brought the missing scouts to light. They raced their mounts toward his troop, more vulnerable than the rest while separated from their pack. Ogodai waved them back, and they changed course, the six of them sweeping in behind the advancing enemy troops and cutting off their retreat.

One man fell midway, his foot caught in the stirrup, dragged behind his steppe pony while his head bounced on the ground. Ogodai shot the scout's attacker between the eyes without a second thought. The pony freed itself and reared, its head thrown back, its squeal audible even against the thrumming background of the kettle drum calling warriors into formation. The scout lay unmoving on the grassy plain.

Of necessity, Ogodai left him there. His troop would retrieve the man later and offer what medical aid they could, but first they had to contain the greater threat. He wished for a larger force, one that included his brother-in-law, Daniil—assigned to a diplomat's duty in Kazan—who used to ride at his side on occasions like this.

A breeze chapped Ogodai's cheeks and laughed at the thin padding of his jacket. Nostalgia would do him no good, so he let the autumn air blow the idle wish away. His men completed their circle, hemming in their opponents as they would a herd of deer.

Raised sabers indicated the captured troop's continued willingness to fight, although the warriors could hope at best for death with honor. Ogodai rode forward. His men had won. Which made it his decision whether to slaughter or reprieve.

Not a place he'd expected to find himself when his troop left the camp right after morning prayers. Men must eat. Horses, too. And months after the July muster, forage for men and beasts had become scarce. When his father's order came down, Ogodai, only half-regretting the necessity—better than the alternative of days cooped up behind walls—had gathered the thirty warriors his father could spare and set out in pursuit of whatever chickens and larks the local populace had not yet swallowed or squirreled away.

He'd expected opposition, but only from others on his own side bent on securing the same chickens. And from the Lithuanians, determined to wear down the Russians and their Tatar supporters, of whom Ogodai was one. Today was the Christians' holy day, which might deter them, but Ogodai had learned the hard way not to rely on others' piety for protection. He'd braced himself for a sprung trap, a cache of fowl hidden in the woods. Sheep or goats, a cow avoiding capture. Not a group of armed men whose accuracy with the bow matched his own. As well trip over a herd of wild pigs.

Which he would, in any case, have left for the Russians. Ogodai lapsed as often as any other man, but he took his adherence to Islam seriously. He'd stand at death's door before he devoured an unclean swine.

As he approached the front of the line, the scout's pony dashed past. Without breaking stride, it leaped the low fence that guarded a farmer's field, running rampant through the ripening rye. *Ai*, another unhappy local to appease.

The kettle drum fell silent. Ogodai assessed his opponents. A scraggy handful of Tatars, most of them dressed in sheepskin coats wool side out, covering not much beyond loose trousers and boots, armed with bows and single-edged Turkish swords.

Then he saw the banner. Tulpar, the winged horse. He knew that design, remembered it from his boyhood. Steppe Tatars. Nomads under the rule of Bahadur Bey, Ogodai's first tutor. Less disciplined and more poorly equipped than his own men but less scrupulous as well. He wouldn't have expected them to come after him: his father and Bahadur were friends of long standing. But they hadn't had much contact in recent years. Perhaps Bahadur had switched his allegiance to Lithuania—or to the Crimean Tatars, most of whom supported Lithuania. Alliances shifted constantly on the steppe in a game with many players, each bent on maximizing his own advantage.

In any case, here the nomads were, enemies bearing the banner of a former friend. Ogodai knew better than to let past loyalties blind him. But how much of a threat did these intruders pose? He had defeated them easily enough, and with twenty-nine skilled warriors he could kill them if necessary. Should he?

His father would order him to take no chances. These warriors would resist capture; in attempting to subdue them, Ogodai risked losing more men. And a father's word was law.

Yet surely Bulat would not demand that his son kill *these* prisoners out of hand—men who served his own *qarïndash*. They might as well be family. They deserved a chance to explain their behavior.

Especially since they were not fighting. They sat with their hands relaxed on their reins, offering no resistance.

Decision made, Ogodai reined in his horse and summoned his most authoritative tone. "What is your business here?"

The leader of the captured warriors, identifiable by his silk robes, doffed his scarlet turban, revealing a shaved scalp with a long strip of light brown hair down the center and more in an arc on each side of his head, ending in small, bound plaits that dangled behind each ear. "Ogodai Sultan," the man said in Tatar. "You have grown. Forgive us, we didn't recognize you."

Six years had passed, but seeing the speaker up close, without helmet or turban, Ogodai identified him without difficulty. So much trouble, for this?

His gloved fist smacked the side of the man's head. "Rafik Argyn, as I live and breathe. We almost sent you to your ancestors, you fool! Even after I recognized the banner, I thought you had changed sides. Have you not?"

Rafik mumbled another apology. "Of course not. We bear a message for your honored father. Bahadur Bey died on the fifth day of Muharram."

The fifth of Muharram, and Safar would soon end. Seven weeks ago, more or less. Ogodai gripped his saber. Let the foraging wait. "I am distressed to hear that," he said. "Did he suffer? What happened?"

Bahadur dead? Impossible.

The man was a giant, a hero. A man like that should live forever.

"He was old, Sultan," Rafik said. "Almost fifty."

The words stopped Ogodai in his tracks. Rafik spoke the truth. Bahadur and Bulat—they were both old. They had been *qarïndashlar* for as long as Ogodai could remember.

And that was an uncomfortable thought—seeing his father as old. Worse than Bahadur's death, almost. "What happened?" Ogodai repeated. "Did he die in his sleep?"

"No," Rafik said. "We don't know what killed him. He seemed fine, then he collapsed. He died within hours. But not in battle. At home."

"Witchcraft? Poison?"

Rafik shrugged his failure to answer.

"Come with me." A jerk of Ogodai's head summoned the two warriors closest to him. "Let Rafik's men go," he ordered. "See to Yadgar. If he's not dead, get him to a healer. If he is, take him to the camp and summon the imam. And by all that's holy, get that horse out of the rye. The farmer will have a fit over it trampling his crop."

The warriors departed. Ogodai beckoned to Rafik, and the two of them led the rest of their combined forces eastward.

Bulat would have plenty to say when they reached the town.

The morning was half-gone by the time they rode past the palisades shielding the small town assigned to the Tatars. In the distance, Smolensk perched on its embankment like a massive bird circled by a wooden nest. Roofed double walls pointed at the sky, interspersed with solid gatehouses topped with what looked like conical hats. From inside, Ogodai heard the incessant pealing of bells, calling the Christians to church. The dissonant chorus distinguished every Russian town—and every Lithuanian one, too. It was one reason he didn't argue with the Muscovite generals who insisted on stationing the Muslim Tatars in camps of their own, although he could not help noting and resenting the prejudice. The same generals were happy enough to accept assistance from him and his kind in battle, including the sacrifice of Tatar lives. Treating their Muslim colleagues *as* colleagues, however, was a different matter—for most of the Christians most of the time, at least. There were exceptions, like his brother-in-law. He mustn't forget that.

The gatekeepers waved Ogodai and his men through. Rafik and his ill-dressed contingent of nomads raised more than a few eyebrows, but when Ogodai swore surety for their good behavior, the guards allowed them to pass. Ogodai signaled for Rafik to ride at his side, and together they led their men through the crowded streets. Their combined group pushed through archers drilling on horseback, watched arrows thudding into the straw targets set up at either end of the run, shielded their ears against the pounding of hooves against the timbers that lined the training ground. They slogged through rutted lanes ripe with refuse and waste, both human and animal, avoiding muddy puddles left over from yesterday's storm. They sidled their horses past hurrying servants bearing baskets and sacks, some piled too high for the bearers to see over. They pressed through the impromptu marketplace that seemed to spring from the earth wherever an army camp established itself for more than a week, dodging peddlers and stall keepers, cooks haggling over bread. Ogodai checked the stalls as he passed: had his interrupted foraging this morning even been necessary?

But the answer, it seemed, was yes. He saw no sheep, no goats, no cattle. Vegetables and grains, cheeses and yogurt, flasks containing various liquids, but no meat to speak of. Once he finished his business with his father and Rafik, he would have to lead another party of raiders into the woods. Troops could not fight without meat.

The group left the market and entered the avenue leading to the more prosperous part of town, where the military leaders had quartered themselves, with or without the consent of the local notables. The noise diminished as the houses grew larger and more elaborate, although even here one could not entirely escape the trundling of carts, the neighing of horses, and the calls of soldiers, servants, and camp followers. Identifying this element or that for Rafik's benefit, Ogodai kept a constant running tally of the sights and sounds, testing each one for danger. But today he heard nothing abnormal.

At last, they reached the two-story house that Bulat had commandeered for his own use. Ogodai ducked as he approached the door, but a question from Rafik distracted him. He swore as the lintel grazed his forehead, but a quick check with a fingertip revealed no blood. Rafik mumbled an apology. Ogodai brushed it off as he pulled his fox-fur cap from his head and stuffed it into his belt. He hated the house, anyway. In addition to having a door that topped out somewhere around his shoulders, the building was colder than a tent. The stove in the corner gobbled fuel to minimal effect, and the windows kept out only the hot air of summer. Fall had barely begun, and he could feel the drafts. In midwinter the place must chill the bones.

He urged Rafik to enter. The sooner they finished their business here, the sooner they could retreat to more pleasant surroundings.

But of course, matters did not proceed as smoothly as Ogodai wished. For starters, Bulat was in the midst of conferring with his hundredmen. Ogodai's arrival with Rafik—a stranger to some, but familiar to those who had served Bulat since his days as khan of Bahadur's horde—set off a flurry of exclamations and inquiries. Bulat's shout brought half-a-dozen servants carrying trays loaded with jugs and baskets of pastries and fruit. The air rang with questions and answers: explanations for the benefit of those who had not met Rafik before; reminiscences of times past; information exchanged about the health of old friends, households expanded or contracted, deaths and births, conditions on the steppe; and comments on how Rafik and his companions had grown/matured/changed. Memories of Bahadur Bey, sparked by the sad news of his passing, dominated the gathering. The sun stood notably higher in the sky before Bulat called a halt to the preliminaries by dismissing both hundredmen and warriors—everyone except Ogodai and Rafik.

With his old mentor fresh in his mind, Ogodai could not help making a mental comparison between Bulat and his sworn brother: both short, both solid, both warriors of renown—but Bahadur, with the build and mentality of an ox, had not adjusted to changing times as Bulat had learned to do.

The thought seemed disloyal, yet Ogodai could not avoid it. His mentor, however loved and respected, had lacked flexibility.

As the warriors retired outside, Ogodai settled into his seat, to the right of and below the khan's platform that his father had occupied throughout. Rafik responded to Bulat's unspoken invitation by dropping onto a large tasseled cushion facing the khan and crossing his legs.

"The council sent you, I assume," Bulat pulled at the side of his mustache, evidence that the news troubled him—although Ogodai could not tell why. Who else would order Rafik here, if not Bahadur's council of elders?

No, not Bahadur's. The new bey's. Bahadur, improbable as it seemed, no longer hunted on this earth. He had fulfilled his allotted time span and moved on.

"Why you," Bulat added, "rather than Shirin's son?"

Oh, so that was what bothered his father. That the council had shown disrespect by sending a less prestigious representative.

Although Rafik was hardly undistinguished. His family had a lineage as ancient as the Shirins—and on Bahadur's council, Kazbek Argyn had wielded more influence than Ildar Shirin, whatever the relative strengths of their lineages. Or so it had seemed to a twelve-year-old Ogodai.

Rafik must have sensed Bulat's displeasure, for he shifted in his seat, visibly uncomfortable. "Malik Shirin has higher status, Khan, I know. But he remained to govern the Shirin clan in his father's absence, whereas I was already in Bahadur's camp, assisting his son. That was why the council asked me to bear the news."

Bulat tugged harder at the abused mustache, but he did not openly dispute Rafik's explanation. "The elders attended the funeral, I suppose."

"Of course," Rafik said. "But Bahadur had summoned them earlier, to plan the summer raids. The sons came for the funeral, but they did not stay."

Everyone could not stay. One area of the steppe could not support the many animals such a combined camp would control. Thousands of sheep and goats, hundreds of horses, cropping the long grass—the memory ambushed Ogodai from the half-remembered past, inflicting a sharp pain that twisted his gut. He had wasted too many years in towns. He should return to the steppe, and soon.

"I would have liked to say farewell to my brother," Bulat said, his tone flat, uncompromising.

"My father apologizes that we did not reach you in time." Rafik dropped his eyes. "But we had no warning of Bahadur's illness. He was healthy, then he died, and we consigned his body to the steppe as soon as the clans arrived. To delay would have been unseemly, since he died in midsummer. The next day, my father sent me to find you, to deliver the news. But it took us some weeks to learn of your whereabouts."

"And how is your honored father?" Bulat asked. "He was not stricken by whatever ailment killed my sworn brother, I trust."

"*Inshallah*, Khan, he is as well now as the day I left the camp."

"I am pleased to hear it. And that your father has not forgotten our friendship." Bulat paused. He seemed to have accepted, finally, that Rafik and his clan had not intended dishonor or exclusion. Yet he did not relax. With his left hand, he tapped the armrest. His eyes remained fixed on Rafik's face.

Bulat did not normally take offense over trifles. Did he express his grief in this focus on protocol?

Bulat spoke again, his voice and gaze steady. "But you bear another message, surely? Bahadur and I had an agreement. He promised his daughter to my son, if I would permit Ogodai to serve as your khan. Do your elders not summon him to that task?"

Rafik rubbed the rich brown fur that lined his sleeve. Frowning, Ogodai leaned forward. His seat on a lower platform denied him a clear view of Rafik's face, but he noted how the visitor squirmed, his reluctance to meet Bulat's eyes.

"Well?" Bulat snapped his fingers in the air.

"It's not quite so simple, Khan."

"Not so simple?" Bulat snorted. "It seems perfectly simple to me, young man. Don't tell me that Bahadur went back on his word. I will not believe you."

"Not Bahadur." Rafik wriggled again on his rug, but Bulat's face remained adamant. "His dying words were to send for your son, to marry him to Lady Firuza as promised and install him to rule over Jahangir Bey. But Ildar Shirin—he says that Bahadur did not name Ogodai. He insists the bey had another son of yours in mind." He flushed, visibly embarrassed, as if describing Shirin's behavior somehow endorsed it.

Bulat pulled the dagger from his belt and hurled it. It stuck, quivering, in the rug about a foot in front of Rafik's cushion. Rafik emitted a yelp of dismay and scrambled backward.

"You see what I think of that suggestion," Bulat snapped. "Shirin knows better than to play such games with me. I *have* no other son of an age to marry."

Rafik murmured agreement and crept forward, resuming his original place. His hand shook as he plucked the dagger from the rug and placed it at the edge of the khan's platform.

Bulat grabbed the dagger and thrust it into its sheath. "Such nonsense!"

"Yes, Khan." Rafik's shoulders rose until they almost touched his ears. "I bear the message; Shirin's views are not my own. My father and I feel certain that Ogodai Sultan can convince the elders to elect him khan. My clan and the Baryns will speak in his favor, and even Ildar Shirin agrees that Ogodai Sultan should appear before the council. But I must tell you that the new bey questions the need for any khan. Many of the nomadic tribes are content to live under Mangyt rule."

"And Jahangir is the Mangyt bey." Bulat ran his thumb over the jewel that adorned the hilt of his dagger. "No surprise that he wants what benefits him. But he too speaks nonsense. My sworn brother recognized that, or why did he send you to me? Even a small horde like yours does better with a descendant of Genghis to lead it."

"Yes, Khan," Rafik said.

Ogodai struggled to follow the quick give-and-take, the names thrown out without explanation. Although he had spent most of his childhood in Bahadur's camp, he had left before he acquired enough experience to recognize the alliances among clan leaders who gathered, at most, three or four times a year. The name "Ildar Shirin" yielded a vague image of an older man, dapper and self-assured, clothes and manners imbued with the cultured air of the south. Kazbek Argyn, Rafik's father—more present, more vocal, straightforward enough for even a boy to read—had left a stronger impression. Him Ogodai remembered well: a solemn fighter with the soul of a judge.

"Very well." Bulat drew his dagger and pointed it skyward, as if toasting the ancestors. "We will humor your elders. Ogodai will present himself as required. He is more than capable, as you and your people will discover."

More than capable? Ogodai straightened in his chair. He hadn't guessed that Bulat saw him that way. Criticism far outpaced compliments from his stern father's mouth.

"That will please the clans. The Shirins and the Mangyts threaten to become over-mighty, and the rest of us would like to rein them in," Rafik said. He kept a wary eye on Bulat's throwing arm as the khan returned the knife to his belt. Ogodai didn't blame him for that.

"Convey my thanks to your honored father for his support," Bulat said, "and tell me what happened to Bahadur." Rafik launched into a long account of the bey's death.

Ogodai wanted to hear the story, but the sounds of tromping feet and horse tackle outside distracted him. The peals borne on the wind from Smolensk had ceased, and with the camp on a war footing, every disturbance merited attention. He listened for the clang of drawn swords, for the thud of battle axes, for screams of rage or pain. He heard everything but the screams. It was difficult to distinguish between the sounds made by his own side at drill and those of the enemy. But if there were no screams, it was not a battle or even a raid. He permitted himself to relax.

The jingling of the horse tackle ceased, and the tromping feet resolved themselves into a single pair of boots. Ogodai looked up as a stolid presence appeared at the door. The head of his personal guard, fully armored and more than usually solemn. Ogodai excused himself, braced for more bad news. The matter must be urgent if it justified interrupting Bulat in the middle of an audience.

Only when his head guard opened his mouth did Ogodai recall that he had asked for an update on the health of Yadgar the scout. "He will live, Sultan." The warrior clasped his hands and stared at the ground, but Ogodai had seen the relief in the other man's face. "Although the healer says he must rest for weeks. His head is very bad, and he dislocated his hip when he fell. There is the arrow wound, too, but that will heal, *Inshallah*."

"Could have been worse," Ogodai said. "If you can take him away from the front, do so. Find a good woman to care for him." He fished a handful of coins from the pouch tied at his belt and dropped them into the warrior's hand. "Pay her well. And if the healer tells you not to move him, use that to make him comfortable in a house nearby." The warrior bowed and retreated, and Ogodai resumed his seat.

Rafik was still talking. "The bey dismissed us—everyone except Diliara, his chief wife, and his daughter Firuza. Not long after that, Diliara left the tent. Firuza emerged last, with something in her hand." He pulled a small felt bag, tied with a knotted string, from his sash and handed it to Bulat. "For you, Khan. A parting gift from your *qarïndash*. His daughter asked me to deliver it to you."

Bulat examined the bag. A puzzled frown creased his brow. "What is it?"

"I don't know, Khan," Rafik said. "The bey ordered her to tell no one. Insisted that you would understand its significance when you saw it."

Ogodai felt a flash of interest. A mystery. And one somehow linked to his promised yet almost forgotten bride.

Bulat fixed his gaze on the unopened bag in his hand. "You have fulfilled your mission. Go, beg what food you can from the camp cooks—we haven't much. Pitch your tents where you see free space, but don't set off for home until I give you leave."

Rafik mumbled agreement and backed from the tent, leaving Ogodai alone with his father. He was considering what to ask first when Bulat forestalled him. "Tell me about the raid."

Ogodai forced himself not to stare at the bag, draped over his father's knee. Surely a mysterious secret was more important than a raid.

"You took a risk," Bulat said as Ogodai finished, "letting them live."

The response he'd anticipated. "I was right."

"This time."

When Ogodai bit his tongue and did not reply, Bulat moved on to address the horse's invasion of the rye field. "Send someone to pay the farmer."

"I already did," Ogodai said.

"Good. And the scout?"

"He will survive, but the healer can't tell whether or when he will recover in full."

"Very well," Bulat said. "You did a good job, son. Let's find out what my old friend Bahadur has sent us."

Chapter 3

BULAT UNTIED THE KNOT, PULLED AN OBJECT FROM THE bag, and held it up. "What have we here?"

Ogodai saw a solid circle about the size of a man's palm, more chain-mail gray than silver. A drilled hole near top center suggested the object might once have hung from someone's neck. A medallion, he guessed, although the front remained hidden. From the back, it looked unremarkable, yet Bulat perused it as if Rafik had handed him a page from a rare illuminated manuscript.

"Interesting," Bulat said. "Unsettling."

He fell into contemplation. As the silence deepened and lengthened, Ogodai's patience frayed. His father had called him capable. And he was capable: his father's second-in-command and chosen heir. Just this morning, he had led thirty men into battle, captured a rival troop, and returned with only one casualty—and that not fatal. Had he not earned his father's confidence?

But Bulat did not like to be rushed. He would talk when he was ready. Rather than fidget like a child, Ogodai surveyed the rustic quarters that made up Bulat's temporary home. As always in this misbegotten town, he kept one ear cocked for potential trouble.

For the moment, nothing untoward pulled his attention away from his surroundings. As a test of his memory, Ogodai closed his eyes and named every item he had observed: Bulat, stockier than usual in leather armor and heeled boots, scratching his thin beard and pondering the medallion; rolled bedding piled atop a pair of sturdy chests; a small table holding maps and documents; a stand for weapons; grandmother poppets arranged in the place of honor behind the khan's platform in the north, facing the door. Had he missed anything?

He opened his eyes and looked around. No. How could he, when the room contained next to nothing of interest?

Except the object in Bulat's hand. Sent by Ogodai's betrothed, at her father's insistence and hidden even from Rafik, who carried it. What did it mean?

In the draft that filtered past the ill-fitted mica panes, Ogodai sensed the ancestors calling him back to Bahadur's camp. It was time. Past time, really. He imagined Firuza and her twin brother, Jahangir, as he had known them then, six years ago. They would have grown up, as he had. What were they like now?

He saw them then, clearly enough, but imagining them as adults proved difficult. Had they become like their father and their sweet-faced stepmother Diliara, who had let Ogodai stay in her tent the night his own parents traveled east, taking Jahangir with them? She had comforted him that night, but afterward their paths seldom crossed. Boys lived and trained with men.

He had last spoken to Diliara—and, in fact, to Firuza— the day after his parents reclaimed him, returning Jahangir to Bahadur's care. He recalled the elaborate betrothal ceremony, himself encased in stiff brocades and weighed down with gold chains, his head swathed in a cloth-of-silver turban adorned with a scarlet feather that swirled dust and made him sneeze, kneeling to face a girl primped and polished until she resembled a small but perfect doll. Murmured promises, hands touching a leather-bound Koran, feasting and speeches—then poof, nothing. His parents had carted him off to another camp, assigned him to another tutor, and Firuza had faded from view until she had no more reality than fronds wafting in the breeze.

The thought evoked an odd, haunting melancholy. Bulat cleared his throat, and Ogodai jumped at the chance to return to the present. At last, he would discover what this was about.

His father turned the metal circle, revealing an emblem engraved with a winged horse in flight. The design was beautiful: sweeping abstract lines polished to the hue of silver against a hollowed-out background lined with tiny beads of blue tile. Vibrant, free, the horse exemplified life reduced to its essence, a style typical of the steppe nomads. Ogodai loved it on sight.

Yet it did not answer his questions. Bahadur had embraced the winged horse as his symbol long ago. The design meant much to him and his people, so much that it was hard to find any specific meaning in it.

"I don't understand," Ogodai said. "Was there no message?"

Bulat tossed him a small sheet of paper, folded into quarters. Unwrapped, the paper revealed two lines of poetry in elegant Arabic lettering: "Storm clouds threaten / To tear eaglets from their nest."

"A woman's hand," Ogodai said. "Lady Firuza herself, I suppose."

Across the years of absence, the paper spoke to him, revealing an unexpected angle. His betrothed's dim outline acquired a new contour: she was a poet.

Examining the exquisite script, he spared a moment to wonder where she had learned to write. His own training in Bahadur's horde had emphasized the practical. The bey had owned no books, had never opened a scroll or signed his name to a document. Bulat had supplied the Koran used in the betrothal ceremony. And Bahadur's knowledge of mathematics stopped with counting sheep and calculating the trajectory of an arrow. That he had sired a poet stretched belief.

Although Diliara had grown up among the Ottomans. Perhaps she had taught Firuza.

"Storm clouds threaten," he said. "A warning."

"Yes." Bulat said. "I recognized that even before I read the verse. Bahadur and I exchanged medallions years ago, when we became *qarïndashlar*. We agreed that each would send his to the other in case of trouble."

Years ago. A prearranged signal, using a symbol that no one would question. Clever.

And Rafik had already hinted at discord among the elders, which would—and should—worry Firuza. If Bahadur had sensed conflict brewing—and as bey he must have constantly monitored the mood on his council—that would explain why he had ordered his daughter to send the medallion in secret. Which meant… "The eaglets are Firuza and her brother?"

"Most likely." Bulat tapped the center of the medallion. "We must respond."

Again Ogodai felt that prickling of interest, that sense that the ancestors summoned him to fulfill his purpose. He strove to keep his voice casual. "I should go. Don't you think? Firuza is my betrothed. I owe her my protection. And the elders have invited me."

Bulat swung the medallion between his fingers, suspended from the hole at top center. "Yes, you go. Honor our contract. Claim your bride. Convince the elders of your worth. Shirin barks loudly, but like a good hound, he yields to a strong, confident voice."

He lifted the medallion and looked sad for the first time since Rafik's announcement, as if he at last permitted himself to feel grief at the loss of his *qarïndash*. "I should have gone back." He spoke to the talisman. "The years flew by, like this horse. But I always meant to visit you, brother. Each time, something got in the way: another deployment, another position. Help out with the eastern horde. Take over Kasimov, fight the Lithuanians, besiege the Poles, stop the Crimeans in their tracks, avenge my son's murder, deal with my daughter's in-laws, travel wherever I'm needed. Who had time for old friends?"

"Will we hold a memorial service?" Ogodai asked. His voice shook. Only seven months ago, he had attended the funeral of his younger brother Girei, slaughtered at the age of fourteen. The pain was still raw.

"We must." Bulat sighed. "He was family. I'll speak to the imam. And when it's over, you leave."

Ogodai blinked. So fast? "Gladly, but what of the Russians? They ordered me here."

"You serve me, not them," Bulat said. "If Ildar Shirin is plotting, we must act swiftly to head him off. And you need Rafik to lead you to the horde. They will be moving east soon, if they are not already, so you will have trouble finding them by yourself. Here, take the talisman. If you need help, send it to me, and I will arrange for reinforcements."

He dropped the medallion onto Ogodai's palm. Like the passing of a standard. Ogodai hefted it, assessing its weight. Heavier than he would have guessed. The prancing horse looked joyous, unfettered—the way he felt galloping across the steppe. It called him to another place, a destiny apart from the Russian forces and Smolensk.

He decided, then and there, not to ask for help. His mission, his bride, his problem to solve. He would show his father that he could succeed without assistance.

Bulat was still talking. "The Russians will understand. They know how volatile the steppe is. Bahadur commanded great respect. Where his horde leads, others will follow. If we can keep them on our side, so much the better."

"And Firuza? The council?"

"Your excuses for traveling." Bulat relaxed against the cushioned back of the platform, extending his legs—the image of a khan in repose. "Secure the girl and the khanate. Then use them to undercut Shirin's ability to sway the horde."

Classic Bulat, that. A khan must not miss an opportunity to advance his cause in the world. He had drummed that lesson into his son's head from the time Ogodai was old enough to listen.

But then, every tutor had made the same point. The acquisition and retention of power required planning and strategy, the exploitation of others' weaknesses—just like a chess match. Ogodai wanted to become khan, so he had to play the game, too. Nothing stopped him from advancing his own interests at the same time. He needed a wife and a place to rule, and here he had a chance to earn them.

"You wish me to spy on Bahadur's camp," he said, to ensure he understood. "To win it to our cause if possible, and report on it if not."

"Yes. Something frightened my sworn brother—and his daughter. Find out what. Keep your eyes and ears open. Ask questions, but don't accept easy answers." Bulat straightened again in his seat, leaned over, and spoke quietly. "And watch your back, son. This whole situation stinks like week-old fish."

Stinks like week-old fish. Ogodai puzzled over that one as he strode through the camp, the talisman clutched in his hand, muttering under his breath. What did that mean, precisely? Something had frightened Firuza, for sure, or she would not have sent the medallion and her poem. Dissension on the council, Bahadur's unexpected death—these things suggested cause for concern. But only Firuza's plea for help could not have an innocent explanation.

A heavy presence brushed his leg. Ogodai jumped sideways as a large dog dashed past, intent on some invisible quest. He shook his head, determined to pay more attention to his surroundings. It was pure luck that he hadn't already stumbled into one of the many messes that dotted the courtyard.

He glanced about and realized he'd attracted the attention of at least a dozen warriors. What a sight he must have made, swinging his arms and grumbling. He pulled himself together and tucked the talisman into his sash. Just for practice, he glared a chuckling archer into submission before resuming his walk at a steadier pace.

As he pulled his fingers from the sash, he felt the folded paper that contained Firuza's two-line poem. The clear handwriting suggested a woman who knew her own mind. It made sense that the girl he had glimpsed around the nomadic camp—competent, intelligent, well-behaved—would grow into such a woman. He remembered her trailing behind her stepmother, doling out food for the servants to cook and bossing people around. Good material for a *khatun*—a khan's chief wife.

She'd been pretty then. Was she still?

It didn't matter, he supposed. He could have as many junior wives and concubines as he desired. But pretty would help, since the point of marriage was to produce children to carry on his line.

Assuming he could win her. He had little experience with virgins, but a man doesn't spend almost four years in the army without encountering a camp follower or six. They'd work it out. At least no one would check the sheets or stand outside the door counting, as they had for his unfortunate sister. He and Firuza could take their time. If things went well, they'd stay in the camp. If not, his mother would welcome her.

And Firuza must have accepted the match, mustn't she? Otherwise, she wouldn't have sent the medallion and her message. A father's deathbed command demanded obedience, yet she could have found some way to circumvent it if she found the idea unwelcome.

At that moment, Rafik Argyn crossed his path. What better chance to get answers to some of his questions? Ogodai grabbed Rafik's elbow. "Have you eaten yet?"

"Not yet." Rafik stopped mid-street. A passing carter grumbled as the sudden halt threatened to topple several of the barrels lashed to his wagon. "I had to settle my men first. Let's dine together. We have much to discuss."

"Indeed we do," Ogodai said. "My tent is nearby, and my man will have prepared food. This way." He gestured to his right, where a group of tents—one finer than the others, with an embroidered awning appropriate to a khan's son—clustered in the lee of the palisades that cut the wind from the east.

He headed that way, Rafik at his side as they crossed the short distance between them and the tents, sidestepping puddles and horse droppings and noxious piles of indeterminate garbage that had even Ogodai, more accustomed to the inconveniences of town life, wrinkling his nose. Rafik, fresh in from the steppe, missed one puddle as he avoided a particularly nasty pile and yelped as he sank up to his ankle in water. Pulling his boot from the mud, squinting at the results and complaining, he looked every bit the friend Ogodai recalled from childhood—a trusty companion ready for any adventure.

Although ... six years was a long time. One-third of their lives. Did he really know Rafik these days?

Never mind. Conversation over dinner offered the perfect chance to sound Rafik out.

Inside Ogodai's tent, the aroma of smoke mingled with stewed chicken and vegetables. Mostly carrots and onions, no doubt, since Ogodai and his band had not had a chance to finish their foraging this morning.

"Take a seat," he told Rafik. "If we eat quickly, we can finish before the midday call to prayer."

"Prayer." Rafik dipped his hands in the bowl of warm water held by Vafa, Ogodai's personal attendant, and dried them on a linen cloth. "We don't do much of that at home. No imam to issue the calls or lead the service. Hope I remember the ritual."

"Yes, of course." Ogodai, washing his own hands, saw in his mind Bahadur's favorite shaman, beaded plaits obscuring her face. Although nominally Muslim, his tutor had favored the old ways. Much devotion to the ancestors, barely a muttered phrase in tribute to the Koran. "It's been so long since I visited your camp. Does the shaman still rule there?"

"She did. A strong woman, not easily distracted or deceived. Although she ran away after the new bey accused her of poisoning his father."

"Did she? Poison him, I mean? By accident if not by design?"

With a shrug, Rafik picked up the boat-shaped ceramic spoon with his right hand. "I doubt it. She defied him the night of his death, refusing to increase the dose on some medicine she was giving him just because he demanded it. Said so right there in front of us."

"Anyone can make a mistake." The stew contained more broth than meat. The acrid taste of elderly turnips overwhelmed the carrots, but Ogodai was hungry, so he ate. Vegetables were no food for a warrior, but Vafa had managed to make these palatable—more or less.

"It's possible," Rafik said. "I don't believe it, though. She knew her potions and her spells. And she had served Bahadur loyally for many years."

"Since his first wife died. I remember." Although too young to recall the shaman's arrival just after his own fourth birthday, Ogodai had heard the story often enough. The previous shaman, too, had left in a hurry, to avoid retribution for his failure to save the khatun. "I'm not surprised she ran away, even if she did nothing wrong. An angry bey makes a bad enemy."

Rafik grunted assent and dipped his spoon again into his bowl of vegetables.

"Sorry there's so little meat," Ogodai said. "I was hunting when I ran into you."

Vafa brought cups of koumiss on a tray. Rafik lifted one in thanks. "There's this," he said. "And we can spare a horse, if you need it. Don't you have extras?"

"We have to keep them for the campaign. These Lithuanians are devils, with cannon that can shoot a horse right out from under you. And the food shortage is temporary. The supply wagons were due four days ago. Delayed by the mud, probably. I appreciate the offer, though."

The bubbly tang of the koumiss fought with the turnips. Ogodai swallowed the last of his stew in a hurry so that he could concentrate on the more pleasant liquid. He didn't want to waste this opportunity to ask Rafik a few pertinent questions, but it was difficult to decide what he most needed to know.

Storm clouds threaten to tear eaglets from their nest. Yes, start there. "Jahangir is the new bey, you said?"

"Yes." Rafik's face twisted into an expression of distaste. "He's the only adult son. Diliara was barren, but Bahadur loved her. He turned to junior wives only when she became so old he could no longer hope for a child by her. And she raised his twins. He had sons and daughters by several junior wives and concubines, but most are still infants. They can't challenge Jahangir."

"So what's the problem?" Ogodai addressed that unspoken dislike. "Jahangir's a good warrior, from what I've heard."

"When he exerts himself." Rafik studied the tent frame, then downed the rest of his koumiss in a single gulp. "Oh, I may as well tell you. You'll discover it for yourself soon enough. Jahangir spends his days drunk and dallying with Bahadur's prettiest concubine. Your lady does most of the work. With a bit of help from the elders, who would rather be off keeping an eye on their own flocks and herds. My father's fed up. That's why he pushed them to send for you. He's hoping—as Bahadur also seems to have hoped—that a strong khan can compensate for Jahangir's vices. The sooner I get you there and you convince them to follow through on the old bey's promises, the better."

The call to prayer sounded. Ogodai handed his empty bowl to Vafa and unrolled the prayer mat kept in the corner. "Very well. We leave tomorrow, " he said. "After the memorial for Bahadur."

After prayers, Rafik withdrew to check on his men. Ogodai summoned his servant. "You heard me talking to Rafik Argyn, Vafa. We're heading south tomorrow. Tell the men to prepare. And I'll need a gift for my bride. See what you can find in the market."

"What sort of gift, Sultan?" The servant—small and elderly, slight of frame—glanced up from the steel helmet he was buffing into gleaming perfection.

Yes, what sort of gift?

Ogodai ran a brief mental survey of the young women he knew. Nasan would ask for a sword or a horse, unless marriage had tamed his tempestuous sister—one could hope. But most girls Ogodai encountered liked feminine things, and Firuza had seemed conventional enough.

Firuza. The name meant "turquoise" in Persian. Perfect. "A set of cosmetic holders," he said, "set in turquoise and jeweled. Or a mirror. Something appropriate for my khatun. You know girls. They like to look good."

Chapter 4

"HAVE YOU RUN MAD?" FIRUZA STOOD, HANDS ON HIPS, and watched her twin brother fondle Roxelana—once his father's favorite concubine, now his. "You can't fool around with your woman. The petitioners are lined up six tents deep waiting for you to hear them."

"Will you stop fussing?" Jahangir dropped onto the padded platform that served as the bey's throne and shoved a brocaded cushion behind his back. "Why don't you get yourself a mirror, paint your face, style your hair—act like a girl? In the name of the ancestors (peace be upon them), you will *drive* me mad with your nagging."

"Take pity on your sister, Bey," Roxelana purred. "She can't help having the chest of a boy and features too strong for beauty."

Insults, always insults from that one. A creature undeserving of notice, so why did her jibes hurt?

Firuza grabbed a gold-tasseled scarlet cushion from the pile and shook it in their mocking faces. "Get rid of her, brother. I need to talk to you."

"And if I don't? You're the bey's sister, Firuza, not the bey. You have no right to boss me around. I rule here."

"Not for long, unless you bestir yourself. Did you ever see *Ata* lose days to carousing and concubines? He ran the horde, and so must you."

He shrugged as if they had not had this argument many times. "The council has sworn to follow me. Not you, sister, fidget and press as you will."

Why could Jahangir not see? The council backed him, true, but it could shift its allegiance in a flash.

Ata had charged her with caring for her brother, whether Jahangir liked her advice or not. "Why should the elders keep you when you make them do all the work? The clan leaders itch to return to their own camps, their own people." The cushion dangled from its tassel. It took every bit of Firuza's self-control to keep from tossing it at his unresponsive head.

"You sound like *Ata*." Jahangir beckoned to Roxelana, who as usual had ignored Firuza's demand that she leave. In response to her master's unspoken command, the concubine nestled on the padded throne next to him. He stroked her cheek. "Doesn't she sound like *Ata*, dear one? Grumbling about some imagined responsibility whenever she sees me enjoying myself."

"Indeed, Bey, a regular Lady Grim." Roxelana produced her sweetest smile, and Firuza clutched the scarlet cushion to her chest, anticipating another attack. "But what else has she to do with her time, poor thing? Even her betrothed has no use for her." She batted her eyelashes at Firuza. "The council had to send Rafik to hunt him down, and still he refuses to claim you."

"Perhaps we should have sent a slave with your picture, instead of a warrior who could scare Ogodai off." Jahangir poked Roxelana in the ribs, and she giggled.

Firuza's self-restraint cracked. The cushion, hurled with a precision that Roxelana would no doubt classify as unfeminine, knocked Jahangir's turban from his head and toppled him backward against the padded cushions. She *would* make him understand, whatever it took. "You must have a death wish, brother." The shuffling of feet outside caused her to lower her voice. "You trust too much in the council's vow of support. There are hawks everywhere. Here, among our half-brothers in the harem—"

"Too young." Jahangir cut her off.

"And in Crimea." Firuza bent double, willing him not to look away. "Kazan. Astrakhan. Moscow. Lithuania. Is Tulpar too young to stay his hand while you amuse yourself with *that*?" She pointed to Roxelana. "Bulat is your last hope, you fool. If he doesn't arrive in force, and soon, how long will the clans put up with you before they seek a bey more to their liking?"

Jahangir laughed in her face. "You are the fool, sister. You know nothing of politics."

It was true. She didn't. Firuza had not received the years of leadership training wasted on her brother. But she had a better sense than he of how the camp operated, and she had no trouble seeing what lay in front of her nose.

"Ildar Shirin backs me," he said. "The others don't matter. Where the Shirins lead, the council follows. You would do better to leave politics to the men and focus on luring your betrothed to your side. You might take lessons from Roxelana here." He rubbed his thumb along Roxelana's collar bone, pressing it into the filmy draperies that both obscured and revealed the exquisite lines of her body.

Firuza fought the urge to abandon her brother and his beautiful concubine to their fate. Her father's last words stayed her feet—and the reality of her own situation. Alone, unmarried, abandoned by her betrothed and his family, Firuza had no choice but to cling to her brother, her twin. If he fell, her future, already murky, looked grim indeed. Whereas Roxelana, desired by every man who saw her, could charm the leader of her choice, Firuza's value depended on her blood ties to the old bey. Any warrior seeking to rule the horde might force himself on her to secure his claim. Was that not why their father had ordered her to stay true to her brother, to advise him no matter what?

Although she doubted *Ata* could have found a more thankless task.

Her stepmother's training pushed Firuza to consider a different approach—difficult for her but worth a try, given that her preferred methods weren't working. She gathered every resource she could find, folded her hands, lowered her eyes, and softened her voice. "Will you not indulge me then, Bey, and hear the cries of your people?" She bit her tongue and bowed.

If she were wise, she would apologize for daring to counsel him unasked. But with the stakes so high, Firuza couldn't muster that level of humility, whatever the senior women of the harem recommended. If Jahangir didn't mend his ways, he faced deposition and exile at best—assassination at worst.

"Oh, very well." Jahangir waved at a second padded platform to his left, less exalted than his own. "But since you're so eager to play judge, you hear them. I'll sit and look bey-like." He patted Roxelana's bottom. "Get me some koumiss, heart's blood. I foresee a long and boring afternoon."

Three hours later, Firuza wished she had left Jahangir to wallow. As she braced her aching back against the cushions, the patterns in the rich hangings that lined the tent frame blurred before her tired eyes. A stray hair escaped her headdress and tickled her forehead. She brushed it into place, impatient with her body's failure to cooperate. The grassy aroma from

Jahangir's goblet lured her, distracting her with visions of food. What had she expected, after needling her brother to agree to this audience?

The responsibility lay heavy on her shoulders; the stream of complaints extended to the horizon. How many goats could stray into the wrong corral overnight? How many brands end up on the wrong horse? Did her people have nothing better to do than make up charges against one another? Briefly, she indulged herself with a fantasy of the council stepping in and taking over, exuding male authority left and right.

But as she had reminded Jahangir, hearing petty complaints was not the elders' job. They had taken time away from their own people to get Jahangir on his feet. If he failed despite their tutoring, they would replace him. Only she cared enough to ensure that he would not require replacement.

Which meant that she had to stop whining and help, whether Jahangir appreciated her efforts or not. Even without the specific training given to her brother, she had experience to draw on. Like all children of the steppe, she had learned to rely on her own abilities, her own judgment. The needs of the herds changed constantly. Whoever happened to be nearby—young or old, rich or poor, male or female—had to step up, make a decision, act for the good of the camp. And her stepmother had shown her how to manage servants and junior wives, to keep the household running no matter the circumstances.

Still, she had reached her limit for today. With a nod, she signaled the guard at the tent door to tell the remaining petitioners to return tomorrow. He glanced at her brother for confirmation, but Jahangir, preoccupied with lust and drink, did not respond.

Firuza kicked his ankle. He glowered at her but waved assent at the guard, who bowed and retreated.

Roxelana purred something inaudible into Jahangir's ear. Firuza winced. Although she did not object in principle to the ancient custom that gave her brother the pick of his late father's wives and concubines, *must* he become obsessed with Roxelana?

Two men stood before the dais, stubbornly talking at Jahangir even though he never looked their way. One—a short, square warrior whose name escaped Firuza for the moment— had arrived from Crimea only in the spring, with Tulpar, and had asked to stay when Tulpar departed under a cloud, a week before Bahadur's death.

Three months ago. It seemed like decades.

The other petitioner she had known all her life. Almas, the village fletcher, a thin man of medium height, a regular sight around the camp because he seldom accompanied the raiding parties. Every Tatar fought when necessary, but armies needed arrows, so Almas's skills were better plied off the battlefield. Although his importance to the horde earned him an equal share of the plunder brought in by the warrior bands and the bey's family ensured that his family did not starve, his herds remained small from lack of careful tending.

But Almas, despite his trade, was a peaceable man. How had he become involved in this quarrel?

The short, square man whose name she could not recall was speaking. "And that my neighbor should accuse me of such a crime!" He pointed a finger at Almas.

"Why would I not accuse you, you dolt," Almas said, "after I found you where you had no right to be?"

No right to be. Which case *was* this? The horse ridden into the steppe and lost? The child conceived during its putative father's absence? The cattle rustled by person or persons unknown? No, she had heard those earlier today, when her mind still worked.

"You attack my honor!" Tulpar's man waved his arms as if winding up for a punch, and she gestured to the guard, who this time obeyed without hesitation—charging forward and slamming his drawn sword between the men at chest level, preventing any attack. Firuza nodded approval. Out of nowhere, her unruly brain spewed out the petitioner's name: Zamam.

"A man who would destroy another's ability to feed his family has no honor," Almas declared.

Ah, that was it. The case of the dog that between one morn and the next had lost its ability to hunt. Because Zamam had poisoned it, Almas insisted.

Why would Zamam do anything so reckless? The man might be quarrelsome and a potential troublemaker, but poisoning a neighbor's animal caused much trouble for small gain.

Still, the death of a good hunting dog was a serious loss. No wonder Almas was upset. Firuza hesitated to demand more evidence, especially after he had waited weeks for the bey to hear his case.

Jahangir raised a languid hand. She had a flash of hope. Would he rule and save her the effort? For no reason she could detect, her mind produced a vision of Ogodai, her absent fiancé, as he had looked on the day of their betrothal. Angrily she brushed the thought aside.

When would she learn? Her betrothed had made his lack of interest clear. He would not help her. She had to take care of herself—and the horde—without his assistance.

"Well, sister," Jahangir said. "What Manduhai-like decision have you reached in the case of the poisoned hound?"

Roxelana snickered. "Oh, Bey, your humor never fails. Manduhai! As if your sister could hope to attain such heights."

Manduhai. Jahangir's capacity for spite constantly amazed her, but what had caused him to revive that old taunt? As

children, they had shared a game in which she played Queen
Manduhai the Wise, the young widow who kept herself alive
and in power by marrying a child to block the claims of rival
candidates, then led his warriors into one battle after another
until she had restored the great empire of their immortal
ancestor Genghis Khan. She had died seven years before
Firuza's birth, and the steppe still rang with sagas of her
exploits.

Depending on who else joined in, Jahangir had played an
enemy commander or Manduhai's chief adviser—sometimes
the Ming emperor. But Firuza had put such dreams behind
her long ago. Even Jahangir, grouchy as a bear robbed of its
honey, must recognize that his sister tried to rule only because
he would not.

While she glared at her smirking brother, Roxelana reached
for the carafe and refilled her lord's cup. They fell back into
murmuring, and Firuza signaled Zamam to continue. He, too,
glanced at Jahangir for confirmation. She gritted her teeth,
wondering whom to shake first. Jahangir? Roxelana? Zamam?

Zamam droned on. To hear him tell it, a lifetime of loyal
military service had inexplicably brought him into conflict with
this suspicious neighbor, bent on calumny and dissension.
Sputters of disagreement from Almas punctuated Zamam's
diatribe like bubbles rising from a stewpot hung over a fire.

Firuza gave these declarations the minimal attention they
deserved. Even under the best of circumstances, serving
loyally as a warrior did not preclude poisoning a dog. But
although tempted to call a halt, she refrained, in the hope that
the two men would resolve their differences more quickly if
she allowed each of them his say.

Grandmothers knew, she had plenty of other problems to
ponder. Why had Bulat not responded to her message? Had he
not understood her poem, not recognized the talisman? Had

Rafik gone astray? Had her betrothed declined to fulfill their contract, because she was as unattractive as Roxelana claimed?

No, that allegation was pure malice. Unattractive or not, Firuza was a bey's daughter, not some importunate servant. Not quite the equal of a khan's son, but close enough, especially when marriage to her would confer leadership of her horde. Even a small group like this could become the starting point from which an able leader could control the steppe.

Besides, if Ogodai had decided he didn't want her, he might at least have the courtesy to end the arrangement.

She conjured an image of Ogodai as she had last seen him. A slim, solemn boy with beautiful dark eyes. Uncomfortable in his stiff clothes but not, she thought, hostile.

Although he hadn't exactly liked her. In the absence of grownups he'd paid little attention to her. He hadn't even dropped frogs down her neck or waved snakes in her face as the other boys did.

Disgusting creatures, boys.

Was that the answer, then—that he had no use for girls? But men with such inclinations married. Everyone married. It was the way of the world. And in her memories, Ogodai was always polite. Almost too polite.

It was a puzzle.

"My courser!" The fury in Almas's voice captured Firuza's attention. She had a flash of recognition, as if she had heard this phrase before, only to realize that she *had* heard it before.

"A beautiful hound," Almas said. "Brought me rabbits and quail. And she sickened and died. Because that man"—he pointed at Zamam again—"gave her foul meat."

"I did not," Zamam yelled. A raised eyebrow from the bey caused him to drop his voice. "I know nothing of poisons."

"Why him?" Firuza asked Almas. "Did you see him feed the dog?"

"He fed her often. She ran to greet him when he passed, and he always had a caress and a treat for her. That day, I saw his back as he left," Almas said. "Within hours, she staggered and fell, and the next morning she died."

"What have you to say?" Firuza extended her hand toward Zamam. "And do not treat me to another rant about your past service. Answer the charge. What were you doing near Almas's tent?"

"Visiting the dog. As he says, she was a beauty." Zamam's fingers moved against his sleeve, as if stroking a pelt. "Far better than such a dolt deserves."

Almas let out another roar of fury. "Don't insult him," Firuza told Zamam. "He has real cause for complaint, and you are not helping your case."

Zamam bowed, hand over his heart. "Forgive me, Lady."

More accusations, more passionate defenses, more details heated the air as Almas and Zamam traded insults.

"Both of you, stop," Firuza ordered. So much for letting them have their say.

She glanced at her brother. He was studying the gourd that held his drink with the owlish expression of one who had already sampled too much of its contents.

Firuza suppressed a sigh. Her problem to handle, obviously. But how?

Almas was a man dedicated to the ancient values of the steppe—absolute honesty, absolute integrity. He would not have made so serious an accusation if he did not believe Zamam guilty. He had suffered a real loss, and she liked him, trusted him, as she did not like or trust Zamam. She hated to rule against her father's old friend.

But Zamam could be telling the truth. He loved animals, dogs included. She had seen him caress his eagle as if it were a favorite child. And Almas's sighthound had been a premier example of its kind—slender but powerful, swift and fierce, with a small proud head and a bond with its owner so tight that it seemed to read his thoughts. Many times she had watched it tearing after game, leading the pack and returning in triumph. It would not surprise her if the dog had attracted the attention of a man who loved animals. That it had died—well, creatures did. Sad but not strange.

Firuza was not her father, able to silence dissent through the sheer power of her personality and the promise of plunder. She ruled, to the extent she did rule, at the sufferance of her brother and the tribal elders. For her decisions to have force, she needed to secure the loyalty of everyone in the horde. What would do that?

Not taking sides, for sure. She pondered her options until a possible way forward presented itself, then raised a hand.

The two petitioners waited—hands clasped and eyes lowered—for the bey's verdict. Firuza again glanced at her brother, murmuring in Roxelana's ear. He did not respond. She smoothed her rose satin skirt, held her chin high, and summoned a mental image of her stepmother putting quarreling servants in their place.

Her cheeks burned at the need to push herself forward. This was not the woman's role for which Diliara had prepared her. Where had Manduhai found the strength to assert her power as empress?

The words tumbled awkwardly from her lips, but she forced them past a tongue grown thick in her mouth.

"I know you to be an honest man," she told Almas. "But Zamam's presence near your tent does not in itself prove that he intended to harm your dog. You did not see him feed it that day, and it may have fallen ill through some other means." Almas opened his mouth, as if in protest, but she silenced him with a raised palm and turned to Zamam. "But we must have peace in the camp, and you are a newcomer among us. You have insulted him, just as he impugned your honor. Your dogs have pups, do they not?"

Zamam nodded, his face glum, as if he could predict what she would say next.

"Then give him one to rear," she said. "The best of the litter, to replace his dead hound. And while the puppy grows, share your food with him. He has many children, and you have none. By aiding him in this way, you prove that you truly wish to live as one of us. To be a good neighbor."

For the first time that afternoon, everyone in the tent stared at her, respect visible in their faces. Even Jahangir held his mockery in check.

She had done it! *Ata* would be proud of her, if he watched from among the ancestors. She was proud of herself, that out of such a tangle she had extracted a solution that worked.

Almas and Zamam bowed and backed from the tent. Firuza straightened her spine and signaled an end to the audience.

Ogodai's horse picked up speed as the circle of felt tents solidified on the horizon. Amid the riffling feather grass, tiny birds cheeped. A bevy of quail, startled by the drumming hoofbeats, shot into the sunlit sky. Invigorated by the gallop across the grasslands and glad to see his destination approaching, Ogodai tossed his cap in the air and howled.

A chorus of howls answered him. Rafik pressed forward till their horses rode side by side, necks stretched toward the tents visible in the distance. Wisps of smoke rose from the hearth fires, and Ogodai's stomach rumbled. He fancied he could already smell the stew pots—rich with mutton and goat, spiced with onions and fragrant grasses. Flat bread, fruit, koumiss—anything but the dried horse meat that had sustained him and his companions throughout their journey. Even that had become scarce, and today the troop had eaten nothing since leaving the temporary camp at dawn, too many hours ago to count. Although on occasion Ogodai had followed Tatar custom and drunk the blood of his horses, he kept that practice for emergencies. His health and that of his men depended on the strength of their ponies.

He'd enjoyed the long ride and the return to the steppe, with its familiar sounds and herbal aromas, the scent of water borne on a passing breeze. The astonishing shapes assumed by fluffy clouds as they raced like steeds across an unblemished cobalt sky, the chance to ride league after league without encountering more than a fox or a rabbit. So early in the fall, the time between dawn and sunset prayers still stretched twice as long as during winter's blizzards, and the weather was perfect for riding—not so hot as to bring on constant thirst, not so cold as to strip away the warmth generated by a full day's exertion. The rainy season had passed, and the ponies' hooves moved swiftly across steppe grasses flattened against parched soil.

Nevertheless, Ogodai looked forward to dismounting, handing over his trusty steed to a subordinate, and settling comfortably around a hearth fire with a bowl of stew. A pail of warm water and some soap would not come amiss either.

Regarding the camp itself, he felt eager to begin yet uncertain of success. Convincing the council of his ability should fall well within his powers, and he had some ideas about how to handle Jahangir. Firuza was another matter. On the brink of wedding a stranger, Ogodai could not help questioning what he would say to her once they became husband and wife. How does one talk to a woman who is neither lover nor sister?

He had not asked Rafik about her, of course. A man did not discuss his women, still less the women of another man.

Rafik would slit his own throat before he dared gossip about the intended chief wife of a potential ruler. But as a result, Ogodai knew little more of his bride than he had six years ago.

The white domes grew larger. Armed warriors poured out of the tents as the drumming hooves came closer. Spirit banners caught the breeze: long staffs circled with stiff leather rounds from which collections of horse tails dangled, one for each male soul. Rafik dug his heels into his pony's flanks and took the lead, lifting his standard high to emphasize that the advancing horsemen were friends, not foes.

The warriors dropped their weapons and howled a welcome. Sheepskin tunics flapped in the wind as arms rose and fell, revealing bare chests and homespun trousers. Sheepskin hats topped heads—fleece outside on some, inside on others. As the sounds of danger yielded to rejoicing, women and children joined the crowd. Boys and girls jumped and hooted while their smaller siblings tugged on the women's sleeves, demanding to be lifted. Some enterprising fellow pounded on a kettle drum, adding to the general pandemonium.

In response to their enthusiasm, Ogodai laughed and swung his quiver in an impromptu salute. Only yesterday, it seemed, he had been one of those jumping, hooting boys, thrilled at the approach of any stranger, eager for a breath of the outside world, for ... what?

He cast himself back to that remote past. Not news—only adults cared about that. For a sense of adventure, perhaps. The knowledge that something existed beyond the confines of daily life.

Odd. In later years the steppe had become, in his mind, the epitome of freedom, the pursuit of simple goals untrammeled by etiquette and culture. But of course, the world of the nomads subscribed to its own rules. As a boy, he had chafed at those restrictions, felt hemmed in by the demands of parents and tutor just as these boys undoubtedly did.

The troop had passed the boundary of the camp. Rafik disappeared among a small mob of Tatars—probably Argyns emerging to greet their returning kinsman. Many of his men were already leading their horses toward one tent or another. Still mounted, Ogodai surveyed the crowd for familiar faces and found half a dozen without trouble. None of them looked as if they could belong to Jahangir or Firuza.

At first, that did not surprise him. Beys do not pile into the street like shepherds to greet any visiting stranger. Nor do the sisters of beys.

But they do greet fellow nobles. Sensing incongruity, he frowned. The council had sent Rafik to Bulat. They would not have acted without the bey's agreement. And Firuza had included a coded message, an explicit request for help. She and her brother must anticipate a response. A woman might have difficulty estimating the length of time such a journey would take, but Jahangir had surely informed himself of Bulat's whereabouts and calculated the distance from the camp's present pasturage to the Smolensk forests. Bulat—senior to Jahangir by virtue of blood, age, and experience—merited a personal welcome from the camp leader. Even Ogodai, as a descendant of Genghis, outranked a bey. Yet no one stood before the largest and most ornate tent other than a lissome brunette with hazel eyes, a come-hither smile, and a body guaranteed to strip a man's mind of any desire to resist her invitation.

Ogodai's gnawing sense of trouble in the horde grew. He swung off his horse and headed in the brunette's direction, shoving his way through the crowd and pulling the gelding behind him.

After no more than a few steps, he felt the reins tug in his hand. He looked down into a pair of bright black eyes, set in a face so similar to his own that he blinked, uncertain whether he beheld a real boy or a spirit.

"I will take your horse to the corral," the boy said.

Ogodai released the reins. "Rub him down," he said. "He has traveled far."

The boy nodded his comprehension and left. Ogodai, wondering, watched him go. Bulat's child? A half-brother? What else could explain the resemblance?

He vaguely recalled his father with a concubine from this camp. How old was the boy, anyway? Five, six, seven? He couldn't tell.

Bulat had left Bahadur's horde eight years ago, returning only briefly, with Sumbeka, for Ogodai's betrothal ceremony. It was possible he had fathered this child.

But Tatar khans did not abandon a son in a distant camp merely because they had not married the boy's mother. If Bulat had sired this child, he would have brought the boy up with his other sons, as he had Tulpar, years ago. Tulpar's mother, too, had been a concubine who enlivened a few winter campaigns. Yet Bulat had taken her into his harem and raised Tulpar to adulthood—until Tulpar's willful disobedience caused the loss of several hundred troops during a battle. The resultant quarrel ended in Tulpar's banishment, and eventually his death. The worst sort of death, abandoned by ancestors and kin.

Ogodai had been eight at the time. He remembered the shouting. The quarrel had taken place in this very camp.

He hadn't seen his older brother since. A hero, then nothing. Not even a body to bury.

Enough. Tulpar had died long ago. Better to focus on Firuza—and whatever had gone wrong in this horde.

Chapter 5

FIRUZA LEAPED TO HER FEET AT THE SOUND OF BOOT HEELS approaching the tent. Force of will had kept her poised on her cushions, hands clasped lest she reach out and shake Jahangir into a proper sense of his responsibilities as bey. Each shriek, howl, hoofbeat, and drum roll threatened to undermine her endurance.

Invasion, her mind insisted. Would she be captured, raped? She had no husband to defend her, and her brother in his present state could not so much as lift a sword!

No. She heard cheering. And the voices of women and children. *Not* invasion then. Friends. Rafik, at last, with Bulat's troops in tow?

Perhaps that was too much to hope for. If Tulpar had returned from Crimea, the horde would cheer for him. He was one of their own.

And what would that mean for her? Ildar Shirin supported Tulpar as khan. If Shirin had his way, the council would bypass Ogodai, negate the betrothal, and offer both Firuza and the khanate to Tulpar.

She'd felt so certain that Tulpar would not return. Not after *Ata* threw him out. That her only hope lay with Bulat and his son.

Suppose she'd been wrong? Would her life be better—or worse? To a woman, the harem agreed that Tulpar was the handsomest, most desirable man any of them had ever seen. And he was, to some extent, a known quantity, a man who had spent much of his life in the camp. Both those things made him a more appealing prospective husband than his distant, uncaring half-brother Ogodai.

Alas, Tulpar was obsessed with Roxelana. *Every* man, it seemed, was obsessed with Roxelana. Every man treated Firuza as his daughter or his sister while casting longing glances in the concubine's direction. Even so, a man obsessed with Roxelana who was also handsome and desirable—and, more important, familiar—might prove a better husband than a man who couldn't spare the time to show his face.

As if she had a choice. The elders would decide, and her wishes would not concern them. They saw her as a womb to continue the lineage of the old bey, not as a potential Manduhai.

They were right. She was not another Manduhai, whatever her brother said. If she had been...

And there, in that moment, a vision flashed before Firuza's eyes, as if sent by the grandmothers. A vision that revealed what her people needed, an idea she had never heard expressed by any man. A vision that neither Tulpar nor Ogodai—and certainly not Jahangir—was likely to entertain for a moment.

Staring like a flummoxed calf at the tent door, she saw a brown hand push the felt covering aside. Her vision would have to wait. Tulpar, Ogodai, Rafik, Bulat? Whoever had caused the hubbub outside would enter at any moment. She grabbed her twin's elbow. "Brother, stir yourself. Will you shame our entire clan? Suppose it's Bulat?"

An intoxicated mumble answered her. Desperate, she gripped his shoulders and shook him.

Too late. She jumped sideways as a boot composed of multicolored leathers joined the hand in pushing the felt door aside. A tall man—black hair tumbling over his forehead; dark eyes every bit as beautiful as she remembered, alight with humor under elegantly curved brows; a pleasing face with high cheekbones, straight nose, well-proportioned mouth, just a hint of mustache and beard; and broad shoulders, surprising in one so slender—stepped across the threshold and ushered Roxelana in.

Not Tulpar. Not Rafik or Bulat, either. Ogodai. Her betrothed. Whose interest in her—and in girls—she had so recently dismissed. Here, in the flesh, as if she had summoned him just by thinking about him. And a lot better-looking than she'd expected.

Surprise robbed her knees of their strength. The grandmothers must have sent him. Him and the vision, at the same time, as if demanding she choose one or the other. She had no idea which she wanted more.

Ogodai inclined his head toward Jahangir, propped against the pillows, then bowed to her. Firuza, her pulses racing, responded in kind.

Ogodai had arrived to claim her at last. And judging from the warmth on his face, he definitely had a use for girls.

He would keep her safe. For the first time in three months, Firuza could imagine life resuming its old, familiar contours.

Yet she couldn't suppress a sigh. Not least when she noticed Roxelana's hand, resting possessively on Ogodai's arm.

With a certain reluctance, Ogodai removed the alluring brunette's hand. *Not* the best way to reintroduce himself to his betrothed, who stood, arms crossed in front of her chest, one slippered toe tapping. Red stained her cheeks, she had compressed her lips, and her black eyes darted back and forth between him and her brother, as if she couldn't decide which of them annoyed her more.

She was shorter than he'd expected. More accurately, she must have attained almost her full height before he left, whereas he had continued to grow. She carried herself very straight, with a confidence he saw reflected in her strong, handsome face. She exhibited none of the pliancy that made the brunette so appealing, but the anger hinted at vivacity and depth. And she was pretty: slim and graceful. Against any competition but the brunette—gliding across the floor, each move an invitation—Firuza would hold her own.

The brunette settled herself next to the man lolling on the bey's platform. That was when Ogodai recognized Jahangir, considerably the worse for drink.

Rafik had warned him. Even so, the situation in the tent shocked him. The bey, prostrate on his cushions, unable to master himself enough to fulfill the most basic courtesy—greeting an honored guest. His sister, clearly uncomfortable, interrupted in the act of shaking him, trying to hold things together against the pull of liquor and the brunette and staring at her brother as if her gaze could infuse him with a sense of propriety. The men, standing around, shuffling their feet, unwilling to draw attention to the bey's incapacitated state but unable either to ignore him or to accept direction from a woman.

Ogodai, raised by a khatun with a mind of her own and with a sister set on emulating the warrior heroines of legend, recognized the men's discomfort without sharing it. Jahangir's condition troubled him more than Firuza's anger. He tried to imagine his former tutor, not to mention his own father, presiding over such disarray. Impossible. How had Bahadur's well-run camp fallen into such a state?

He didn't ask. He had nothing to gain from undercutting his soon-to-be brother-in-law. But watching his bride struggle, head high, to bring Jahangir to a sense of his responsibilities, Ogodai decided on the spot to offer her every assistance. If the Argyns and the other clans supported him, good. He would marry her, become khan, and, by hook or by crook, do what seemed to be beyond the capacity of everyone else here: sober up Jahangir.

And if the clans did not, he would marry her anyway and take her away from here.

Vafa's arrival, preceded by a small group of men, including Ildar Shirin and Rafik's father, gave Ogodai an opportunity to circumvent the awkward moment. He greeted the newcomers, then beckoned to Vafa, who dodged a solid-looking warrior clad in brocade robes and a lambskin hat to hand Ogodai two wrapped parcels. One, bound in red silk, contained a filigreed and jeweled goblet—far too appropriate a gift, Ogodai thought wryly. He stepped forward and laid the red silk at Jahangir's unresponsive feet. Which put him in the perfect spot to hold out the other package to Firuza.

"With my compliments," he said. "To mark the occasion of our wedding."

A simple speech, carefully rehearsed, designed to match the exact level of their relationship—neither strangers nor intimates, long bound together yet mere acquaintances. He could imagine no reason why so straightforward and accurate a statement should cause his betrothed to shudder as his hand brushed hers.

She recovered quickly—so quickly that he doubted his initial impression. "Thank you," she said, her voice clear and well modulated. Strong, as he remembered it, but not shrill. A pleasant voice. While he watched, searching for the source of her obvious discomfort, Firuza turned back the forest-green velvet.

Her mouth dropped open, and Ogodai felt his chest warm with satisfaction. The set of combs—pure gold embedded with turquoise ovals and circles arranged in sweeping lines to create an impression of the winged horse—had enchanted him when Vafa procured them. Against her black hair, they would look spectacular; even the brunette might have cause for envy. "They will suit you," he said. "I hadn't realized how much."

Firuza stared at him as if the winged horse in person had assumed his shape. "Thank you," she said again. Her voice had acquired an appealing, throaty gurgle.

He picked up one comb, then the other, and pressed them gently on either side of the silken bun piled high on her head. "Lovely." His fingers grazed her ear as he stepped back.

The red in Firuza's cheeks deepened—and not, he thought, with anger. She transferred her gaze to his boots, and her air of confidence vanished in what could only be maidenly confusion. Ogodai, pleased, returned his attention to Jahangir.

The brunette, whose name he still had not learned, looked quite put-out. Too bad.

But since she clearly belonged to the bey, it would not do to chase her. He would concentrate on his bride, since the wedding was, if not the whole purpose of his trip, his justification for making it. Sultry brunettes could wait.

He glanced at Firuza again. The winged horses glittered in her dark hair. She had recovered her composure and stared at him, chin elevated in an unspoken challenge. Long turquoise earrings swung on either side of her elegant neck, and her eyes flashed fire. She licked her upper lip, as if unconscious of how such a gesture would affect a man. Her mouth, since she'd stopped compressing it, had an appealing shape, like a composite bow. He imagined caressing her—a privilege only he had the right to claim. The brunette's obvious charms looked cheap by comparison. His fleeting attraction to her faded.

Jahangir, still incapable, lay in the brunette's arms. Ogodai ignored the woman's sultry smile and watched as, with admirable efficiency, Firuza took charge. She snapped her fingers at one servant and handed the green velvet—long enough to become a tunic or sleeveless coat—to a second, then issued a series of orders that ended with Jahangir's removal to another pile of cushions and Ogodai's installation in the place of honor facing the door. In response to her summons, the brunette sauntered from the tent. Both women withdrew, and the four elders came forward to greet him.

Ogodai took mental notes on the four as they exchanged courtesies, comparing today's council members with the men he had known six years before. He assumed they were assessing him in the same way, although they had far more experience than he did in concealing their feelings behind a mask of courtesy.

As befitted the senior statesman of the council, Ildar Shirin approached first. "I trust that your journey went smoothly, Sultan. We have awaited your arrival with great"—he paused, with what Ogodai suspected was a deliberate attempt to rattle him—"anticipation." With one hand he indicated the older man standing next to him, who bore a distinct resemblance to Rafik. His father, Kazbek. No doubt about that. He had not changed a bit in six years.

"My friend Argyn, in particular," Ildar Shirin finished.

Ogodai inclined his head, showing respect for an elder, and wondered how best to respond. For a man whose crown reached Ogodai's shoulders, Ildar had a surprisingly intimidating air about him. How would Bulat handle this?

He settled on basic courtesy. "It pleases me to see you in good health, Ildar Bey, after so long. I look forward to spending some time renewing my acquaintance with your horde—and with my betrothed."

Despite intense awareness of the elders' scrutiny, he managed to deliver this speech with barely a tremor. Bulat would have approved. Ildar, although his demeanor did not thaw in the slightest, indicated satisfaction by bowing and withdrawing to his assigned place on Jahangir's right. Ogodai suppressed a sigh of relief and turned to greet Kazbek Argyn, whose acceptance seemed far more likely. Kazbek welcomed him with a bear hug worthy of a Russian officer. "How you've grown, Sultan! You're quite the warrior these days, Rafik tells me." Released, Ogodai saw Rafik himself grinning, two council members back.

After that, conversation became easier. The two other clan heads—Baryn and Kipchak—had ascended to their present positions after Ogodai had left Bahadur's tutelage. He remembered seeing them from time to time, accompanying their fathers to one meeting or another, as Rafik was doing now. Although they were five to fifteen years older than Ogodai— hence not true friends—neither of them matched Ildar Shirin or Kazbek Argyn in authority. Ogodai sensed them weighing his carefully chosen words, withholding judgment, sounding him out.

"Your presence honors me," he told them. "Will you not take your seats, and we can begin to learn more about one another?"

A group of slaves spread felt mats before those attending the impromptu banquet. Others arrived with one dish after another, spreading them on the carpets until they hid the patterns from view. The members of the council arranged themselves around the bey's platform, and the other men performed a complicated dance that ended with them sorted into concentric arcs, beginning near the khan's platform and extending south toward the door. Ogodai watched them, memorizing the seating pattern. Because it was based on their relative status within the horde, it would help him rank them going forward.

His mouth watered at the array before him. Although the problems in Bahadur's camp had revealed themselves as both real and serious, they did not extend to its hospitality. He saw bowls of meat accompanied by carrots and deep-fried dumplings, baskets of flat bread, plates of glistening melon, frothy koumiss in long-handled jugs. And for Ogodai, the guest of honor, an entire sheep's head on a platter, which he would dole out as required by custom just as soon as someone identified each attendee by name. Jahangir should perform that office, but the ritual was clearly beyond the bey's powers at present.

Ogodai signaled to Rafik, who hesitated until his father urged him forward with a gentle push. Rafik rose and navigated a path around the arcs of men, assuming a place on Ogodai's left.

When the crowd settled, Ogodai raised both hands before his forehead, palms in, and moved them slowly down until his fingertips touched his chin. The rest of the room repeated his gesture, blessing the food and the spirits who had bestowed it. Ogodai lifted the basket of bread, honoring the sustaining force of life, then removed one flat grilled piece and passed the basket to his right. He inhaled its scent—smoke from the clay tandoor, flour, garlic—before tearing it into pieces. As he savored the yeasty texture against his tongue, waited for the introductions that would let him perform his role as honored guest, and treasured the sour/sweet potency of the koumiss, Ogodai reveled in the sense that he beheld his future people. His home, his wife.

Viewed from the perspective of a khan, the camp could use some improvement. Here, inside the bey's tent, the style was rich but old-fashioned. Horse tackle lay in a heap next to a pile of bedding, visible at the edges of the screen designed to shield it. The carpets masking the trellised frame had a threadbare look. The leaders who chatted over the bread wore silk and satin, velvet and furs, but the reek of unwashed clothes and bodies caused Ogodai's nostrils to twitch. The smell would fell a camel.

The servants and common people showed evidence of neglect: ragged clothing and missing shoes. Bahadur had, no doubt, provided for his people, but a horde required a constant flow of loot to ensure its well-being, and Jahangir's sorry state made it improbable that he had launched the necessary raids. Ogodai would remedy that at the first opportunity. If nothing else, the camp would benefit from having its warriors occupied. In Ogodai's experience, raiders at leisure amused themselves by picking fights with one another.

A lesson learned from Bahadur—and therefore taught to Jahangir, too. That the new bey had not acted on the information told Ogodai everything he needed to know about the situation in this camp.

Rafik, prompted by Ogodai, launched into a long list of names. As he responded to each declaration by dispatching another piece of the sheep's head, Ogodai listened carefully, fixing in memory each name and the face that went with it. He had done this several times—in the army, in Kasimov, and before that in Astrakhan. Here it was easier, because he recalled many of the faces and most of the names and needed only to build a structure into which the information would fit. One that included alliances, friends and enemies, the loyal and the less trustworthy—a task that demanded more than a single day but must become his top priority.

So Ogodai listened, observed, and learned even as he enjoyed the feast. His campaign to become khan and help Firuza—even his survival—depended on it.

Firuza slipped away from the women. Roxelana had jibed at her departure—and a headache *was* a poor excuse, Firuza admitted to herself, but in this case she'd spoken the truth. Ogodai's arrival had unsettled her, in more ways than one.

Sidestepping the occasional servant bearing food and drink, she headed for the far side of the camp, to the ancient shrine of the grandmothers—a frayed tent on a cart that traveled with the horde throughout the year, connecting her group of nomads with its female ancestors. Firuza came here often, seeking a respite from the endless demands of the wives and concubines, stepmothers, servants, and members of the camp who surrounded her, waking and sleeping, every hour of the day.

The setting sun coaxed an orange shimmer from the battered felt, smoothing its imperfections and giving the shrine an otherworldly glow. The men feasted in one tent, the women and children in another. Alone, Firuza approached the black wooden cart, tossing milk from her ladle to feed and honor the grandmothers.

When she reached the cart, she propped the ladle and small pail against a wheel and climbed onto the platform. With one hand, she pulled back the felt covering and pressed her palm against the wooden door. Dipping her head, she stepped over the threshold. Small rips in the felt allowed gleams of light to penetrate, but otherwise the interior lay still and dark.

She settled herself on her knees before the raised seat in the center. Silence enfolded her. Spirit dolls representing the ancestors—small poppets of wood about the length of a man's hand dressed and coiffed like Tatar matrons, arrayed in a line against the back of the platform—accepted her homage as she bowed. Her forehead touched the woven mat. She pressed her hands against the floor and pushed herself upright, then drew a package of dried meat from her sleeve and dropped it in the clay bowl left for the use of pilgrims. She offered it to the spirit dolls for their sustenance. Touching her new combs for inspiration, she murmured greetings to the grandmothers while she waited for the right words to form in her head.

A brass plate, balanced on end, sat behind the dolls. A previous offering, no doubt. Its gleaming surface highlighted the exquisite gold and turquoise combs, their winged horses set off by the glossy black of her hair.

Words came without prompting. "He said they would suit me," she told the grandmothers. "'I hadn't realized how much,' he said. 'Lovely,' he said. To *me*, not Roxelana. He took her hand off his arm. She's been pouting ever since. And he stroked my ear."

Firuza's stomach clenched beneath her robes. Was it possible that one man in the universe found her more appealing than her father's favorite concubine?

Surely not. And if he did, what then?

"He won't understand," she said. "How can I tell him? He's a khan, like any other. Men think only of raiding and fighting, but the horde needs more, Grandmothers. You must agree. You sent me the vision."

A breeze brushed her face, and she listened, because in just this way the spirits spoke to their descendants. But the grandmothers' intent remained cloudy.

"It is true," she said, acknowledging the thought sparked by the breeze. "You sent Ogodai, too. I must marry him now. Our fathers intended it. To refuse would dishonor them and ourselves. But how can I agree, when the horde needs so much more than he and Jahangir can give it?"

She had reached the essence of her vision: raiding and plunder would not ensure her people's prosperity.

"Even under *Ata*," she reminded the ancestors, "the camp declined. The herds produce fewer offspring each year; the grasslands have become less lush; the winters grow colder and longer, the summers shorter and more arid. Our world is changing, but we have not changed. We continue to live according to the old ways."

Of which the grandmothers were a part. Yet they had sent her a vision.

"Teach me," she said, "how to lead my people along the path you have set for them. Show me how to overcome their divisions, prevent the injustices and squabbles I saw today, find new trade routes for them, turn them toward something besides violence. Open the milk road to me, and I will do what Manduhai did not—seek peace, not war. Give me your blessing, as I give you my word. I will put my people first, above the petty interests of the council. If I do not, I give you leave to separate my soul from my body. To rend me limb from limb."

She shivered, for the oath was a powerful one. With her body broken, her spirit could not join the ancestors. Her existence would end with her death.

A breath of air grazed her ear, as Ogodai's finger had earlier. The soft hiss of the breeze evoked his whispered voice. Her cheeks flushed anew. She sensed something unfamiliar but alluring, the promise of pleasure. The hollow feeling in her stomach strengthened; her thumbs brushed the turquoise combs in her hair.

"The winged horse," she murmured. "The forces of air, of change. Is that what you want me to hear, Grandmothers— that because you sent Ogodai *and* the vision, I must find a way to combine them?"

Could she combine them? There would be real advantages to having a man share her journey. A man to advise her and support her, whose children she would bear. Without heirs, her achievements would die with her. And a man who saw her as pretty, who stroked her cheek, who brought her winged horses made of turquoise and told her that they suited her—such a man would make a good companion.

If she could trust him to fulfill her vision. For that, she needed to learn more about him. She would request a delay, to become better acquainted with him. A delay dishonored nobody. The elders might even welcome it, since they still had to vote on whether to accept Ogodai as khan.

"Would that be acceptable?" she asked the spirits. "To postpone the ceremony for a while?"

Light danced against the platform. She sensed only calm. They agreed, then.

She bowed to the spirit dolls, again letting her forehead touch the battered mat. "Enjoy your meal, Grandmothers," she said, then retreated from the tent the same way she had entered it.

Outside, the sun was setting. The men's voices, loud amid the silence of the enveloping steppe, boomed from the reception tent where she had spent so much of the afternoon. They would continue to feast for hours, but the women were already dispersing. Firuza picked up her pace, determined to reach her bed before anyone noticed her missing. The grandmothers had revealed what they expected of her.

She must marry Ogodai, after a permissible delay. Somehow that would lead her to her goal, although she did not see how.

Confide in him? Not yet. They were near-strangers still.

Although an ally *would* make her quest more attainable. Slipping into her home and finding it free as yet of busybody sisters and friends, Firuza dropped onto the nearest seat and covered her face with her hands. Life seemed far more complicated than it had yesterday.

Chapter 6

OGODAI KICKED THE INNER TENT FLAP ASIDE AND HELD IT open, letting the early morning light fall on the tent's sleeping occupants. "Get up," he announced at top volume. "We're riding today."

Jahangir groaned and dropped one arm over his face. "Go away, Ogodai. I'm sick. And don't talk so loud."

"Don't drink so much." Three days of exchanges like this one had convinced Ogodai not to waste his time on sympathy. Being the only person in the camp who outranked Jahangir made him the one person who could safely ignore the bey's orders and tantrums, and he intended to take full advantage of that. His childhood friend might have disappeared into some internal hell, but if Ogodai could find a way to winkle him out again, he would.

Roxelana (it hadn't taken him long to discover her name) stirred and sat up. Ogodai averted his eyes as a gesture of respect for Jahangir, although he couldn't help sneaking a peek at those magnificent breasts.

"Cover yourself, woman," he said to hide his lapse. "And get your master some tea."

"Tea? We don't have tea here." The sneer in her voice implied that no real man drank tea—the most recent in the series of insults that had replaced her initial attempts at seduction as soon as she realized those attempts were not working. She wasn't accustomed to men spurning her, he guessed.

"Vafa brought it in his saddle bags. My man. He's expecting you," he said.

She rose, defiantly naked, taunting him with her beauty. Even Jahangir in his weakened state could not ignore that piece of impudence (or flirtation). He threw her a robe. "Put that on, woman, at once." With a sulky expression, she complied.

"I'm going to see to the horses," Ogodai told Jahangir. "Be dressed when I get back, or I'll return with a full bucket. It wouldn't hurt you to bathe."

"You're a heartless bastard," Jahangir yelled as he struggled to a sitting position.

Good. Jahangir didn't want a repeat of yesterday morning, when Ogodai had tossed half a jug of water over the bey's head.

Come to think of it, Roxelana had caught her share. No wonder she was mad.

"Yes, but not a drunken one." Ogodai grinned as he let go of the tent flap and heard Jahangir moan once more as the felt thwacked into place.

Like it or not, Jahangir would soon become bey in fact as well as in name.

The small boy who had taken Ogodai's reins three days ago was playing in the makeshift street between the tents. Ogodai beckoned to him, and he came running.

"What's your name, lad?" he asked. He hadn't seen the boy since the day of his arrival. The child's resemblance to himself at around the same age struck him with renewed force.

"Timur," the boy said. A good Tatar name.

"Well, Timur," he said. "I am Ogodai Sultan. Do you know how to prepare a horse for riding?"

Timur had been shuffling his feet, staring at the ground as if a lizard might pop up amid the grasses, but when challenged he threw his head back and held it high. "Yes, Sultan." He glanced down again. "I can't quite lift the saddle, though."

"I'll help," Ogodai said. "You can hand me the gear as I need it. Come." The child skipped at his side as he moved away.

In the corral, Ogodai's men already mingled with members of the horde, readying the horses for work. Ogodai soon established an amicable rhythm with Timur. The boy stuck out his tongue in concentration as he separated the horse tackle, but he had no trouble selecting what Ogodai needed or identifying the pieces when asked. They had saddled and bridled Ogodai's horse and begun on Jahangir's when the sound of an approaching troop interrupted them.

The clang of metal mixed with thrumming hoofbeats as the men in the corral drew their weapons. Ogodai grabbed for Timur and missed as the boy raced for the gate in the latticework fence. "Wait," Ogodai shouted, but Timur paid him no heed. Instead, he waved one arm wildly and screamed something Ogodai could not quite make out.

It sounded like *Ata*—Father. Was this a returning raiding party, then? Timur appeared to live here, in the camp—with his mother, one assumed. Which implied a father somewhere.

Not Bulat, either, if this was Timur's father riding in. Too bad, in a way. Ogodai missed his younger brother, and Timur was an appealing child.

But still a child, too young to foresee danger. Just because he thought he saw his father didn't mean he had.

The horses within the corral pressed forward. Men reached for dangling reins. Determined to find out what was going on, Ogodai vaulted into his saddle and surveyed the approaching warriors.

And nearly fell off at the sight of the leader, waving the white banner of victory above his turbaned head. Whether Timur's father rode among the incoming troop or not, Ogodai had no way to tell. But he recognized the leader, despite their long separation.

Tulpar. Bulat's oldest son, his own half-brother, presumed dead for the last decade.

Anger, shock, bewilderment, joy—Ogodai couldn't disentangle his emotions enough to name them, much less direct them. Tulpar was *alive.* But what brought him here? And why had no one mentioned his affiliation with this camp?

Worse, why had his father said nothing? Bulat had scouts watching camps and cities throughout the Tatar lands. He must know that his eldest son lived, and where. Yet he had not warned Ogodai, even when ordering him here. He'd allowed everyone to think Tulpar dead.

Which Tulpar, obviously, was not. He looked much the same, in fact, allowing for the ten years of separation from his family. Ogodai watched his half-brother dismount and pick up Timur, who stopped shrieking once he had both arms around Tulpar's neck.

Because the child had found his father. Hence the family resemblance. Not a half-brother via Bulat but a nephew. One mystery solved.

Preoccupied with the boy, Tulpar had not noticed his brother on horseback. As Ogodai examined Tulpar more closely, he saw that there had been changes, if superficial ones. Tulpar had never lacked self-confidence, but his adolescent cockiness had matured into something more like assurance. His body had filled out, his face slimmed down, his mustache grown more luxuriant. But his dark brown hair, with its tendency to wave; his eyes, so closely matched in color to the hair under dense, often-frowning brows; and his symmetrical features—these things had not changed. Women had thrown themselves at him at sixteen. They probably still did.

Roxelana certainly did. She dashed—robed, her hair veiled—from the bey's tent and hung on Tulpar's arm. Laughing, Tulpar returned his son to the ground and lifted her off her feet, rubbing her nose with his own.

Jahangir, also dressed, stumbled through his door and winced as the sunlight hit his face. At almost the same moment, Firuza emerged from her tent across the way from her brother's. In a rare act of symmetry, the twins turned as one to face the new arrival, placed their palms together, and bowed. As Tulpar moved to greet them, they smiled—Firuza more warmly than Jahangir, who gazed owlishly at the sky.

The smiles fueled Ogodai's sense of injustice, his conviction that the world—the twins, their camp, his father— had deceived him. Bereft of speech, he opened his mouth in a wordless roar.

Amid the hubbub of welcome, the roar caught Tulpar's attention. His head snapped toward the sound. The blankness of nonrecognition gave way to a shock that mirrored Ogodai's own. Then that, too, faded, leaving a sardonic grin. Tulpar crossed his arms across his chest, cocked his head at the angle used in issuing a challenge, and waited.

Ogodai stared, wheels spinning in his head as he tried to make sense of his brother's behavior. The Tulpar of his childhood had treated him with casual affection, tolerating his hero worship and sporadically intervening on his behalf. They had yet to exchange two words, but *this* Tulpar had already declared himself, in expression and pose, an enemy. Why, Ogodai couldn't tell, but he could see that it was so. He bit his lip, fighting a sense of loss. It was ridiculous to grieve for a brother long believed dead.

Jahangir snapped his fingers at Roxelana, who sauntered toward the bey.

"So, Tulpar," Jahangir said, "I suppose I need not introduce Ogodai Sultan." Tulpar inclined his head to the minimum level required by courtesy. Ogodai dismounted, wishing he could keep his seat. The height offered him an advantage, and in the present uncertainty he needed one. As he walked toward Tulpar and Jahangir—not so fast as to seem eager, not so slow as to indicate reluctance—he turned over in his mind what to say.

But it was hard to choose the right course. Everyone in the camp had a better grasp of the situation than he did. Jahangir and Roxelana made no bones about enjoying his confusion. The elders watched from a distance, withholding judgment. Among them, only Kazbek Argyn had offered full support. Rafik, whom Ogodai had trusted to advise him, had failed to mention Tulpar's existence. Firuza, although in general friendly, had asked for a postponement of their wedding. He had agreed, of course. He had no desire to force her. But as a result, he was not sure where he stood with her, either. And Tulpar looked outright aggressive. In short, no allies here.

"*Ené*," Tulpar said when Ogodai reached him. Younger brother. The most basic greeting he could make. "You have grown. I did not recognize you for a moment."

"We thought you were dead." Ogodai blurted out the first words that came into his head. He flexed and released his hands, then forced himself to stop. It felt strange not to greet his brother with a hug, but Tulpar's crossed arms repelled any embrace.

"No thanks to you that I'm not." Tulpar ignored Timur, tugging at his coat. His stance, the way he thrust his shoulders back and his chin forward—everything about him suggested a man preparing for a duel.

"No thanks to me? What are you talking about? I was eight." Ogodai felt himself imitating his brother's pugilistic pose. "I had nothing to do with the fight between you and *Ata*. Couldn't you have sent word, at least?"

"You think Bulat allowed that? He made sure I had no contact with any of you." Tulpar produced an angry, gruff sound somewhere between self-mocking laughter and a grunt. "Not that I wanted it. I'd had enough, thank you. So don't give me that wounded expression. I've followed your career, you know. You're a good little soldier, Bulat's faithful shadow. You do what *Ata* wants."

Deterred by the glee in Jahangir's and Roxelana's faces, Ogodai bit back the desire to point out that being a good soldier was a virtue, not a vice. Firuza looked worried. He needed to impress her, not defend the obvious.

"Why pick on me?" he asked. "I wasn't much older than Timur there when you left. I would have liked to hear from you. So would my mother and sister. We missed you."

Tulpar's expression softened at that declaration, then hardened again, as if he were forcing himself to cling to long-nurtured grievances. "Then why not investigate my supposed death? You're what—eighteen, nineteen? Old enough to think for yourself. Instead, you stand by while Bulat tells you who your friends should be. Who your family should be. What your life should be. You're a puppet, not a man."

Ogodai felt his patience slipping. "Go to hell, Tulpar," he said. "Nurse your grudge. I don't have to justify myself to you."

He headed toward Firuza, but Tulpar stopped him in mid-stride. "Don't you want to hear what I did to get on your blessed father's bad side?"

Ogodai glanced at him. "He's your father, too."

"Not these days. He made that clear." Tulpar had uncrossed his arms and planted them on his hips, elbows out, the picture of intransigence.

Ogodai mimicked his pose, jutting chin and all. "And why was that? Because you defied an order in the midst of battle. Men died. Hundreds of good warriors killed to puff up your vanity."

From off to one side, Ogodai heard someone gasp. It might have been Firuza.

Tulpar's face darkened. "That's Bulat's version. Which you swallowed, of course. It's not true. Men died, yes. I regret that. But Bulat loses men in every battle. He takes the losses in stride, as every commander must. It was for having had the temerity to question the khan's orders that our father banished me from his sight."

Speechless, Ogodai stared at him. Bulat was autocratic, as most Tatar fathers were. Ogodai himself chafed under *Ata*'s demands for complete, unquestioning obedience. But exile his oldest son for defying an order? That sounded extreme, even for Bulat.

So extreme, in fact, that Ogodai didn't believe it. Tulpar had concocted a story that absolved him from responsibility. He would defend that story to the death. If Tulpar could blame an eight-year-old for his disgrace—or an eighteen-year-old for not investigating a decade-old death report—Ogodai had little faith that talking could change his brother's mind. At this point, he wasn't sure he cared.

Tulpar spoke again. "But you don't need to worry about that, do you, *ené*? You are the khan's favored son. Why beat your head against the door to ensure justice for others?"

His scorn was unmistakable. Jahangir unleashed a cackle that bordered on the maniacal. Roxelana curved her lips in a snaky smile and glided into the bey's tent. Only Firuza gazed at her betrothed with anything that might be considered sympathy.

He was wasting his time. But for the sake of their past brotherhood, Ogodai made one last effort. "I didn't come here to fight you. The council requested my presence, and our father asked me to honor the contract he made with Bahadur. To marry his daughter."

"Marry his daughter?" Tulpar burst out laughing. "Oh, that's rich. I will be the one marrying Bahadur's precious daughter. He promised her to me long before he offered her to you. And I assure you, *ené*, that I have every intention of collecting my prize. Prizes, rather. Firuza *and* the khanate. You won't rob me twice."

Tulpar had designs on Firuza, Ogodai's betrothed since they were twelve? That was too much.

Firuza made a sound like a hen fluffing its feathers. "You lie. On his deathbed, *Ata* ordered me to summon Bulat, and I did. To marry Ogodai, and I will."

She had spoken up for him! Ogodai twisted to face her once more. She had a hand clapped over her mouth, and her eyes looked huge, but when he smiled at her, she dropped her fingers and blushed.

Tulpar grinned. "Another good soldier. You'd make a fine pair. But it won't be your choice, poppet. Your father is gone, and the council will select your husband." He inclined his head.

"Bahadur promised his daughter to the eldest son of Bulat. Me."

"Not you." Ogodai struggled to keep his temper. "*Ata* disowned you, and you were always a concubine's child. *I* am the eldest son of his chief wife. You can strut like a peacock, but it doesn't change anything."

"We'll see about that." Tulpar reached past him and clasped Firuza's hand, as if staking his claim to her. "Ildar Shirin backs me, and the council knows me. So the bey's daughter is mine. Aren't you, poppet?"

She flinched. How dare Tulpar touch a woman who was not his! Ogodai surged forward and wrapped a protective arm around Firuza's shoulders. "Leave her alone," he told his brother. "And don't call her poppet. She belongs to me!"

His betrothed trembled under his hand, the way a mare quivers when facing battle for the first time, but she did not pull away. One good thing to come out of this mess.

Because it was a mess. Even if Tulpar lied—and Ogodai wasn't sure he did, because the two sworn brothers *could* have made such an arrangement long ago, even if they changed it later—the truth hardly mattered. By questioning Bahadur's intentions, Tulpar had forced the council to intervene. And the elders might well favor him. He was older, more experienced, and familiar to them. Three days had not given Ogodai enough time to prove himself to anyone.

"Tut, tut," Tulpar said. "Little brother is upset. Go home, little brother, and leave the khanate and the girl to someone who knows what to do with them. You'll inherit Bulat's horde. You don't need this one. As you put it so charmingly, you are the son of his chief wife." He sidestepped Ogodai and took Firuza's chin in his hand, as if his younger brother had no more presence than a spirit. "Quite attractive, aren't you, poppet? I will enjoy introducing you to the arts of love."

Firuza jerked her head out of his grasp and stomped with her foot, but he pulled his boot out of range and stood laughing at her discomfort. Ogodai, furious beyond words, dropped the arm consoling his bride and aimed his fist at Tulpar's midriff. Tulpar blocked the blow with one hand and retaliated with the other. His fist connected with Ogodai's chin. Ogodai sailed backward through the air and landed in a heap outside Firuza's tent. As the laughter reached a crescendo, he sensed her trying to drag him inside.

Damnation. So much for impressing his girl.

That was his last conscious thought for quite a while.

Tulpar strolled away, cradling his grazed fist in his other hand. Firuza hissed at his departing back, then grabbed Timur and ordered him to find the shaman who had arrived last month to replace the runaway blamed for Bahadur's death. "And send Vafa to my tent at once," she called after the boy. "Tell him his master is hurt."

Ogodai lay as if dead at her feet, but she saw his chest rise and fall. Not serious, then.

Men. Infuriating creatures. Why must they always solve problems with their fists?

Although Ogodai *had* been trying to protect her. No one had stood up for her like that since her father died. And the fight would have gone nowhere if Tulpar hadn't hit back. As the elder, he had a responsibility to keep the peace. Instead, he had pushed his brother as far and as hard as he could, even pretending to find Firuza attractive.

For a moment there, he'd almost convinced her. But she had spent too many days watching him flirt with Roxelana to believe he felt a genuine interest.

It didn't matter anyway. *Ata* had betrothed her to Ogodai, whatever Tulpar said. They had his blessing—and the grandmothers'. And at this moment, her betrothed needed her attention. She pressed a hand to Ogodai's forehead and found it cool to the touch. A good sign.

Alas, he was too heavy for her to lift, or even to drag. She signaled to the closest pair of warriors, then followed them as they carried Ogodai into the tent and laid him on the bed in the corner.

In these domestic matters, no one questioned her authority. Jahangir, chortling, had retreated to his own tent. Tulpar had disappeared into that of Timur's mother.

Diliara bustled in, eager to help and to gossip. "I told Vafa we would care for your young man, dearest," she said. She sailed over to a group of trunks that stood against the far wall, her veil floating from the tip of her pointed cap, her silk skirts swishing against the carpeted floor. Firuza joined her, and together they removed a pair of coverlets from one of the trunks and spread them over Ogodai.

By the time the shaman arrived, Ogodai was stirring and mumbling. She couldn't make out his words. "He's coming to," Firuza told the healer. "Just smudge and leave, then stay nearby. I'll call if he needs you." Her stepmother passed her a small bowl of warm water and a cloth, and Firuza sat on the bed next to her betrothed and patted his forehead with the damp towel.

The scent of sage from the smudge stick, the shaman's chant, the weight of the bowl in her hands, the male form (younger, slimmer, more handsome!) lying before her— Firuza's mouth dried as the scene thrust her back to the night of her father's death. Raw panic rushed through her. She had cared for *Ata*, just like this, yet *Ata* had died, upending her world, initiating changes bound up in the person of this young warrior who lay on her bed, his black hair soft under her fingertips, his eyelids fluttering.

"Leave us," she repeated, and the shaman did. As the scent of sage faded, Firuza's heartbeat slowed. "He will awaken soon." Her hands shook as she dropped the cloth into the bowl and handed it to her stepmother, but she managed to keep her voice steady.

"Indeed." Her stepmother perched on an inlaid chest, sturdy enough to support her ample frame. "What brought him low, dearest?"

"Himself," Firuza said. She would have liked to share the story, ask Diliara's opinion, seek advice and comfort. But her betrothed's eyes had opened, and he gazed blearily at her. She leaned on her heels, creating distance between them, but the position was too uncomfortable, so she compromised by letting her thighs shift to the side.

Ogodai pushed himself to a sitting position. He rubbed his chin where Tulpar had struck him but otherwise appeared unharmed. Upright, his body was no more than a few inches from hers. If she wanted, she could touch the pulse that beat in his throat.

Unsettled by his nearness, she edged away. He caught her hand. She stared at their clasped fingers, wondering how he could make her feel nervous and excited and shy at the same time.

He addressed Diliara. "I wish to speak to my betrothed alone. Please give us leave."

Alone. He had something to say to her that others shouldn't hear? The fluttering in Firuza's stomach intensified.

Diliara, ever obedient to male commands, rose to her feet. But she didn't leave. Instead, she hovered. "Your reputation, dearest."

"We are betrothed," Firuza reminded her. "And will marry before long."

"I won't take advantage of her," Ogodai said. "Wait nearby, if you like. I just need to ask her a question."

Question. Firuza bit her lip. What sort of question?

The assurance appeared to satisfy Diliara, who bowed and withdrew. Ogodai tightened his clasp on Firuza's hand, startling her. She didn't pull away. He was her betrothed; he had the right to hold her hand.

Only none other had. Not like this. Except her father and her brother, and they did not count. And Tulpar, earlier today, but he didn't count either. He was not her intended.

Was he?

"You nursed me," Ogodai said. "Thank you." He raised the hand he held to his mouth and brushed his lips across her fingers. She dipped her head, too flustered to speak. The fluttering yielded to a stranger, stronger sensation, as if her insides were dissolving. If the simplest caress had such an effect on her, how would it feel when he kissed her?

Did he want to kiss her? Was that why he had asked to talk to her alone?

"But I must know," Ogodai said. "Why did you hide the truth about my brother?"

For sure, the ancestors had deserted him this day. A straightforward question, plainly stated, with no accusation, even an implicit one, other than the frustration lingering from this morning's altercation with Tulpar. He had even remembered to thank Firuza for her care before he asked it. With her hand nestled in his, the sweet memory of her fingers rubbing his forehead fresh in his mind, her delightful blush and lowered gaze, it had seemed like the perfect moment to introduce the issue at the forefront of his mind. Get it over with as soon as possible and with the person least likely to have a nefarious motive for her silence. Then he could tackle Rafik, Jahangir, and the council.

No point in talking to Tulpar. His brother had left no doubt that he would refuse to cooperate. Ogodai reflexively rubbed his jaw with his knuckles. No doubt whatsoever.

Only nothing was going as planned. Firuza dragged her hand from his and sat flattened against the tent wall as if she sought to push her way through the felt. He hadn't said anything *that* dreadful, had he?

Her face suggested he had. "I hid no truth about your brother. I have no idea what you're talking about."

"I'm talking about Tulpar. He has a son here. He appears to live here. You can't have forgotten his quarrel with my father. He must have told you we haven't seen him in years. I would have said, 'Your brother Tulpar visits us sometimes.' Isn't that natural?"

Firuza's blush deepened. "He doesn't live here. He hasn't come here in ages. Last time I saw him was when he left for Crimea, the week before *Ata* died."

"Which happened three months ago," Ogodai reminded her. "Forgive me, Lady"—he could not keep the ironic tone from his voice—"but that seems recent enough to merit a mention."

He expected an apology, but he didn't get one. Firuza yelled, "You don't understand anything," and ran out of the tent.

Well, she'd got that right. When it came to women, he didn't understand a thing.

Ooh, the nerve. When she'd been expecting ... well, she didn't know what she'd expected, to tell the truth, but not that Ogodai would ask for time alone just to pester her about his family. How was *she* supposed to know he had no idea his brother frequented this camp? And if she had known, what did he imagine she could have done about it? They'd barely seen each other since he arrived, and he thought she'd blurt out that Tulpar used to visit until her father banished him three months ago?

Besides, Ogodai was her betrothed. He should show *some* interest in her as a woman.

A vain hope, that. He might not moon over Roxelana—at least not where his betrothed could see him—but obviously he was like every other man. He'd played her up when it suited him, only to chide her the first time she disappointed him, not wasting a moment in wondering how life looked from her point of view.

Roxelana must have it right, whether Firuza liked it or not. She really *was* that unattractive to men.

Diliara called to her as she dashed past. Firuza acted as if she hadn't heard. She couldn't ignore her stepmother for long, but right then, she had to get away. The prospect of sitting among chattering women demanding, speculating, and advising made her want to throw something. They'd assume Ogodai had flirted with her, press for details, prod and pry. She would *not* give them the satisfaction of telling them what he'd said. Not when they still teased her over how long it had taken him to show his face.

The corral beckoned to her. Perfect. She whistled for her mare. Kubelek trotted toward her and nuzzled her shoulder. She led the horse out of the corral and mounted bareback, tangling her fingers in the mare's creamy mane.

Soft, but not as soft as the caress of Ogodai's lips against her hand. Firuza shook her head to clear it and dug her heels into the horse's side. "*Chu, chu,*" she said, urging the mare into a canter.

She shouldn't let him affect her that way. Who was he besides a courteous stranger? The man her father had picked for her, true, but no one whose touch should cause her flesh to melt. What kind of idiot entertained fantasies that he might care for her?

No woman expected fidelity. But the daughter of a bey did not accept less than the status of chief wife. If Ogodai did not respect her, she might do better with Tulpar, now that he had declared his intention to fight for her. He'd behaved badly today, but mostly to annoy his brother. She'd seen him charm and coax when it suited him. At times, he had even made the effort to charm and coax *her*, although he usually didn't bother. If he wanted her as his wife, though, that would have to change.

She didn't have much power, but she had more than the men thought she did. If she signaled a preference for Tulpar to Ildar Shirin, he could use that information to persuade the council to do what he wanted it to do anyway. If she told Kazbek Argyn she favored Ogodai, he could do the same. She might even strike a bargain with Tulpar: banish Roxelana, and I'll ask them to make you khan. Although if she chose Ogodai, she wouldn't have to worry about Roxelana at all. Which man should she pick?

Ata had been a sound judge of character. He'd backed Ogodai, whom he had known only as a child, over Tulpar, who had served him in adulthood. Tulpar's claims to the contrary were nonsense. And *Ata* had sworn her to obedience before he died. The ancestors would disown her if she broke her oath.

Although Tulpar *was* quite attractive...

But then, so was Ogodai. He'd worked wonders with Jahangir, and he'd treated her with unfaltering courtesy. She sensed she could trust him, but she didn't, not yet. She needed more than three days for that.

The mare broke into a gallop. Firuza clung with fingers and knees as they flew across the grassy plain, scattering birds and small animals as they passed.

The sensation of wind on her face exalted her. Even the odd sensations that reduced her to simpering idiocy at Ogodai's touch dissipated among the swift-moving clouds. So must *Ata* have flown to join the ancestors.

As the mare slowed, she realized she didn't have to choose. She could bide her time and watch. The council was divided: the Shirins against the Argyns, with two elders susceptible to persuasion and Jahangir poised to cast the deciding vote. By accepting Tulpar's claim, Ildar Shirin would unleash negotiations that could last for months. The Argyns hated the Shirins' dominance; they would insist that the council respect the old bey's choice. The clan leaders controlled her marriage, yes, but that was secondary. They would give her to the man they selected as khan.

Either way, Jahangir would be safe and Firuza would retain her standing and her freedom. She had time to sound the two men out, to test her vision, to pray to the grandmothers for guidance. She just had to ensure that, in the end, the council made the right choice. As soon as she discovered what that was.

Firuza turned her horse toward the camp. But Kubelek had not taken more than a few steps before she reined the mare in. Negotiations. Divided council. Ildar Shirin.

Why had Tulpar returned? Had someone told him about Ogodai's arrival? It seemed too much of a coincidence that he would decide, after not visiting the camp in months, to show up three days after his half-brother arrived—and with a chip on his shoulder the size of the steppe, to boot.

Ogodai hadn't summoned him. He had been astonished when Tulpar rode in. So who? Not Kazbek Argyn. Jahangir? Shirin?

If Tulpar had not arrived, the elders would have proclaimed Ogodai khan within days—or, at most, weeks. They had no reason not to, and they were eager to return to their own flocks and herds.

Yet someone—most likely Shirin—had decided to complicate things by introducing a rival. And if Shirin had summoned Tulpar to challenge Ogodai, maybe Shirin planned to tip the election in his favor, depriving Firuza of the opportunity she needed to influence her own destiny.

She kneed her horse in the ribs and raced for home, determined to find out more.

As the camp loomed large before her, she recalled that she had run away from Ogodai. She would have to apologize. Which was awkward, given that she would die before she blurted out that she'd expected him to kiss her instead of quizzing her about his brother.

She began constructing stories in her head, but in the end she didn't need them. By the time she reached home, Ogodai no longer occupied her tent.

Chapter 7

IRINA BULATOVNA KOLYCHEVA—KNOWN TO EVERYONE IN Kazan by her birth name, Nasan—inhaled the lemony aroma of chypre with a pleasure she would not have believed possible six months ago. Then she had longed to escape the scented palace courtyards, the dew-bright fountains of Kasimov—to ride into the steppe and never look back. She had not imagined that fate might force her along an entirely different path: into marriage to a Russian nobleman—imposing on her a new language, a different faith, and surroundings so unfamiliar that she rejoiced to put them behind her and return to the luxurious draperies, the grilled windows, the spice-rich air of the Tatar lands. Each time the muezzin called from the minaret, marking a new stage in the endless cycle of days, Nasan felt a small bubble of happiness rise from her middle to her throat, as if she could break into song like the skylarks so prevalent in the grasslands.

Each time she refrained. Not so much because khans' daughters should not carol about the palace like peasant girls binding hay—Nasan had little patience with such conventions—but out of respect for the feelings of the man sitting next to her, elbows on his knees, body leaning forward, his face taut. Her husband, Daniil. Nineteen years old to her sixteen; tall, with tawny hair and brown eyes, strong and quick-witted, full of good humor and blessed with a smile that had lured Nasan from their first meeting, when she had wanted to hate him. Four months into her marriage, it still amazed her that, somehow, out of the catastrophe of her younger brother's death the grandmothers had crafted an ending in which she returned to live among the Tatars with Daniil Kolychev at her side.

For Daniil, though, Kazan signified not home but alien territory, filled with hidden enemies bent on his and his wife's destruction.

He had reason to worry. The familiar customs and appearance of Kazan did not blind Nasan to the signs of something awry at the royal court. She felt the tension as she strolled the tiled passageways, sensed half-heard quarrels and secrets borne on the air like sandalwood and cinnamon. From Queen Gulnara and her chief henchman, Gazim Shirin, to the lowest stablehand, the Kazan court hummed with rumors and plots.

And like it or not, Nasan and Daniil found themselves tossed into the center of the maze, with few clear indications of which paths might lead to the exit or even what constituted a path. They had traveled here at the orders of Grand Princess Elena, regent of Russia, who had assigned Daniil to accompany her diplomatic mission to Kazan, which she saw as a rogue khanate ripe for Russian domination. A junior envoy in the train of Alexander Makhmetovich Sultan, the converted Tatar who headed the mission to recover Russians captured in Kazan's recent series of slave raids and to procure reparations for the damage done to the captives' lives and health. A mission that seemed less likely to succeed with every day that passed—news guaranteed to annoy Elena if delivered.

In truth, Nasan found the current arrangement disconcerting. Whereas Daniil was not in the least distressed to find himself a humble attaché, Nasan, a khan's daughter from a lineage even more distinguished than Elena's, envisioned herself and her kin at the fore of every undertaking. Never mind that her husband did not speak Tatar (although he practiced at every available moment), ranked at least four steps in the court hierarchy below any Tatar sultan, and could not hope to match Alexander Makhmetovich in experience. Nasan remained unconvinced. Her rank equaled Alexander's, and *she* spoke Tatar, did she not? Why, her uncle Jan-Ali was the khan of Kazan!

Daniil laughed when she said this, declaring his complete lack of interest in becoming an ambassador. If it were up to him, he'd send troops to rescue the captives, although he hoped the negotiations would drag on for years if living here made her happy. Meanwhile, could she keep an eye on what might be going on behind the scenes, because if he'd ever seen a place roiling with hidden currents, Kazan was that place? As a woman, she could enter areas barred to him.

He did not add that no court had a use for a female diplomat, regardless of rank. And why should he? Nasan knew the rules, whether she liked them or not.

At least Daniil appreciated her help, so she did what she could. Her safety depended on his, and vice versa. Moving around the palace, she felt as if she and her husband walked a rope across a canyon, surrounded by fog, while dragons roared from below and eagles stooped from above.

But she learned enough to tie the underlying problem to her uncle Jan-Ali, appointed by the Russians—and hence, in the eyes of many Kazan residents, too close to the enemy. Although no one openly spoke of deposing Jan-Ali and reinstating his predecessor, Safa-Girei of Crimea, Nasan overheard restless whispers that hinted at such a possibility. She confided each intercepted murmur to Daniil and plunged back into the fray. Keeping Jan-Ali on his throne not only fulfilled her duty to her family but guaranteed the future health and prosperity of the Russian envoys. Fair or not, Grand Princess Elena would blame her diplomats for any weakening of her grip on Kazan.

Today, Nasan and Daniil planned to discuss their concerns with her uncle. As family members, they could spend time with Jan-Ali without arousing suspicion—at least, less suspicion than a session with the ambassador. Alexander Makhmetovich had issued strict instructions, but he approved of their plan. He, too, wished to keep the meeting unofficial.

So here they were, in mid-afternoon on this autumn day. Nasan glanced around at the exquisite sitting area, a niche set into one wall of a larger reception room, lined on three sides with sofas, their rose-patterned silk and rolled cushions brilliant against the gray-streaked marble of the walls. Carved folding tables filled each corner, and the sun, already tinged with gold, refracted through the iron arabesques that lined the one window. The grassy aroma of green tea filled the air, mingled with chypre and sandalwood. A curl of smoke spiraled toward the ceiling from the charcoal brazier that occupied the center of the room. Nasan and her husband shared one divan; Jan-Ali sat cross-legged on another, to Daniil's left. From there, the khan could monitor the comings and goings in the room beyond. He had ordered the reception area cleared, but the frequency with which he glanced at the entryway suggested that he didn't trust his servants to obey him. His anxiety underlined who held—or in his case, did not hold—real power in the Kazan court.

Nasan wondered what her uncle knew that he was not saying, whether she could get it out of him by the end of the meeting, and how she felt about him in general. None of these questions had easy answers. She had grown up on the steppe, moving to Kasimov only after Jan-Ali left the town, so they had met only at the occasional family gathering: his wedding to Aslanbika the year before; his installation as khan the year before that—both public events at which uncle and niece had few opportunities to interact. He remained a stranger, and a disturbing, secretive stranger, at that.

He was gazing at her now, his fingers steepled under his chin, his face impenetrable. A short, slender man with Asiatic features like Nasan's own, his skin light brown where hers was ivory, his eyes smaller but just as dark, his hair thin where hers lay thickly coiled beneath her veil—he was her father's half-brother but not much more than a year older than she. These generational overlaps occurred often in Tatar families, where multiple wives meant that siblings might be far apart in age.

The meeting had just reached the point where the routine exchange of courtesies could end and the real business begin. Daniil was speaking in Russian, and she listened with care even though she knew, for the most part, what he planned to say. He had asked her to translate for him, and she had jumped at the chance to prove herself useful. Her Russian had improved a lot since her marriage in Dhu'l Hijja of last year, which the Christians counted as June 1534. It was painful to remember how isolated she'd felt when she first reached Moscow. By the time she returned, she'd be able to hold entire conversations!

"My husband wishes to know," she said in Tatar to Jan-Ali, "what Queen Gulnara and her chief adviser, Gazim Shirin, expect to gain from an alliance with Sahib-Girei Khan of Crimea."

Nasan and Daniil had selected this question in advance. They'd picked it because, in effect, they had already guessed the answer. Gulnara and Gazim sought to maximize their own power and the power of Kazan by ridding the throne of someone they perceived as a Russian puppet. But by asking the question in this nonjudgmental way, they could discover where Jan-Ali stood and what kind of ally he might make. If he gave a straightforward answer, good. If he appreciated the subtleties of the situation, so much the better. If he pretended ignorance, they would know that he distrusted them. In that case, they would have to convince him they had his best interests at heart. Nasan slipped her hands into her long, loose sleeves and gripped her elbows, fighting the urge to push her uncle in one direction or another.

Jan-Ali's fingers tangled in the embroidered fringe he had loosened from the side of his turban. "Gulnara and her minion Gazim," he said quietly, "seek to play both ends against the middle. They acquiesced to Russian power, telling themselves they had won because they pushed the grand prince to appoint me instead of my older brother. But the situation has changed with the grand prince's death. The Russians are weaker now than they were two years ago. So Gulnara and Gazim toss out lures to Sahib-Girei of Crimea and to his nephew Safa-Girei, hoping they will draw the Russians' fire while Gulnara and Gazim expand their influence here."

Nasan nodded, relieved. Of the responses he might have given, this was the most honest and therefore the best. She murmured his explanation in Russian for Daniil's benefit. "He does not hide the truth from us, at least," she finished, only to bite her tongue as she intercepted a glance from her uncle.

Did he understand Russian then? He'd given no sign of it until now. Her father and brother both spoke Russian fluently, as did her uncle Shah-Ali, but Jan-Ali had spent his life among the Tatars. Like most khans, he had mastered Arabic, Persian, and Turkic—the diplomatic language of the khanates—but Russian, no. Or so she'd thought.

She must take care, just in case—at least until she could talk to Daniil in private. Her sense of walking on quicksand grew. Did no one in this court speak his mind?

Daniil tapped the empty porcelain cup on the carved wooden table at his side. "There must be more to it," he said, also keeping his voice low. "Whatever Gazim and Gulnara want, the khans of Crimea won't oblige them. They see Kazan as one piece of the Great Horde, which they have sought since my grandfather's day to subjugate to themselves."

Impressive. She hadn't expected him to grasp the complexities of the situation so quickly. There were advantages to military training.

Even so, he had missed a few of the subtleties that plagued Tatar politics. "Unless Gazim negotiates with Crimea on his own behalf, not Gulnara's," Nasan said. "As the old khan's sister, she has a certain power, and she has used it well. But as a woman she can command only so much respect; and Gazim, as head of the Shirin clan, may have decided that he can do better with Safa-Girei restored to the khan's throne."

Daniil rocked back in his seat and crossed his arms. "You think Gazim speaks for himself? That would change things, wouldn't it?" He gestured an apology to Jan-Ali. "Translate, please."

She fulfilled his request, then added, "Is it possible, Uncle?"

"Of course." Jan-Ali tucked the fringe back into place across his head. "Gazim Shirin is a dangerous man. He uses Gulnara every bit as much as she does him. And even if he does speak on her behalf to the khan, we can assume he is also dealing directly with his own kinsmen in Crimea. Tell him."

Nasan did as ordered. "The Shirins are the dominant clan among those not born of Genghis," she added. Daniil probably knew this, but it didn't hurt to make sure. "In every khanate they control the council of elders, which includes one representative of each Mongol clan. And they connive without ceasing to increase their power by playing one khan or sultan against another. Their politicking is not the only reason Kazan has had five khans in the last twenty years, but it is a major reason."

"Look." Jan-Ali picked up a piece of paper and scribbled on it with a piece of charcoal, then held out the paper to his niece.

1. FRIENDS	2. ENEMIES	3. OPPORTUNISTS
Jan-Ali	Sahib-Girei of Crimea	Queen Gulnara of Kazan
Nasan and her family	Safa-Girei, his nephew	Gazim Shirin
Alexander Makhmetovich	Saber rattlers convinced	Aslanbika Khatun
and Russian envoys	they can defeat Russia	and her father
Loyal servants		Clan elders seeking power
Peace-loving citizens		Disloyal citizens
		of Kazan
		Troublemakers
		on the steppe

Nasan examined the list. Allowing for Jan-Ali's understandable bias, it did a pretty good job of identifying the parties involved. Like most Russian nobles, Daniil could not read, and Jan-Ali had in any case written the names in Arabic script, so she pointed at each group of names as she explained. "Think of it as three armies," she said. "Groups 1 and 2 both want Kazan to remain independent, but they disagree on how to achieve their goal. Those in Group 3 think in terms of what's good for themselves. Here we are, in Group 1, with my uncle and the Kazanians who support him. These are the people who believe that the path to avoiding Russian conquest is to accept limited interference from Moscow in Kazan's internal affairs."

Daniil touched the second group. "This represents those who seek an alliance with Crimea?"

Good. He had understood her metaphor. "Yes," Nasan said. "The Crimeans see Kazan as part of their territory, as you noted. But this column also includes Kazanians who fear that allowing Russia to appoint their khan encourages Moscow's desire to rule Kazan. This group doesn't care about Queen Gulnara and Gazim Shirin. They support Crimea because they think a strong khan can fight off the Russians, and they oppose my uncle only because they see him as too close to Russian power."

"And the third group?"

"The last group lists those whose loyalties shift according to circumstances. That includes the Nogai tribesmen on the steppe, where every bey calculates which balance of power among the khanates gives him the greatest leverage. Individual clan leaders who seek to expand their power. Kazanians who have not yet picked sides, or who change their minds as the wind blows. And those who have switched sides in the past: Queen Gulnara, Gazim Shirin, and ..." Nasan stopped, staring at the third name in the last group. *Aslanbika? Really?*

Whether he spoke Russian or not, Jan-Ali obviously had no difficulty following her recitation of names. "Go on," he prompted. As if to demonstrate his complete indifference to the words on the page, he lifted a sweetmeat made of almond paste from a platter left by the servants and raised it to his mouth.

Nasan studied the name and the improbably complacent khan until Daniil prodded her in the ribs. "And?"

"Aslanbika," she said. "My uncle's chief wife. He suspects her of disloyalty, perhaps because her father is a prominent Nogai prince." She translated, looking to her uncle for confirmation.

"For that and other reasons," the khan said.

Nasan considered, then discarded, the idea of asking about those other reasons. She wanted to talk to Daniil before probing further into her uncle's disputes with his wife. Instead, she offered the paper to Jan-Ali. He shook his head and pointed to the charcoal brazier. Nasan crumpled the paper and fed it to the flames, watching it curl and blacken as flickering orange tongues lapped at its edges. The last word she saw as the list collapsed into ash was "Aslanbika."

"Are you sure, Uncle? She's very young." Indeed, Aslanbika, married at thirteen, was still two years younger than Nasan herself. And in Nasan's few—admittedly superficial—conversations with her, Aslanbika had shown not a whiff of interest in court intrigue. She chattered on about clothes and hair as if world events had no importance. Nasan had dismissed her as the usual harem favorite, unable to see beyond cosmetics and veils.

Although Nasan *had* overheard Aslanbika complaining that her husband showed no interest in her, an odd comment from the lips of a young woman who showed promise of becoming a legendary beauty.

Nasan had dismissed such claims as pique, but perhaps Aslanbika had spoken no more than the truth. For at the sound of her name, a moue of distaste distorted Jan-Ali's face. The bite of sweetmeat he was swallowing went down the wrong way, and he choked. Nasan sprang to her feet, intending to help him, but Daniil moved faster, dislodging the problematic chunk with a hearty slap on the back. Not the most respectful way to assist a khan, but effective.

Jan-Ali could have objected to Daniil's rough-and-ready response, but he did not. Nasan was rejoicing in her uncle's forbearance when she noticed how Jan-Ali looked at her husband. As Daniil returned to her side, Jan-Ali's eyes followed him. And while he stared at Nasan's handsome husband with the kind of yearning better reserved for a wife, Daniil, discomfort visible in every line of his body, alternated his gaze between the ceiling and the far wall.

Nasan again gripped the insides of her sleeves. This was not good.

"Find out," Jan-Ali said. "We are expecting envoys from Sahib-Girei Khan this week. Watch them. Watch her. Bring me your answers."

With that, he dismissed them. The meeting could not have ended too soon for Nasan.

Back in their quarters, Nasan checked behind each gauzy drapery before taking a seat next to her husband. Inlaid tiles, inviting sofas, velvet cushions tasseled in gold, soothing waterfalls endlessly recycled through twisted pipes, soft greens and blues: the full panoply of the palace decorators' efforts to induce serenity failed to calm her.

She sank onto a pile of cushions and addressed Daniil. "I don't know what to believe, do you? My uncle spoke frankly, most of the time. He seems to recognize the dueling political factions and the danger they pose. We must support him. Yet I don't trust him."

Because he desires you.

She hesitated to say that. Daniil had sworn fidelity to her, and she to him. It shouldn't matter that the khan yearned for him.

To warn him, though?

Nonsense. Her husband had spent four years in the army. If Nasan, despite her sheltered life, had heard more than once of rulers who kept catamites or wrote odes extolling the young warrior of their fancy, Daniil must have encountered such situations before. He would have ways of dealing with them.

Although khans could prove notoriously difficult to resist.

She should ask him. They would have to discuss it sometime.

Not right now, though. The conversation was certain to prove awkward, and they had other points to cover. More important points, on which their own safety, her family's future, and Russia's interests depended.

"I don't trust him, either," Daniil said. Her thoughts had led her so far astray that it took a moment to recall that "him" referred to Jan-Ali. "I don't trust anyone here. Half of them see us as the enemy, and the rest as their saviors. But that doesn't matter. We have to back him whether we trust him or not, because we have no alternative. That means I need to tell Alexander Makhmetovich what happened today."

"Yes." In her mind Nasan reconstructed her uncle's three-part list. "Jan-Ali counts on our support. That's good. And he's guessed our true purpose for being here." Although the diplomatic mission addressed a real problem, the negotiations were mostly an excuse to assess the lay of the land. "The two sides won't surprise your ambassador, I'm sure, but I suspect he will want to hear about the list of opportunists. Especially that it includes Jan-Ali's wife."

"You'll have to investigate her," Daniil said. "I can't get into the harem. I'll warn Alexander Makhmetovich to prepare for the arrival of envoys from Crimea."

"Agreed." Nasan experienced a thrill of pleasure. Marital partnership was a rare gift. "The ambassadors won't speak before a woman, even a khan's daughter—unless I can ingratiate myself with Gulnara."

Daniil, rambling around the room, stumbled into a low table. A pile of books went flying, and Nasan dove to rescue them. Her precious medical texts, gathered from the palace library and diligent searches through the local shops. She spent every free moment studying them. Her finds would accompany her back to Moscow at the end of this stay. Medical books were scarcer than hens' teeth in the Russian capital—and anyway, she had yet to learn the Cyrillic alphabet. The thought of convincing Daniil's law-abiding mother that Nasan needed to read Russian, especially to study medicine, was daunting.

Daniil muttered an apology, took the pile of books from her, and returned them to the small table. "Tell me about Aslanbika. Why would your uncle suspect her?"

So much for putting things off. Nasan mustered her courage and took the plunge. "He claims to distrust the nomads, and she grew up among them. But I think he dislikes her for other reasons. From the way he looks at you, I can guess what those are."

Daniil started like a tiger surprised in the woods. "Oh, you saw that." His cheeks crimsoned. "I thought you ... girls in Russia don't ... ah, it happens with some men. Not to my taste, you know, but I've encountered it from time to time."

None of which would have enlightened her a bit, if her mother had not already schooled her in how attraction worked. Christians were so easily embarrassed! Islam castigated men like Jan-Ali as sinners, too, but gossip was the lifeblood of the harem. Men and women, men and men, women and women—these combined with the arts of sensual appeal to form the essence of harem conversations.

"Not to your taste?" She laughed, grateful for this tiny release of tension. "You still think you need to convince me of that?" Women flocked to Daniil as birds to a feast, and until Nasan arrived on the scene, he had responded to them with enthusiasm.

He grinned. "I can prove it, in case you've forgotten since this morning."

"Later," she told him. "Can you keep my uncle at arm's length? Khans don't take refusal very well."

"Watch me," Daniil said. "I will be amazingly stupid, missing every cue. In a pinch, I'll remind him that I have married his niece, but with luck, I can prevent him from ever raising the topic."

"I hope that works." Nasan wrapped both arms around her knees. "The last thing we need is another complication."

"Indeed," Daniil said. "Enough of that. We have a plan. I talk to Alexander Makhmetovich and, if he agrees, try to figure out what the Crimeans want. You befriend Aslanbika." He paced from door to window and back, then returned to face her.

Whatever he had meant to say was lost when a servant appeared in the doorway. Nasan, startled, addressed her sharply. "What brings you here?"

The servant bowed. "Apologies, Khanim. Aslanbika Khatun sent me to request that you join her on the roof, to observe the beauties of autumn."

How providential. Well, if her job was to sound out Aslanbika, she might as well get started. "Very well. Tell the khatun I will join her shortly."

The servant withdrew. Nasan returned her attention to her husband, only to find him prowling toward her. "Later," he said. "You promised. Well, later is now."

She let him slide his arm around her waist and nuzzle her neck. "Aslanbika," she mumbled. "Didn't you hear? I'm supposed to join her on the roof to admire the autumn leaves." If the words came out sounding less than forceful, well, what could one do when a husband was sending rippling waves of fire down to one's toes?

☙ *109* ❧

"The leaves won't fall before you get there." Daniil swept her off her feet, preparatory to carrying her to a room that no servant would dare invade.

Nasan stopped protesting. The rules of the harem were clear: a husband could not be denied. Even if she wished to deny him—which, given Daniil's skill at his chosen pursuit, she most certainly did not.

Indeed, the leaves remained attached to their trees when Nasan reached the flat portion of the roof some time later. Cream porcelain tiles adorned in blue and russet brown, arranged in intricate patterns, spread in all directions and up the sides of the waist-high walls that framed the balcony. Above, a tent-like canopy composed of red tile, sloped to resist the weight of winter snows, extended out from its high point in the center, held up by pillared brick arranged in regular columns along the balustrade, itself topped with matching tile. A distance of about six feet separated the wall from its canopy, and this lay open to the sky—in reality, a room connected to the outdoors or an enclosed balcony, but everyone called it the roof.

By the time Nasan arrived, Aslanbika and her ladies had abandoned their study of the foliage—with the exception of one young lady-in-waiting who stared intently at an oak branch as she tried to capture its pattern with charcoal on paper. The others clustered around a group of dovecotes that lined the south wall. Gauzy veils and long false sleeves of brocade in many shades fluttered in the breeze. Nasan hugged her elbows, glad she had worn her lined jacket.

As she circled the walls, the sun kissed her face, and the cool air exhilarated her. She raised her arms and spun in place, wishing for her mare, Sorkhokhtani, restored to her a few weeks ago as the ambassadorial party passed through Kasimov and lodged in one of the stables below.

Oh, to leave the city, find the grasslands, and gallop!

Could she talk Aslanbika into agreeing to such a plan? Surely a Nogai princess must miss the open plains—clouds and feather grass, quail and eagles, hares and foxes and endless, endless sky.

"Nasan," Aslanbika said. "At last. Where have you been? I sent for you ages ago."

A stolen hour did not seem like ages, but one did not contradict a khatun. "I went to meet with my uncle," Nasan said. "So that my husband would have a translator." Kinder than telling a woman suffering from neglect the true reasons for her tardiness. Even this hint of connection, she noticed, caused Aslanbika's beautiful lips to twist. The khatun's glossy hair, long and straight, resisted the pull of the wind, but scattered tendrils blew across her face, obscuring, then revealing, her clear black eyes until she tucked the wisps under her headdress.

"So I heard," Aslanbika said. "I thought the meeting ended sometime ago. Perhaps I was mistaken."

The anger in her voice shocked Nasan. "I came as soon as I could," she said.

Aslanbika frowned. "And what did you discuss with my husband?"

The ladies fluttered around her, human replicas of the cooing doves that swooped down on fragments of bread and cast shadows across the women's cheeks as the birds returned to their perches. Nasan hesitated. Securing Aslanbika's confidence required an offer of information. Yet who knew how many spies, and for whom, fluttered among the gauzy veils and rich brocades?

She temporized. "The usual talk, Auntie. Who plots with whom. Whether Crimea can be persuaded to shift its allegiance from Lithuania to Russia. What the Nogai will do."

"Men's business." Aslanbika waved a languid hand. "I pity you, wasting a glorious afternoon on such trivia. They talk and talk, yet nothing changes. The Crimean khan promises his support to anyone who asks, hoping each court will lure him with gifts while he sits safe at home, laughing and fat with booty to reward his troops."

It was the most observant remark she'd made yet. Nasan felt her interest spark. Aslanbika had more in her head than she'd let on, it seemed.

Another keeper of secrets, playing her own game. Just what she and Daniil needed.

"An apt description," she said. For no reason she could detect, the khatun's dark eyes narrowed. Was Aslanbika testing her?

"But of course, the Tatar hordes do not act as one," Aslanbika said. "Each bey, sultan, and khan makes his own decisions. I'm sure Alexander Makhmetovich understands that. Speaking of which, why did the ambassador send your husband to represent him at this meeting? Is Daniil not a rather junior member of the team?"

"I told you, Auntie. It was a family meeting."

"I'm not family?"

Nasan winced. What had happened to the beauty-obsessed harem darling? This conversation became stickier by the word. "I didn't ask my uncle to exclude you, Auntie."

"No." Aslanbika snatched a dove from the air and held it, quivering, between her long fingers. "I don't suppose you did. But you *are* in the thick of it, aren't you?"

"I don't understand," Nasan said, and she didn't. Aslanbika had used the singular "you," but Nasan had no official position at the Kazan court. "I'm here as a wife. I just translate when asked."

"I didn't mean here." Aslanbika released the dove, which made a mad dash for the far side of the roof. "Your brothers are battling for control of a steppe horde, the one formerly led by Bahadur Bey. I heard it from Queen Gulnara, who had the news from Gazim Shirin." She leaned forward and grabbed Nasan's wrist, gripping hard enough to hurt. "Do you expect me to believe you didn't discuss *that* with my husband? That you could put me off by babbling about men's talk?"

Nasan pulled at her wrist, but the khatun held her fast. "That can't be true. I have only one brother. His name is Ogodai. My half-brothers are too young to battle for a khanate." She fought off a surge of grief, for she *had* had another, closer to her even than Ogodai, until Girei died in a revenge killing last year. "Ogodai is stationed near Smolensk, with our father. I learned that when we passed through Kasimov on our way here."

"Not now. He left last month, heading south to collect his bride." Aslanbika's raised eyebrows gave her an odd resemblance to an egret.

"I assure you, I have heard nothing of this," Nasan said. "And if my mother knew, she would have mentioned it. She receives couriers once a week. Why would Ogodai hide his journey from her, or from me? It doesn't make sense."

Her bewilderment had the happy effect of dispelling Aslanbika's anger. A royal wave dismissed the ladies to the far corners of the roof, and a royal hand on Nasan's elbow drew her to sit among the abandoned doves.

"You really hadn't heard?" Aslanbika asked.

"Not a word."

"But it must be true, Nasan. No one would make up such a story. It's too complete." Aslanbika told her of Bahadur's death, the mysterious message, Jahangir's incompetence as bey, and Ogodai's journey in search of his betrothed.

"How do you *know* all this?"

"I told you. Gulnara had the tale from Gazim Shirin, who has spies in every horde. The other candidate is Tulpar. He's not your brother?"

Tulpar. The name, seldom heard for almost a decade, called forth a hazy image of a tall, laughing, young god—bestower of gifts, teller of stories. Nasan gulped for air. "I had a half-brother named Tulpar. Ten, twelve years older—I don't recall, exactly. He died when I was six.",

"I don't think so." Aslanbika's eyes softened in sympathy. "It would be unlike Gazim to mistake both the relationship and the name. Are you certain he died?"

Nasan nodded, then stopped. *Was* she? She didn't recall a funeral, like the one so recently endured for Girei. Even a child would attend a funeral for such a close relative.

"Maybe I misread the situation," she said. "My parents rarely speak of him, and when they do, they act as if he died. Ever since the quarrel."

"What happened?"

"An argument on the battlefield. I don't know the details. Tulpar refused to follow orders, and *Ata* cast him out. My father doesn't tolerate disobedience."

"What father does?" Aslanbika shrugged. "But to cast off a son—it seems extreme."

"Yes," Nasan admitted. "My mother said once that they were too alike. Two male eagles trying to share a nest, each convinced he had the answers."

"So the old eagle pushed out the young one," Aslanbika said.

"Without his clan," Nasan said. "Without the ancestors to guide and protect him. How could he survive?"

"But he did." Aslanbika sounded wistful. "I met him once, at the summer games. He is quite gorgeous." She giggled, sending Nasan a mischievous glance. "Just ask him."

Nasan laughed, too, but she was only half-listening. If Tulpar had taken refuge in the horde of their childhood, how surprised Ogodai must have been to find their half-brother there. How was he coping?

Nasan yearned to talk this new information over with her husband. He and Ogodai were sworn brothers—friends until the family feud that ended with her marriage ripped that friendship apart. Since then, they had been brothers only in name, but she sensed a certain guarded affection between them, even so.

She could use a friend, in truth. She missed her mother. And time spent together would help her learn more about Aslanbika—which would be fun, now that her aunt had revealed the Nogai princess hidden inside the harem beauty.

"Could we ride together?" Nasan asked. "I have my mare in the stables here. She would love to gallop on the plains outside the city."

Aslanbika's eyes brightened. "Tomorrow." She waved a hand. "With as many of my ladies as desire to ride."

Nasan had hoped for more private conversation, but any ride was better than none. She bowed to Aslanbika and circled among the chattering women until she could manufacture an escape. As she passed from group to group, she kept an ear open for gossip, details, scraps of useful information, but she heard only the familiar concerns of the harem. How to make hair shine and teeth gleam, to allure with perfume and come-hither glances, to drape a gauze so that a man thought of nothing but its removal, to spice a tea and feed a sweetmeat to a willing lover.

She might as well be back in Kasimov. Although Daniil might enjoy the perfume and the gauze...

Chapter 8

OGODAI WOKE TO THE CRASH OF TREES FALLING AROUND him, as if some unseen giant had picked up handfuls of poles and scattered them willy-nilly across the steppe. Catapulted out of a deep sleep, he lay on his back, staring at the smoke hole above his head, trying to marshal his thoughts. Outside the tent, children's voices—high-pitched with excitement— mingled with adult shouts and the bleating of goats and sheep, snapping wood, jingling harness, neighing horses, and spinning wheels.

What is going on?

From the grayness of the light entering the smoke hole, he guessed that morning had the night in retreat, but not by much. The dew would still glitter on the grasses, sunrise shimmer in the east. Making the furor outside even less comprehensible.

He sat up. It didn't sound like battle. No screams, no war cries, no hissing arrows in flight.

Vafa appeared in the doorway. "Sultan," he said. "You're awake. Good. We must get ready."

Get ready. Truth dawned. Short of a full-fledged battle, only one event could account for this level of noise.

"They're breaking camp." Ogodai sprang to his feet. "I should have guessed. Winter is coming." Indeed, the nights had become frigid—the cold locked in perpetual struggle with the hearth fire, mediated by the smoke hole that must stay open if the tent's occupants were to breathe, the heat of other bodies the main armor against the approaching snows.

Snows that would soon cover the prairie, leaving the herds without protection against the driving winds. Despite his years away from Bahadur's camp, Ogodai knew the rhythm of the seasons as well as anyone here. The nomads had left their summer pastures a month or more ago, but they had not reached the end of their journey. They must move the animals back to the winter grazing grounds, where the grass had had half a year to regrow and mountains and forest would shelter man and beast from the Arctic winds that blew straight from Siberia while guaranteeing enough snow in the right places to provide a steady supply of water. This horde's ancestral lands lay in the hills south of Kazan, east of the Sura River. If Ogodai had not allowed himself to be distracted by Jahangir's sorry state, his betrothed's ambivalence, and Tulpar's unexpected appearance yesterday, he would have wondered why the camp had stopped here as long as it had.

So he understood the move itself. But why had no one said anything last night at the feast to welcome his half-brother— which he had attended over Vafa's protests, because a man does not let a punch to the jaw keep him down? Refusing to look weak before Tulpar, Jahangir, and the horde, Ogodai had engaged many warriors in conversation, drunk and laughed and danced with the rest. Yet no one had mentioned plans to tear down the tents and depart at first light. Somehow, without his knowing, the bey or the council or both—as if they had been waiting for Tulpar's party to return—had ordered the horde to move. And if Ogodai didn't pull himself together, and fast, they might leave him behind.

"Yes," he said, before Vafa could ask for instructions. "Pack up. I'll find people to help you."

Easier said than done. Ogodai slept in his clothes in camp or on campaign, but even a man who slept fully dressed had to wash face and hands, say his morning prayers, don armor for the journey, buckle on his sword, and break his fast with a bowl of soup. He could still taste the warm mutton and onions as he strode through the camp looking for the soldiers who had accompanied him from Smolensk.

As he passed through the camp, he kept a running tally of how far the horde had progressed in its preparations to depart. On every side, groups of three or four stripped the tents of their felt, rolled and bound it into squat, fat cylinders. Some tied the rolls to patient Bactrian camels while their fellows pulled off the rings that kept the smoke holes open, releasing the roof poles with the singing snap that had jerked Ogodai from sleep. Others untied poles and folded trellis frames, loaded down the waiting camels with yet more sections of dwelling, or packed household goods onto wheeled carts. Most impressive were the huge wagons pulled by oxen, carrying the four large, undismantled tents that would house the bulk of the horde throughout the journey. Two for the women and children, two for the men: he anticipated lots of company from here to the winter grazing area.

Off to the right, Ogodai saw Firuza, in her element as she directed servants carrying portable trunks here and children dragging reluctant sheep there. He noticed she had dressed for riding, leather trousers visible under her quilted robe and a sable hat atop black braids curled at the nape of her neck.

She greeted him with a big smile, which he returned until he glanced to his left and saw Tulpar lounging against a fence. Was she smiling at him?

Jahangir, completely and improbably sober, vaulted a trailing tent pole and smacked Ogodai on the shoulder. "Well, well, if it isn't Khan-in-the-Making. I thought we'd be on our way before you stirred yourself."

Such an obvious insult didn't merit a response in kind. Ogodai smacked Jahangir in turn, addressing him with equally false bonhomie. "If you'd given me a hint of your intentions, I too would have leaped from my bed before dawn. But don't worry, I'll be ready."

Beyond Jahangir, Ogodai spotted the head of his own troop, saddling horses in the corral. Ignoring Tulpar, still grinning and lounging, he went to fulfill his promise to Vafa.

Jahangir's call stopped him in his tracks. "Too bad you got up late, Ogodai," he said. "I already assigned the vanguard to Tulpar. You and your men will defend the rear."

Ogodai turned. His fists clenched at this new insult. Jahangir had no right to order him to do anything. And the rear was the least prestigious place in any excursion, military or otherwise. He belonged in the vanguard, or at least on one of the flanks.

Tulpar collapsed in open laughter. Firuza looked anxious. Timur, whom Ogodai had not noticed until then, glanced his way before hiding behind the skirts of his father's coat. Jahangir pretended to cringe, but the glee in his face gave him away. Ogodai heard the air catch, as if the entire nomadic band was holding its breath. Behind Jahangir, Rafik Argyn, who had also escaped Ogodai's attention, raised his hand, palm out.

But Ogodai didn't need a signal to restrain his worst instincts. Punching Jahangir would express his anger, but to repeat the scene with Tulpar so soon would make him look like a hothead. That could only undermine his goals to become khan and to seal his contract with Firuza.

"I'll tell my men," he said, denying his adversaries the satisfaction of admitting they had riled him while withholding any acknowledgment of Jahangir's right to rule.

The camp exhaled. Firuza relaxed. Rafik bowed, hand over his heart. And Ogodai noted that his response had wiped the grins from Jahangir's and Tulpar's faces.

Not much, perhaps, but a beginning. It will do.

Firuza's intention, so firm the day before, to find out what had brought Tulpar back to the nomadic camp had suffered one setback after another. Diliara grabbed her as soon as she crossed the threshold, demanding to know what Ogodai wanted while scolding her for running off. By the time she freed herself, the men had begun their celebration, placing everyone who could answer her questions out of reach. At least Ogodai had recovered sufficiently to attend—or so Diliara told her as she dragged Firuza off to join the other women. Then, while grudgingly fulfilling her obligations, she learned that her brother had ordered the horde to break camp at dawn—without consulting her!

Moreover, when she tracked Jahangir down and pounded on his door after the carousing and dancing at last abated, he refused to talk to her, claiming that Roxelana required his attention. From his state of partial undress, she could guess what kind of attention, and for reasons she didn't want to examine too closely, the knowledge that he was amusing himself in that particular way added to her list of grievances.

She told herself she should feel grateful that for once he had not over-indulged in drink. It had been obvious from his unslurred speech and the energy with which he shut the door in her face. But Firuza did not feel grateful as she glared at that closed door. While her brother reveled in debauched pleasures, she had a fiancé she barely knew, a challenger with questionable allegiances, and an unsolved mystery that might help her chances or undermine them—she had no way to guess.

Grumbling under her breath, she stormed back to her tent. The ancestors' shrine beckoned, but the hour was advanced, and she had a lot to do if the horde planned to leave in the morning. The grandmothers would understand.

She worked for several hours before retiring among her mothers and sisters for the night. Even then, her brain tormented her with lists of chores that she must supervise. Roxelana haunted her dreams. Otherwise, she would have sworn that her eyes never closed.

But somehow they must have. A gentle hand on her shoulder woke her, and Diliara's unmistakable scent, composed of ginger and pomegranate, lingered in the air. Swishing fabrics alerted her that the other women were already packing, and soon the ginger and pomegranate gave way to rose petals and jasmine, citrus and lavender, wafting from veils, tunics, robes, jackets, and more. Servants folded clothes and rolled rugs, stowed cosmetics in boxes and larger items in trunks— which they locked and bound with protective straps to prevent the goods inside from bursting loose if a container fell off its baggage cart. By the time Firuza had washed and dressed, paid her respects to the grandmothers and eaten, everything was packed. A dozen men arrived to dismantle the tent, and she moved outside.

Ogodai's appearance amid the throng while she was organizing the distribution of goods on the baggage carts took her by surprise. She smiled. At first, he responded in kind, but soon his friendliness vanished. He hadn't forgiven her for running away from him the day before.

But there was nothing she could do about it then. With the camp in disarray, she had no time to talk.

By the time the sun reached its zenith, the nomads were on the move. More than two hundred people—accompanied by herds of horses, sheep, goats, and heavily laden camels—they straggled across the steppe like an army of ants. Jahangir and Tulpar rode at the front, whence they could dispatch groups of scouts to pick up advance warning of hostile bands or rustlers looking to swoop down and carry off cattle, maidens, or youths for the slave market.

Ogodai had caught a glimpse of Roxelana as she climbed onto the foremost of the large wagons. No riding for her. No packing either, from what he'd seen. She'd glided from the bey's tent just as servants removed the outer felt and installed herself on the wagon without more ado. Women drove most of the felt-covered baggage carts and large tented wagons, but Roxelana evaded even that responsibility. Ogodai wondered if he'd misunderstood the male/female segregation of the sleeping arrangements, since the foremost tent presumably belonged to the bey, his entourage, and honored guests like Ogodai himself—not the bey's concubine, however alluring.

Ah well, he'd find out the answer soon enough. His attention shifted as Firuza galloped up and fell into line beside him. At that moment, the advantages of guarding the rear became apparent. His spirits rose.

With winter closing in, the tramping herds no longer kicked up a whirlwind of dust, choking those who followed the moving animals. Rafik and his Argyn kinsmen had chosen to declare their support by accompanying Ogodai and his warriors.

If Firuza decided to join him, so much the better. Perhaps they could at last have a real conversation, uninterrupted by hovering stepmothers and the endless tasks of household management and administration that had occupied her since his arrival.

And Tulpar, stuck up front, could not interfere.

Firuza assessed her betrothed as she reined in her mare at his side. His voice held a certain warmth as he greeted her; his eyes regarded her kindly. Perhaps she had imagined his withdrawal this morning.

"You're better," she said. No doubt of that. The color had returned to his face. He looked calm and collected, although an upward glance revealed the bruise from his brother's blow outlined against his jaw.

"Yes, quite well. And you?" Not warm. Neutral, guarded even.

Perhaps he expected an apology. She didn't owe him one, really. But he did have a right to hear her conjectures about his brother.

And it had been her own fault, hadn't it, that she became upset with him yesterday? Imagining—not to say wishing for—something that had not occurred to him. If it gave them a chance to talk, if it showed her how his mind worked, an uncalled-for apology would serve her purpose. It wasn't like being forced to express sorrow to Jahangir for having the nerve to save his skin.

"Yesterday," she said, and stumbled. Where to begin? With Ogodai inches from her right elbow, conversation seemed much more difficult than when she had blithely ridden up to join him. She couldn't blurt out some disconnected story. He would think her demented.

And she had to watch her words. His men, the Argyns, other warriors—listening ears surrounded them.

"Yesterday," Ogodai said. His voice sounded encouraging again. "I didn't mean to offend you. My thoughts were somewhat muddled."

He was making it easy for her. She appreciated that. "No, I'm sorry. I should have answered your question. Of course you wondered why no one had said anything about Tulpar—especially me. I just assumed you knew. I think we all did."

"No, my father told me he died," Ogodai said. "I don't understand the lie. It seems pointless."

The bitterness in his voice reminded her of his greeting to Tulpar. What it must have meant to him to see his brother alive! And despite the shock of discovery, he had tried to reach out, only to be rebuffed. It spoke well of him, that he had made the effort—and not so well of Tulpar that he had pushed Ogodai away.

She and Ogodai had both lost a brother—hers to self-indulgence and drink, his to exile and anger. She felt a real connection to her betrothed for the first time.

"How terrible for you," she said. "You mourned him, when you didn't need to. Jahangir is … difficult, but at least I can hope he will return one day."

"Jahangir leaves too much on your shoulders." Although Ogodai didn't explicitly acknowledge her empathy, she sensed a release of tension in him that heartened her. "I will help, if you let me. My father showed me your poem. That's why I came here. Not only to marry you, but to assist you however I can."

A chill breeze caused Firuza to shiver. He offered to help, but what did that mean? She didn't know what to ask, what to say. Perhaps she'd have done better not to approach him yet.

No, she'd made the right choice. To decide which man she wished to marry—him or Tulpar—she had to draw them both out, test their limits, judge their characters. Right now, she saw a perfect opportunity to do that.

Rafik and his warriors had set off on a long foray up the flanks of the roaming mass—heading off sheep and goats, nudging cattle and horses into formation, grabbing the occasional child oblivious to danger. Seeing Ogodai's fingers tense on the reins, Firuza caught his hand. "Wait."

He glanced at her, visibly startled, and her tongue again tangled up. No wonder Roxelana wooed men away from her with such ease.

But she'd stopped him from leaving. She couldn't sit there like a straw man set up for target practice. She released his hand and said the first thing that came into her head, sparked by his earlier comment about Jahangir. "My brother is sober today."

Ogodai's eyebrows vanished behind his black fringe. Whatever he'd expected her to say, it wasn't that. "I noticed. It's a good sign. Does he usually stop drinking when the horde moves from one pasture to another?"

Firuza pondered that question—and his reason for asking it. "Yes," she said after a while. "I hadn't seen the connection before, but he does. And before leaving on a raid."

"He should raid more often, then." Ogodai shifted his gaze to the distance briefly, then returned it to her. "He's not the man I expected. He used to take charge, like your father."

"Yes. Something changed when he turned fifteen. It's as if he wants to fail."

Rafik's men were shouting. Ogodai surveyed the herds, then turned his head toward her once more. "And your father sat back and did nothing? Had he lost control of the horde?"

"Lost control? *Ata?*" Her hands clenched on the reins, and Kubelek reared. Before Firuza had time to realize what had happened, Ogodai grabbed her harness above the bit and forced the horse's head down. He held on, stilling the mare with the power of his grip, until Kubelek quieted. Only when he released the harness did Firuza hear herself breathe.

"Thank you," she said, shaken. Her serene, courteous stranger—a sparrow to Tulpar's peacock—had acted without hesitation. To rescue her, his betrothed.

Not a sparrow. A kestrel. The spark that proximity to Ogodai lit in her stomach burned anew.

"She's a beauty." Ogodai patted the mare's neck. "A Turkmen palomino. A golden horse. What a sheen! Can you handle her?"

"I've had Kubelek since she was a foal!"

He grinned at her. "Don't get huffy. I wasn't insulting your riding. Your Butterfly has spirit, like any good horse."

Firuza, tempted to kick the mare into motion and show him how well she rode, bit her tongue. He was laughing. Reflected sunshine lit his black eyes. He looked relaxed, charming, handsome. She couldn't help smiling back.

Her instinctive defense hadn't bothered him one bit. Did he not expect submission, then? What a strange man she'd found.

He had saved her from a fall. And he'd raised a serious question, one she had not yet answered. What was it about Ogodai that turned her into a muttonhead?

She pulled herself together. "You asked about *Ata*," she reminded him. "No, he controlled the horde until the night he died. He allowed Jahangir to drink in the evenings so long as he remained sober during the day. They quarreled about it—quite a lot, in fact—but Jahangir didn't dare defy him." Her throat caught, and tears pricked at the back of her eyes. "No one did."

"He died suddenly, your father. Of no known cause. So Rafik told me." Ogodai raised her hand to his lips, then held it between his own. "Could the trouble with Jahangir have brought on an apoplexy? Your father was no longer young."

She gulped for air, hoping her voice would not break. "No. The symptoms were wrong."

"Some other disease, then?"

"The shaman thought so, but even the plague doesn't kill as fast as that. I suspect poisoning. Accidental, maybe. Only I can't prove it. The shaman swore she didn't misjudge her dose."

"So Rafik said. And although Bahadur must have had enemies—what leader doesn't?—I doubt any of them had a reason to kill him after so long. Especially with Jahangir as the alternative." He produced a rueful shrug. "Sorry. I'm being rude, but let's speak the truth to each other, shall we?"

The offer, with its suggestion that Ogodai saw her as an equal, soothed and pleased her, giving her the courage to say what must be said. "There is *your* brother. He desperately desires to become khan. He left the week before *Ata* died, though."

He shifted his grip, clasping her right hand in his left, and tapped the end of his whip against the pommel of his saddle—gently, so as not to disturb his horse. "Rafik told us, you know, in Smolensk. He said Ildar Shirin favored another son. My father threw a knife at him. To shut him up, I see now. At the time, I had no idea." The bitterness had returned to his voice. His father's silence cut deep, she thought. "Tulpar has support on the council, just as I do. But his supporter carries more clout."

Politics, always politics. His thumb caressed her palm, distracting her. She forced herself to concentrate. "Yes, the Shirins like him. They always have. But he and *Ata* argued a lot. That's why *Ata* threw him out."

Ogodai dropped her hand. "Threw him out? Tulpar left because your father threw him *out*—despite his ties with Crimea and support from your chief elder? And a week later, Bahadur dies, and no one makes a connection?"

Firuza gaped at him. Why hadn't they linked the timing of Tulpar's departure and *Ata's* sudden death?

Because they had wandered in a fog of grief and shock. Herself, Diliara, the other women. With Jahangir intoxicated, Roxelana bent on securing her own future, and the clan elders jockeying for power, no one had spared a thought for Tulpar.

In the distance, Rafik's men yelled louder. "Something's happening," Ogodai said. "I have to find out what it is."

"I'll come with you." She raised her chin, testing him.

He nodded and kneed his horse into motion. Firuza urged Kubelek forward, and the two animals walked side by side.

The questions Ogodai had raised tumbled in her brain. *Could* Tulpar have killed her father? *Would* he have?

"Tulpar would challenge *Ata* in battle, surely," she said, thinking it through. "Not poison him in secret like an enraged concubine."

Ogodai glanced her way. "I would hope so. He is a warrior."

Whereas... "Roxelana desires him. Your brother, I mean. More than she does mine. Even before *Ata's* death, she flirted with him."

He reined in his horse and turned to face her once more. "And few arts of the harem remain concealed from Roxelana, I suspect. We must keep an eye on her. But we can't accuse her on possibility alone, any more than we can accuse Jahangir or Tulpar."

"No," she said. "But we can investigate. You among the men, and I the women. Agreed?"

She was taking a risk. If they worked together against Tulpar, was she not, in effect, casting her lot with Ogodai? But what was the alternative? She couldn't marry a man who might have murdered her father.

"Agreed." Ogodai caught her hand again and squeezed it. "But investigating a murder can be dangerous. We are betrothed, whatever my brother says. The entire camp witnessed it. Will you not move into my tent, so that I can protect you? I won't force myself on you." The gold flecks lit his eyes again. "My mother, I promise you, will take care of the celebration later."

For a moment, she felt tempted. If Ogodai swore to guard her, he would. For the first time since *Ata*'s death, someone would watch over her and keep her safe—as safe as a woman could be in a world where powerful men saw others' wives, sisters, and daughters as goods for the taking. But in accepting, she would lose her brief moment of freedom.

The earth trembled under her horse's hooves. Off to the left, the shouts of Rafik's men mingled with a low, booming sound. Firuza rose in her stirrups, but the herds blocked her view. She returned her gaze to her betrothed.

He seemed as restive as the distant herds. His fingers tensed around hers. He controlled his own mount with his knees; his free hand grasped her horse's reins once more, as if to ward off another outbreak by Kubelek. He was looking at the animals, not at her, as if he could obtain the information he sought through will alone.

"I can make no promises until we reach our swinter pastures," she said. "Until then, you have no tent, and I will be quite safe among the women."

She braced for an argument, but the ancestors intervened. Rafik tore up on his pony and skidded to a halt in front of them. "Sultan," he said. "We need your help. The herds are scattering!"

Ogodai dropped her hand. "Very well," he said. "But remember, my offer stands. I can always pitch a tent."

Firuza watched him gallop off, shaking her head in confusion. Did she want to marry him or not?

Her mare danced with impatience, eager to join the other horses as they chased down the maddened sheep.

Wait. What maggot possessed her brain? *The herds were scattering.* If her people didn't stop them, their wealth would vanish in an afternoon. And here she was worrying about marriage!

No need to press her heels against the horse's sides, or even to urge Kubelek with a muttered *chu, chu.* Firuza relaxed her hands, and the palomino broke into a gallop. Ogodai and Rafik were already far ahead. She rose in her stirrups, committing herself to the challenge ahead.

Chapter 9

OGODAI, HIS THOUGHTS IN TURMOIL, RACED AFTER RAFIK. First and foremost, they had to stop the stampede. It was the bane of nomadic life, the uncertainty that afflicted herds on the trail. What had set them off? The scent of a predator—wolves?

It could be anything. A shift in the light as the clouds scudded across the sun, an odd configuration in the ground, and animals went tearing in all directions as if driven by demons. Sheep and goats panicked, horses fled. Only the camels, monitored and heavily laden for transit, plodded along as if nothing had changed.

Whatever had spooked the herds, he and his men had to surround them and drive them back before they became too dispersed to retrieve. That was the job of the rear guard: to watch from behind and respond if needed. Ogodai had performed this task many times, but not since he attained adulthood and not as the one in command. As his horse galloped across the supple grass, he dipped into past experiences and twisted pieces of them into a workable plan.

Rafik, a few horse lengths ahead, had reached the other leaders. Already, warriors fanned out around the edges of the roiling animal mass. Good. Ogodai rode into the midst of the small group and issued a stream of orders. As soon as he had most of the men deployed, he dispatched two scouts: one to Jahangir, who had the right as bey to be kept informed; and the other to Ildar Shirin, head of the council, with a suggestion that he notify the other elders.

About to give chase, Ogodai caught sight of Firuza. The gorgeous palomino—her coat agleam in the overhead sun, her creamy mane and tail flying in the autumn breeze—galloped toward him. On her back, Firuza rose and sat with the fluidity of a natural horsewoman. Her black eyes shone, and bands of rose painted her cheeks. She looked magnificent.

And entirely out of place, as he told her as soon as she and the palomino skidded to a stop at his side. Behind him, the calls among the troops were already fading as the warriors moved off along their assigned paths.

"I'll ride with you," she said. "I know what to do. I won't slow you down."

He should argue. Send her home. Chasing panicked animals was no job for a sheltered girl.

Only she wasn't that sheltered. She had grown up here. A vision of his younger sister on horseback flitted through his head. How disappointed Nasan would be if he turned *her* away under similar circumstances. Why not humor Firuza? He trusted his own ability to keep her out of trouble if necessary.

Besides, he didn't have time to quarrel. Every moment counted. "Stay with me," he said. She stared at him, as if astonished. As he kicked his gelding into a canter, he laughed. "Come on then, or you'll be left behind."

She didn't answer, but he heard the palomino's hooves pounding against the prairie behind him.

It took hours of hard riding and constant changes of plan before Ogodai and his warriors reestablished control of the herds. Rafik's father arrived midway with the Baryn and Kipchak leaders, and—more important—a train of horses kept in reserve for such emergencies as this. Ogodai switched mounts and persuaded Firuza to replace her palomino, whose head hung at an alarming angle as breath bubbled through the mare's nostrils. He hated to see harm come to so exquisite a horse.

Firuza looked not much better off, her face pinched with exhaustion. His own muscles ached with fatigue. But he wasted no effort on convincing his stubborn bride to return to the camp. She had maintained the pace admirably—and anyway, he'd made three such suggestions already, and she'd turned him down flat every time.

Her stamina and determination impressed him. If he stayed here, her strength as khatun would prove invaluable. Wherever he went, in fact, he liked the idea of a passionate, committed wife at his side, an ally who would not only run his household but defend it against the enemies who threatened every khan.

He still had to win her, though. Her response earlier had underlined that point. She could have made life easier for both of them by accepting his proposal to move into his tent. Surely she understood that he didn't take her acquiescence as permission to treat her however he pleased—although in truth, the more time he spent with her, the harder he found it to keep his hands to himself.

Yet she had refused him. He tried not to let that thought depress him. He didn't want to lose her—and when had *that* happened? But marrying her against her will, to defeat Tulpar or for any other reason, didn't appeal to him either.

For the moment, though, the herds demanded his full attention. "Ready?" He lifted Firuza onto her saddle— transferred to a serene and elegant roan—and mounted the piebald gelding supplied by Rafik's father. Together, they trotted toward the panting herds. A ring of mounted warriors hemmed the animals in. At the outer edge, he saw Rafik waving.

Ogodai reached for Firuza's reins, but she turned her horse on her own. Rafik said something over his shoulder to the man next to him and rode out to meet them.

"What have you found?" Ogodai asked when Rafik came within range.

Rafik held up an arrow—broad, almost flat at the tip, with an arrowhead of bone, not the steel tips needed to puncture armor—a weapon intended to wound or frighten rather than to kill. "This," he said. "In the bellwether. It left a slash across her back, then lodged behind her left shoulder. Otherwise, we'd have assumed the sheep injured herself running. But we discovered a similar slash on two of the others. Someone set out to scatter the sheep—hoping the goats and horses would follow, I suppose."

"Which they did." Ogodai took the arrow from Rafik and twisted it in his fingers, examining it from every angle. "Raiders?"

"We didn't see any," Rafik said.

Firuza pressed her horse forward until her knee touched Ogodai's. When he handed her the arrow, she didn't study it as he had. Instead, she flicked the far end of the shaft, where the propelling feathers lay. "It's one of ours." She held out the arrow to Rafik. "Didn't you recognize it?"

Recognize it? At thirty arrows per quiver and at least a hundred mounted warriors in the camp?

Yet Rafik flushed. "The blue feather," he said. "Almas's signature. I missed it."

Ogodai plucked the arrow from his bride's fingers and examined it anew. Sure enough, amid the white goose feathers on either side of the shaft, one shone faintly blue.

"Who is Almas?" he asked. "One of the warriors? I don't remember him."

"Not a warrior," Rafik said. "Our fletcher."

"Our best fletcher," Firuza added. "This arrow could belong to anyone in the camp."

"Including Almas himself." Rafik surveyed the herd, as if he expected the culprit to stand up and declare himself.

"Almas gave full allegiance to my father." Firuza sounded shocked. "How can you suspect him? Scatter the herds? He might as well slay us all while we slept."

"Someone did," Ogodai pointed out. "If not Almas, then another of your people. My men and Tulpar's have their own arrows." Firuza and Rafik nodded grimly in response.

No rustlers to deal with. He tried to take comfort from that, but in truth, treachery from within was more disturbing than rustling by outsiders, a common enough occurrence on the steppe.

On the western horizon, the setting sun cast fiery trails across the sky. Orange clouds warred for attention with grasses as molten gold as the palomino's coat. A fine riding day tomorrow.

But not today. Chasing down the herds had consumed the short afternoon.

"Let's get these beasts back to the camp," Ogodai said. "Send a messenger to Jahangir Bey, advising him that his people need to build a temporary corral to restrain the animals while they recover. And let him and the elders know what you found. I'm sure they will agree to stop for the night."

Firuza dipped her hands into a bowl of warm water and raised them to her face, relishing the heat against her chilled skin.

Her fingers and cheeks felt numb. Her ears, protected from the steppe winds by her furred cap, pricked at the murmurs she heard from the other side of the screen; her toes tingled as life returned to them. More than anything, she wanted to don clothes that didn't smell of horse and sweat, eat a warm meal, relax, sleep. The women's tent wouldn't fall silent for hours, but after expending so much effort on the trail, she doubted an invading army could keep her awake. She reached for a square of linen left out for her use, wet and soaped the cloth, and passed it over her body, moving swiftly to retain the warmth. Many layers of felt barricaded the interior from the evening air outside, yet tendrils of cold never failed to seep beneath the trellis frame.

Suppose she had accepted Ogodai's offer? She might be snug now in his arms. He'd promised not to force her, but she knew he desired her. She sensed it in the brush of his lips against her fingers, the way his hands lingered on her waist when he lifted her onto the saddle, the light in his eyes when he laughed. And here, in this rare moment of privacy, Firuza admitted that she wanted her betrothed to desire her. Wanted to feel his arms around her, press herself against his body, experience his kiss. Roxelana obviously enjoyed the act of love. Diliara, once upon a time, had enjoyed it too. Why not Firuza?

And Ogodai was special, different. Exhilaration coursed through her veins as she recalled how they had raced after the stampeding herds. He led the way, but at the same time, he encouraged her—no, expected her—to match him in speed and skill. He didn't slow down for her or condescend to her, as her brother so often did. She wondered where it came from, that ability to treat her as an equal.

He had mentioned his mother. Firuza scrunched her forehead, recalling Sumbeka, a lady of decision and beauty. And he had a sister—Nasan. A girl who rode and handled a bow and a sword better than most of the boys, even at eight, when Firuza had last seen her. Did they explain his ability to tolerate strong women?

She needed time to talk to him! Foolish to think of moving into his tent before she had learned the first thing about him.

Yet, try as she might, the appeal of Ogodai's offer continued to tug at her.

She dressed in scarlet silk trousers and a matching quilted tunic that reached to her knees, with a high Chinese collar and embroidery portraying glowing phoenixes and strange warped trees like those that clung to the edges of the steppe. Her hair, thick and straight, fell to her waist. Tomorrow, she would order her servant to wash it—right after the day's trek ended, so she had time to dry it over the hearth fire. For tonight, though, braiding it would suffice.

The slave girl waited for her on the other side of the screen. Firuza told her to fetch Ogodai's winged combs and sat on a cushion near the fire to sip goat stew while she waited for the girl to return.

She had barely finished her meal when a male voice summoned Diliara to the tent door. The chatter that filled the tent in response reduced all previous whispering, muttering, and gossip to a mere hum of sound.

Diliara turned and beckoned to Firuza, who felt her stomach tighten. A man at the door. A summons from her stepmother.

Ogodai, surely. No other man would call here in the evening asking to speak with her. Had he pitched a tent as promised? Would he ask her again to move in with him?

She pushed herself to her feet. It wouldn't do to keep him waiting. Her knees didn't seem quite steady, but somehow she picked her way around the many mattresses that lay between her and Diliara and reached the door.

A man stood there, sure enough. A tall, handsome man dressed in layers of fur-trimmed brocade and boots of multicolored leather, his trim waist cinched with a golden belt and a feather adorning his white satin turban.

She had no doubt it was the latest style from Istanbul. Because the man who sought her company was not Ogodai but Tulpar.

Trailed by her maid—for propriety's sake, but not so closely that the girl could hear everything said—Firuza accepted Tulpar's arm as they strolled through the camp. The evening chill made her glad she had stopped to don hat and coat before agreeing to walk with him. In truth, the drag of tired muscles had caused her to hesitate. But she suspected Tulpar would talk to her more readily than to his brother, whom he so obviously disliked, and she might have no other opportunity. Under normal circumstances, unmarried men and women spent little time together.

Except with Ogodai, Firuza seldom found herself at a loss for words. She began by asking Tulpar about his son, in part because she knew he loved Timur and would be eager to talk about him, and in part to remind him that he *had* a son, as well as a tie to the woman who had borne that child.

He answered her questions readily enough until she brought up Ogodai. "Is it not strange," she asked, "that he thought you dead?"

Tulpar's face tightened. Even in the dimming light, she couldn't mistake his tension. "Why do you detest him so?" she asked. "He seems nice enough."

He shrugged. "He sits in my place. My son's place, one day. Who cares if he's nice, when he claims what is mine?" He squeezed her fingers, resting lightly on his sable-trimmed sleeve. "You, for example." He raised her hand to his mouth and brushed his lips across its back, just as Ogodai had earlier.

The gesture didn't affect her in the same way, though. Odd, when Tulpar was even more handsome than his brother.

She jerked her hand away. Undeterred, he gazed meaningfully into her eyes. "You're becoming quite the beauty, are you not?"

Words she would have yearned to hear him say a week ago! Even now, she couldn't suppress a tingle at being showered with praise by this good-looking older man who had previously reserved his smitten glances for Roxelana.

Yet a swift self-appraisal revealed thoughts still clear, tongue untangled, and a body for the most part unmoved. His caressing gaze, the brush of his lips—she liked the *idea* of bringing him to his knees, but the reality? Not so much.

Still, he had given her an opening. "*Ata* didn't promise me to you, Tulpar. On the very night he died, he ordered me to wed Ogodai."

"Ah, but he did, my sweet. You were a toddler; you don't recall. But Ildar Shirin does. So does Kazbek Argyn. The council plans to take up the discussion tomorrow morning."

"A toddler?" That worried her. Most Tatar women were the same age as their husbands or a few years older, but Bahadur had saved Bulat's life the year before Firuza's mother died. Their sworn brotherhood began then. They *might* have promised her to Tulpar.

"Three," Tulpar said.

Yes, that was the right age. But... "That means nothing, Tulpar, and you know it. The elders did not oppose my betrothal to Ogodai, so don't pretend there was some previous ceremony that I have forgotten. Our fathers changed their plans."

A flash of annoyance lit his eyes, but his smile did not alter. "*My* father set out to cheat me of my birthright, yes, and your father went along with it. And Ogodai benefited, as ever. But I had you first, my sweet, and I will have you again. Ildar Shirin has already agreed to help me."

His threat stiffened Firuza's spine. He hadn't changed one bit. He'd been using her all along!

She knew why Shirin backed Tulpar. Shirin had assisted Tulpar in the first place out of dislike for Bulat Khan—a man too straightforward, too blunt in his opinions, too sure of his standing as khan to tolerate Ildar's attempts to expand Shirin power. Ogodai seemed to share his father's distaste for intrigue. It didn't take a shaman to predict that Ildar would favor Bulat's older, cast-off son. If installing Tulpar as khan annoyed Bulat, so much the better.

"Ildar doesn't control the other clan leaders," she said. "And *Ata* can speak for himself. We will hold a feast for him, and his spirit will guide us."

"Old wives' tales," he scoffed. "What kind of Muslim are you, holding feasts for the dead?"

Hands on her hips, she stood her ground. "The old ones still guard us. They are not gods but ancestors. No threat to Allah. And *Ata* rides among them."

Tulpar shrugged. "No doubt. He had less respect for the faith than a camel does. But I thought better of you."

He had stopped trying to woo her. She could and did heave a sigh of relief. "I'm not for you, Tulpar, and the entire camp knows it. Shirin's backing will not silence the other clans. Rather the reverse."

Tulpar again brushed her cheek. "Charming. The bey's daughter plays at politics. But you're wrong, Lady. The clans want booty. The horde depends on a steady stream of plunder, and I'm just the one to provide them with it."

But a future based on plunder and war was the opposite of her vision.

She didn't say that. The hint of opposition would only divert him further, and her most urgent questions still required answers. The camp had quieted for the night. She couldn't stay much longer.

"You were away when *Ata* died," she said. "What do you know of that night?"

She'd expected anger, astonishment, denial, outrage—even befuddlement at her abrupt switch of subject. Instead, Tulpar burst out laughing, swept her into his arms, and kissed her soundly on the mouth.

Had the man run mad? When she smacked his chest, he lifted her until her feet no longer touched the ground. Her blows had no effect. Where was her maid?

She heard feet, running in the wrong direction. Tulpar's mustache scratched her upper lip. His mouth pressed against hers. His tongue touched her teeth, probing for an opening.

Firuza swung her booted foot and kicked him in the shins. When he staggered, she wrenched her mouth from his. "How dare you!" she said. "Let me go this instant!"

For one horrible moment, she thought he would refuse. Then he dropped her. Her feet hit the grass with unnecessary force, but she managed to stay upright.

"Hussy," he said. "I'll enjoy taming you, when you're my wife. And don't think you won't be, my girl, because your father gave you to me, and I intend to take you, little brother be damned."

Heat blazed in Firuza's cheeks. Rage stripped her mind of every acceptable word—and every unacceptable one, too. She scrubbed her mouth with the back of her hand.

"I will *never* marry you," she choked out at last.

"Indeed not," Ogodai's voice said from behind her. "She belongs to me, whether you like it or not. So keep your hands off her. I won't warn you again."

"Ooh, I'm terrified." Tulpar opened and closed his fingers, as if readying for a punch. "You must have forgotten the other day, if you're so hot for a repeat."

As Ogodai moved to her side, Firuza could see only his profile, which looked grim, and with good reason. Tulpar was being deliberately obnoxious, hoping Ogodai would snap, she guessed, and alienate the horde. Or fail to act, which would make him appear too weak for a good khan.

Ogodai did neither. He touched a hand to Firuza's waist and said, "Let's go."

Without hesitation, she turned toward the women's tent. Ogodai strode at her side. The sensation of Tulpar's eyes boring into her spine was, she assured herself, a girl's silly fancy.

Ogodai didn't stop at the women's tent. At the doorway, he dismissed her maid. Only then did Firuza realize the woman must have fetched him. That explained the running feet—and why they'd headed in the wrong direction.

A finger touched Firuza's lips, stilling her protest before it could form.

"I need to talk to you alone," he said. His voice sounded strained. "Before you return to the others."

In the light of the torch that kept the night at bay, she studied his face. What did he want of her at this hour?

"Trust me?" The grim expression provoked by his brother's chivvying had vanished, leaving him wistful, boyish, charming. And although she had freed herself without his help—without even knowing he was present to offer help—he *had* stepped forward to challenge Tulpar on her behalf.

"Yes," she said. Her insides had broken into the odd little dance they did in his presence. She had no fear that he would try to take advantage of her. He didn't lack self-control; she had learned that much.

Besides, she knew the perfect place for their discussion. Taking his hand, she led him toward the grandmothers' shrine.

They did not enter. She carried no milk to spray in greeting, no food to offer the waiting spirits. But the shrine stood apart from the other tents—silent, sacred. From there, the ancestors cast their net, gliding on the cool breezes of the autumn night to infuse the present with the serenity and wisdom of the world beyond. From the center of the camp, fires of dried dung purified the air with their smoke, and the sizzle of fat from meat cooked earlier in the evening occasionally painted red-gold flashes against the dark.

Ogodai held her hands and looked deep into her eyes. "You know your own business best, my bride, but was it wise to walk with Tulpar—and unescorted at that?"

"I had my maid." He had spoken quietly enough. So why did she feel herself under attack?

He raised his eyebrows, and she bit her lip. "I saw it as a chance to find out what I could about his role, if any, in *Ata*'s death. He stopped at the women's tent and asked me to go with him. Most of the time, I have no opportunity, no reason, to talk to him. It seemed heaven-sent, and my stepmother gave her approval."

"Why?" he asked. "She barely let me talk to you, despite our betrothal and me being flat on my back at the time."

"Because of the maid, I assume. We were not alone." Her voice caught on the last word, as the memory of Tulpar's assault began to crack her defenses.

"He seems to have thought so."

"I didn't ask him to kiss me!"

"Didn't you? What would any man think if you wandered off with him in the twilight?"

He thought she had brought it on herself?

Apparently so, for he added, "Did you enjoy it?"

"How can you ask me that?" He must have seen her struggling. He didn't understand her one bit!

"How can I not?" His face hardened. The wistful boy who had begged for her trust might not have existed. "You refused to stay with me. You chose to walk with him. Is it not reasonable to conclude that you prefer him to me?"

Firuza recoiled. "Your brother never showed the least interest in me until tonight. How was I to guess he would dishonor me so?" And with that, she pulled her hands from his grasp and ran to join the women. Ogodai called after her, but she ignored him.

He didn't follow her. The silk trousers gave her a speed her usual robes couldn't match, but Firuza had no doubt he could have caught her if he'd tried.

Chapter 10

WELL, HE'D MUFFED THAT ONE. WHAT WAS IT ABOUT FIRUZA that caused him to lose the few skills he possessed in handling women whenever he tried to say anything important to her? Ogodai kicked a tuft of grass, swearing at the unresponsive earth. He'd made real progress with her today, for the first time since he arrived, and what must he do but throw it away!

When he asked her to walk with him, he'd meant to suggest, calmly, that she might have given Tulpar the wrong impression. A hint to keep her on her toes before finding out what happened. Nothing that would upset her.

Then he heard her voice catch, and for one crazy instant the memory of her in Tulpar's arms overwhelmed him. And there he was, attacking her without justification, hearing the ugly words tumble forth, unable to stop them.

He knew why, too: he was jealous of Tulpar. The skilled older man, better-looking, more experienced, more seasoned in combat. He'd worshipped Tulpar as a child, and some of the earlier awe lingered. He had to get over that, stand up for himself, accept that Tulpar saw him as a rival and that their father, for reasons best known to himself, had set his two sons at odds. And stop alienating Firuza, who at times seemed to like him. Otherwise he would lose her.

He didn't want that. The khanate didn't matter. If not this one, he'd find another. But Firuza was a different story. The more he saw of her, the more he desired her. He would not pack up and go home without Firuza. He would not permit his brother to force her.

Which Tulpar had. Ogodai recognized that in retrospect. He had seen her fighting—before he lost his mind and accused her of luring Tulpar on.

His brother had taken a big risk. Ogodai could have killed him, and no one in the horde would have censured him. Laying hands on another man's woman was the ultimate insult.

Of course, Tulpar claimed the woman, as he did the khanate. He could argue that no insult was intended—or possible.

He'd raised the stakes, though. No deal, no quarter, no appeals to brotherhood. Tulpar had declared war—and so far, Tulpar was winning it.

Time to develop a plan.

He must apologize to Firuza, for starters. But he couldn't invade the women's tent at this hour. He'd have to talk to her tomorrow.

He should get inside. But where? Not a chink of light showed beneath the four great tents on their wagons. Even if he hurried, he would wake the other warriors as he stumbled to the pallet spread for him in the place of honor farthest from the door.

Yet he lingered, despite the cold that intensified with each breath he took. The thought of sharing space with Tulpar, taunted by Roxelana and Jahangir's lovemaking, repelled him. If he went to his assigned space, he couldn't avoid the reminders of what he didn't have. But to sleep among the men of lesser rank, which might have worked as a solution if he'd thought of it sooner, would throw the entire camp into turmoil now that everyone else had retired to bed. Even ordering his own men to raise a tent must wait.

Ogodai turned in a slow circle, assessing the alternatives. The bonfires would keep him warm, and he had slept on the ground often enough not to rule that possibility out. Not comfortable, for sure, and he'd have to rise before dawn.

A shabby, moth-eaten tent stood nearby on a small wagon of its own. The traces dipped to touch the ground, holding the two wheels still. From its size, he judged that it couldn't hold more than a single family, the only such tent left standing. Yet throughout his conversation with Firuza not one sound had emanated from the tent, as if it were deserted. The whole area appeared set apart, abandoned.

Memory stirred. He'd seen the tent before. It was the home of the clan ancestors, the shrine that accompanied the nomads on their travels. So many years had passed since he'd lived here—years spent in lands rich in the traditions of the Crescent and the Cross, where the ancestors lived on only in doorways and firesides. He'd forgotten how central the grandmothers remained to nomadic life, especially to women. Even among his own people, his mother and sister communed with the old ones more than the male members of the family did. Why had Firuza brought him to this place? What had she wanted to tell him that he'd been too caught up in his own fears and jealousy to hear?

No matter. That, too, could wait. For she had solved his problem. The ancestors were loving spirits, who took a close interest in the lives of their descendants. They didn't stand guard like the Christian saints, barring unbelievers from entry. They didn't demand sloughed-off shoes and perfect performance of complex rituals. An obeisance and some food to succor the hungry ghosts, and a man could seek shelter among them for the night.

Ogodai patted his belt, glad that he had retained his riding clothes rather than matching his brother's finery for the evening. A flask of koumiss provided mare's milk to spritz the air in greeting; he dropped dried meat left over from the trail into the spirit bowls on entry. He touched his forehead to the mat in veneration and, sensing acceptance, stretched out. His booted toes touched the far corner of the tent; his head just cleared the dais where the grandmothers sat. From that angle, he could see that someone had left a rolled quilt behind the stand. He sniffed it and, satisfied of its cleanliness, wrapped himself in this unexpected bounty and prepared to sleep.

The ancestors communicated through dreams. Dreams of warning, dreams of revelation, dreams of longing. Ogodai had heard their whispering since infancy. Some dreams came in scattered fragments, others entwined in symbols too complex for anyone but a shaman to untangle. And some—not many, but a few—shone clear as a mountain lake, perfect and unforgettable as the pink/violet glow of twilight on the winter steppe.

Even asleep, Ogodai recognized that tonight's was such a dream. He had the odd sensation of watching himself that marked a true spirit message. Bahadur Bey approached on a winged steed, its coat so pure that it gleamed translucent against the night sky, stars like pinpricks visible through the spirit flesh. Bahadur waved his saber as he swooped and dove among the stars, the horse's wings rising and falling, obscuring the bey, then revealing him.

The horse came close, closer. Bahadur sheathed his saber and leaped from the animal's back, landing with a whisper of spirit boots against the mat on which Ogodai lay. The bey sat cross-legged beside the quilt and prodded Ogodai in the shoulder. "Rouse yourself, boy," he said, "or you will lose what I have set aside for you."

The watching Ogodai saw his spirit sit, bringing him face to face with Bahadur. The bey had not changed from their farewell six years ago, but Ogodai remained his adult self. In the dream, that did not seem strange.

"What must I do?" Ogodai's spirit asked. "How do I win her?"

Bahadur laughed, the hearty guffaw Ogodai remembered from a hundred such exchanges, earnest questions that in their naïve sincerity had amused his no-nonsense tutor. "Not my daughter, young fool. The khanate."

Had he already lost her then? "I want her," he said. "The horde can choose its khan. If your people pick my brother, I will go elsewhere. But I will take Firuza with me."

Bahadur slapped Ogodai's spirit on the back with a force that even death could not, it seemed, reduce. The entire tent rocked on its wagon frame. "You will have my daughter," the bey said. "I summoned *you* to wed her, not your brother. But you must do more than that to earn my blessing. Tulpar must not become khan. Stop him, or others besides myself will die."

The bey rose and whistled. His turban, topped with a spray of black swan's feathers, brushed against the roof of the tent and penetrated the shabby felt. In the distance, Ogodai heard the beating of wings, growing louder. His spirit sprang to its feet and confronted Bahadur.

The winged stallion swept between them, and Bahadur vaulted into place, tucking his knees under the wings.

"Wait," Ogodai cried. "Why must Tulpar not become khan? What do you mean, others besides yourself will die? Were you murdered?"

Bahadur clasped the horse's wings, slowed its flight, turned his head—astonishment visible in his face. "Of course," he said. "Why else would I come here?"

Before Ogodai could rally himself to ask his next question, winged stallion and bey were gone. His spirit reentered his body. His eyes opened, and he stared at the silent dais—home to the grandmothers, Givers of the Dream.

Secure among the women, warm, comfortable, sated, Firuza couldn't sleep. She strove not to toss and turn. Restlessness would lead to an interrogation in the morning, with her mothers and sisters speculating about the cause of her discomfort.

She told herself she needed sleep after today's long ride, needed it if she planned to ride tomorrow. It made little sense to thrash about, wide awake, worrying about losing affection she'd never had from a man who didn't care a jot about her. Why couldn't she get it through her head that Ogodai saw her only as a pathway to the khanate?

Just like his brother. Two men, both uncaring, one of whom she inexplicably preferred. Had she at least chosen the better-looking one, the one with more experience, the one she'd known her whole life who had the support of the council leader? No, *she* had to fall for the newcomer, for no better reason than because *Ata* had ordered her to like him.

And if that was not a lie, then she had never uttered one. Tulpar had shown no interest in her. Her fantasies about him had had little grist to feed on; they could not prevent her from noticing that she represented, for him, at best a means to an end.

Whereas Ogodai had appealed to her from the first. The winged horses for her hair, his comment that they suited her, his refusal to flirt with Roxelana, his willingness to accept her as an equal partner, the possibility that he might share her vision of her people's future—were these things not the tinder that lit flames inside her every time they spoke? She could pretend that he meant no more to her than a commitment honored, but the words rang hollow even to herself. From the moment he strode, unexpected, into the audience hall, he had drawn her to him like a lodestone.

If only he felt the same! Just this evening, she would have sworn he wanted her, but twice now, he had had her entirely to himself, and while she waited expectantly like some dimwit from the harem, he held her hands and chided her for some shortcoming to do with his brother. Whom she didn't even like.

Yes, once she had prayed Tulpar would notice her. And she had felt a brief thrill when he asserted his claim to her. A childish desire to spite Roxelana, she suspected. But she had *not* asked him to kiss her, and she hadn't enjoyed it when he did, whatever Ogodai supposed. Whereas Ogodai had only to brush her fingers with his lips to send her into turmoil.

And why *had* Tulpar kissed her? To distract her, perhaps, because her blunt question had surprised him. Because what sane man would laugh when asked about another's death?

Either way, the kiss left no doubt that Tulpar would take her if he could—to profit from her connection to the old bey, to prevent his brother from enjoying her. And to secure his position as khan. Tulpar wanted to keep his brother from enjoying *that*, too.

Which meant she couldn't afford to wait for the council to decide. She must declare her loyalty, and soon.

But to which man? Since neither wanted her for herself, she had only her own feelings to go on. Her feelings and the possibility that Tulpar had killed her father. And her father's command, which a good daughter must honor. Maybe Ogodai would learn to love her in time.

She had some pride, though. She would control her words and expressions lest she reveal how much he already meant to her. Let *him* show some interest for once.

The next morning, before Ogodai had time to do more than straighten his clothes and climb down from the ancestors' cart, Vafa arrived in a state of great agitation. "Sultan, I could not find you. I feared you had left. I searched throughout the camp, but no one had seen you. Fortunately, I spotted your horse, so I knew you must be nearby. The elders request your presence in the bey's tent!"

Request? Summons, more like. Ogodai reassured his servant with a smile. "The day's hardly broken, Vafa. Can they expect me so soon?"

"At once, Sultan, they said." He bobbed his head. "If it pleases you."

"It had better please me, it seems." Ogodai ran a hand through his hair and wished for a bowl of warm water. No matter. Soon the camp would set out again, and he would be covered with sweat before they had traveled the length of two cows. Most likely, the desire to finish its business without delay explained the council's haste. The elders would not expect him to show up in full court finery. "Very well, Vafa. Does my appearance disgrace my father's name? If not, I suppose I should present myself as required. No point in raising their hackles."

With a flourish worthy of a sorcerer, Vafa produced a wooden comb and handed it to him. Ogodai subdued his unruly hair, returned the comb to his servant, and went off to face the council.

As he walked, he wondered what the leaders wanted. His interactions with them—except for Kazbek Argyn, Rafik's father—remained cordial but distant. He observed their scrutiny without particularly liking it, but a mere five days after his arrival, their wariness didn't surprise him. Tulpar's appearance had made them, if anything, more cautious. He would bet on a pair of knuckle bones that they hadn't called for him to announce that they had decided whom to appoint as khan.

To discuss yesterday's near-disaster, maybe. Working together, he and Rafik had saved the herds. The elders would want to hear what they both had to say. A spring lightened Ogodai's step as he made his way through the awakening camp.

Wisps of steam from fires tended outside the large tents carried aromas of mutton and herbs. With luck, his stomach wouldn't growl during the meeting.

Before long, he mounted the steps at the back of the wagon holding the bey's tent. Two guards stood at the entrance, their black-fringed spears crossed, each point almost touching the other's turban. As he approached, they snapped the spears upright. He nodded at them, lifted the felt door covering, and stepped over the threshold.

Dim light suffused the interior. The central hole was covered, since there could be no hearth fire with the tent loaded for travel. Lanterns placed on flat stones shone in four spots arranged equidistant outside the circle of men. In the middle of the circle, a tablecloth supported bowls of braised meat, baskets of apples and flatbread. A pair of silent slave girls moved among the men, filling cups from the long-spouted ceramic jugs they carried. A small part of Ogodai's tension evaporated. The elders had not skimped on their hospitality, and he need not fear embarrassment caused by the demands of his body.

Five men rose at his entrance; Tulpar, at the far end, did not. Ogodai moved forward, addressing each clan leader in turn and inviting him to resume his seat. Those present included only the four tribal elders, plus Jahangir Bey, Tulpar, and Ogodai himself. No Rafik. Perhaps not a question-and-answer session, then.

Tulpar had taken the place of honor, which he occupied as though born to it. He greeted his half-brother with a flick of the wrist, as if acknowledging the unwelcome entrance of an inferior. Whereas Ogodai still wore yesterday's riding clothes, his brother had dressed as if for a celebration. Brass armor emitted a dull gleam as he shifted position; his white silk turban glowed like a moonbeam in the dim light.

Irritated by Tulpar's casual assumption of authority, Ogodai communicated his displeasure with a chilly nod before addressing the elders. "Forgive me, beys. I came as soon as I received your message. I hope you won't take it amiss that I didn't keep you waiting so that I could change my clothes."

Tulpar sniffed, and Ogodai felt a flash of pride. He was learning. Tulpar needed the occasional jab.

"Not at all, Sultan. You honor us." That was Ildar Shirin. "Will you not be seated?" He extended his arm, indicating the empty place to Tulpar's left. Jahangir sat to Tulpar's right, and Shirin next to him.

Ogodai nodded acceptance and made his way around the circle, grateful to note that the elders had placed him and Tulpar at the same level, side by side.

The leaders viewed them as equals then. He had been right: they hadn't yet decided whom they wanted as khan. If they had already made their choice, their preferred candidate would take precedence over his rival.

Over Tulpar's left shoulder, Bahadur's spirit banner stood upright in a chased iron holder. A comforting sight, as if the former bey attended unseen.

The banner resembled the tufted lances carried by the guards but was more elaborate. A rimmed, decorated brass disk topped a long trident, creating the impression of a helmet. White horse hair collected from Bahadur's favorite steeds, a good foot in length, dangled from the disk. Ribbons of white brocade attached to the disk supported another ribbon that ran horizontally around the hair, constraining its first few inches but allowing the remainder to blow free. Brass disks connected the horizontal and vertical ribbons, which formed a crude cross on either side. So long as the spirit banner remained with the horde, so, too, would Bahadur's soul retain its place in his people's hearts.

Ogodai sat, putting as much distance as possible between himself and Tulpar yet acutely aware of Bahadur's spirit presence hovering behind his own right shoulder. Last night's dream tugged at his thoughts. Should he mention it to the council?

Better to find out first what they wanted, perhaps.

Kazbek Argyn resumed his place at Ogodai's left. "Greetings, Sultan," he murmured, and Ogodai responded in kind. He wanted to ask what this meeting was about, but to do so would reveal his anxiety. He asked about Rafik instead.

"He's getting ready for the festival," Kazbek said.

"What festival?" Honestly, did these people revel in secrets? They couldn't tell him they planned to move, they couldn't share plans for a festival?

"We'll discuss it in a moment," Shirin said.

A festival didn't sound ominous. Ogodai quelled his nerves, tried not to look at his half-brother, and accepted a cup from the slave girls, which turned out to contain mare's milk. He sipped the rich, grassy liquid with appreciation and reached for a piece of flatbread.

Opposite him, the heads of the Baryn and Kipchak clans sat cross-legged. Baryn reminded him of Bahadur Bey: short and well-fed, with a set face. He seldom contributed to any discussion, even at dinner. In personality, he appeared stolid and unyielding, lacking both Shirin's quicksilver deviousness and Argyn's straightforward practicality.

Kipchak was more volatile, with the massive biceps and thighs, the barrel chest of a fighter. As the youngest member of the council, he had the least authority. Neither he nor any of the other clan leaders rivaled Tulpar in splendor. They wore riding dress or, in the case of Argyn and Kipchak, leather armor. Even Jahangir sported a chain mail shirt similar to Ogodai's under an unfastened coat of red wool. A peaked, embroidered felt hat with a broad, turned-back rim adorned his head.

As Ogodai struggled to conceal his impatience, Kipchak sliced pieces from an apple with his dagger and popped them, one by one, into his mouth. A servant passed a bowl of braised meat, and Ogodai ate. The mutton was warm and the sauce thick, but if they had a taste, anxiety overwhelmed it.

After the prolonged exchange of pleasantries that accompanied every meal, the council at last settled to its purpose. Jahangir took the lead—his right as the representative of the Mangyts, the most powerful clan among the nomads, but startling given his usual state of intoxication. Although Ogodai saw no evidence of that today, just as he had seen none yesterday. Clear, coherent, decisive—Jahangir again resembled the friend Ogodai had once known. But he saw no friendliness in the malicious dark eyes that stared at him from Jahangir's face.

"Please don't take offense if I speak plainly and on behalf of the entire council," Jahangir said. "Although we are, of course, flattered by the interest in our camp shown by the sons of Bulat, and while we are bound to honor the commands of my deceased father, as the current guardians of this people we must proceed with caution before naming a khan. Some of us believe that we can succeed without a descendant of Genghis to lead the way. Some support the more experienced and familiar candidate"—he indicated Tulpar—"whereas others prefer the one who can deliver reliable and powerful assistance from outside. My sister's fate also remains to be determined.

Tulpar argues an earlier betrothal than the one most of us remember."

"I can attest to the earlier betrothal," Ildar Shirin announced. "Argyn, you recall it also. Don't pretend otherwise."

"Of course I recall it." Argyn, his face taut, leaned forward. Shirin had his full attention. "Nor have I forgotten when and how Bahadur broke it. Let us not create confusion where none exists. Tulpar moved among us for a while. He defied his father's commands, with dire results, and Bulat banished him. He had the right, for a son owes absolute obedience to his father and Bulat had already endured much defiance from Tulpar. And Bahadur, who led us always with great sense, responded by breaking that prior contract. He could do that in good faith, since his daughter was still too young for marriage, the arrangement had not progressed beyond the stage of promises, and breaking the contract showed his loyalty to his sworn brother. He then agreed to betroth her—more suitably, I would argue—to Ogodai Sultan."

"And that union we celebrated," Baryn added. "I also remember that on the night of his death, Bahadur begged us to summon Bulat's son and wed our Lady Firuza to him."

"Yes, but which son?" Jahangir asked. "We have two to choose from."

Ogodai felt his head whirling. He had been right, then, to suspect that Tulpar had not made up his story of a prior betrothal. His half-brother *did* have reason to consider Firuza his own.

Not a good reason, admittedly, but perhaps sufficient justification for Tulpar, burning with a sense of injustice.

Had Bahadur once promised Tulpar the khanate as well? It wouldn't be surprising, with Tulpar the older and once-favored son. Clearly, the bey had withdrawn that offer, too, if he had ever made it.

He couldn't let Jahangir's last comment go unchallenged. Ogodai pulled the medallion from his sash and showed it to one council member after another, beginning with Ildar Shirin. "Bahadur sent this to my father," he said. "It was a prearranged signal between them, as sworn brothers. That if either needed help, he would send for the other. If your former bey wished you to ally yourselves with Crimea, why did he summon me, not my brother?"

Jahangir shrugged. "A likely story. I never saw that before in my life."

Shirin frowned but didn't speak. The two younger members of the council looked puzzled. But Kazbek Argyn's face lit up, and he reached for the emblem. Ogodai dropped the winged horse into his hand.

"You wouldn't have seen it, Bey," Kazbek said. "I had no idea your father still had it. He must have hidden it somewhere to keep it safe. But it is true: Bahadur and Bulat exchanged talismans when they became sworn brothers. If my son carried the winged horse to Bulat at Bahadur's orders, then there is no doubt that he intended Ogodai to become khan, as I have believed from the start."

"Except," Shirin said, "that if you look at the medallion, you will see that it does not reference Ogodai but Tulpar. The winged horse."

"Because they favored me first." Tulpar abandoned any effort to convey lounging indifference and straightened his spine like everyone else. He held his hands tightly clasped in his lap. "Why else did my father name me after Bahadur's symbol?"

"But they changed their minds," Kazbek reminded him. "And you have only yourself to blame for that." The glare that Tulpar shot his way seemed not to bother him one bit.

The tense, angry silence lasted no more than a few seconds, although it felt much longer to Ogodai. Jahangir broke it with laughter that he didn't bother to explain.

At the far end of the circle, Kipchak rose to his feet. "I may be the least among you," he said, "but I propose that we delay the decision. Both candidates have strong points and weaknesses. We know Tulpar Sultan better, true, but Ogodai Sultan proved his worth during the stampede yesterday." He bowed in Ogodai's direction, and Ogodai returned the courtesy by placing his hand over his heart and lowering his head. At the same time, he marked Kipchak's careful attempt to maintain equality between the brothers. Until now, only Shirin had given Tulpar the title conferred on him by birth. The others had withheld it, Ogodai assumed, in deference to Bulat's decision to banish his eldest son.

"I agree," Baryn said. "I suggest that Bulat's sons prove to us, during the contests today, which one we should follow—if we choose to accept either of them as khan."

"And Lady Firuza?" Ogodai asked. He couldn't escape the memory of Bahadur ordering him to secure the khanate, but he still saw Firuza as more important than power.

"We can't let a woman's whims decide the fate of the entire horde." Baryn sounded regretful, but he spoke without hesitation.

"Well, not entirely," Jahangir said. "One of today's contests is 'Chase the Girl.'"

Kipchak held out his painted cup, and a servant hurried to fill it. "You jest, Bey, but I like Baryn's proposal. Let these two young men show us who will make the best khan."

This was the moment to share his dream, except that Ogodai could not. What good would it do at this point? If he must prove himself on the field, then he would.

"Jahangir, do you agree?" Kazbek said. "And you, Shirin? I see no reason for delay, but little harm in it either."

"Very well." Shirin looked unhappy.

Jahangir smiled as if he had gained a point; Ogodai wasn't sure why. He drained his cup and placed it upside-down on the rug before him. "Now, can we dismiss them and discuss yesterday's attempt at sabotage? At this rate, the morning will be half-over before we get down to business."

Tulpar doffed his turban, laughing. "As the bey would have it," he said before striding from the tent.

Ogodai followed more slowly, taking time to bid farewell to and thank each council member—even Ildar Shirin, who looked glum, and Jahangir, whom he desperately wished to reach out and shake, not least because of Jahangir's disinterest in his sister's welfare.

He was still fuming when he reached the outside, where Vafa waited with news of the day's planned events.

Chapter 11

FIRUZA WOKE TO THE NEWS THAT SHE NEED NOT WORRY that her troubled night would leave her falling asleep on the trail. The council, with Jahangir's approval, had ruled that the herds must rest after their wild run. To keep the warriors out of trouble, the clan leaders had ordered a day of celebration: wrestling matches and a poetry competition, races and contests on horseback, a feast that would cull sheep and goats likely to die during the journey. And, for the maidens and unmarried men of the camp, the game of "Chase the Girl."

Firuza couldn't have asked for a better opportunity. On a good day, she and her palomino could beat any other pair in the horde. Before nightfall, Ogodai and Tulpar would both learn the results of her deliberations last night. Evading her stepmother's demands for information about the walk with Tulpar, Firuza grabbed her best set of riding clothes and slid behind the screen to wash. The grandmothers must have arranged to give her this chance. They would understand why she laughed silently as she readied herself for the day.

By the time she had dressed and eaten, the wrestling matches had begun. Firuza wandered among pairs of shirtless men, their tight trousers tucked into high boots, their bare chests revealing muscles honed by a lifetime preparing for war. Manduhai the Wise was not the only Mongol queen who had exercised power in a male-dominated world. Lady Khutulun, the bards said, had so excelled at the art of wrestling that no man could win her, because she refused to accept any suitor she could beat. To the great distress of her parents, she defeated more than a thousand heroes and died unwed rather than settle for an unequal partner. To prevent any repetition of their disgrace at Khutulun's hands, the warriors had adopted an outfit in which no woman could deceive them—or so the story went.

Ogodai, stripped like the others, threw Rafik without difficulty. Firuza stopped her prowl to admire her betrothed's fine physique. She had made her choice, and it didn't hurt to look. Today the sun shone, and exercise warmed the men, but it remained cold enough to raise veins like ropes in the warriors' arms. Oiled bodies gleamed. The scent of male sweat caused her nostrils to twitch, but the deft motions of Ogodai's feet, the quick thrust of his hip, the speed with which he assessed and downed his opponent could not fail to please.

Tulpar strode into the ring and dragged his tunic over his head. Firuza's booted toes dug into the grass as Ogodai turned to face his brother. Would he challenge Tulpar again—and lose again?

No, because Tulpar had already challenged him. The two men crouched, facing each other, shifting left and right. Out of nowhere, the playful atmosphere of the wrestling circle hardened. The brothers' faces set in deadly seriousness; their eyes fixed on each other.

Tulpar charged toward Ogodai, arms hooked around his head like a bull's horns. The force of that run threatened to bowl Ogodai over, but he danced sideways, then leaped on Tulpar's back as he went past. Tulpar fell forward, cursing as his hands hit the packed earth, and rolled. Ogodai rolled with him, and for a moment, Firuza thought him trapped under his brother's weight. But he dug his heels into Tulpar's ribs, wrapped an arm around his opponent's neck, and continued to roll that crucial half-turn that returned him to the top. Firuza held her breath as her betrothed hauled on his half-brother's chin.

Tulpar thrashed and writhed, but the pressure on his windpipe limited his range of motion. He should yield—even a girl could see that—but he refused, even as his face darkened from lack of air. Did he hate his brother so much?

Rafik stepped in, awarding the victory to Ogodai, who released his hold on Tulpar's throat and sprang to his feet. Firuza allowed herself to breathe again.

Tulpar stormed out of the ring without acknowledging defeat. Everyone else in the circle milled around the victor, shouting congratulations. Amid the hubbub, Ogodai glanced her way and grinned. His chest rose and fell with exertion, but he looked as if he hadn't a care in the world. Had he already forgotten their squabble last night? Had he forgiven her? Or was he just so thrilled with his victory that nothing else mattered right then? Firuza, caught in the snare of her own emotions, smiled, blushed, and moved on.

The poetry competition drew her, and she blended into the crowd—as much as the bey's sister could blend. On another day, she would have pushed forward to the center, where the poet-contestants vied to outdo one another in quatrain and couplet while the crowd cheered on its favorites (and placed bets behind the scenes). Firuza loved poetry, hearing it and creating it. It seemed like magic, the way the right word sprang to the tongue and a phrase dropped into place, twisting something familiar—a breeze or a bird—into a truth precious as a newly minted gold piece.

Idly, she wondered if Ogodai liked poetry, too. She would find out, she supposed. He had mentioned her poetical plea for help but not how he felt about the art itself.

No matter. Today was for listening. Her scattered thoughts wouldn't settle into the clarity needed to produce verses, and she had no desire to tie herself down in this contest. She had other plans. She might not wrestle like Khutulun or rule from horseback like Queen Manduhai, but Firuza had skills of her own, and she intended to use them.

At last, her moment came. Jahangir raised their father's staff and ordered the two sides to take their places for "Chase the Girl." Firuza had long since left the poets to their own devices and stationed herself near the corral, where her palomino, already saddled and bridled, grazed. She led the horse to the race area and mounted, scanning the lines of men.

Her brother, of course—flask and Roxelana at his side but not yet, so far as Firuza could tell, drunk beyond utility. Not riding either: the council had pleaded with him to referee the races, and he had agreed. No doubt Roxelana had added her own means of persuasion. The concubine didn't want her lord chasing and kissing other women.

On the far side of the field, Firuza saw Tulpar, as she'd expected, magnificent in brass armor and crisp white turban, a jeweled feather at its tip. As usual, he stood out among the crowd, outshining even Jahangir yet oddly inappropriate for his setting, like a peacock misplaced among a flock of wrens.

So many others, each familiar to her since birth. Firuza scanned the expanding lines of men. Suppose Ogodai had decided not to race? He would undo her plans!

Then she saw him, off to one side. Her betrothed hadn't attempted to compete with his brother's finery. He wore a simple tunic, high-collared and long-sleeved, in a velvet the color of the sky as it settles into night, the deep purple that precedes the stars' emergence, so close to black that she recognized the true shade only when he nudged his chestnut gelding forward into the sun. He stopped next to Tulpar, their horses shoulder to shoulder ahead of the others. Tulpar turned his head toward his brother, then shrugged and looked front once more. Ogodai did not acknowledge Tulpar in any way.

Perfect. He couldn't have placed himself better if she'd confided her intent to him this morning.

The maidens formed their line and began to move toward the warriors. Firuza kicked her palomino into a trot, placing herself in the lead.

Her chance. Her man. No one would dare get in her way.

Ogodai watched the advancing line of girls, Firuza at their head. She still surprised him, this bride of his. What was she up to now? Would she humiliate him by picking Tulpar?

His victory earlier still cast a glow about his heart. One contest down, and he had won. Tulpar had underestimated him.

Of course, his undisputed triumph hadn't lasted longer than it took for the sun to rise above the lowest clouds. Tulpar had wrested Ogodai's sword from him in their duel, and the judge had voted them exactly equal in the archery contest— although Jahangir had presided over the latter, and Ogodai suspected him of favoritism. He supposed he should be glad even to have tied.

Which meant that the current race would determine who came out ahead today. But did Firuza know that? Tulpar's display, which Ogodai had dismissed as excessive to the point of ridiculous, now appeared ominous. Tulpar might anticipate— had he secured Firuza's agreement beforehand?—a public declaration of their future relationship and her consent to it. The nomads offered few means for women to indicate their preferences in a mate, but this game was one. Ogodai hadn't played it since he left the camp, and then he'd been so young it had seemed to him to be a contest a boy would rather lose than win. But he had grown, and the rules were easy enough that no one could forget them. A girl chose the man she wanted by tapping him with her whip. He then chased her to the far end of the field. If he caught her, he kissed her—and continued to kiss her as they rode back to the starting point. If she evaded him, she whipped him back to the beginning while the spectators laughed at his discomfiture.

If Firuza picked him, Ogodai didn't intend to lose. But would she? Their confrontation last night still haunted him. She might have decided to show him that he couldn't take her for granted.

Tulpar inched his horse forward as the line approached. Ogodai matched him, nose for nose. They were like a pair of fighting cockerels, each determined not to yield.

Firuza had stopped to watch him wrestling this morning. And when he caught sight of her, she'd blushed like the maiden she was and slipped away, bemused. There was hope.

Firuza, still in the lead, looked left, then right. She nodded to the girls behind her, and they drew up alongside her, forming a single line stretching the whole way across the field. Ogodai braced himself. Hard as he tried not to care, he felt his stomach tighten as it did before a battle. Because this was a battle, of sorts. Between him and his brother, but also between him and Firuza. Would she pick him, or not?

The slap of her whip against his hand came almost as a relief. Tulpar roared in outrage, but Ogodai had no time to worry about his brother. Firuza had turned her horse, and the gorgeous palomino dashed for the far end of the field as if eagles swooped from the sky, ready to carry off horse and rider. He hadn't slowed for her yesterday; she would give him no quarter today. He had to win her, fair and square.

As he took off after his fleeing bride, Ogodai realized that his brother had joined the chase, just as if Firuza had chosen *him*. As if Tulpar had not already lost.

That did it. Ogodai relaxed his hold on the reins, howled into the sky, and urged the chestnut after Firuza's palomino until they flew like the winged stallion of last night's dream.

The wind whipped past his face. The sun ducked behind a passing cloud, and the effect of its temporary disappearance opened the borderless expanse as if the steppe rolled on forever—an ocean of grass. Ogodai rose in his stirrups, relieving the chestnut of his weight, increasing the distance between himself and Tulpar and closing with Firuza, smaller and lighter as well as blessed with the advantage of a head start.

He would reach her in time. The same part of his brain that calculated the flight of an arrow, the movement of soldiers in the field, and the deployment of horses for the hunt clicked through the relevant factors without distracting him from the task at hand. The palomino was spirited, her rider exemplary, but his chestnut had greater endurance. And Tulpar had miscalculated when he decided to make a statement by donning his showy armor. The extra weight slowed his horse. He was already more solid than Ogodai, which here worked to Ogodai's benefit.

He didn't turn his head to check. Amid the mêlée of men racing after the young women who'd picked them, no one could detect a single set of beating hooves. But as Ogodai gained on Firuza, he hoped that his brother was falling farther and farther behind.

He caught her not far from the finish line. As he grabbed her around the waist, she twisted toward him. Her face—flushed, laughing, alight with joy—was so adorable that Ogodai didn't hesitate. He kissed her hard, pulling her off her slowing horse and onto his saddlebow. She flung both arms around his neck, and he tugged her closer, in no rush to turn for the ride back. The cheers of the crowd filled his ears.

Someone tapped his shoulder. Ogodai raised his head and glared into his half-brother's dark eyes. How far would Tulpar try to push him this time? Would he insist Firuza had picked him instead?

To head off any such plan, Ogodai held up his left hand, tightening his grip on Firuza with his right, and showed the milling crowd the mark that Firuza's whip had left across his fingers. "I told you before. She is mine. And today she has chosen me herself. Relinquish your claim."

Firuza nestled into his hold, as if in confirmation. Tulpar bowed, his exaggerated air turning the courtesy into a mockery. "Enjoy her then, *ené*, while you can." He moved off, allowing his horse to amble as if no other idea had entered his head.

Ogodai watched him go. Was that a threat?

He held his bride close, enjoying the feel of her in his arms. She wriggled on the pommel, and he kissed her again, controlling his horse with his knees as it wandered back to the starting point. The palomino trailed them, her reins dragging on the ground until Ogodai leaned sideways, caught them, and looped them about his left wrist.

Midway, he stopped kissing Firuza long enough to murmur, "Forgive me. I had no right to say what I did to you last night. I'm jealous of my brother. The way he takes what he wants, no matter who had it first. But I let fear drive my words. Fear that you would prefer him, I mean. Most women do."

"Many do," Firuza said. Her honesty surprised him, as so much about her did. "I don't. He says whatever suits him at the moment. What I told you last night was true. As long as he's lived here, he's had no use for me—only for women who amused him, seduced him, adored him. Even last night, he didn't kiss me because he desired me. He wanted to shut me up, I think, to stop my questions. I had asked him about *Ata*'s death."

"I dreamed of your father last night." He told her the essence of the dream. "He gave you to me, Firuza. He said so. We have his blessing. Will you not come to me?"

She hesitated. He held his breath. Too far, too fast? Had he misread her again?

"Yes," Firuza said. "Tonight." Her arms tightened around his neck, and they were kissing once more.

Ogodai must have ordered his men to pitch a tent as promised, because before the celebration ended—as soon as the crowds thinned, in fact—he led her away from the others. Just inside the ring of wagons, a single tent stood in the shadow of the ancestors' shrine, smoke curling from the center of its roof, door ajar, inviting them to enter.

Firuza swallowed. Her insides swirled and spun like scarves in a wedding dance. She had taken a chance, and it had paid off. Her fear that Ogodai, like his brother, might care more for her lineage than for her seemed silly in retrospect. Those long, drawn-out kisses promised a night of splendor and discovery. She welcomed the prospect. It was time she became a woman. No going back now.

But where would forward lead? She wanted to learn and dreaded discovery, both at the same time. Ogodai's strong grip tugged her toward the future. Her father approved; and so near the shrine, she sensed that the grandmothers, too, blessed them. Nothing but peace emanated from the ancient tent. Somehow, crossing this threshold would lead her to her vision. Firuza, obedient to the commands of her ancestors and her own heart, ducked into the tent.

Inside, brass lanterns cast filigreed shadows on the felt coverings. A fire blazed in the central hearth. Someone—a servant, presumably—had balanced a tray of sweets, somewhat precariously, on the flattened half-cylinder that formed the top of a brass-bound leather chest. Perfumed steam rose from a long-spouted brass teapot near the fire. Two cups of Chinese porcelain, almost transparent in their jade glory, sat next to the pot. The tent contained nothing else but a pallet on a low stand, covered with blankets and furs, and a small, square table that held a wash basin, jug, and towels.

Ogodai led her to the pallet and bade her sit. When she did, he offered her tea, which she accepted, and sweets, which she refused. She felt too tense to eat.

She cradled the fragile porcelain cup in her hands. The tea tasted of grass and flowers. Ogodai, in his rich but understated velvet, sat next to her. Her thoughts darted from one detail to another like bees: the slight curl of her betrothed's black hair as it lay against his cheek; the curve of his ear, of the lips so soft at times, so demanding at others; the line of his jaw; the bruise still visible on his chin. Impossible to believe that a week ago she had believed he wouldn't complete their contract, that he didn't like girls. The memory of his kisses after the race robbed her of words.

"I saw you watching me earlier," Ogodai said. "At the wrestling match. That's when I decided you might not dislike me as much as I feared."

She blushed, remembering how he'd looked stripped to the waist for the contest.

He reached out, removed one of the winged horses from her hair, and placed it on the tray next to the sweets. "The whole time you rode toward me, I kept wondering if you would choose my brother, to show me how I'd offended you."

"Choose your brother? I told you, I don't trust him." Then again, why wouldn't he have expected her to choose his brother? They had argued over Tulpar. She had run away and left Ogodai standing outside the shrine. Earlier, too, when he questioned her about his brother, she had run away. Because it had been too humiliating to explain that she wanted a near-stranger to kiss her. Even with the certainty that he would, very soon, do much more than kiss her, Firuza couldn't bring herself to admit what had upset her that day.

"It doesn't matter." Ogodai brushed tendrils back from her face, removed the second winged horse and placed it beside the first, pulled off the net that held her braid coiled at her neck, untied the end of the braid and ran his fingers through her hair. "This time, I'm the one who gets to kiss the girl."

Firuza handed him the porcelain cup, still half-filled with tea. He returned it to its place by the fire and resumed his seat on the pallet. Under her palms, his cheekbones felt solid and smooth. "The only one," she said. "No other man has ever beaten me in a race."

His face lit up, boyish laughter so close to the surface that she saw it reflected in his eyes. His arms encircled her waist. "No other. Really?"

"Really." She let him pull her closer, until their lips almost touched. "I never wanted to lose before. But I didn't let you win. I can only respect a man who plays fair."

"You have my word," he said. "I will always play fair." Then he kissed her, at last.

Ogodai eased his bride down into the furs. His fingers brushed her cheek, tangled in her hair, stroked silk-covered mounds, undid cloth fasteners. Her skin—warmed by fire, warmed by tea—slid petal-soft under his roving mouth.

Her responsiveness to his touch moved him. He could hardly believe his luck. This morning he would have sworn he'd lost her. And now—well, suffice it to say that his wildest fantasies had not encompassed this passionate yielding.

As he surrendered to pleasure, Ogodai allowed himself a moment of triumph. Firuza belonged to him, and had since she placed her hand in his six years ago. But marriages were made by parents. Her decision to come to him, to stay with him—that meant more than an old debt acknowledged.

She had chosen sides. She had chosen *him*. Firuza wanted this. She wanted him, as much as he wanted her. It was up to him to make it a memorable experience for her.

He peeled back her tunic, her trousers, her soft silk undergarments. Her clothes fell away, dropped in soft piles, mixed with his own. Her body opened beneath his probing fingers. Murmuring endearments, Ogodai claimed his wife and, with her, his future.

Sometime later—she had no way to tell how long and didn't much care—Firuza lay on her back, surrounded by blankets. Her clothes mingled with Ogodai's, strewn over the makeshift bed and floor. Her body was sore in places that she hadn't previously considered capable of pain, but on the whole, she felt wonderful. And the fleeting pain had come as no surprise. Diliara would have considered herself remiss if she had failed to prepare her stepdaughter for the most momentous event, barring childbirth, in a woman's life. Nor had the harem gossips refrained from passing on every tidbit they believed a virgin bride should know. Yet their chattering hadn't captured half the blissful satisfaction that weakened Firuza's limbs, her sense of being cherished as no one had cherished her before.

Ogodai propped himself on one elbow beside her and kissed her cheek. His free arm embraced her. "You are contemplative. Did I hurt you?"

She turned to face him. With the heels of her palms, she kneaded the muscles of his chest, the smooth skin that covered them, the sparse black hair. He smelled of sweat and soap, the smoke from the hearth fire, even a lingering, wispy hint of tea.

"I am well," she said, answering the intent of his question rather than the words. He must know he had hurt her a little. Blood streaked her thighs, mixed with his seed. "And glad to be your wife in truth. Will I sleep here, in your tent, from now on?"

"Indeed you will. Even your stepmother can't object." He nuzzled her nose. "We belong together."

"And the council?"

"The council knows that, too. The elders test me—and my brother. It's their right to choose whom they will follow. But whatever happens, I will keep you with me."

He kissed her again. Firuza, eager to believe his assurances, edged closer, reveling in his closeness. Her breasts pressed against the same muscles she had just kneaded, and she luxuriated in the sensation of his full length against her belly, her thighs, his hands stroking her back. No more questions.

The door crashed against the trellis frame, jerking them awake as the tent shook. Ogodai bolted upright, identified the intruder as an enraged Jahangir, and reached for his trousers. The fire flickered as cold air poured into the tent.

Firuza emitted a small, shocked sound. He pressed her shoulder into the furs, checking that the blankets covered her, then pulled on the rest of his clothes and placed her silken pile within reach. By standing in front of her and spreading his coat with both hands, he created a makeshift screen. No one would doubt what they had been doing, and Ogodai felt no guilt. But confronting an angry brother-in-law would go better without the disadvantage of nakedness.

He had turned out the lanterns before they slept, so the only glow came from the hearth fire. In its dim orange light Jahangir loomed, a menacing outline. "Close the door, can't you," Ogodai said, "before you kill the fire? If you have an issue with me, say so. We can discuss it like men without freezing your sister."

Jahangir growled, but he did shut the door, using the same unnecessary force. Grumbling, he stomped into the circle surrounding the hearth fire, which emitted a thick smoke redolent of cattle before settling back into its usual steady glow.

Ogodai handed Firuza her gold combs and hair net before resuming his seat on the pallet next to her. She had pulled on her clothes and was again fully covered.

Without looking at him or her brother, she pushed the combs into her hair, then fastened the last of the cloth loops that closed the high collar of her robe. The heightened color in her cheeks and her refusal to meet the men's eyes suggested embarrassment.

"It won't work, you know," Jahangir said. "The council will decide her fate. You have no right to take matters into your own hands."

"I have every right. Your father gave her to me six years ago. You witnessed it. Your entire camp witnessed it. The council witnessed it, as the elders acknowledged this morning.

More important, your sister chose me today, although no one forced her." Ogodai strove to sound reasonable, to keep his own anger in check. "Tulpar needs to face reality: your father changed his mind."

"The clan leaders can still take her away from you." Jahangir scoffed, but his eyes moved from side to side like a thief's. "They can refuse to name you khan. You have dishonored them, Ogodai, by ignoring their demand that you wait."

Firuza trembled in his hold. He patted her back but spoke to Jahangir. "I won today. Two contests to one. Does their word mean nothing? But whatever they do, they will not take my wife. I won't stand for it."

Jahangir stormed from the tent. The wind created by the door he slammed doused the fire, casting the interior into gloom.

"Damn," Ogodai said. "Now where's the flint?"

Firuza shivered as she listened to her betrothed—no, her *husband*—stumble about in the dark, searching for the flint. Residual heat still warmed the tent; her shivering was a reaction to Jahangir's anger and to the realization of the enormity, in his eyes, of her choice. She didn't question that choice, but she hadn't expected such opposition from her brother.

More illusions. Despite the many disappointments of the last three months, of the years that preceded the last three months, she had hoped for better from Jahangir. That her brother, if he couldn't ensure her happiness, would rejoice if she attained it.

Instead, his resentment knew no bounds. He would deny Ogodai the khanate, take her from the man she desired and respected and give her to another, force her to live in exile or bend before his spite. He didn't care if he destroyed her.

Very well, she would live in exile, if the ancestors required it. But she would not bend. Never again would she clean up Jahangir's messes or risk her happiness to protect him from his enemies. Her father had blessed her marriage to Ogodai, and a wife owed allegiance to her husband more than to her brother.

A shriek of pain split the night, followed by the sound of scuffling feet. Firuza saw the door open, a shadow outlined against the frame. Ogodai, she guessed, because the shadow vanished into the darkness, lit only by starlight.

She leaped for the door. That cry had sounded like a wounded animal. Could wolves have attacked the herds, or yesterday's troublemaker have returned to cause new mischief?

Not wolves. She would have heard them howling. Another type of predator, then, human or animal. Silent, like a cat.

In the still-lightless interior, she couldn't find her jacket. She had no time for that, anyway. Using the trellis frame as a guide, she circled the tent until she reached the opening, where the night concealed everything but a long shape flat on the ground and a man-sized hillock next to it.

The hillock spoke with Ogodai's voice. "Quick," he said. "Get help. I think your brother's dead."

Chapter 12

NASAN AND ASLANBIKA RACED THEIR HORSES NECK AND neck across the field west of Kazan. The wind knocked their caps from their heads and tore their hair from its pins, but Nasan didn't care. The sheer joy of galloping in the open air made concerns about tangles seem paltry. This was the third time since her arrival in Kazan that she'd had the chance to give Sorkhokhtani her head and toss propriety into a corner for an entire glorious afternoon.

And with a friend, no less. When had she last enjoyed a friendship with a girl close to her own age? Before her father had dragged his family to Kasimov two years ago, for sure. And not for lack of contact with women: the harem courtyards had overflowed with wives and concubines, half-sisters and cousins. Nasan just had nothing to say to people whose concerns ended with the drape of a veil and the arch of an eyebrow. In Aslanbika, she had found someone who shared her own irritation with the pampered beauties who reveled in the perfumed luxury of the Kazan court.

Too soon, they reached the forest edging the field. Nasan pulled on the mare's reins, but Sorkhokhtani was already swinging into a wide circle. She had learned the routine. Nasan patted her neck and bent forward to reward the horse with a piece of carrot.

As Aslanbika drew up beside her, Nasan giggled at the sight of the ragged line far behind them. "Look at our pathetic ladies. We will have crossed the field twice before they pass the gate!"

A slight exaggeration. The court ladies had ambled their sedate ponies perhaps a quarter of the way onto the field.

Aslanbika didn't point that out, as Nasan had guessed she would not. Instead, she joined in the laughter. "Pathetic *riders*, you mean. See how they straggle across the grass like so many snails. Are we not cruel, Nasan, forcing them into the saddle day after day?"

"It's good for them," Nasan said. "What would they do, if we didn't require them to ride with us? Eat sweetmeats and gossip from dawn to dusk?"

"No doubt." Aslanbika was still laughing. "They live and breathe scandal." She stroked her horse's mane. "Shall we take pity on them and turn back, or wait for them to join us here at the edge of the woods?"

At the rate the ladies were traveling, twilight would shade the skies to purple before they caught up. Nasan and Aslanbika had never pulled so far ahead before, and so fast. "Riding with you, I feel as if I'm back in my father's camp," Nasan said. "How I miss the steppe!"

"I too," Aslanbika said, her voice wistful. "Your brother is lucky, to have a chance to rule a nomadic horde. And his bride, that she need not leave her home, whichever brother she weds. Sometimes I hate the city." She reached out and clasped Nasan's hand. "Until you came. Can you not stay with us?"

"I wish I could," Nasan said, in what was at best a partial truth. As much as she enjoyed the rides with Aslanbika, and little as she looked forward to her return to the isolation of Moscow and the jabs of her resentful sister-in-law, Maria, Kazan had not offered the refuge she had hoped.

A thought too depressing to entertain for long—especially when, for the moment, she had Aslanbika to talk to. "The horses shouldn't stand in this wind," she said. "Let's walk to meet the others, but not too fast. It will give us a chance to chat free of the palace's listening ears. Do you not sense them everywhere? It drives me crazy, feeling hemmed in all the time. Rather than stay here, I would wish us both returned to the steppe."

"Oh, if only I could! Yes, let's talk. I have much to tell." Aslanbika nudged her horse into motion with her knees. The pure white mare lifted her dainty hooves and stepped over the grass as if clouds billowed under her feet. Nasan urged Sorkhokhtani to follow, and soon the two animals walked side by side. Would Aslanbika answer the questions Nasan didn't dare to ask outright—or at least create an opening where asking became possible?

"I wrote to my father," Aslanbika said. "I told him that my husband doesn't like me. *Ata* wants heirs for Kazan, through me. That's why he married me to your uncle. I don't think it will happen. I don't want him to blame me."

"Of course not." Nasan, recognizing a fear common to every wife, reached out a comforting hand. "Don't despair, Auntie. My uncle knows his duty. And if he has forgotten, you could ask Queen Gulnara to remind him."

Aslanbika shuddered. "What humiliation! To have to ask *her*, in particular. She and Gazim Shirin don't support my husband, you know. Not really. They buckled to pressure from the Russians, then bargained for the best deal they could get. Besides, the marital act is unpleasant enough. I want no man who must force himself to complete it."

It seemed impolitic, even unkind, to point out that she enjoyed it a great deal. Nasan bit her tongue, but she couldn't suppress the flush that warmed her cheeks.

"Oh, not for you, I see." Aslanbika slapped Nasan's hand. "I should have guessed. Half the harem swoons at the sight of *your* husband, who has eyes only for you. I swear, I'm jealous."

So much for her attempts at deception. Her aunt's impish expression belied her last comment, and Nasan giggled again in appreciation and relief. "Can we blame them, Auntie? Think how dull their futures are. They have no hope that my uncle will ever visit them, even as a matter of duty."

"True," Aslanbika admitted. "And yet, I would prefer not to be someone's duty, wouldn't you?"

"Yes," Nasan said. "In fact, I would hate that. I feel for you. Truly I do."

She did, too. At sixteen, Nasan had seen many arranged marriages. She recognized that Aslanbika's experience, if not her exact problem, was more typical than her own. It made her more grateful than ever for Daniil. And to think that she had once reviled him as her enemy!

What she didn't know was why Aslanbika had chosen to confide in her. Idle chatter, or something else? The khatun didn't have many equals she could trust neither to gossip nor to use her unhappiness against her. That might explain her decision.

Or it could be a test of sorts. Nasan decided to push the conversation a little farther. "Did your father respond to your letter?"

"He did." Aslanbika sounded dissatisfied. "But not to reassure me. Instead he rambles on about Crimea."

"Crimea?" Nasan couldn't contain her surprise. Why should Aslanbika care about Crimea, so distant from Kazan?

Then she remembered her uncle's chart, and her question answered itself. The Crimeans had designs on Kazan, as they did on all the lands held by their fellow Tatars. Their belief that the entire legacy of Genghis Khan rightfully belonged to them made them a constant irritant to every other ruler in the region. Even the Russians couldn't govern their state without fending off the Crimeans' demands and preparing for their not-infrequent assaults. Aslanbika had to worry about them, too. Her standing here depended on her husband staying one step ahead of the Crimeans—and their supporters in his court.

"Crimea," Aslanbika confirmed. "The civil war there has resumed. Safa-Girei, who ruled here before the Russians forced the Shirins to accept my husband—"

"Don't speak to me of Safa-Girei," Nasan said, unable to contain herself. "That bandit! How many times has he raided my father's people in Kasimov? Last summer he killed hundreds and carried off five times as many, and this spring he and his cousin launched another great raid on our region. Of all the Tatar khans, he is the worst."

"Tut, tut," Aslanbika said lightly. "Such passion. I remember when he visited my father's camp, the year before I left to come here. A terribly handsome bandit is Safa-Girei, and only twenty-four. He wrestles. He rides. He fights like a man inspired. I'm sure *he* would give me sons." She heaved a mighty sigh. "Not that it will ever happen."

Nasan, hands tight on her reins, glared at her aunt. Sons with Safa-Girei? Yes, she sympathized with Aslanbika, stuck in a wretched marriage, but yearning for a bandit who would kill her husband as soon as look at him—that was too much. No wonder Jan-Ali had put her on his list of suspects!

But one couldn't yell one's frustration at a queen. Biting back her anger, Nasan said, "I spoke out of turn, Khatun.

Your honored father writes of civil war in Crimea, but the war has been raging, on and off, for a generation. How does that affect you and me?"

"Don't sulk." Aslanbika leaned over and pinched the back of Nasan's hand. Sorkhokhtani shook her mane and sidled. "Safa-Girei isn't the one causing trouble in Crimea. I'm sorry he inflicted violence on your father's people, but it was his uncle Sahib-Girei who sent him on those raids: to annoy the Russians, no doubt. What else could he do, if the khan ordered him to raid? At least he is no weakling. I mention him only because he sent information to my father."

A weakling—like *my* husband. Aslanbika didn't say that, but Nasan heard the unspoken comparison. "The Girei dynasty is a plague upon the land," she said. "They fight among themselves. They fight my family—and yours. They use Crimea as a base from which they raid the Russians, the Lithuanians, the Poles. No amount of plunder satisfies their greed. That hasn't changed since I sat my first pony. Does your father write only to say that their quarrels continue?"

"No." Aslanbika pulled on her mare's reins, forcing Nasan to do the same, lest she outpace her aunt, an unpardonable discourtesy. "So long as the Crimeans fight among themselves, they have no energy to spare for Kazan. *Ata* wants me to know that we are safe for the moment."

"*Are* we?" Curiosity dispelled the last of Nasan's anger. "With due respect to your honored father, the Crimeans are here. That is, they have sent envoys to my uncle. Why, unless one side seeks support against the other in this fight of theirs? They came from Sahib-Girei Khan, did they not?"

"They did." Aslanbika edged her horse into motion again. A frown creased her perfect forehead. "That wouldn't endanger us, of course, so long as the envoys are focused on their enemy at home."

"Unless my uncle refuses to get involved. He has no love for the Girei dynasty, nor they for ours. If not Safa, then who is Sahib's opponent?"

"Islam-Girei," Aslanbika said. "Sahib's heir apparent."

"Again?" Islam-Girei rebelled—and reconciled—every other year, it seemed.

"Again. My father says he has formed an alliance with the Russians and turned against Lithuania. And Nasan, I suspect you don't know that Islam-Girei has the support of your older brother Tulpar." She shot Nasan a mischievous glance. "Now there's another man guaranteed to turn making children into a pleasure. You haven't seen him recently, have you?"

"I barely remember him." Nasan called up a vision of the young man who used to toss her in the air and tease her. "He was always good-looking, though." It was hard to change her thinking. She had considered Tulpar dead for so long. Yet he remained her brother.

Their father had severed that connection. Had let them think Tulpar dead, although if Aslanbika knew otherwise, surely Bulat had known, too. Not a brother, then.

Except that he still felt like one. She couldn't feign indifference to his fate.

"My uncle might back Islam-Girei, then, if he fights on the side of the Russians," she mused out loud. "Sahib's envoys would not like that. I must ask my husband what happens when the ambassadors meet. Perhaps your father's right, and the dissension keeps us safe. But it could sweep us up as well."

"It could." Aslanbika waved a hand. "Ask your husband, yes, but we need not wait for him. Gulnara will attend the meeting. So can we. Let's head back."

She nudged her horse. "*Chu.*" The mare picked up its pace, and Sorkhokhtani matched it step for step. Ahead of them, the gaggle of ladies drew nearer. The time for uninhibited chatter was drawing to a close.

"Tell me about Tulpar," Nasan said. Although the tortured politics of Kazan was of more immediate moment, this topic seemed less problematic in a crowd.

"He fights for Islam-Girei, as I said. He has for years, through many rebellions. When the rebellions fail, as they always do, Tulpar seeks refuge among the horde that once belonged to Bahadur Bey and to your father. He regards it as his own."

"But it isn't his." Nasan turned her head to focus her full attention on Aslanbika. Sorkhokhtani pranced and shook her mane, impatient with the slower pace. "Bahadur Bey promised it to Ogodai."

"Who now challenges Tulpar for the right to rule it," Aslanbika said. "This much you know."

"Yes, you told me a few days ago."

"I did. But until my father explained it, I didn't understand why I should care which of them won the contest. Now I do." She clasped Nasan's hand, then dropped it almost immediately. "If Tulpar wins, he will take that horde into battle, to support the cause he favors."

"Islam-Girei."

"Yes." Aslanbika smiled, as if pleased with a slow student.

Nasan puzzled it out. "If Ogodai wins, he won't take sides. He has most to gain by consolidating his rule, even expanding it by winning the support of others. But that horde is small. Too small to tip the balance, surely."

Aslanbika shrugged. "My father believes it matters—not in itself, perhaps, but for the influence it could have on others. Bahadur had many friends and commanded much respect. Where he led, others followed. Your father, too—and through him, his sons. If Tulpar says fight, many will fight. If Ogodai says stay, they will stay."

"That affects me. They are my brothers. But it affects you only if their intervention makes it possible for the Crimeans to solve their conflict. Then we must again worry about their intentions toward Kazan."

"So my father believes."

Nasan, hearing the careful phrasing, wondered. Wheels within wheels, and the outcome far from certain. Even if Tulpar did take Bahadur's horde into battle, his intervention might not guarantee success for Islam-Girei, the survivor—as Aslanbika had noted—of many failed rebellions.

But, right or wrong, Aslanbika had provided much useful information. Even if every piece didn't fit into its proper place, she had given Nasan many more pieces to work with than when they set out. Pieces to share with Daniil, whose grasp of military matters far surpassed Nasan's own.

Yet one question remained. As Nasan saw the court ladies break into a shambling trot, she reached out and grasped the white mare's harness. "Your father is wise. Thank you for sharing his counsel with me. But I must know. If Crimea attacks Kazan, where do you stand—with my uncle or the bandit who can give you sons?"

Aslanbika jerked so hard on the reins that the horse reared, tearing the harness from Nasan's grip and leaving a burning strip across her palm.

"You *ask* me such a thing?" Aslanbika said.

Nasan cursed her own impetuous nature. How could she have undone all the good of the past week in one rash moment? *Stupid, stupid, stupid.*

"Forgive me, Auntie. I didn't think," she mumbled.

Aslanbika scowled. Nasan dropped her eyes, mentally chastising herself in four languages while holding Sorkhokhtani steady with her knees. The ladies—drawn, no doubt, by the scent of conflict—cantered up and circled them in a swirl of chypre and silk. Elegant boots constructed from patches of multicolored leather in intricate geometric patterns filled Nasan's lowered gaze, completing her state of dejection.

Having given offense, she couldn't look up until her aunt responded. Protocol required humility, even for a question that in retrospect seemed ever more apt—whether asking it had been appropriate or not. Where *did* Aslanbika stand, with the husband she despised or—as that husband believed— with the handsome interloper from the south?

The ladies' chatter surrounded her, excluding her. Nasan's cheeks burned, from anger more than guilt. Her aunt had decided to make her squirm. The harem would buzz with rumor for the rest of the week, glorying in the new favorite's swift fall.

Then Aslanbika laughed. "Always and ever," she said, "I stand with the Nogai. Stop staring at the grass, Nasan. It's not going anywhere. Our horses are restless, and we'll miss the meeting with the envoys if we dally. I'll race you to the palace."

Aslanbika urged her horse into a trot. Sorkhokhtani needed no persuasion to match pace with the white mare, and soon the wind was again tangling Nasan's hair. The staccato percussion of hoofbeats as the grass gave way to wooden streets assured her that their unhappy entourage hadn't fallen too far behind. And from the conspiratorial glance she received from Aslanbika as they galloped side by side up the hill, it seemed that their friendship might have survived her ill-advised candor.

The thought pleased Nasan more than she liked to admit.

The time spent in conversation caused the women to arrive after the ambassadorial meeting began, but fortunately the requirements of diplomatic protocol delayed negotiations long enough for Nasan and Aslanbika to exchange their riding gear for court robes and mingle with Queen Gulnara's attendants. When they reached the hall, the ambassadors were exchanging flowery perorations that boiled down to heartfelt wishes for the good health of the envoys, their leaders, their kinsmen—indeed, everyone associated with them in any way—combined with assurances of the speakers' utter trustworthiness. None of these statements impressed Nasan.

She spared a moment to sympathize with Daniil, dimly glimpsed amid a mass of boyars in splendid costumes. She could already anticipate his complaints; his forthright mind rebelled at the convolutions of diplomatic practice, despite his attempts to master them. He and Ogodai were much alike under their surface differences, both honest to a fault. It was too bad that the feud between their clans had undermined their friendship. By nature, they were truer brothers than Ogodai and Tulpar could ever be.

It was, of course, unfair to regard Tulpar as duplicitous merely because he opposed Ogodai—or supported Islam-Girei, for that matter. Men aligned themselves with this ruler or that for many reasons, and she hadn't seen Tulpar in so long that she had no basis for judging him. Only Aslanbika's word aligned Tulpar with one side or the other in the dispute among the Crimean Tatars, let alone indicated what he planned to do with Bahadur Bey's horde if he happened to defeat Ogodai in their contest.

Yet Nasan couldn't help hoping that Ogodai would win in the end. Unlike Tulpar, a hazy presence at best, she knew Ogodai and loved him. She trusted him to make the right choice, the honorable choice. Here amid the treachery of Kazan, where statements of support had no more permanence than spring flowers and motives lurked hidden beneath veils and behind screens, her brother's unswerving honesty called to her like one of the winged horses soaring above the clouds that raced in endless progression across the steppe. Even Jan-Ali, her own uncle, couldn't escape the taint of subterfuge that permeated this exquisite, sin-filled palace.

Jan-Ali looked virtuous enough at this moment. As khan, he sat in the focal point of the crowded hall, legs crossed under him on the raised platform that set him above and apart. Scholars in layered robes and turbans flanked him, ready to offer advice if asked. The Russian envoys sat forward of the platform on his right, the Crimeans knelt in packed ranks to his left. A signal that he regarded the Russians as of higher standing—a slur that Sahib-Girei would resent, no doubt, when he learned of it.

The women clustered near the door, behind Queen Gulnara and Aslanbika, who shared a lower but just as richly decorated platform. As a descendant of Genghis, Nasan had the right, if she chose to claim it, to share the queen's space. She preferred to remain in the background, preserving her freedom of movement and picking up hints of muttered conversation from both sides. In her elaborate silk gown and loose jacket, a floor-length gauze veil drifting from the point of her jeweled cap, Nasan couldn't slip unnoticed among the men. But by edging around the arc of women with the skill and silence she had mastered during her outings as the Golden Lynx, she observed more than a few promising exchanges. Those skills had once helped her save a divinely appointed ruler; she trusted them not to fail her here. In a sense, those skills had brought her to Kazan.

Of her observations, the most important to her, if not to the task at hand, included the attention her uncle focused on the youngest member of the Crimean delegation, a boy of such extraordinary beauty that he quite eclipsed Daniil. Nasan released a long, relieved breath. For an instant, her eyes met her husband's. He winked at her. He'd seen it, too.

She searched the crowd for Gazim Shirin. Such an important adviser should sit on the carpet to the khan's right, next to the Russians, but Gazim was, for whatever reason, not there. Nasan edged around the arc in the opposite direction, wondering at Gazim's absence. Although the queen's adviser, he wouldn't openly ally himself with her in this very male arena.

No, there he sat on the Crimean side, hands folded on his ample lap, at an angle that placed him halfway between the khan and the Crimean ambassador. Interesting, especially since he had no counterpart mediating Jan-Ali's interaction with the Russians.

Because Jan-Ali, assured of the Russians' support, needed no representative there? Or because Gazim had in this subtle way indicated his interest in a new alliance? Nasan stored her questions for future discussion with Daniil and turned her attention to Gulnara.

The double doors opened, and servants clad in knee-length beige tunics and red tights arrived, bearing wrapped parcels. A sigh ran round the hall. The initial courtesies had ended, and the presentation of gifts could begin. In the resulting commotion, Nasan wriggled her way past the tight knots of women, pushing steadily forward until she stood on Gulnara's side of the shared platform. There she dropped to the floor.

She had chosen the spot with care. It seemed unlikely that Gulnara, an old hand at pulling strings from behind a curtain, would reveal her true thoughts in a crowd as large as this one— although Aslanbika had promised to encourage confessions with a leading remark or two.

If Aslanbika told the truth. If they were really friends, and Nasan could trust her aunt as she wanted to do and as her instincts told her she could. This was, in a sense, a test. Nasan hoped Aslanbika would pass it, that their friendship could grow, but the conversation this afternoon had shaken her faith. Safa-Girei, her own family's enemy—could Aslanbika really imagine having children with such a man? Or had she said it to provoke, as she had mentioned Tulpar?

Tulpar would be more acceptable as a husband, so long as he didn't stake his claim by arranging Jan-Ali's murder.

Nasan pulled herself back to the present. In a sense, the results of the test didn't matter. If Aslanbika succeeded in provoking Gulnara, Nasan had placed herself in a position to hear without being seen. If she did not, Nasan retained the advantage of an angle that allowed her to monitor the two queens' movements while keeping an eye on the men.

Although it would help to have a clear sense of what she sought. Nasan wrapped her arms around her bent knees and settled in for a long wait. The stuffy, overheated room pressed on her eyelids. The pleasant fatigue caused by her mad gallops across the field didn't help her resist the pull.

So tempting to nap. She must not give in.

Then the servants set out the gifts, and the desire to sleep left her. The Crimeans had outdone themselves with jeweled swords and rich silks, tasseled brocade cushions and cloth-of-gold robes, sweetmeats in boxes constructed from folded paper, silver-gilt Ottoman helmets glistening with richly decorated nose pieces, even a fully caparisoned bay stallion that provoked gasps throughout the chamber, including one from Nasan. Seldom had she seen a more elegant horse. He would enrich her uncle's stables for generations.

The Russian ambassador, she saw, was seething. His presents, although fine, had not equaled these. Jan-Ali wouldn't switch his allegiance—not toward a group of envoys representing two men who wanted his head—but Nasan suspected that Jan-Ali was not the real target of these gifts. Gazim Shirin leaned forward to caress the ruby-encrusted hilt of the sword closest to him, and she imagined she could watch it pulling him toward the giver. Better presents indicated greater respect—and a man who, as

Aslanbika had noted earlier, had accepted Jan-Ali only under duress would be ripe for persuasion.

The servants departed, leading the stallion and piling the other gifts on a mosaic table set up for the purpose. The details of the negotiations caught Nasan up, and she followed the quick give-and-take with interest, admiring the ability of Alexander Makhmetovich and his Crimean counterpart to yield without giving the appearance of weakness and to stand firm without causing offense.

Nasan had long recognized that subtlety was not her forte. Here she had a classroom ready made. She watched, riveted.

The spectacle drew her so far into its spell that she almost missed her ally's murmured provocation. "What do the Crimeans want?" Aslanbika asked Gulnara.

"I sent for them," Gulnara said. "They need us now."

"Was that wise? Suppose they attempt another invasion?"

"So what if they do?" Gulnara dropped her voice to a whisper, and Nasan strained to hear. "We Tatars must stand together. Accepting Jan-Ali was always a temporary measure to convince the Russians to leave us alone. Now their child ruler weakens them. If we bring back Safa-Girei, he will teach the Russians to mind their own business."

Nasan moved as close to the platform as she dared. Her breath came too fast, and she fought to control it. Safa-Girei would kill Jan-Ali, attack her family and Kasimov. She couldn't permit that to happen.

Gulnara continued her murmur. "Consider, girl, what will best serve your interests. Everyone knows Jan-Ali can't appreciate your beauty—and what prevents him from doing so. Why not take a husband who can give you sons before the men decide that you're barren? A divorced wife lives a miserable existence."

Silken words, sticky as a spider's web. Nasan clutched her knees and waited, but try as she might, she couldn't catch Aslanbika's response.

But Aslanbika had already made her position clear. Nasan's belief that she could trust her aunt evaporated. For Gulnara had identified Aslanbika's problem with precision and offered the very solution that the khatun herself preferred. After hearing that promise, only a child could convince herself that Aslanbika would continue to support Jan-Ali.

Nasan had never been gladder to have an hour or two with her husband. Back in their quarters, she prowled around their suite, bent on ensuring their privacy. Listening ears might be everywhere in this palace of conspiracies, but even listening ears could reach only so far. With the rooms cleared of servants, she settled among the cushions that marked the center of the main reception area. Daniil handed her a cup of apple juice and a fried meat turnover. She set them in front of her, gesturing with her hands while she filled him in on her morning's conversation with Aslanbika, her observations of the conference hall, and Gulnara's overheard remarks. They spoke in Russian, a further deterrent to eavesdropping.

"This war isn't new," Daniil said when she reached the end of her tale, confirming what she already knew. "Islam-Girei has been fighting first one uncle, then the other, for supremacy in Crimea this past decade. It keeps the Crimean court occupied—no bad thing, since the Gireis oppose us more consistently and more aggressively than any other Tatar group. Nor do your half-brother's allegiances worry me. I doubt that this horde you mention poses much of a threat."

"Except to Ogodai." The shock of Gulnara's treachery had driven awareness of her brother's danger from her mind. Daniil's dismissive comment brought it back full force.

His rueful smile acknowledged the tartness she had failed to keep out of her voice. "Except to Ogodai," Daniil said. "That does concern me, dearest. But his fate affects our family more than our government. Whereas if Sahib and Safa make a play for the throne of Kazan, we must take immediate action to protect your uncle and Russia's interests. And if they enmesh Aslanbika..."

He left the sentence unfinished. "Gazim, too," Nasan reminded him. "He sat with the Crimeans. When I saw him, he certainly looked willing to negotiate with them."

"Indeed." Daniil bit into a turnover and swallowed. "The unhappy wife, the ambitious counselor, the aging queen eager to hang on to the power she has. A powerful trio—and a dangerous one, if it falls into the hands of Sahib-Girei. More so if he can use it to resolve his problems at home. We can't rule out the possibility of a conspiracy."

"Which would cause trouble for us all, but my uncle first and foremost." Nasan hesitated before adding, "I had begun to think of Aslanbika as a friend."

"You can't trust her," Daniil said. She heard sympathy in his voice. "Not until we find out where she stands."

Had she not told herself the same thing, there in the council hall? Daniil was right, whether she liked his advice or not. Nasan ate the rest of her turnover in two bites and dipped her fingers into a bowl of water. "She says she stands with the Nogai."

"Most of whom favor the Russians."

"Yes. Hence her father's choice of a Russian-backed candidate for her. But she dislikes Jan-Ali—and with good reason, I must admit. He has put her in an impossible position.

If she sees a way out, even if it means his death, I don't think we can count on her to refuse. Jan-Ali listed her among those whose loyalties he questioned. I didn't understand why, but in this wasps' nest of rumor, who knows what he's heard."

"My thoughts precisely." Daniil refilled her cup from the tall brass jug. "I've never encountered a place so seething with plots."

"Nor I," Nasan said. "So how are we going to smoke out the wasps?"

Their conversation led to other, more pleasurable activities. Freedom from surveillance had its advantages. Nasan felt thoroughly relaxed by the time a strangled cry sounded from the direction of the corridor, followed by the sounds of running feet, shrieks of dismay, and unfinished exclamations that included phrases like "The khan," and "Doctor, quick!"

She reached for Daniil, intending to shake him awake, but he was already on his feet. She rolled sideways and stood, straightening her robes. A glance in the brass mirror revealed hair that, although releasing tendrils around the edges of her pointed cap, wasn't *too* impossibly mussed for propriety. She tucked in the worst offenders before letting Daniil grab her hand and tug her into the hallway.

There pandemonium reigned. Servants dashed in all directions, robes flapping, hands waving, carrying odd assortments of bowls and cloths, knives and vials, and, for no reason Nasan could discern, a small drum in a wooden frame. Amid the crowd, three solemn dark-robed men with plain white turbans strode unheeding. One carried a large book bound in plain calfskin.

"Doctors," she told Daniil. "Follow them. They seem to be heading for my uncle's quarters."

Daniil's height, coupled with his years of command on the battlefield, gave him an advantage over the panicked servants. He tightened his grip on Nasan's hand and cleared a path through the throng, at one point sweeping an arm around her waist and lifting her bodily over a woman too addled to yield.

Inside Jan-Ali's suite, the furor intensified. As Daniil set her down, Nasan noticed the beautiful Crimean boy huddled terrified in a corner. Jan-Ali lay on the divan, clutching his hand and moaning. Servants fluttered around him.

The three doctors had entered just before Nasan. A barked order from the oldest of the three froze the servants in place. In the ensuing silence, Nasan heard the Crimean boy sobbing. She stood on tiptoe to whisper in Daniil's ear, "Get closer to my uncle. See if you can follow what the doctors say."

When he nodded, she released his hand and indicated her intended destination with a jerk of her head. "I'll talk to the boy."

Renewed hubbub had broken out among the servants, each trying to tell the doctors what he or she had observed. As Nasan circled left, she saw Daniil moving forward, calm and purposeful. Servants fell away to both sides as if parted by a wand. It must be nice to be big.

She crouched beside the Crimean boy. "What happened?"

He rubbed his eyes with his sleeve and sniffed. "Who are you?"

"The khan's niece," she said. "My name is Nasan. What's yours?" Close up, she saw he was older than she'd believed—close to her own age, she guessed, just a year or two younger than her uncle. His slight frame had deceived her.

"Oraz," he said.

Oraz. The name meant "happiness." A wholly inappropriate name for him at this moment. "You don't look happy," she said, hoping to jolly him into confiding in her. "Did my uncle mistreat you?"

Oraz shrugged, an eloquent gesture that implied either low expectations or painful past experience—Nasan couldn't be sure.

"I'm sorry," she said, feeling her way. "He seems to have injured his hand. Did you see what happened?"

The boy blanched. Nasan grabbed his arm before he could flee. "Tell me. Did you hurt him? By accident, perhaps?" She opened her mouth to utter reassurances, only to close it again as she realized she could make no promises to protect him until she knew what he'd done. Attacking a khan was a capital offense.

Oraz shook his head violently. "Not me," he said when she prodded again. "Spider. In the sweetmeats. I handed the khan the box because he asked for it. He took one, then he screamed and threw it across the room." He mimicked the gesture. "I saw the spider and stomped on it."

"Spider? What kind of spider?"

The boy shrank from her vehemence. "Don't know." He tried to pry her fingers from his arm, but she held tight while scanning the floor for a smashed spider.

"What did it look like, then?"

He turned his right foot, covered in a green leather boot with gold embroidery. On the sole, near where the boot toe began to curve, she saw a small black spider with mashed, crooked legs and an unmistakable collection of red spots.

This was bad. "Did it bite you?"

"No." Oraz grabbed her hand with his free one. "I swear, I had no idea it was there. It must have crawled into the box before we left."

Maybe. Maybe not. But either way, they had only one patient to worry about. Nasan dragged the boy to his feet and looked around for her husband.

Daniil had followed her instructions and moved into position to one side of the three doctors, who hovered over Jan-Ali, still moaning and thrashing. Her uncle's left hand covered his belly; his right hung by his side. He shook as if chilled, although braziers blazed about the room. The symptoms fit.

Nasan handed her captive to the nearest servant who looked large enough to handle him. "Hold him," she said. "He's probably not responsible, but the doctors may have questions for him."

She pushed through the crowd until she reached the clear area surrounding Jan-Ali. The doctors frowned at her approach, but her court robes gave them pause. They turned back to their patient.

Nasan imagined herself as her mother, Sumbeka—a lady as imperious as she was elegant. "My uncle the khan," she said.

The three medical heads snapped as one to face her. Good. Her declaration of kinship had made an impact.

Nasan straightened her shoulders, staring them down. "My uncle the khan was bitten by a karakurt spider concealed in a box of sweetmeats. You must cauterize the wound at once."

The uproar caused by Nasan's announcement outdid even the previous noise level. Maidservants squealed and lifted their skirts, searching in vain for the spider. Manservants converged on the hapless Crimean boy and on the khan, whose moaning had given way to wailed protests against his own imminent death. The three doctors shouted for calm while beating servants away from the khan, even as they selected four husky specimens to hold him down. Nasan took the opportunity thus offered to join her husband.

"Karakurt spider?" he asked. "What's that?"

"I don't know the Russian." Like the other women, Nasan held her long skirts at ankle length. Oraz had killed one spider, but it might not have traveled alone. At least she still wore her riding boots. If cauterized quickly, the bite of a karakurt spider did not always prove fatal, especially in young, healthy people like herself and Jan-Ali. But treatment options were few, and Nasan wanted to take no chances.

"It's black with red spots," she told Daniil. "And a mark on the abdomen, also red." With her forefinger, she drew a shape like two triangles, touching at the tips, on the back of his hand. "Only the females bite, but their bite is poisonous. They live on the steppe."

"Black widow," he said. "Nasty creatures. We encounter them sometimes on campaign, near the southern grasslands."

"Black widow," she repeated, memorizing the Russian. "A good name. The boy stomped on the one that bit my uncle. I saw it on his boot, but there may be others." She gestured in the direction of the Crimean lad, expecting to find him held fast.

She gasped. "Husband, where are they?"

He bent over her, touching her waist. "Who?"

"The Crimean boy. The one I went to talk to. I left him with another man, but they've gone."

The three doctors had restored order to the roiling mass of servants. The space around Jan-Ali cleared once more, and the four selected assistants advanced to hold the khan down while the doctors dosed him with a potion of some sort. A knife handle protruded from one of the braziers.

Daniil surveyed the room. "No boy." He caught her hand. "Quick, wife of mine. Let's go after him."

A goal easier set than met. Since they last braved the corridor, the members of the court whose response to the commotion had been delayed—Gulnara, Aslanbika, Gazim Shirin, Alexander

Makhmetovich and the entire Russian delegation (although not the Crimean envoys, Nasan noted in passing)—had arrived. As a result, even more people obstructed Nasan and Daniil's passage. His best efforts enabled a halting progression worthy of an intoxicated tortoise. Nasan clung to his robe like a child, lest the crowd separate her from him.

The odor of burning flesh struck her nostrils as they pushed their way out of Jan-Ali's room. Her uncle's scream pierced the air. Whatever drugs the doctors had administered had not proven sufficient to sedate him.

Even at the end of the corridor, Nasan and Daniil found no trace of the Crimean boy and the servant to whom Nasan had entrusted him. Instead, they heard the rapid pounding of hooves.

They ran to the window. Far below, through the main street of Kazan, the party of Crimean envoys raced at top speed for the city gates.

"Stop them," Daniil shouted, but his voice didn't penetrate the grilled screen, never mind reach the street below.

Nasan smacked the window embrasure. White stone bruised the side of her hand, but frustration numbed the pain—for the moment. "It's too late," she said. "They're almost at the wall. No one can reach them in time."

She turned to face Daniil. "The negotiations were a ruse. The envoys came to assassinate my uncle."

"I agree," Daniil said. "Time to have a chat with Alexander Makhmetovich."

Chapter 13

"HE WILL LIVE." THE SHAMAN SAT BACK ON HER HEELS AS she pronounced her verdict. "The bey is strong, and the wound has closed. I see no signs of infection. So long as nothing putrid lurks within, he will survive."

Firuza dropped her head onto her knees as her spine sagged. With relief? She hoped so, but after a week of sleepless nights, she had lost the ability to tell. Her twin would live. She couldn't regret that, not after a lifetime spent loving and protecting him—even if his determination to break her emerging bond with Ogodai threatened her future.

Rain lashed the tent roof. Beneath her feet, the cart rocked, swinging her braid from side to side. The horde had rested in place for three days after the attack on Jahangir, waiting to hear whether its bey would live or die, searching for clues that would point toward his assailant. So late in the evening, it should have been easy to identify which man had not taken his appointed place by the fire, but with two dozen sentries guarding the herds and watching for marauders, settling on one miscreant had proven harder than the council expected. The investigation had winnowed its list of suspects down to ten, but even that result seemed questionable. Every man in the camp carried a knife. Anyone could have delivered the blow that felled Jahangir—a slice through the chest that struck an inch or two above the heart. The horde would watch the ten from here on, but that in itself couldn't undo the damage already done.

Tulpar had proven unexpectedly competent during the crisis, taking charge of the investigation (which seemed to Firuza rather like allowing the wolf to count the sheep, but no one except Ogodai asked for her opinion, and he agreed with her). Tulpar stayed away from Firuza and her deathly ill twin, but during her occasional trips to the women's tent to rest, she heard glowing tales of his interrogating this warrior or that. She hoped that those interrogated were in fact guilty and that his prowess wouldn't sway the elders in his favor, but Jahangir's needs consumed her, leaving little energy for politics. Ogodai visited her once or twice a day, but their time together was precious. She couldn't bear to waste a moment quizzing him about Tulpar. Ogodai, too, spent his days working on behalf of the council, which must reach a decision soon. But until Jahangir's fate was known, the elders would not rule.

Winter closed inexorably in, and eventually the nomads resumed their trek. Firuza, Diliara, and the shaman nursed the bey around the clock in his tent, mounted on a huge flat cart dragged by half a dozen oxen, steadied from behind by four times that number of slaves. A pair of armed guards, sent by Ogodai, stood before the tent door, balancing themselves against the rocking motion, their crossed spears a deterrence to potential enemies. A third man held her brother's spirit banner— its nine horse tails defiantly white to symbolize peace despite the near-state of war prevailing in the camp. The spirit banner of a khan or bey was a sacred trust. Without going outside to check, Firuza knew that the trident that formed its shaft would point to the lowering sky, its horse tails swing free in the rising wind, constrained only by the helmet of brass and the embroidered straps that kept the whole together.

Roxelana had removed herself to more congenial surroundings, much to Diliara's and Firuza's relief. Their tented wagon rolled slowly across the unending feather grass, but roll it did. Before the snows made the steppe impassable for wheels, Bahadur's horde—the name stuck, despite the change of ruler—must reach its winter pastures.

A hand tapped Firuza's shoulder. She raised her head to find her stepmother kneeling beside her. Diliara held out a small bowl. Fragrant steam, meat mingled with herbs, tickled Firuza's nostrils. Assorted vegetables floated in the broth, mixed with small dumplings made from precious flour. "Eat," Diliara said, "then rest. I will feed your brother, if he can swallow. The shaman will help me."

Firuza tried to argue, but the words tangled in her throat. Her eyes watered from the steam. Exhaustion dragged her down, the result of too many nights spent dabbing her brother's face to reduce his fever, mopping his wound with potions designed to prevent infection, replacing spider webs and bandages and propping him in position so that he didn't tear out his stitches or even lie on his injury. Too many nights spent praying to Allah and begging the grandmothers—to save his life, yes, but also to change his heart, to restore him to the warm and fun-loving brother of her childhood.

She drank the soup. It slid past her lips and down her parched throat, carrying with it a sense of release from her burdens. "It will be all right," Diliara said as she took the bowl away again. "Sleep, daughter, and trust that life will work itself out in the end."

Firuza lay back and closed her eyes. She felt Diliara wrap a quilted cover around her. Work out in the end, yes. But for whom?

Stinging rain mixed with sleet chapped Ogodai's cheeks as he rode behind the herds. His sheepskin coat, turned fleece inside for warmth, blocked the assault of the weather, but every inch of exposed skin felt as if some enemy flailed at him with a corded whip. He missed Firuza, imagined her riding at his side as she had on that one glorious day. But he did not wish her exposed to this driving rain. Better that she travel in warmth and safety, even if it meant hours bent over a dying man.

Caring for Jahangir took a lot out of her. On the brief occasions when Ogodai saw her, her face looked pinched, the circles under her lovely eyes dark, her shoulders hunched in anticipation of bad news. He had offered to carry her off to rest, but she refused every suggestion of comfort except to press her face into his chest—a concession that Ogodai enjoyed a great deal. Last night, the shaman had indicated that Jahangir was approaching a crisis. Perhaps by tonight, the bey would have rallied. Or not. Either option seemed preferable to the current uncertainty.

The ground grew slick under the horses' hooves. Ogodai plodded on, hands loose on the reins, allowing the chestnut to choose its own pace. Around them, the grass bent at unnatural angles, sculpted by falling ice. Men brushed impatient hands across their brows, squinted into the distance, buried their chins in the high collars of their coats, pulled hats lower to shield their eyes. Nothing helped.

Ogodai considered whether, if he were khan, he would call a halt and wait for the sleet to ease. The decision wasn't his to make: with the bey incapacitated, the council ruled by decree. But on the whole, he thought not: as the calendar moved through Rabi el-Thani, the weather would only worsen. As yet, water continued to war with the ice. The sure-footed horses, accustomed to the vagaries of the plains, would find their way. The Tatars should push on, urging the herds as close to their destination as possible before the snows arrived in earnest. At this rate, they'd be lucky to reach their ancestral lands without encountering at least one blizzard.

Rafik cantered up to him, racing his horse faster than the weather warranted but somehow keeping the dapple gray upright. A brief exchange followed. Rafik, it seemed, had been asking himself similar questions.

"I agree," Rafik said, when Ogodai shared his thoughts. "I could talk to my father, but there's little point in stopping. This sleet will turn to snow before dawn. At least the animals have enough to eat." When Ogodai nodded, Rafik wheeled his horse and took off again, still riding too fast, to prod the rest of the men onward.

Ogodai tightened his collar and reined in his chestnut gelding, stamping its feet in its eagerness to dash after Rafik. He felt the animal's powerful neck strain under his grip before the chestnut resumed its plod. Ogodai went back to scanning the horde.

A squat warrior caught his eye. One of the ten on the council's list of those who might have attacked Jahangir. This man, Zamam, stood out because he rode with a hooded eagle perched on his forearm, its talons pressing into the thick sheepskin of his coat. A grand gesture, Ogodai assumed, for the bird must weigh heavy as the horde pressed on, mile after endless mile. The Don lay far behind them, and they would stop before they reached the Volga, but great swaths of grasslands still separated summer from winter pastures. It would take two or three weeks, he estimated, to reach their destination. A good rider on a series of swift horses could cover the distance in four days. But sheep and goats meandered at the pace of a man walking, and Jahangir's wagon could travel only half that speed without pushing the critically ill bey closer to death. Zamam would regret carrying his bird the whole way.

Thoughts of dates and times jolted Ogodai with the realization that today was his birthday. The fifth day of Rabi el-Thani. He had turned nineteen this morning, to no fanfare whatsoever. Of course, no one knew except Vafa; and servants, however long established with a family, didn't take it upon themselves to observe their masters' birthdays.

Childish to wish for one friendly face—one family member bearing koumiss, cakes, gifts, and good wishes—summoning everyone in the vicinity to celebrate.

Ogodai turned his eyes back to Zamam, but the man was doing nothing worth watching. Plodding across slick grass, steadying his horse from time to time, doing his best to keep icy water from trickling down his neck. Like everyone else.

After a while, passive watching exhausted Ogodai's patience. Deciding to join Rafik, who could be counted on to enliven the ride with conversation, he angled his horse to the right, so that the driving rain from the north would not blind the animal. The chestnut moved with surprising swiftness across the treacherous grass, and they soon caught up with Rafik, about to set off on another long swing to check on the herds. Ogodai nudged his gelding into place, and the two horses moved forward together.

"Any news on your fletcher?" Ogodai asked. Because of the arrow that had scattered the herds, the council had placed the fletcher, too, on its list of suspects. Ogodai had forgotten the man's name, although he had a general sense of someone tall and thin, more reedy than robust—an unlikely assassin of Jahangir, who whatever his faults had shown no reluctance to defend himself.

Rafik held a hand to his hat, palm down to shade his eyes, and squinted at the herd. "Almas? No. Shirin put him on the list out of excessive caution. He's loyal."

"Despite the arrow we found?"

"Yes, despite that. Oh, he made it, I'm sure. And I did suspect him for a moment. But your lady was right. He didn't fire it. Still less attack the bey. He's not the violent type, Almas. Never in any trouble—well, except for the squabble between him and Zamam, but that seems to have blown over. Zamam, now—he's a man deserves watching."

Ogodai's task. "I watched him for miles," he said. "But what can he do in the midst of this storm?"

"Not much, I suppose." Rafik slewed his horse sideways. Ogodai's chestnut, caught off-guard, reared.

"Watch it," he said. Rafik apologized, but Ogodai barely heard him. From his vantage point above the moving horde, he saw Zamam—impossible to mistake because of the eagle— still plodding forward.

He brought his horse down. "Zamam is where I left him." A new thought occurred to him. "But why? He doesn't belong with my men. No one assigned him to me."

"Keeping an eye on you, maybe." Rafik shrugged. "He's your brother's man, or has no one mentioned that? Was, anyhow."

"Tulpar's?" This camp never failed to surprise him. "I don't remember seeing them together."

"They arrived together, though," Rafik said. "From Crimea, right when we reached the summer pastures. Zamam stayed when Tulpar left. Claimed he preferred the old bey's service, but I always wondered if Tulpar left him to spy on us. Your brother grumbled like mad when Bahadur Bey threw him out."

Ogodai frowned into the pelting sleet and shook back the hair that dripped into his eyes. Pieces of information clicked into place inside his brain. Zamam had been Tulpar's man. He'd stayed behind when Tulpar left, in an uncommon if not unheard-of departure from custom, and not long after that,

Bahadur died, leaving his daughter and his horde in the hands of a bey incompetent to protect them.

If Bahadur hadn't sent the talisman to his *qarïndash*, Tulpar would have had an opportunity to ride in, lay claim to Firuza, establish himself as khan, and rule by force of arms. By the time Bulat discovered what happened, it would be too late to undo the damage.

And once in control of these Nogai, Tulpar would do what? Pledge them to Crimea, where Tulpar supposedly had connections?

Not clear. Tulpar might use Bahadur's horde as a base to increase his own power or as a springboard to another, more prestigious Tatar court. But one thing seemed certain: wherever he went and whatever he did, he would oppose Bulat and Ogodai.

"Would Zamam attack Jahangir?" he asked, before the silence could become oppressive. "Near as I can tell, Jahangir seems to favor Tulpar."

Rafik turned his head sideways. Sleet stung Ogodai's cheek as he matched Rafik's gesture. The weather was growing fouler by the moment.

"I doubt he would," Rafik said. "Attack Jahangir, that is. Do any of our ten suspects *not* support Tulpar?"

"Suppose I was Zamam's target?" Ogodai strove to keep his voice level, as if a brush with death had no meaning. "No one expected the bey to come pounding across the camp to confront us. Could it have been a case of mistaken identity?"

Rafik's horse jerked in response to sudden pressure on the reins. Ogodai's gelding, its patience shredded by the driving sleet and stolid gait, broke stride and lunged at its fellow, teeth bared. Ogodai wrestled the animal back into submission, but he didn't miss the shock on Rafik's face. If such a plot existed, Rafik had not taken part in it.

"It could have," Rafik said. "Why didn't we think of that before? If you were the intended victim, that would explain why the blade went in above the heart. You're about that much taller than Jahangir."

Ogodai wanted to kick himself for being so slow. How many Tatar courts had he attended? How many Tatar rulers had he seen dispatched by enemies? What made him think himself immune to treachery just because he was the protected son of a powerful khan ruling a relatively peaceful province, where Russian suzerainty ensured that assassination could not in itself secure the throne?

Here among the nomads, halfway between Astrakhan and Crimea, with that beautiful traitor Kazan guarding the gates to the northern forests—here he couldn't afford naïveté. Here the threat was real and present. He was eighteen—no, nineteen. He had to grow up, and fast, or he would not live to become khan, to see Firuza bear his children, to grow old with her. Tulpar would kill him, then steal her away.

And to think he'd imagined that he could take Firuza and leave the horde to its own devices. No wonder Bahadur had called his dreaming former pupil a fool.

"The red robe," Ogodai said. "No, not that one. The crimson velvet with the jeweled collar. And my hat of black fox. The council members treat me as if I were in truth the boy they remember. I want them to see me as a khan."

And my former brother, who would crush me under his heel like a snake in the grasslands—he, too, must see me as a rival to reckon with.

"The cloth-of-gold would convey that point even better, Sultan." Vafa held up a robe on which phoenixes and lions romped against a brilliant yellow backdrop. Sable edged the collar and the sleeves.

Ogodai laughed, the tone harsher than he had intended. His tension this evening was not Vafa's fault. "Save that one for my installation as khan, Vafa, if it ever happens. Or for my wedding. Tonight the velvet will serve well enough. I wish to impress them, true, but I must retain the ability to impress them more later."

Vafa nodded and bent over the chest once more. The cloth-of-gold vanished, replaced by velvet the deep red of the Frankish wine served at his sister's wedding. Long strings of pearls dripped from Vafa's left hand. "But you will wear these, Sultan?"

Ogodai took the folded robe from his servant and donned it. The robe, lined with felt, raised a barrier between his silk shirt and the chill seeping in from outside. "Assuredly." The robe fell to the top of his boots, concealing his loose trousers.

When had Tulpar decided to kill him? Had he planned an assassination from the first, or had it been a spontaneous decision—a response to Ogodai's winning the race and Firuza, just as Jahangir had responded with the angry, unannounced visit that had turned him into the unintended victim of Tulpar's assault? Because it had to be Tulpar who had ordered the killing, didn't it? No one else had as much to gain.

Vafa produced a length of pleated sky-blue silk, which Ogodai used to secure the crimson robe. He bent his head to allow Vafa to toss the six strings of pearls over his head, added a pair of gold rings to each hand, and pulled the black-fox hat over his ears—glad of its warmth.

"The Ottoman dagger," he ordered.

The servant dug into the chest again and returned with the dagger, a gorgeous curved object chased in gold, rubies twice the size of Ogodai's thumbnail embedded on each side of the sheath. The jewelry was for show, but the knife was no toy, the blade fashioned from Damascus steel. Tulpar had tried to kill him and failed; he might well try again. Bulat had said, "Watch your back." Ogodai would watch it tonight—and every night from now on.

He slid the weapon into his sash, adjusting it when it clanked against Bahadur's talisman—stored there in case of need. He was ready.

He left the tent, glad that Vafa had ordered it raised as soon as he heard of the council's summons to his master. The certainty of privacy as he prepared himself, mentally and physically, for what amounted to a public performance was the only thing that made his efforts tolerable. He thought wistfully of the brother he'd once worshipped, now bent on his destruction. And of Firuza, exhausting herself to save a twin who showed precious little concern for her welfare. Families shouldn't be so complicated.

The rain had stopped, although ice clung to the ground. The white horse tails of his spirit banner, firmly planted before the makeshift tent, stretched almost horizontal in the howling wind. The breath of nature, bringing strength and energy to his soul. He spoke to the man who guarded his tent, one of those who had accompanied him from the camp near Smolensk. "My bride. You have men protecting her at all times?"

The man placed his hand over his heart and touched spear tip to forehead. "Of course, Sultan. As you ordered. She sleeps, Lady Diliara tells me."

If anyone could sleep through this noise. The rejoicing that had greeted the bey's turn toward recovery caused the large tents to vibrate. "Watch her yourself," he told the guard. "Our enemies won't sleep."

"Yes, Sultan," the man said.

It was the best Ogodai could do, for the moment. He set off to beard the council in its den.

The council met in a tent set up for that purpose. The attendees' opulence contrasted sharply with the bare lattice walls and plain felt overthrow of their meeting place. Ogodai couldn't help wondering—while he greeted the ancestors and exchanged pleasantries with each of the four beys in turn—what hidden currents their bland surfaces concealed. His brief experience with this horde had convinced him that much went on that he discovered only after the fact.

Yet he was not without allies. Ildar Shirin, resplendent in a tall felt hat that matched the hue of his gold-embroidered robe, was unlikely to abandon his opposition to Bulat and therefore to Bulat's chosen heir. But Kazbek Argyn, equally distinguished in turquoise silk and an ermine-trimmed cap shaped like a helmet, had backed Ogodai from the beginning. Jahangir, whose words and behavior seemed more hostile than not, attended only in spirit.

Ogodai assessed Baryn and Kipchak, fourth and fifth in importance. Perhaps because they did not often wield the deciding vote, they had guarded their neutrality so far, treating Bulat's sons with the same courteous distance. Perhaps they would declare themselves tonight. Ogodai needed them both.

A set of bolsters arranged in a semicircle to the north of the hearth fire indicated where the meeting would take place. Still chatting about the weather, the group of beys moved toward the bolsters.

Tulpar had yet to arrive. Ogodai stood near the place of honor, easily recognizable because, as before, the setup placed him and his half-brother side by side. He decided to stand, rather than scramble to his feet when his brother deigned to make an appearance. He could, of course, repay Tulpar in kind for his brother's crassness at the last council session, but such discourtesy didn't speak well for a man's ability to rule.

As Ogodai reached this conclusion, Tulpar strode in. Always a peacock, he had outdone himself this evening. His purple-swirled brocade and emerald-studded belt surpassed in magnificence even Ogodai's crimson robe and black fox.

Ogodai decided he didn't mind. He looked more like a warrior than his brother, whose scented person suggested too much time spent at court.

An illusion, as Ogodai had every reason to know. He had not forgotten their various contests, from that initial punch through the wrestling, swordsmanship, archery, and riding matches—not to mention their ongoing struggle for the khanate. Even so, illusions had meaning in a world where the strongest ruled.

The four beys bowed. Tulpar greeted his half-brother with a tip of the turban. Ogodai responded in kind, then took his seat. Kazbek Argyn dropped into place on his right. A solid declaration of support, and Ogodai smiled in appreciation.

He glanced again at his older brother, settling himself on Ogodai's left. The bolsters of the two khan's sons ran exactly parallel, as before. The council had still not decided which son it supported, then, despite its promise to accept the one who excelled at the festival. Although by arriving first, Ogodai had managed to secure the seat to the right. No one suggested he yield it to his older brother. A small victory, but one worth savoring.

Hair brushed his cheek. He glanced left to find the spirit banner of Bahadur Bey again positioned behind his shoulder. Its white horse tails drifted in the draft that pierced the smoke hole, its point a hand's width higher than the head of its one-time owner while standing, its chased iron holder as solidly planted in the grassy floor as Bahadur's boots had once been upon the earth. The reassuring presence of his mentor heartened Ogodai as he pondered the confrontation to come.

The remaining council members took their places—Baryn to Argyn's right, Kipchak next to Shirin. More signals? If the council split evenly down the middle, what then?

But someone had to sit next to Shirin. And Jahangir could cast the deciding vote, if necessary, when he recovered. Ogodai's task hadn't changed. He must still convince both Baryn and Kipchak to stand with him.

Servants arrived bearing platters of food: the same bread and mutton stew served in the large tents, here presented in elegantly woven baskets and brass tureens lined with glazed pottery; the mugs of frothy koumiss that graced every feast.

The shaman entered, shaking her beads and pounding her drum as she offered the first taste to the hearth spirits and the ancestors, thanking them for allowing Jahangir to remain with the living. Then, still chanting, she left. The servants followed.

Ogodai began his meal simply enough, engaging Argyn and Baryn in a discussion of information learned during the ride today—Zamam's decision to join Ogodai's men and Rafik's insistence that Almas the fletcher had borne the former bey no ill will. He asked for their opinions, sounding Baryn out, and discovered him to be a sensible man. Ogodai didn't even need flattery; his admiration was sincere.

While they talked, he listened with one ear to Tulpar's conversation with Shirin and Kipchak. Shirin and Tulpar traded stories of the Crimean court, of the renewed struggle between Sahib-Girei Khan and his heir apparent, of the disagreements that weakened the Shirin clan, and the beauty of certain Shirin daughters who would make excellent wives for deserving warriors. Kipchak listened, his face impenetrable.

Argyn and Baryn ran out of suggestions just as Tulpar waxed lyrical about one of Ildar's nieces. Ogodai couldn't resist. He shot a look of pure mischief at Argyn, then asked, "Why not wed one of these gorgeous Shirin daughters, *aby*, since you find them so appealing?"

Argyn's mouth twitched. Tulpar downed a shot of koumiss before retaliating. "Why don't *you* wed a Russian, *ené*, since you're so fond of them? Just imagine, a whey-faced Christian for your very own."

"No accounting for tastes, is there?" Shirin added.

"I already have a wife," Ogodai noted dryly. "She pleases me well. But you're showing your ignorance. Not all Russian women are whey-faced. I saw a glorious blonde at our sister's wedding, and another woman with hair like copper. The *padishah* in Istanbul would have spent a fortune for either of them. Suleiman has a weakness for Slavs, from what I hear. Although the redhead might prove too much even for him. What a temper she has!"

This time, Kipchak was the one who burst out laughing—the first evidence he'd given that he was not a block of wood. The others joined in, Shirin a beat behind the rest.

"Now that I would like to see," Baryn said. "Who is this maiden of fire?"

"Widow," Ogodai said. "We killed her husband in a raid, then married Nasan Khanim to the surviving brother. You might say the redhead had reasons for not welcoming us to her house."

More laughter. Tulpar produced an exaggerated shudder. "You can keep your fire maiden—or widow. I'll stay with flashing Tatar eyes, thank you. Unless I can find myself a Chorasani as fair as Roxelana, that is."

"May you be so fortunate, *aby*," Ogodai said lightly. Before Tulpar could come up with an answer, Ogodai addressed Kipchak. "Tell me, Bey, who is taking care of your camp while you so graciously volunteer your time to aid those here?"

Kipchak looked grateful for the change of subject. "I have three sons, Sultan. The oldest should have gone to his tutor this year, but I kept him back and assigned a warrior to teach him. I hope to rejoin them soon, though. One of my wives is due to deliver any day."

"May Allah bless you once more." Ogodai ran calculations in his head. A ten- or twelve-year-old son—not surprising, but it emphasized the extent of the man's commitment to Bahadur's cause, if he would leave his camp in the hands of a child and his tutor for months. "May you soon return to them."

Kipchak nodded, a wistful expression on his face. The conversation continued until the servants removed the plates, leaving the jugs and cups of koumiss. Ogodai braced himself. His half-brother undoubtedly had something up his sleeve.

He hadn't long to wait. "Our Sufi," Tulpar drawled as the last slave left the tent, waving his right hand to remove any doubts as to whom he had in mind. "Religion keeps him sober where fellowship requires him to empty his cup. I ask you, lords, do you seek an imam or a warrior as your leader?"

His voice slurred enough to suggest that he might have done better to emulate a Sufi himself, but Ogodai tensed at the implied insult. He knew the demands of his religion as well as his brother did—and no doubt respected them more— but whatever Tulpar said, his accusation here had nothing to do with the Prophet (on whom be peace) and everything to do with declaring himself a man and Ogodai less than one.

"The horde has one leader who values fellowship above duty." He kept his voice level, neutral. "It can profit from not electing another of the same bent." He stared hard at Tulpar, who smirked and did not drop his eyes.

"Moderation in all things," Tulpar said. "And there is much to gain here through fellowship, do you not think? A horde. A woman."

Ogodai gritted his teeth, determined not to let his brother's needling get under his skin. "*Not* a woman. Even by the council's rules, I won Firuza fair and square."

That swayed them, he saw. Not Tulpar or Shirin. But the other three—Baryn, Argyn, Kipchak—remembered the challenge issued at the last meeting and its outcome.

To tighten his grip on them, Ogodai pulled the talisman from his sash and held it out. "But she was already mine, as you know. Her father gave her to me. You witnessed our betrothal. Bahadur is here. He wants you to choose me. Ask him."

Shirin's eyes narrowed at the sight of the emblem. "We discussed this last time. The needs of the horde take precedence, and the horde fares best under the strongest leader. Why else would we even bother with a khan? The Nogai do well enough with their beys."

"You challenged me to defeat my brother in the games," Ogodai retorted. "And I did. That makes me the stronger."

"Faster, not stronger," Tulpar put in. "I was holding my own until that last race. Besides, you cheated."

The nerve! Ogodai stopped trying to hide his anger. "I did not. You were the one who pretended she had chosen you, and even so, you lost."

Kazbek deflected their emerging squabble. "You both did well in the contest, but Ogodai Sultan came out ahead. Still, strength rests on more than a fast steed or a powerful sword. Bahadur's alliance with Bulat protected us for decades, and the talisman symbolizes their brotherhood. The winged horse carries much power." He held out his hand.

Ogodai passed him the medallion. Argyn raised it in homage to the watching spirit banner, then returned it. "Bahadur's summons reveals the trend his thoughts took on his deathbed, his hopes for us. We honor his spirit by following his commands."

"We harness the power of the winged horse by electing Tulpar Sultan as khan," Shirin said. "These symbols are open to many interpretations. Do we not honor older sons over younger ones? Tulpar has the advantage of his brother by eight years."

"Years spent in battle," Tulpar added, a smug expression on his face.

Ogodai's palms itched. "I'm not a novice. I've spent four years in the field. And unlike my brother, I have not lost half an army through my inability to profit from the wisdom of my elders."

Tulpar hissed. Shirin's face assumed a supercilious expression. "A khan needs initiative. He cannot merely follow orders."

The words might have come from Tulpar's mouth. Ogodai strove to respond with the courtesy this elder statesman deserved. He doubted he could convince Shirin, but he wanted to convey to the others his maturity and readiness to become khan. "I've led missions—and done so well enough that my father believes I can succeed as your khan. Initiative has its place, I agree, but my father wouldn't have cast off Tulpar because of one misjudgment, however serious the consequences. Nor would Bahadur. We have already established that Bahadur changed his mind about betrothing his daughter to my half-brother. That he sent the talisman to my father as a warning— against Tulpar. Think, Beys, how grave a pattern of misdeeds must have stained my brother's name for my father to declare Tulpar dead to our clan and to our ancestors."

"Lies," Tulpar said. "My father wanted an obedient slave, not a son."

Shirin winced. Three shocked faces turned toward Tulpar. "A son must not gainsay his father," Kazbek Argyn said, his voice as chilling as the ice that had flattened the feather grass.

A mistake, at last. Ogodai felt the tension in his stomach ease. He hadn't won them yet, but Tulpar might have lost them. From time immemorial, the peoples of the steppe had embraced the principle of complete obedience to one's elders, especially one's father. By defending the indefensible, Tulpar had eroded their sympathy.

To push them farther in the right direction, Ogodai reiterated the points he had made during the last meeting. "My father ordered me to fulfill his contract with his sworn brother by wedding Bahadur's daughter. If you refuse to accept me as khan, then I will leave with her and celebrate our marriage in Kasimov. In that way, I honor the ancestors."

Horse tail snapped against his cheek, as if Bahadur sought to add his voice to the argument. Smoke billowed from the hearth fire, its scent acrid with burned meat and milk, bearing hints of the shaman's herbs.

Trust me, Ogodai thought, hoping his mentor understood that he hadn't changed his goal, only his means of achieving it.

Shirin tipped his head in Ogodai's direction, his expression sour. "With all due respect, Sultan, your honored father doesn't decide who weds our lady. Nor can you and she force our hands by what you choose to do in private. Marriage is an agreement between clans. It doesn't depend on the whims of the young— and rightly so."

"You seem to have few friends and fewer allies," Ogodai pointed out. "Can you afford to anger a leader as powerful as Bulat?"

"We cannot," Argyn said. Ogodai let him have the floor, glad of his support. "You forget, Beys. Despite the years Tulpar has spent among us, Bahadur didn't send the talisman to him. Instead, he sent Tulpar away, just as Bulat himself did. And for the same reasons: defying orders and scheming." He gestured at the spirit banner. "If we overrule our former bey, we will have more than Bulat to worry about. Bahadur can turn the wrath of the ancestors against us, and I for one don't wish to see that day."

Shirin opened his mouth, but Tulpar intervened before he could speak. "A fine speech on behalf of a man who serves the Russians. Whose *father* serves the Russians. We need not fear Bulat if we have ties to the Crimean throne."

"Bah!" Baryn said. "You offer us another overlord. And one not friendly to our cause. Sahib-Girei Khan uses the nomads when it suits him, but he has little patience with us. Why would an alliance with him benefit us more than one with the Russians?"

"Not Sahib-Girei," Tulpar said. "His nephew Islam-Girei, who already controls the steppe north of the Crimean Peninsula."

"And who works with the nomads," Shirin added. "He honors the clans and respects the old ways. And like his uncle, he can wring rich booty out of the Poles and the Lithuanians. They give him lands and gold and wagons filled with cloth."

"A man who rebels often but wins seldom," Baryn said, his voice curt. "And on the rare occasion when he succeeds, he can't hold what he has seized for more than a few months. I don't bend my neck to Islam-Girei."

"He would be an overlord of our own religion, our own kind. One indebted to me for years of support." Tulpar raised a languid hand, ignoring Baryn's objection. "That seems preferable to me."

"Neither Islam-Girei nor his uncle can rule without approval from Istanbul," Ogodai said. "You would subject yourselves to a vassal. And for what gain? The grand prince of Moscow doesn't restrict our customs or our faith."

"He hasn't yet," Shirin said. "One day he will. In any event, that's a matter for us to decide. We have the right to confirm our own khan."

"Me." Tulpar ducked as the horse tails, propelled by a new blast of air from the chimney, whipped across his cheek. Ogodai nudged the spirit banner, steadying the spear with his left hand, holding it so close to the base that it appeared to move of its own volition. Tulpar pulled back, muttering, and Ogodai suppressed a grin.

Kazbek Argyn spoke up again. "Ogodai Sultan speaks the truth. That conflict renews itself as regularly as the seasons, and the Ottomans stoke the flames instead of dampening them. They like seeing their vassals divided. Why else did they appoint Sahib-Girei, when his nephew had already declared himself khan? They will fight until one of them dies, and if we join either side, we will be in the thick of it. Do you want that for us?"

"The Ottomans are Muslims, too," Tulpar argued. "The game is changing before our eyes, Beys. Do we join our brothers in the eastern steppe and spend our lives, when we're not scrounging for food and for pasturage, beating back whichever people chooses next to cast its eyes on our grazing lands? Or do we defend and expand what is ours by accepting the suzerainty of others like ourselves? Crimea has an impregnable fortress, a defensible peninsula, the backing of a great empire, and"—he cast a disdainful glance around the tent—"greater luxury than we enjoy."

"Moscow also has impregnable fortresses and riches of which nomads don't even dream," Ogodai said. "But if I were khan, I would not suggest that we subjugate ourselves to the Russians. I would argue that we should preserve our freedom for as long as we can." He leaned forward, focusing on the three he had a chance of convincing, and fixed each man in turn with his eyes. "Remember that Bahadur set up the alliance with Bulat. For thirty years he ruled you, and the horde remains strong because of his leadership. Surely you trust him to lead you still." He grasped the spear supporting the spirit banner, showing them that he didn't fear Bahadur's soul, that he drew strength from his mentor's symbol. "You remember me from boyhood. You know that Bahadur taught me well. Accept me as khan, and you will have Bulat at your backs, which is no small thing. But there is more. The night before Jahangir was attacked, I slept among your ancestors. Bahadur came to me in a dream and ordered me to accept the khanate and to take his daughter to wife. Call the shaman. She will confirm it."

For once, Tulpar remained silent. Under the fingers of Ogodai's left hand, the spirit banner thrummed, as if with approval. He addressed the beys. "I am a good Muslim, as my brother noted earlier." He lifted the cup of koumiss before him and drained it, upending it to show that not one drop remained. "Although not so good that I ignore the demands of hospitality. And Muslims, too, recognize the power of the ancestors. When one speaks from beyond the grave, surely it behooves his horde to accept his guidance. Fetch the shaman."

Chapter 14

THE TINKLE OF SHELLS SIGNALED THE SHAMAN'S ARRIVAL.
They dangled from the brim of her fur-trimmed hat, shirring
together as she moved like a flock of tiny birds crying for food,
their clinking an accompaniment to the seed-filled gourd she
shook in rhythm with her pounding feet.

The braids that usually obscured her face tonight lay tight
against her skull, emerging from the crown of her calfskin hat
to fall in a ragged tail halfway down her back. Each braid ended
in more beads, which added a soft *ssh* to the medley of shells
and gourd, the stamp of felt boots against the carpet. Amid a
company resplendent in silk and velvet, the shaman's ragged
collection of skins—adorned with tufts of rabbit fur and
ancient symbols formed from strips of leather, the implements
of her trade dangling amid a profusion of ropes and bells—
emphasized her connections to the other world of ancestors
and spirits. Even in this camp, where water was too precious
to waste much of it on bathing, the body odor that emanated
from those damp and musty skins made Ogodai's nostrils flare.

She hummed and chanted, her words a tangled mumble
of Arabic phrases long familiar to Ogodai and references as
ancient as the grandmothers in the cart where he had dreamed
his encounter with Bahadur Bey. He saw that she had already

entered her trance. The sight reassured him. The council would have no chance to influence her with its questions.

Unless, of course, Ildar Shirin already had. But Ogodai thought not. He had startled them when he revealed the dream. Those who opposed him had had no chance to prepare a defense.

If his vision had been a true one. If Bahadur chose to appear tonight.

If, if, if. The possibilities would drive him mad.

The shaman circled the fire, rattling her gourd, chanting the spirits into attendance. She sprinkled milk into the flames, releasing another blast of sour-smelling smoke that tickled Ogodai's throat and caused his eyes to water. Puffs of sage and thyme came next, then meat fat. He coughed. Everyone coughed.

The thickness of the smoke, the steady beat of stomping feet, the harmony of beads and shells pulled the audience, too, into a version of the shaman's trance. Ogodai felt lightheaded, his thoughts far away as if he had returned to the ancestors' cart, to the place of his dream, while still awake. Shells, beads, rattle, stomp blended into the lift and fall of the white stallion's wings. Bahadur, responding to the shaman's call.

An unearthly shriek broke the thrum of sound. The white horse tails curled upward until they stood straight out below the spear point, pointing right, toward Ogodai. The shaman's voice took on the timber of a man's, and her mumbled chanting became thunderous, its mixture of languages yielding to the clear, common speech of the nomads. "I am Bahadur Bey," she announced. "Have you forgotten me already, my people, that you can defy my wishes and fall prey to the schemes of my murderer? Make Ogodai khan, and give him my daughter. I, Bahadur Bey, command you!"

"Murderer?" Argyn, Baryn, and Kipchak spoke with one voice. "What infamy is this?"

Shirin scowled at the shaman as if he regarded this accusation from beyond the grave as a personal affront. Or perhaps he was reconsidering his support for Tulpar.

"Don't look at me that way. I did not kill Bahadur!" Tulpar leaped to his feet and grabbed the spirit banner, whirling it above his head as if calling the clan to war. The shaman, her trance shattered by the uproar, cringed before them. She obviously had no idea what she had said to provoke Tulpar's anger.

"Calm yourself, *aby*." None other would dare, so Ogodai stood and gripped the spirit banner just below the point. The white horse tails felt rough under his hand.

Tulpar held on, and the two of them wrestled for a while before Tulpar released his grip and staggered backward. He rubbed the palm of his hand against his elegant coat as if it burned him.

Perhaps it did. Ogodai sensed forces greater than himself gathering in the tent. The white stallion's beating wings, his mentor's voice, the spirit banner throbbing with life in his hands. And his brother thought him capable of this display?

He said as much as he restored the spirit banner to its holder. A hum of chatter broke out. Ogodai strained to listen. *Murder. Tulpar?* He couldn't blame the beys for their astonishment.

Shirin pointed at the shaman, rage cutting harsh lines in his face. "Get you gone, woman. Take your croaking elsewhere."

She retreated in a cascade of beads and shells until only her scent remained to remind them of her message. Shirin turned his attention to his fellow clan leaders, whose chatter had stilled when he dismissed the shaman. "Listen to me. Bahadur ruled well, but every man is fallible. Bulat won't live forever. And the grand princes are a rapacious lot, each more intent on acquiring territory than the last. Are we to place our fate in the hands of the Muscovite bear?"

"Or in this case, cub," Tulpar said. His voice shook with fury. "More dangerous than a bear, since we have to take it on faith that young Prince Ivan will not change as he grows. Become his lackeys, and what value have we to him?"

"The same applies to the Crimeans," Ogodai said. "Nothing in life is certain. The next khan might be a monster, the young grand prince grow into a saint. We can make decisions based only on the information we have. And in any case, I don't suggest that you serve Russia. I told you that before. If I were khan, I would fight to keep the horde independent of outside powers, as Bahadur did. Then both the Russians and the Lithuanians will value us; both will pursue us and offer us plunder. Even the Crimeans won't be able to ignore us. My father would support such an effort. But he makes a dangerous enemy, and he will take it ill if you choose the son he has cast off over the one he regards as his heir."

He lifted his left hand to touch the closest horse tail. "As the honored Argyn Bey has noted, Bahadur, too, makes a dangerous enemy. More dangerous than my father."

Kipchak spoke. "I agree with Ogodai Sultan. The Crimeans benefit from pitting Lithuania against Moscow, and we must do the same. That will profit us most." He tipped his turbaned head toward Shirin. "I trusted Bahadur Bey in life, and I trust his judgment in death. As Argyn Bey has reminded us, Bahadur sent Tulpar away for defying his orders and arguing with him. The same sins Tulpar committed against his own father. If Ogodai Sultan swears to place the interests of the horde first, he has my vote."

Ogodai bit his tongue, lest he emit an exclamation of joy that he would later regret. Shirin's face reddened. Argyn, who had sat upright as any soldier since the meal ended, leaned against his bolster, a small smile on his face. "And you, Baryn?" he asked.

"I was inclined to vote with Shirin. Tulpar Sultan has more experience in battle, and I have seen much of him in manhood, not only as a child." He bowed in Ogodai's direction—a genuine obeisance, not Shirin's pseudo-courtesy. "No disrespect intended, Sultan. You handled the stampede well. Yet age brings wisdom."

Not always, Ogodai thought.

Baryn continued. "But I want no alliance with outside powers. No leader with a record of poor judgment. No ruler who must defend himself against accusations of murder. Bahadur treated us well. He kept the horde together and helped it prosper. If someone removed him before his time, I have no desire to reward such evil. We should investigate."

"Investigate? On the word of a shaman, when if anyone killed Bahadur, it was another of her kind?" Tulpar shot upright as if the spirit banner had pierced him with its steel point.

Ogodai forced himself to swallow, to breathe, to keep his emotions hidden. "Yes, investigate. If my brother speaks the truth, you will discover it. Look into the attack on Jahangir as well. They may be related."

If he had been the target, they almost certainly were. He didn't raise that possibility. Let them investigate. They should have done so already.

But the memory of his own danger pressed in on him. The long, tense evening became oppressive, and he wished for it to end.

To end well, but soon.

He couldn't rush it, though. The stakes were too high. Events must run their course.

Baryn extended a hand, palm up, then slowly turned it toward the spirit banner. "Ogodai Sultan offers good counsel. And let us remember. He had no contact with us before our bey died. We can be certain *he* did not kill our ruler."

"I wasn't here either when Bahadur died," Tulpar reminded them. "And murderers can kill from far off."

Ogodai pounced on the slip. "Except that I had no contacts within the camp. *You* could have killed from far off. Not I."

Four clan leaders frowned. Even Shirin looked concerned. "Yes," Baryn said. "Let's investigate. I served Bahadur from the day I reached manhood. If someone killed him, I want to know who. If someone attacked his son, we must discover that, too, and punish those responsible. But I have made my decision. I stand with Argyn and Kipchak."

He rose to his feet, stately in his formality, placed his hand over his heart, and tipped his head to Ogodai, who bit the inside of his lip, lest his jaw drop open. Had he really won?

Tulpar snarled. Perhaps it was true, then.

Baryn was still speaking, explaining his choice. "Ogodai Sultan has impressed me. He responds well to crises. He can organize men, as we saw during the stampede. He has a steady head. He reminds me of his father, whom I respect. A man who tells you where he stands—like the old bey. I vote to honor Ogodai's betrothal to our lady and—if he swears to place us first and to work with Jahangir—install him as khan."

It was true. He had won. Three in favor, one opposed, and the bey unable to cast a vote. A howl of joy pressed at Ogodai's throat. He didn't utter it.

Tulpar lunged, falling on Ogodai like a dead weight. Ogodai kicked him in the stomach, shoved both arms upward to separate the hands closing on his throat. Blood pulsed in his ears—or was that a roar, coming from outside his head?

Quick as a cat, he twisted free, kneeing Tulpar in the groin for good measure, and rolled to his feet. He stood over his half-brother, hands clenched, breathing hard. Tulpar curled into a ball, groaning.

Ogodai glanced around the circle of men, who sat relaxed, waiting for the brothers to work out their differences. Kazbek gave him an approving nod, Shirin a grudging one. At least, Ogodai imagined them thinking, they hadn't picked a weakling.

"Thank you," he told them. "I will do everything I can to justify your faith in me."

Firuza awoke to the sensation of a thumb caressing her cheek. Whose? Her eyes flew open, and she pushed herself upright.

Ogodai. Why had she been afraid? The stress of the last four months must be catching up with her.

"Sorry, did I startle you?" Her betrothed looked even more handsome than usual in his elegant crimson robe. The smile she was coming to love lit his eyes as he bent and nuzzled the side of her face, caressing her cheek with the slow sweep of a lover, allowing his lips to brush across her skin. Firuza released a soft sigh.

"I hoped to persuade you to come back with me," Ogodai said. "We have much to celebrate."

Firuza, remembering the last time she'd been alone with him in his tent, blushed. The maidenly reaction annoyed her. How unsophisticated he must think her!

"My brother," she stammered, knocked further off-balance by her own reaction.

Ogodai's smile widened. He bent sideways, revealing a figure in gauzy draperies with a sulky expression on its beautiful face. "As you see, now that the hard work is done, Roxelana has recollected her responsibilities as the bey's favorite concubine. She has come to nurse him. You can safely leave him in her loving arms."

He must be joking. Firuza stared at him, torn between desire and obligation, unable to find words that would express her utter lack of faith in Roxelana's ability to cope while the concubine remained with hearing range.

His lips twitched. "And your stepmother has promised to relieve her soon." His thumb stroked the line of her cheekbone once more. "The council backed me, beloved. The leaders have accepted our marriage. Your brother is out of danger. And it's my birthday. Will you not come and share my joy tonight?"

There was only one answer she could give to that. "Yes," Firuza said. "Just give me a moment to adjust my dress."

Early next morning, the camp resumed its trek to the northeast. With Jahangir on the road to recovery, the horde could pick up its pace a bit. It might reach its destination before winter after all.

Today the skies had cleared, although cold continued to make one grateful for fur hats and lined jackets. Ogodai dispatched one of his warriors to keep an eye on Zamam and escorted his bride back to the covered cart where her brother lay. Somewhat to his surprise, Roxelana remained in attendance on her fallen lord.

Not for long, though. Diliara, whose rapid and incautious handling of piled clean cloths betrayed her impatience with

Roxelana, shooed the concubine from the cart under the pretext that she had done enough and needed to rest. Roxelana writhed sinuously and cast pleading glances at Ogodai as she launched into a long and impassioned protest, but when he failed to intervene, she departed, grumbling. It took his entire stock of self-control to keep from laughing.

"What a performance," he said when Roxelana at last moved out of earshot. "She is wasted on this camp. She deserves a royal palace, I think."

"Or a group of traveling players," Diliara said wryly. "I thank you for the guards, by the way. Do you stay with us this morning, Sultan?"

"For a few hours." Ogodai pressed his bride's hand, still nestled in his. "After noon I will resume my place. They need every man to watch the flocks. But I wished to see for myself how the bey is recovering, to speak with him if possible." He released Firuza's clasp to brush a loose strand of hair behind her ear, provoking that adorable blush of hers. "And to spend a little more time with my bride."

Diliara regarded them with pursed lips but signaled approval with her eyes. "I'll put you both to work," she announced.

"I'm ready," Ogodai said. "What would you have me do?"

She looked him up and down, then nodded. "Yes, you will be useful. I must change the dressing on his wounds, and you can turn him far more easily than Firuza can. Please, come with me." She handed him her pile of cloths and addressed Firuza. "Meanwhile, you, my sweet, fetch that water skin."

The cart lurched into motion as she spoke. Firuza, reaching for the goatskin filled with water strapped to the right side, stumbled as her foot caught in a trailing blanket. Ogodai, bent almost double as he moved toward Jahangir, reached to grab her.

He missed. She went down, clutching her ankle. Her face drained of color.

Ogodai thrust his pile of cloths at Diliara and knelt beside Firuza. When he tugged at the boot that was the usual footwear for often-muddy campgrounds, she moaned. She covered her mouth at once, but he could see tears forming in her eyes. "It hurts?"

Without waiting for confirmation, he pulled his dagger from its sheath, sliced the boot along its seam, slipped it off Firuza's foot, and tossed it aside. Gently he probed her ankle, the delicate bones of her feet. Across the arch he saw the skin reddening, and Firuza emitted a suppressed wail when he rubbed her sole, but he sensed no shifting, no break, in the bones themselves. "You've strained the muscles, beloved. Or so I think. You'll limp for a bit, but it should heal well."

He glanced at Diliara, who had dropped cross-legged onto the rolling carpet protecting them from the planks of the cart. "Have you another bandage, Lady?"

Silently she handed him a long thin cloth. He placed it around Firuza's foot, folding it over her toes before wrapping it around the arch and heel, then splitting the rest with his dagger so that he could secure it at the ankle. She made not a sound. He kissed her lightly in tribute to her bravery. "No shoe for a while," he said. "And no walking unless you have to. If you get cold, ask for another layer."

"But Jahangir," she said.

Ogodai stood and lifted her, testing his balance against the steady trundle of the rolling wagon. Diliara slid sideways as she recognized his intent, and Ogodai carried his injured betrothed until he could set her down at her brother's left side.

"I'll stay with you for today," he said, "and return to the flocks tomorrow. We'll find someone to help your stepmother."

He didn't try to keep the mischief out of his voice. "Roxelana, I'm sure, will be happy to oblige."

Diliara groaned. Firuza giggled. "Thank you," she said. "I can do enough, just not everything."

"Indeed," Diliara said. "But I'm glad you will stay with us today, Sultan. Let's take care of the bey."

Chapter 15

WITH OGODAI'S HELP, DILIARA REMOVED JAHANGIR BEY'S bandages. Firuza collected the used cloths and set them aside for cleaning. As she watched her husband lift and twist her brother as if Jahangir weighed less than a child, she hoped Diliara would beg for Ogodai's help every day. Although the bey had passed the crisis point, he faced weeks of recovery. Which meant that Firuza couldn't look forward to riding with her husband-to-be anytime soon.

An idle wish, better left unspoken. She would enjoy his company while she had it. Whether Jahangir recovered quickly or not, her fall this morning would keep her off a horse for some time. Throbbing pain ran from her big toe to her heel, intensifying across the middle of her right foot, fading as it approached her ankle. The whole area felt hot to the touch. Even the slightest pressure reminded her of that moment when she'd clutched at air as the blanket tangled her in its folds.

"Such a stupid mistake." She pointed to her bandaged foot as she passed her stepmother a small pottery bowl and a clean piece of felt. "So unnecessary."

"That's why we call them accidents." Diliara pointed at the ugly gash that she dabbed with mint and vinegar to prevent infection. "You see how much better this looks. Your foot will heal, too."

Firuza examined the deep slash above her brother's heart—its enflamed edges and scabbed center. To an untrained eye, it didn't look much better. But she saw no red lines radiating from the wound, no yellow pus or puffiness. "It seems clean," she said.

"Yes," Diliara said. "Our task is to keep it that way. Sultan, if you would raise the bey's shoulders, Firuza and I will wind the bandage around him."

Firuza didn't argue, but inside she raged at her own clumsiness. Who could afford accidents when her brother needed care, duty kept her betrothed away from her, and evildoers roamed the camp looking for their next target? When had she become the one making idiotic missteps?

The memory of Ogodai's fingers rubbing her foot caused her stomach to riffle like the feather grass in spring. However much the unsolved mystery of her brother's near-assassination terrified her, at least she need no longer fear that the elders planned to drive Ogodai away from her. A blessing from the grandmothers, that.

If he would soon be khan—here, in this horde—should she not tell him about the vision she had received at the moment of his arrival? At first, she hadn't wanted to take the risk, lest he mock her. But much had changed in the short time they had spent together. It seemed only fair to share her hopes and dreams with him.

Diliara poked her head through the tent door and ordered the guard to stop. The heavy wagon ground to a halt.

"The bey must rest," she told Firuza and Ogodai. "I go to supervise the women. Send a man if you need me. Otherwise, the two of you can handle him until we stop for the night. Keep him warm, if you can." She brushed Firuza's cheek.

"Since the council has ruled in his favor, you no longer need me to chaperone you."

Keep him warm. Easier said than done, although at least rain and sleet didn't trouble them today. Even so, as the door shut behind Diliara and the wagon resumed its roll, Firuza felt suffused with a warmth of her own, the gentle glow of gratitude. The ancestors had granted her a rare opportunity, one she must not waste. Jahangir lay quiet, felled by illness and pain. She was alone with Ogodai. If she was ever to trust him with her insight that the horde needed more than raids to ensure its survival, here was her chance.

The words came out haltingly at first. Her brother and father hadn't encouraged her to express her views on what would help their people; the council neither sought nor heeded the opinions of women. But Ogodai listened without interrupting, his chin resting on one lightly clasped fist. Her voice grew stronger, more confident, fired by his interest.

"We must find lands closer to running water," she said. "With better grass for the herds. More goods to trade and partners to trade with, so that we can depend less on raids, which cost us in men and mounts. The Nogai hordes support themselves by selling horses to the Russians. Why don't we?"

"No extras," Jahangir mumbled.

Firuza started like a quail surprised by a roaming wolf. She'd been wrong to think herself alone with her husband. Her brother lay with his eyes closed, but he wasn't unconscious or asleep.

"Leave it, sister," he went on. "Not women's work."

She would have snapped at him, but the lines of suffering turned his face into a caricature of how he would look in extreme old age. The sight gave her pause.

Besides, Ogodai was laughing. "Not *women's* work?" he said. The corners of his mouth twitched. "Don't say that to your stepmother, Bey. Still less my mother. *Or* my sister, unless you want her to hand you your head in a bag. The future concerns women as well as men. Perhaps more, for they bear the children on whom our survival as a people depends."

Jahangir snorted. Ogodai touched Firuza's hand. "You make good points, sweetheart. I have a way to go before I secure my position as khan, but I'll keep your thoughts in mind. Why should this horde not find better grazing lands that will breed fine, fat horses? The Wild Field is a big place, much of it untamed. And my father and I know many Russian commanders eager to buy strong stock."

"Sweetheart, khan—you run too fast," Jahangir said. "She isn't yours yet. Nor is the horde."

His voice didn't waver, and he had formed three complete sentences. Yet Ogodai touched a finger to his lips. Firuza nodded. No need to reveal the council's decision. Her brother would learn the truth soon enough.

"Tell us what you remember," Ogodai said to Jahangir. "About the man who attacked you."

"Why?" Jahangir touched the bandage that circled his chest, as if it connected him with the night when he received the injury.

Still truculent. Firuza sighed. Would her brother *ever* grow up?

"Because we haven't found him," Ogodai said, calm as a tutor instructing a fractious child. "He almost sent you to your ancestors, and as yet we have not discovered why. Or who. Do you want him to try again as soon as you're on your feet?"

Jahangir grumbled something inaudible under his breath.

"Louder." Ogodai poked the reluctant bey gently in the shoulder, above the bandage.

"I couldn't see anything. It was dark."

"Yes." Ogodai maintained the same patient rhythm. "Very dark. Otherwise we would have caught the man that night. Or woman, I suppose. I was out the door right away, stumbling over you. But you must have gathered some sense of him or her. The knife went into your chest, not your back. Tall, short, bulky, powerful?"

Jahangir opened one eye, then the other. "Tell us, brother, please," Firuza said. "We want to stop this person before he strikes again. Or she."

The bey hesitated once more. His creased brow slowly relaxed, lessening his resemblance to an ancient. Firuza had the impression that he was sifting his memories. Or perhaps persuading himself of the need to cooperate. She waited, careful to say and do nothing that might distract him. Until the very moment when he spoke, she couldn't predict whether he would confide in them.

"Not a woman," he said at last. "The height was right for a woman, but the arm that drove the knife, no. I grabbed it, trying to divert the blow. Those were the muscles of a warrior. A man. A woman could match the speed and the accuracy, but not the force."

"A man." Ogodai rubbed his chin. "Well, we guessed that much. You can tell us nothing else?"

Jahangir closed his eyes once more. Ogodai forced himself into stillness, silence. Firuza, beside him, sat rigidly straight, as if the strain of dealing with her recalcitrant brother would become too much to bear if she relaxed for a moment. He caressed her cheek with the back of his hand, and she shivered like a newborn lamb.

"The blade came from below," Jahangir said. The truculence had seeped from his voice, just as the unnatural energy of a few moments ago had drained away, leaving only fatigue.

From below. Not in a straight line, not from above. "Someone shorter than you?"

"Shorter, yes," Jahangir said. His right hand touched his shoulder, as if indicating a possible height. Even if he couldn't see clearly, he must have received some impression of the presence in the dark.

"Not Almas, then." Ogodai ran a rapid mental check of the ten potential suspects. Almas was the tallest and thinnest. Several stood around the same height as Jahangir. About the same number ranged in height between him and Almas. Only two or three were shorter. Which improved their odds of catching the suspect quite a bit.

"No," Jahangir confirmed. "Stockier than he. More muscular."

From where Ogodai knelt in the jouncing cart, Firuza sat between him and her brother. He saw her open her mouth, then shut it again, a thoughtful expression on her face. He wondered what she had meant to say, which question she might have asked, and what she considered important to keep from Jahangir. Whether she would confide in him, Ogodai, when he had her alone. As she had confided her vision of her people's future. Her faith in him touched him.

"Ten men can't confirm their presence among the others." Ogodai drew the words out, trying to recall exactly what Rafik had said and phrase it in the way best designed to keep Jahangir responsive. "We've had warriors monitoring them. The one that best fits your description is Zamam, the man who rides with an eagle."

Firuza gasped. Jahangir frowned. "Zamam," he said slowly. "Perhaps. He fits the description, as you say. But he wouldn't attack me. We both support Tulpar Sultan." There, it was out. A flat declaration of an allegiance previously only suspected.

Zamam has reason to attack me, if Tulpar ordered it. Ogodai fought the queasiness thoughts of his brother's treachery evoked. He saw no reason to share that thought with Jahangir. Better to push the bey to reconsider, if possible.

"Tulpar wants Roxelana, you know." Ogodai forced himself to say it lightly, as if the statement had no importance. "If he becomes khan, he can take her from you. Are you so sure he has no reason to want you out of the way?"

Jahangir grunted, then fell silent. His eyes closed once more, his brief flash of energy extinguished.

Ogodai wrestled with his conscience. He hated to leave Firuza alone, especially injured as she was. Yet it would be irresponsible of him not to share what he had learned with Rafik and his father, his staunchest supporters among the horde.

"I must pass on to the elders what your brother has said," he told Firuza. "We have to move against Zamam before he realizes we suspect him. But if you need my help, I'll do what I can before I go." He indicated the bey with one hand.

Her face tightened, and she looked sideways, at the floor. "I'm sorry," he said. "I'll return as soon as I can."

"It's all right." She turned her eyes toward him as she spoke. From her expression, obviously it was far from all right, but he could see that she had decided not to argue. "I need only pour some drops into a bowl, then watch him as he sleeps. But if you raise his shoulders while I dose him, so that he doesn't choke, that will help."

"Of course. Where are the drops?"

She pointed to the small basket that held cloths and medicines. "There. A stoppered vial made of white jade."

He rooted through the basket, found the vial, and handed it to her, together with a small cup. With Diliara gone, the bey's right side was free. Ogodai moved behind Jahangir and, avoiding the bandages, raised him to a half-sitting position.

Across from them, Firuza unstoppered the vial and dripped a milky liquid into the cup. Even frowning with concentration, she was lovely.

Ogodai sighed. He wanted to stay with her. They had so little time together, and here a whole day lay before them. And while he was with her, he needn't fear for her safety.

Yet his duty was clear. A potential khan couldn't sit and gaze at his future wife while danger threatened. He must do what he could to defend her—and the horde.

Firuza stilled the trembling in her hands. The vial of poppy juice came from Roxelana, who had obtained it from a traveling peddler by means better left unexplored. In handing it over unasked, Roxelana had shown a magnanimity rare for her. Perhaps the concubine did care for Jahangir after all.

The potion required careful measurement, or Firuza would send her brother not into restorative sleep but into a rest far more permanent. Any such recurrence of her father's death—and at her hands—was unthinkable. Yet it was hard to concentrate while her emotions roiled like clouds in a storm-laden sky. Joy—Ogodai had *listened* to her, taken her suggestions seriously. Fear—if Zamam did prove to be the attacker, then his natural target was Ogodai, surely? She had almost blurted out the identification, before recalling that her brother would reject the idea if it came from a woman. And in the end, her silence hadn't mattered, because Jahangir supplied the name himself. Anger—how dared these hidden strivers undermine her happiness?

And although it seemed trivial by comparison, Ogodai's departure ended her hopes of their spending an entire day together for the first time.

A thought so wrong she hesitated to admit it, even to herself. Her future husband was a leader, and a conscientious one—not a pleasure seeker like Jahangir. He wouldn't fail to do his duty because he preferred to spend time with his betrothed. She respected him for that. How could she resent him for being competent and responsible?

Firuza glanced at the cup. The amount seemed right. She added honey to hide the bitter taste and water to make it less viscous. Inching forward on her knees, she positioned herself across from Ogodai, who steadied Jahangir against the rocking of the wagon.

Her brother swallowed the potion and grimaced. More honey next time.

Jahangir's head was already lolling. Ogodai lowered him gently back to the bed of felt and furs.

Firuza knelt, hands clasped in her lap, her teeth touching the tip of her tongue to keep from pleading with her betrothed to stay. She would soon be a khatun. She must act like a queen, not a seductive concubine desperate for the khan's attention.

Ogodai stepped over her brother's legs and knelt at her side. His lips traced a path from the corner of her mouth to the lobe of her ear. She inhaled his unique combination of soap and sandalwood, tea and fresh air—the scent of rain, although it wasn't raining. Then, with one last endearment, he passed through the door.

She heard him speak to the guards outside, ordering them to maintain their posts with extra vigilance. Heard their firm response. Boots hit the ground running, although the wagon never slowed. She guessed that Ogodai had jumped: not an extraordinary feat for a young man in fighting trim, since the oxen couldn't plod faster than the drivers who walked alongside them or the slaves who steadied the cart from behind.

He was gone. Firuza sat alone with her sleeping brother. And with the treachery rife among the horde, she had to wonder when—or if—she would see Ogodai again.

Chapter 16

Kazan, 6 Rabi al-Thani 941 A.H./15 October 1534

AFTER TWO DAYS OF PAIN AND FEVER, JAN-ALI RECOVERED. Even before he rallied, the investigation into the attempt on his life had begun. The palace hummed with rumors like a forest filled with bees. At the khan's request, the members of the Russian delegation assisted in gathering information. Nasan found it sad that her uncle placed more trust in his Russian backers than in his own court—even his chief wife—but she understood his reservations. She had her own reasons to doubt the reliability of Gulnara, Gazim, and Aslanbika.

As a result, those on the ambassadorial staff most fluent in Tatar fanned out throughout the palace. Daniil made use of his rudimentary grasp of the language in questioning the one or two servants who had spent the most time with the Crimean delegation. Nasan monitored those interviews from behind a handy screen. Once it became clear that her husband didn't need her help to follow the conversations, she left him to his own devices and focused on the harem.

Just as loss of sight sharpens hearing, the confinement of the palace women heightened their sensitivity to the world outside their grilled windows and paneled doors. Gossip flew about the blue-tiled rooms like doves fluttering from perch to perch. Which fragments were true? Which grew like tangled weeds from fantasy, desire, or dreams? Nasan took note of every tale that passed her ears, no matter how absurd. Queen Gulnara had summoned the envoys. No, Gazim Shirin, seeing an opportunity to advance the power of his clan, had forestalled the queen even as he pretended to represent her interests. The spider bite had been an accident. No, the *spider* had traveled to Kazan by chance, but the boy had tossed it at the khan in self-defense. No, the Crimeans had intended from the beginning to assassinate Jan-Ali. No, Gazim and Gulnara had seen in the Crimean delegation an opportunity to rid themselves of a khan they no longer wanted and had persuaded—no, manipulated—the Crimean envoys (or just the boy) to perform the evil deed on their behalf.

There was no making sense of it, Nasan concluded at the end of three exhausting days. She had heard every possibility thrown out and discussed, including some too bizarre to merit more than fleeting consideration (Jan-Ali had kept the spider in reserve to threaten the boy, only to suffer the black widow's bite himself, the result of divine chastisement for his illicit lust?). Unless Daniil returned from his latest ambassadorial session with some information worth pursuing, the investigation, it seemed, had reached a dead end. Not too few clues but too many veiled the truth.

After another fruitless morning of listening to harem chatter, Nasan could no longer contain her exasperation at her lack of progress and fled for the stables. She wished she could order Sorkhokhtani saddled and bridled, to ride off her frustration in the open field, but awareness that her situation had changed deterred her. No longer the wild girl of Kasimov, Nasan had to protect her husband's honor as well as her own, and hauling Daniil's men away from their work to escort her would win neither of them any points with the Russian ambassador—or her uncle the khan, for that matter. Jan-Ali became ever more desperate for answers as one fruitless day passed into the next. Aslanbika, to her credit, had spent most of the intervening time with her husband, but her show of devotion made it even less acceptable for Nasan to burst in and beg her to go riding.

Perhaps she could talk Daniil into accompanying her later. The elaborate protocol that governed court life irritated him, too. Until then, she planned to murmur in her horse's ears the many things she couldn't say out loud to anyone but her husband. Sorkhokhtani always listened, her brown eyes warm with sympathy, her head cocked to one side as if she understood how it felt to live confined in a box constructed from others' expectations, forced to pretend to be someone one was not.

On this day, however, Nasan didn't get so far as confiding in her mare. As she approached the main doors leading out of the harem, a hissing whisper caught her ear. She slid behind the nearest pillar, holding her breath as she tried to identify the source of the sound. Was someone calling her name?

She saw no one in the courtyard. The mornings had become frosty, the sun slow to rise and eager to set, although here in the early afternoon bright days permitted pleasant walks and even the occasional garden excursion. Today, though, the sky glowered with impending rain, and a distinct chill chapped her cheeks. Not a day for casual lounging around the fountain.

Or for riding. A point she should have considered before.

The sound came from a grilled window to her right. In Kasimov, she would have known from the placement of the opening whose rooms lay beyond, but the Kazan harem was much larger and its layout less familiar to her.

The pillar wouldn't conceal her if she moved to stand in front of the window. Anyone who entered the courtyard would see her eavesdropping, and the way rumors spread in this place, the person behind the grille would have a full report before Nasan had time to invent a reason for her presence there.

Then she noticed a clay planter, a vase big enough to hold a thousand djinn—never mind one relatively small young woman. Nasan recalled a child she had rescued from such a container back in Kasimov. That one had stood upright, waiting to receive its plants for the season; this one lay on its side, its soil and greenery already removed for the winter.

Easy in, easy out. Before anyone could enter the courtyard and wonder what she was doing, Nasan ran to the planter and crawled inside. Peering around the opening, she was pleased to see the grilled window right above her head. She had made almost no sound. The voice beyond the grille went on unchecked. She pulled her head inside and prepared to listen.

After a short while, she identified the voice as Queen Gulnara's. Despite her skill at subterfuge, the queen seemed not to have entertained the possibility of being overheard from the direction of the window. Finally, something was going Nasan's way.

"You bungled it," Gulnara said. "A spider! What fools were these? The envoys had no need to kill the khan. After they deposed him, they could have done with him as they willed. Instead, they have put him on the alert—and the Russians, too."

"The boy panicked." A man responded—Gazim Shirin, matching the level of his voice to the queen's. "The envoys told him to leave the box in the room. Jan-Ali would have discovered it long after they left, if their luck held. Instead, the boy shoved the box at the khan as if urging him to take it. As soon as he opened it, the spider jumped out."

"You need to choose your servants better."

"Yes, my queen." Gazim—soothing, placating. Nasan imagined him bowing, rubbing his hands in that irritating way he had. Nor had his story matched the boy's, but she assumed Gazim was lying to protect himself. "But the boy succeeded in overcoming the khan's defenses. No other member of the delegation could have entered that room without a guard."

Someone grunted. Gulnara, presumably. "At the cost of arousing Jan-Ali's suspicions," she said. "And the Russians'. Alexander Makhmetovich, that traitor to the Tatar cause, has his men trailing our people like so many hunting dogs. And that little bitch from Kasimov has spent the last three days quizzing every woman in the harem—although they've sent her in so many directions, her head must be spinning by now. I told them to mix her up, and they have outdone themselves. I never heard so many ridiculous stories in my life. Meanwhile, Aslanbika, the silly girl, has been peppering me with questions, as if a new husband were not the best present I could give her."

Little bitch from Kasimov? How dare she!

Gulnara had ordered the harem to lie. Infuriating. She'd nearly gotten away with it, too, which was embarrassing as well as infuriating. Nasan had guessed something was wrong, but she hadn't come close to figuring out what. She bit her tongue to keep from swearing and gripped the edges of her sleeves until the knuckles of both hands showed white.

Keep quiet and listen, she told herself. Discovery now would be fatal.

At least she could stop worrying about Aslanbika's loyalty. The khatun, from the sounds of it, was as much in the dark as Nasan.

Gazim Shirin murmured agreement. Nasan listened, but soon the voices above her head faded, then ceased. With great caution, she edged forward enough to peer past the rim of the planter.

The courtyard remained deserted. No one watched from the windows nearby. She waited, barely breathing. Nothing. They must have left the room.

A clatter of pots sounded on the far side of the courtyard. Servants, heading this way. Nasan scrambled out of the planter, shook the hem of her robes to remove any lingering dirt, and left the harem, determined to find Daniil as soon as possible.

Tracking her husband proved more difficult than Nasan had expected, but at last he returned to their quarters to change. It wasn't long before sunset prayers, and he was grumbling about being required to attend yet another state dinner. Nasan dismissed the servants with a clap of her hands as soon as they had poured warm water for him and laid out his court robes. "I will assist my lord," she told them, ignoring Daniil's grin at her lofty tone.

"Yes, Khanim." They backed from the room. As soon as the door closed, Nasan, murmuring in Russian, told Daniil what she'd overheard that afternoon.

"We must share this news with your uncle," he said at once. "Conspiracies within his court are his problem to solve. We have no jurisdiction here."

"So long as he is well enough to order the arrest of Gazim and Gulnara," she said. "Or whatever he decides to do. We mustn't tip our hand before he has the capacity to act on what he hears from us."

"I understand he feels much better today." Daniil rubbed her temple with his thumb. "Don't look so worried, wife of mine. Your uncle is sitting up. He ate fruit and cheese this morning. He will recover."

"I'll be glad when this is over and we can leave," Nasan told him. "I wanted so much to come home, but this is not home. Plots, betrayal, conspiracies—I hate it. Moscow is better than this."

"I agree," Daniil said. "We will leave soon, I think. As envoys, there is little we can do to protect the khan. We must report to the grand princess and let her decide how to handle the threat from Crimea. Sahib-Girei will not stop with Kazan."

Nasan sighed. So she had guessed. More wars, more raids, more attacks.

Daniil squeezed her hand, then placed it on his arm. "Let's go and talk to the khan. With luck, what we learn will hasten our departure."

They found Jan-Ali sitting on the long divan in his room, swathed in blankets and Aslanbika at his side. When Nasan and Daniil arrived, the khan and his wife were engaged in a game of chess. From Jan-Ali's gleeful expression and the relative numbers of pieces on his side and Aslanbika's, Nasan deduced that her uncle was winning. It seemed odd, yet pleasing, to see them interacting like any couple, talking and laughing. A *dombra* lay to one side. The two-stringed instrument of the steppe—the sight of it brought back, with a fierce nostalgia that made Nasan's eyes sting, the nomadic camp of her childhood.

"Do you play, Auntie?" She pointed at the *dombra*. "I haven't heard one of those since I left for Kasimov."

"Not I," Aslanbika said. "My maid was playing it, but we sent her away. Greetings, Daniil Nikolaevich."

Daniil bowed, hand over heart as the nomads did. "Greetings, Khatun. Greetings, Khan."

Nasan greeted Jan-Ali, then Aslanbika, with a sniff to the cheek. "My husband said you felt better, Uncle. I'm pleased to see that you've recovered even faster than we hoped."

"My wife has proven herself a capable nurse," Jan-Ali said. "And a devoted one. She has scarce left my side."

Nasan's eyes met Daniil's in an unspoken question. She hadn't anticipated Aslanbika's presence, still less the khatun's apparent bond with her husband. Could they share their news? It seemed clear that Gulnara had plotted to assassinate Jan-Ali without assistance from his wife, yet Nasan hadn't forgotten the light in Aslanbika's eyes when she spoke of marriage to Safa-Girei of Crimea.

Daniil answered her unspoken question by accepting the khan's waved invitation to join them. Daniil's court robe, amber velvet with a russet sash, parted as he sat, revealing leather riding trousers and boots. He leaned forward, his face intent and his chin supported on one hand. Nasan settled into place beside him, arranging herself at an angle so that she could watch both her uncle and her aunt.

They stared back—curious but not, so far as she could tell, fearful of what they might hear. That spoke well for their innocence.

"We have information for you," Daniil said. He told them in brief what Nasan had overheard, although not how she had learned it.

"Clearly, Gazim and Gulnara are guilty of something," he finished. "Although the queen appears not to have endorsed the attempt on your life. And your own queen—forgive me, Khatun—had no involvement whatsoever in their scheme."

Aslanbika's dark eyes flashed. "You suspected me? Even you, Nasan? I thought we were friends!"

"I, too, thought that, Auntie," Nasan said. "But your name came up as a potential enemy before I'd spent more than a few hours with you. I wanted to believe you innocent, but I couldn't take it on faith."

"I suppose not," Aslanbika said quietly.

Had she really understood the dilemma Nasan faced? Perhaps their fragile friendship had died stillborn. That would be sad.

Jan-Ali patted his wife's knee. "My wife has sworn fealty to me. I accept her word."

A lukewarm endorsement, to Nasan's ears, but Aslanbika clasped his hand and lowered her eyes. "My own dear husband," she murmured.

Nasan bit her tongue, unwilling to interfere as her aunt and uncle felt their way to a better relationship. She hoped that the information overheard from Gulnara would lessen Jan-Ali's suspicions of his wife and turn today's camaraderie into a regular, not an occasional, event. But unless Jan-Ali's brush with death had changed him fundamentally, it seemed unlikely her uncle would strive to provide sons now when he had not before. And whether he did or not, Safa-Girei would continue to wait and plot.

"You have done well," Jan-Ali said. "We must attack the vipers in our midst before they can slither from sight. Niece, order my guards to bring Queen Gulnara and Gazim Shirin here for questioning. And you, Daniil Nikolaevich, fetch the Russian ambassador."

Daniil returned with Alexander Makhmetovich before the guards arrived with their prisoners. Nasan and Aslanbika retired to a window seat, leaving the three men in command of the room.

They made an odd trio, Nasan concluded. Despite his Russian dress and the cross that hung around his neck, Alexander Makhmetovich looked like an older version of Jan-Ali—slender and of medium height, with a close-trimmed beard as black as his hair. The khan's features were more delicate, the ambassador's mouth and chin more forceful, but otherwise they could be brothers, ten years or so apart in age. Daniil—tawny, broad-shouldered, a head or more taller— stood in sharp contrast to the pair of Tatars.

The men exchanged courtesies. Nasan, murmuring to Aslanbika, kept an ear directed at their conversation. From the sounds of it, Daniil had already shared their news with Alexander Makhmetovich. She tensed each time he glanced at them, but he didn't suggest they leave the room. Good. She had no intention of going and felt reasonably certain that Aslanbika would refuse as well, but it made life easier if no one asked.

The clank of steel and the tromp of leather on tile signaled the guards' approach. The door opened, and Gulnara strode through, a half-dozen soldiers tramping in her wake—not daring to touch her yet dogged in their determination not to lose track of her. She stopped an arm's length from the khan, let her long skirts fall, and shook the floor-length veil back from her face. "What is the meaning of this outrage, Khan?" She ignored Alexander Makhmetovich and Daniil altogether but spared a glare for Aslanbika and Nasan.

Another half-dozen soldiers entered, Gazim Shirin in their midst. Clearly he didn't intimidate them as much as the queen did. Nasan saw signs of manhandling in his mussed hair and misaligned robes, usually so neat. Even now, a guardsman restrained Gazim with a hand above his elbow. At the sight of Jan-Ali's implacable face, Gazim bowed low, hands extended in a pleading gesture, cupped with the palms up. He didn't speak.

"The outrage is not mine but yours," Jan-Ali said. "You have betrayed my trust, both of you, by negotiating with the Crimean envoys to bring about my death."

He had decided to make no distinction, then. Interesting. Nasan sat on her hands, as if doing so could keep her from speaking. It wouldn't do, here, to push herself forward. With any luck, her name wouldn't even come up. But "that little bitch from Kasimov" would have the last word.

"I did no such thing!" Gulnara pointed at the cringing Gazim. "I suggest you look to that one. I already questioned him on your behalf, Khan, after the lord of your chamber came to me with a strange story."

"And I told you I had nothing to do with it," Shirin yelled.

Jan-Ali made a chopping motion with his hand. "The envoys came up with the plan themselves," Shirin added in a more normal speaking voice.

"So he told me," Gulnara said. "But how does he know what the envoys decided? I say they involved him, and he seeks to rid himself of blame."

Some ally, ready to sacrifice her henchman to save herself.

Aslanbika touched her hand, and they exchanged glances. "Will it work?" Nasan mouthed. Aslanbika shrugged.

Gazim raised his head as Gulnara reached the end of her speech. "So that's the way of it, my queen? I slave for you, carry messages for you, talk on your behalf with the men from the south—only so you can wash your hands of me if need arises? Don't listen to her, Khan. She's been working against you since the day the Russians sent you here. Would I take it on myself to negotiate such a scheme?"

"For the sake of your clan, Gazim Shirin, I believe you capable of any effrontery," the khan said.

Gulnara, fingers extended like talons, surged toward him. A guard extended his long spear between them, and she pulled back. But her foot tapped the elegant black and white tiles of the floor, and her crossed arms spoke of anger barely contained.

"Enough," Jan-Ali said. "You condemn yourselves out of your own mouths. I favored you, relied on you, and you thought nothing of betraying Kazan to its enemies." He gestured to the guards surrounding Gazim. "Take that one and behead him in the courtyard. Immediately. Summon the troops and the servants to watch. Let everyone see that I will not tolerate traitors."

Gazim flung himself face down on the floor, pleading, his arms outstretched, but Jan-Ali turned his head away and gestured for his removal. The guards wasted no time in dragging Gazim from the room.

Nasan, watching Gazim hauled away, shuddered. To fall so far so fast, to die without honor—these things she couldn't wish on anyone.

Gulnara and her escort remained. The queen regarded Jan-Ali with hauteur, but Nasan detected a trembling in the royal hands. Gulnara must wonder how long *she* had to live.

"Remove her," the khan told the guards. "No longer will she see the light of my bright eyes. Imprison her in the harem and let just one trusted servant in to feed her and care for her."

The guards bowed and departed, an unhappy Gulnara in their midst, her protests unheeded.

Nasan released her clasped hands. Her shoulders felt lighter, her breath came more evenly. "A fitting punishment," she said quietly to Aslanbika. "For a moment there, I thought my uncle would order her executed, too. That he considered them equally guilty."

"I suspect they *are* equally guilty," Aslanbika replied. "Whatever Gulnara says. But to order the public execution of a queen is a serious matter. Better to immure her and permit death to find her in its own way at its own time."

Or at the convenience of the khan, Nasan added in her mind. Gazing at her uncle, effervescent as he accepted the congratulations of the Russian ambassador and Daniil, she couldn't avoid the suspicion that she had witnessed no more than round one in an ongoing game.

But for the moment, her uncle had won—and because of information she had provided to him. Russia's interests in Kazan were secure, and the grand princess in Moscow would reward her envoys instead of punishing them.

A piercing wail sounded from the courtyard below, followed by the swish of a sword through the air and a loud collective sigh. Nasan, with Daniil on her left and Aslanbika on her right, ran to the window and peered through the iron grille.

A headless body, wearing Gazim's robes, lay next to a pool of blood. More blood dripped from the sword raised in the executioner's right hand. Gazim's face, distorted in death, hung by its hair as the man exhibited it to the crowd. "Thus are traitors punished," he called, over and over again.

It was justice. A fitting end to one who had dared to attack a ruling khan.

Chapter 17

WITH OGODAI GONE AND HER BROTHER SEDATED, FIRUZA had little to keep her occupied. She stoppered the vial and considered what to do with it. Her foot throbbed. The effort of returning the vial to the basket seemed excessive when she would have to retrieve it later, so she propped it against Jahangir's pallet and secured it with a bolster.

A book and writing materials lay nearby. Firuza looked at the book, but Diliara had selected it for Jahangir. A mirror for princes, designed to bring her brother to a proper sense of his responsibilities—a quest unlikely to succeed at the best of times, in Firuza's opinion, and entirely a lost cause with him so ill.

If boredom made her desperate, she might take a look at it. Even a dull book was better than nothing. But the sight of paper and pen had sparked an idea. She had prepared no gift for Ogodai's birthday yesterday. Why not write him a poem?

A blissful hour followed as she considered and rejected various combinations of words. What image did she want? Spring, sunshine, flowers, bees? The steppe?

At last she decided on five lines and scribbled them down. Not much, but they would do for a beginning. From the look of things, she would have plenty of time to work on them.

She replaced the pen in its leather bag, checked the ink pot to prevent spills, and left the paper on the rug to dry.

What next? She picked up the book and tried to decipher the words, but the looping script crawled across the pages like a drunken snail, blurring before her tired eyes. Last night with her husband-to-be had been delightful but not restful. Lulled by the trundling wagon, Firuza curled up at the end of the pallet and let her drooping lids close.

A sound woke her. She rolled into a sitting position, uncertain of what she'd heard. Felt covered the smoke hole in a vain attempt to contain heat within the rolling tent, and the lantern in the corner had burned out. When she turned to check, a smooth hump—not unlike a small hill glimpsed faraway on the horizon—showed her brother still snug in the arms of the poppy potion.

Had the sound come from him? Surely not.

A thud, a gurgle. The tent door swung open, and a man strode in. With the light at his back, she saw only a dark outline with glittering jewelry at neck and arms, a gleam of weaponry at his side.

Startled, Firuza sprang upright, arms spread wide to protect her brother. Pain shot through her injured foot, and she collapsed with a cry. Tears she couldn't control soaked the high collar of her jacket. She clutched her bandaged arch, fighting nausea and faintness. When the intruder knelt beside her, she couldn't muster the strength even to push him away.

"Why, my sweet, what happened to you? Did my brother mistreat you?"

The voice, the reference to his brother. Her muddled thoughts supplied a name: Tulpar. Gradually her vision cleared, and the light from the open door revealed his face. She shook her head. He was jealous—possessive, rather—but how could he imagine for a moment that Ogodai would mistreat her?

He reached across her, scooped up the paper, and scanned it. "Swans swim alone," he said. "How touching." His snide tone left her in no doubt of his true feelings.

Firuza felt her cheeks flame. "Leave that alone!" How dare he read a private message, then mock her for writing it? She tugged at the paper, but he hung on. The paper ripped. She glanced at it, saw that her poem had survived intact, and threw it as far from Tulpar as she could.

"Temper, temper, my sweet. A fiery piece, aren't you? In need of a man's direction. Well, never mind. I'm up to the task."

"Task? Me? You arrogant oaf!"

"Save the protests, my dear. You're coming with me." Tulpar reached out to caress her throat with one hand.

"No!" She jerked her head away—or tried to. His hand tightened on her neck, and his thumb pressing into her chin made speech impossible.

"Yes," he said. "My annoying younger brother has secured the council's support; and the Argyns, damn them, stick to him like burrs to a saddle. I have no chance to get close to him, but if I 'borrow' you, he will have to respond. Maybe I'll bargain. Maybe I'll keep you. You're quite appealing, even when you're spitting at me."

His fingers pressed harder against her throat. Firuza tugged at his hand, but he responded by tightening his grip. Spots flashed before her eyes; breathing demanded her full attention.

He had accused Ogodai, but he was the one mistreating her. Throttling her. Planning to kidnap her. He thought he could use her to wangle his way back into the council's good graces. Or did he plan to kill Ogodai and ensure his own succession that way?

Probably. Why else would he want to get past the Argyns? Fear shot through her, sharper even than the pain from her injured foot. She could lose her betrothed as she had lost her father, be forced to wed this wicked man who had killed them both.

Well, she wouldn't stand for it. She was not Roxelana, not one of his pampered beauties from Crimea. She was Bahadur's daughter.

Firuza thrashed in Tulpar's hold as she fought for air. With her good foot, she braced herself against the floor, giving her a small but secure base of support. Even so, she almost blacked out before she managed to snatch the eating knife from her belt and slash at his wrist.

His fingers fell from her throat, and she propelled herself toward the door as fast as she could, shouting, "Help me!"

Where were the guards? Her voice sounded husky, strange—and far too quiet, no more than a whisper. Perhaps they didn't hear her, for no help appeared. Instead, Tulpar came after her. She continued her scramble, refusing to whimper even though pain turned her foot into a bed of embers and sent flaming tendrils up her leg.

If she could run… Too late. She was still a mat's length from the door when he grabbed her once more and backhanded her across the face. "Hussy!"

A sob escaped her as her head hit the floor. He wrenched the knife from her hand, and she heard it spin across the carpet, thwack against the wooden frame.

She twisted toward the sound, only to discover that the knife lay far beyond her reach. Tulpar hauled her across the tent, wrenching her upper arm until she felt certain he would pull it from its socket. Her thigh hit the pallet holding Jahangir, and her brother moaned.

Tulpar plucked the vial from the floor. "What's this?" He flicked the stopper off with one thumb and sniffed. "Poppy juice. How convenient."

Firuza writhed in his grip to no avail. Tulpar wrapped his arm more tightly around her shoulders and tipped a healthy dose of the opium down her throat.

She spat in his face. He laughed. "Not so high-and-mighty now, are you, my khatun?"

Not his wife. Ogodai's. She wanted to tell him that—again—but her mouth didn't work. Her arms and legs no longer served her. The world became fuzzy, then faded.

The sun stood near its zenith by the time Ogodai finished his consultation with Rafik and his father, Kazbek. The perpetual wind of the grasslands hinted at the winter ferocity to come, but here at the height of the day a warrior could ignore its bite. The lowing and baaing drowned out the whistling breeze. Everywhere Ogodai looked, sheep and goats, cattle and horses shoved and strolled. Jogging camels maintained a rough barrier on either side. His horse and those of his two companions kept pace with the camels, but at a respectful distance outside their line. Camels had nasty tempers, especially when crowded by horses.

"We should interrogate Zamam right away," he said.

"Tonight." Kazbek stared straight ahead, his brow furrowed as he monitored the straggling herds. "When we stop."

"Suppose he makes a run for it?" Ogodai clenched his hand on his sword hilt. He wanted to shout in Kazbek's face, tell him he'd had enough of old men urging restraint, but he wasn't khan yet, despite last night's triumph.

Kazbek's horse shook its mane in time with its rider's head. "We're late as it is. I think this journey is cursed. We can't afford further delays. Zamam will go nowhere without one of our men trailing him, and any attempt to escape will proclaim his guilt."

He was right. Although Ogodai itched to act, he understood that the horde needed to progress as far as possible toward its destination, still more than ten days distant.

"Very well," he said. He heard reluctance in his voice, but he could do little about that. "We'll wait. But as soon as the horde stops for the night, we move."

"Agreed," Rafik chimed in. Ogodai gave him a friendly buffet on the shoulder, nonverbal thanks for his support.

Kazbek regarded them both with the air of a stallion chivvied by a pair of restless colts. "Patience, you young hotheads. A few hours, and we'll have our answers." He aimed the point of his spear, decorated with black horse tails, at an eddy of white-fleeced animals up ahead. "Meanwhile, I don't like the look of that flock. Let's investigate before one of the sheep decides to make a break for it. They worry me more than Zamam."

It took a long time to settle the flock, to keep humans and animals moving in the right direction. As he dashed from one side of the roiling mass to the other, Ogodai glanced from time to time at the bey's tent trundling far in the rear. At least Firuza was safe. His men would guard her with their lives.

The riding and the camaraderie restored his spirits. By the time purple streaked with gold cast shadows rich as a khan's robe on the ice-tipped feather grass, he looked forward to checking on Firuza, then grabbing a bowl of stew and wringing some satisfactory answers out of Zamam. Sensing Rafik's horse nose to tail with his own, Ogodai urged his mount through a winding stream and turned the chestnut toward the spot where the servants were already hobbling horses and camels, penning sheep, placing stones behind the giant wheels of the tent-bearing carts, and preparing food.

He found Vafa, dispatched a pair of warriors to keep an eye on Zamam, and ordered the rest of his men to pitch his tent.

The ancestors had chosen to lure Ogodai away from his bride for yet another day on the trail, but he was determined to spend the night in her arms. The bey's cart would soon arrive, and he planned to meet it when it did and see for himself whether Firuza's foot required attention. She needed someone to take care of her, did Firuza, whether she recognized that or not.

Firuza's temples pounded in a throbbing rhythm that seemed familiar, although she couldn't identify it. Her cheek stung, and not only from the wind she felt snapping past her face. The back of her head ached. A ball of flame encased her right foot. An odd bitter taste filled her mouth, and fuzz covered her teeth. When she opened her eyes, pink and yellow spots danced against the flowing grass, making her dizzy.

She closed them again, but the dizziness remained. An image of brown cloth trousers ending in a leather boot, a stirrup crossing under and over the arch, appeared etched against her eyelids.

Horse, her mind said. *I am on a racing horse.*

Another part of her mind insisted that she couldn't ride, that she was in a tented cart looking after her brother, that the weight around her waist couldn't be an arm holding her on a galloping horse. Because who would hold her so close except Ogodai?

Those are hooves, the first voice said. *Feel the rhythm. We're moving fast.*

The powerful shoulders under Firuza's trousered legs bunched. Instincts bred during a lifetime on horseback warned her as the horse gathered itself to jump.

Hooves hit the ground with stunning force. Firuza gasped in pain as her much-abused body absorbed this new shock. Then darkness descended once more.

More than an hour passed before the bey's cart caught up with the settled horde. By then, Ogodai's men had his tent frame constructed and the door tied in place. Layers of felt obscured the latticework. The light had faded to the point where, outside the narrow circles cast by hearth fires and lanterns, the camp appeared to consist of no more than dim shapes, some shifting as people settled into their evening routines. Vafa split his time between supervising the boys he had decided to train as cooks and ensuring that the women tying straps to hold the tent coverings in place took their job seriously.

"In short, Vafa couldn't be happier." Ogodai told Rafik, who had joined him for dinner—not that dinner had yet had a chance to appear—so that they could discuss how best to approach a certain-to-be-taciturn Zamam.

"Unlike that youngster." Rafik pointed at one of the nearer circles of light, where Timur stood scuffing his booted toe against the grass, a troubled expression on his face. "What's bothering him, I wonder? He's usually a cheerful lad."

"Let's find out."

Ogodai called the boy's name. Timur had seldom shown his face except in his father's company since Tulpar's unexpected arrival weeks ago, and Ogodai accepted that the child owed his first allegiance to his father. But Timur did indeed look troubled. Ogodai liked the boy. It wouldn't hurt to ask if something worried him.

Timur started like a high-strung colt at the sound of his name. Ogodai beckoned to him. The child glanced over his shoulder, back at Ogodai and Rafik, over his shoulder again. Then, as if making up his mind to tackle a difficult task, Timur dashed from his own circle of light to theirs.

"Sultan," he said as he skidded to a stop before Ogodai.

"*Salaam aleikum*," Ogodai said. The formal greeting might calm the boy, focus him.

Timur gulped, then inclined his head and placed his right hand over his heart. "*Aleikum salaam*, Sultan, Rafik."

Good. Timur had learned basic courtesy. Ogodai surveyed the settling camp and decided that his own tent had progressed far enough toward completion that he could safely invite guests inside. With any luck, the servants had arranged carpets over the grassy floor and lit the hearth fire. "Come with me," he told Rafik and Timur. "We can talk in comfort."

Relative comfort, at least. No cushions yet, and only one carpet, but smoke did drift upward from the circle of stones in the center. Still, they needed only a place to sit, and they had that. Ogodai dismissed the servants with a wave of his hand and positioned himself north of the fire, facing the door. In response to his gesture of invitation, Rafik and Timur took seats to his left and right, respectively.

He considered and as quickly dismissed several possible openings. Timur was young—how young exactly, Ogodai had yet to determine, but six or thereabouts. Subtlety would confuse such a small child.

"Do you know why I called you in here, Timur?" He leaned forward to make himself less threatening, but Timur was staring at the floor and shaking his head.

"Yet you came," Rafik said.

The boy looked up. "He's a sultan."

"And your uncle." Ogodai patted the child's hand. "You needn't fear me. We noticed that you seemed unhappy. Can we help you?"

Timur flinched. "*Ata* has gone."

"Gone?" Rafik and Ogodai spoke in unison.

"Gone where?" Ogodai added. "When did he leave?"

Timur squirmed against the rug. Fear darkened his eyes.

Rafik stretched out an arm as if to grab the boy and shake him. Ogodai knocked the arm aside. He'd have liked to grab Timur himself, but a frightened child—or a frightened colt— would not respond well to rough treatment. Save that for Zamam.

Instead he forced himself to speak gently. "Tell us, Timur. I won't hurt you. Where did your *ata* go? And when?"

It took more cajoling and reassurance and even the appearance of Vafa with a piece of honey candy before Ogodai could persuade Timur to talk, but at last the child yielded. "I don't know where, Sultan. He rode away this afternoon with the bey's daughter, and when the guards challenged him, he said she was ill and he would take her to Lady Diliara. But he didn't come back."

A crushing load of shock mixed with guilt tumbled over Ogodai, beginning at his furred cap and descending to his booted feet. "Firuza? Tulpar?"

Timur bolted to his feet. Rafik, unrestrained this time, grabbed him and pulled him down again. "Not so fast, youngster. How did you see this? Why didn't you stay with the herds like you were supposed to?"

"The boys always ride off," Ogodai said. "You remember, Rafik. Few tasks, fresh horses, and a bundle of energy. Why wouldn't they ride back to check on the stragglers?"

He touched Timur's elbow. "You did well to tell us, Timur. And well to notice. But I need you to be braver still. Speaking the truth demands great courage. So answer me. Did your *ata* indeed take the bey's daughter to Lady Diliara?"

"I didn't see." Timur looked less wary. "Shirin Bey caught us and scolded us, then sent us back to the herds. But *Ana* was surprised when she heard *Ata* had left." He picked at a loose thread in the carpet fringe. "When he goes, he stays away for a long time."

"That makes you sad, I'm sure." His building anger made it ever more difficult to maintain the air of quiet interest most likely to produce results. Somehow, Ogodai managed. "Was it you who told your mother that your *ata* had left?"

Timur's face cleared. His mouth widened in a sticky grin, as if the question absolved him of guilt. "No. The driver. He's one of *Ata*'s men, and he came to collect *Ata*'s things."

"Tulpar's man was driving the cart?" Ogodai asked Rafik. "How did that happen?"

"I don't know, Sultan. We must find out. The boy will be safe here."

"Or with his mother." Ogodai reached for Timur's wrist, avoiding the sticky fingers, and clasped it lightly. "Go home, and stay there until morning. If you remember anything more, ask your *ana* to send for me, and I will visit you."

The child's face crinkled once more. "But *Ata*?"

What worried him? That his father would be angry if he knew Timur had talked to Ogodai? That his father might never return?

"You did the right thing," Ogodai said. "No one will harm you—or your father."

Except Ogodai himself. He'd tear his brother limb from limb if Tulpar had hurt Firuza.

A thought that would terrify Timur if spoken aloud. Ogodai walked his nephew to the door and summoned Vafa. "Make sure he gets home," he told the servant. "Good night, Timur. Don't worry."

The child left. Freed of the need to exercise self-restraint, Ogodai returned to the fire, muttering every insult he knew in every one of his five languages.

Eventually he noticed Rafik, waiting, an appreciative grin on his face. "I wish I had a tenth your fluency, Sultan."

"He's driven me to the breaking point." Ogodai resumed his seat. He assumed he had no need to identify Tulpar.

"That's been his goal since he arrived," Rafik said.

"Yes. Well, he succeeded." Ogodai caressed the hilt of his sword. "Let's start with the bey's tent. I left four guards there. What happened to them? There were slaves steadying the wagon, as well as the driver. Did Tulpar replace them all?"

"And the bey? What of him?"

Ogodai winced. "He was drugged—and too weak to move even if the poppy syrup wore off. He also favors Tulpar. Although I sowed a few seeds of dissension there, they haven't had time to sprout. He may have given Tulpar his blessing."

"And what of Zamam?"

"Have him brought here under guard. I doubt he connived at my wife's abduction, but he seems to have attacked the bey, and he used to serve Tulpar, you said. So he may know where we should look for my lady. We'll check the wagon, return here, and beat the truth out of him if necessary." Ogodai kicked the fringe, sticky from Timur's handling, to show he meant business.

"Beat him?" Rafik sounded approving but skeptical. Had Tulpar convinced *everyone* that Ogodai lacked the guts to be khan?

"If we have to." He stood. The need to find Diliara, to *move*, consumed him. "We'll try other forms of persuasion first. We have enough trouble on our hands without him lying to protect himself from pain."

He thought of Firuza as he had left her this morning: beautiful, injured, vulnerable. She'd counted on him to protect her, and he'd failed.

Tulpar must have killed the warriors charged with guarding her. But where had he taken her? Ogodai's hand tightened on his sword hilt. If Zamam knew, he would rue the day he underestimated his khan-to-be.

"On second thoughts," he told Rafik. "You start on Zamam. I'll talk to Diliara and check the tent. It shouldn't take long. Vafa will bring you something to eat. Don't share it with our 'guest.' I'll be back to give you a hand before you know it."

Rafik had risen to his feet when Ogodai did. He placed his right hand over his heart as Timur had done. "Yes, Khan." Ogodai left to seek out Diliara, his anxiety lightened by that clear declaration of support.

Perhaps Timur had misunderstood what he saw. The boy was so young. Surely Firuza had spent the afternoon with her stepmother after all.

She hadn't. Ogodai's first exchange with Diliara confirmed his worst fears.

"Sultan!" she greeted him when he ran her to earth in the women's tent. "The grandmothers have sent you at just the right time. I am about to go and see to our darlings. The bey's tent has arrived."

She wore a heavy coat over her elaborate robes and a fur hat in place of her usual headscarf. A girl trailed her, also dressed for the outdoors and carrying a covered basket. He assumed it contained medicines and bandages.

"Then you haven't heard? One of the boys saw Tulpar ride off with Firuza. He said he was bringing her to you."

Diliara wailed like a tigress robbed of its cub. "He did not! What has he done with her? Where has he taken her?" Before he could answer, the tigress turned on him. "I left her with you. You promised to protect her! How could you leave her unguarded?"

He had not. In fact, he had doubled the guard. But he hadn't stayed on the cart himself. Diliara's anger shamed him.

"We must check on the bey," he said. "Find the guards and question them—if they live. I assure you, I will retrieve your daughter for you. For us both." She acknowledged this with a curt nod.

A shriek interrupted them. Roxelana ran toward them in a swirl of gauzy draperies and scent. "What are you saying?" she cried. "Tulpar wouldn't take that puling thing and leave me behind! What has *she* to offer a man?"

"More than you can imagine," Ogodai retorted. Her callous disregard for his betrothed's safety made him furious. "But don't think I will give him time to find out."

Roxelana stamped her foot and hissed a phrase in Persian. He stared her down until she stomped away, muttering insults pitched loud enough to ensure that he heard them.

Diliara had dropped to the floor, just inside the door, and wrapped her arms around her head, sobbing, "My darling, my baby girl, where is she?" The maid knelt beside her, patting her mistress on the shoulder.

"I will find her," Ogodai repeated. "I will bring her back."

He left then, weighed down by his sense of having failed Firuza. He should have predicted Tulpar's attack, not clung—like an idiot, like a child—to the belief that his older brother wouldn't fall so far as to steal Ogodai's bride.

Well, he had learned that lesson. What remained was to protect his wife-to-be from the consequences of his own shortsightedness. He signaled to the warriors bearing torches, and one pair fell into place ahead of him. Next stop, the bey's tent.

Signs of trouble struck his eye as soon as he drew close. The bey's spirit banner lay sideways under the tent frame, when it should fly strong and free in the hands of a sentry.

He saw no guards, no driver, no slaves. Someone had unhitched the horses. Otherwise, the cart appeared deserted, although it had traveled throughout the day in the wake of the herds. A stain marked the planks to the left of the door, where a warrior would stand to forbid entrance, of the right size, shape, and (possibly) color to indicate a pool of blood.

Why was the camp not in an uproar? Even though the cart had arrived not long before, in such a small horde it seemed inconceivable that no one had noticed. Although if the slaves and the driver served Tulpar, then they could blend into the crowd without attracting attention.

According to Timur, the driver had not blended. He had gathered Tulpar's belongings and left the camp. Someone else familiar with Timur's destination—but, alas, out of reach.

Ogodai turned to the warriors who had accompanied him. He ordered one man to stay, then took the torch from the other and told him to fetch reinforcements. "From our own comrades-in-arms," he said. "I want not even a whiff of treachery tonight. And when you find them, send a man to alert Kazbek Argyn. The council must learn what happened here as soon as possible."

The bearer ducked his head and left. Ogodai straightened his shoulders and climbed onto the platform to examine the stain. It was larger than he'd thought at first: irregular, dark in the torchlight. He touched the edge and felt damp, extended his tongue to lick at the drop that clung to his finger. Metallic. "Blood," he told the warrior who remained.

The man joined him. Careful to avoid the stain, Ogodai pushed open the door and entered, wondering what he would find. Tension compressed his throat.

The interior of the tent lay in darkness, lightened only by the torch he carried. Even the smoke hole was covered. The heat had dissipated throughout the day, and his breath formed small clouds before his face. The air was far too cold for a man as sick as Jahangir, although the torch revealed another breath cloud, indicating the bey still lived.

A snapped command brought his man into the tent. Ogodai took that torch, too, and set the warrior to stripping the cloth over the smoke hole and kindling a flame in the brazier. Soon he could distinguish the outlines of shapes in the dark.

A petulant Jahangir scowled at him from the pallet. "You. Where's my sister? My stepmother?"

He hadn't known in advance, then, what Tulpar intended. One point in his favor. "Tulpar rode off with your sister this afternoon," Ogodai said. "You didn't see him?"

Jahangir shook his head, frowning. Whatever he mumbled under his breath, Ogodai didn't hear. "I plan to go after them," he said. "But I came to check on you first."

"And Diliara?"

"She will arrive soon." He hoped. When last seen, Diliara hadn't looked capable of tending to any needs but her own. "It's hard to believe you heard nothing."

Jahangir retreated into his shoulders like a turtle. "I woke from the opium, and my sister was gone. No explanation. No one came when I called. I couldn't move." He shivered. "It's cold in here."

Sulky but sincere, as far as Ogodai could tell. "We're building a fire. You'll be warm soon." He handed one torch to the bearer and held the other above his head as he circumnavigated the tent, looking for evidence of what had happened. Firuza hadn't struck him as a young woman who would meekly consent to an abduction—unless Tulpar threatened to kill her brother if she refused. She did seem devoted to Jahangir, despite his poor treatment of her.

Still, a struggle was more likely. She would have had some warning: thuds as the warriors succumbed to Tulpar's attack;

the arrival of Tulpar himself. She might not realize the danger at first, but then she must have screamed, pushed him away. She was no frail harem blossom; she had made that clear in the way she rode.

A piece of paper, ripped across one corner, caught his eye. He picked it up. In the elegant female hand he recognized from the note sent to Bulat, Firuza had written five lines.

> *Swans swim alone*
> *Until they find the perfect mate.*
> *Wings touch, souls meet,*
> *As ours have done, my husband.*
> *Happy the day when you swam to me.*

She had written it for him. And she had compared them to swans—sacred birds at home on earth, in air, in water; birds that mate for life. Touched, he stared at the poem, memorizing the five lines.

Running feet signaled the arrival of his men. Ogodai rolled the paper into a scroll no thicker than his finger and tucked it into his sash, then summoned them to join him. A dozen armed warriors pushed through the tent door, Kazbek Argyn hard on their heels.

"Get fresh horses," Ogodai told his men. "As soon as the moon rises, head back the way we came. You're looking for bodies. Of our guards, definitely. Of the slaves who accompanied the cart, possibly. And keep your eyes open for any hint that a horseman left the trail and headed into the steppe."

The warriors bowed. The odds against their finding anything were high, but they would search diligently. The twelve of them belonged to his personal guard, bound to him by an oath to serve until death, and those killed—because nothing else would explain the sentries' absence—had been their close companions since he assumed his first independent command four years ago. They would follow his orders to the best of their ability. He tapped two of them to stay at the tent and sent the other ten on their way.

Kazbek nodded approval. Ogodai dipped his head in that direction. "Argyn Bey," he said, "please tell the council what we've discovered here. Someone, most likely my half-brother, attacked and carried off my betrothed. I'll meet with you as soon as I have news."

Kazbek surveyed the tent. "Of course. I'll send men to search the camp for the missing servants. And the driver?"

"Gone," Ogodai said. "To serve my brother."

"A bad business." Kazbek moved to the door, then turned before exiting. "We will await you in the men's tent."

"Yes."

With Kazbek gone, Ogodai resumed his survey of the wagon while the remaining guards did what they could for the bey. Some distance from the door, a gleam alerted Ogodai to the knife stuck under the trellis frame. He pulled it out. Yes, unsheathed. And Firuza's—he recognized the hilt. The blade bore a stain. Rusty red. More blood. Hers or her attacker's?

He turned in place. Carpets covered much of the surface. Their bright colors and interwoven patterns masked stains in the dim light, but there, near the bed where Jahangir lay, the gold diamond looked asymmetrical. And was that not the jade vial that had contained the poppy potion, unstoppered and on its side, as it hadn't been when he left the tent those fateful hours ago?

In the morning, the carpets would reveal their secrets. But Ogodai intended to be far away by then.

"Care for the bey," he told the guards. "Don't leave him unattended for a second, no matter what. Let no one in except our own men, Rafik Argyn and his father, and Lady Diliara with her servants."

"You won't catch him," Jahangir said, unappreciative as ever. "He's long gone. By the time you track him down—if you ever do—he'll have her with child."

Ogodai, already at the door, stopped to stare at the sneering bey. "What is wrong with you? She's your sister! She cares for you, and you do nothing to protect her."

Jahangir lowered his eyes, as if abashed.

"Let me be clear," Ogodai said. "If Tulpar forces himself on Firuza, he dies. And whether he does or not, I will take her back. She is *my bride*. One day, you'll get that through your skull. No one but Firuza herself will ever convince me otherwise."

He didn't wait for an answer. From the look on the bey's face, Jahangir had none to give.

Chapter 18

Ogodai would gladly have set out right away, trusting the moon to illumine his quest. But he had promised to consult with the council, and without a destination he could search the steppe for months without finding Firuza. Which meant that he must first wring at least that portion of the truth out of Zamam.

In short, time to check in with Rafik.

The sentries guarding the door uncrossed their spears as he approached. He ducked under the lintel and entered. Inside, two men pinioned Zamam's arms behind his back while another pair held his ankles straight out in front of him. The prisoner looked as if he would like to kick them, the warriors as if they dared him to try. Rafik, taking advantage of the additional height offered by the khan's platform in the center of the tent, had been lounging in exaggerated contrast to Zamam's discomfort—an empty bowl in front of him and a jug of koumiss at his side. He sprang to his feet when Ogodai entered.

Ogodai waited near the door and gestured for Rafik to join him. If they kept their voices low, Zamam wouldn't overhear them.

"What have you learned?" he asked as Rafik crossed the last carpet.

"Nothing." Rafik looked as dissatisfied as he sounded. "He keeps muttering some nonsense about needing to take care of that damned eagle of his."

Ogodai blinked. He couldn't help it. "Tulpar has abducted my betrothed, and Zamam expects us to care about his eagle?"

Rafik shrugged. "You see why I called it nonsense."

The rage Ogodai had bottled up since his conversation with Timur surged through his veins. He spun on his heel and marched toward Zamam.

The man cowered as he approached, so his anger must show on his face. Good. While the four warriors restrained Zamam, Ogodai straddled the man's legs and reached forward to grab the collar of the prisoner's jacket. He twisted it in one hand and held the other, clenched, inches from Zamam's jaw.

"I want to know where my brother took my bride," he said in his best battleground snarl. "When he leaves here, where does he go? And don't pretend you can't answer the question. I'll wring your blasted eagle's neck myself if I don't get some cooperation out of you."

As a ploy, it left much to be desired. It shouldn't have worked, especially with a hardened fighter like Zamam. Yet Zamam loved his eagle. Or so Ogodai guessed when their captive flinched.

"Tell me," he snapped. "Make it quick. Where does my brother go?"

Zamam bit his lip, looked aside. Ogodai tightened his grip, moved the fist closer, then dropped it and said to Rafik, "Kill the eagle." He made his tone casual, as if he ordered the slaughter of trained hunters without a second thought.

"Yes, Khan," Rafik said. He stood behind Zamam, and Ogodai saw him grin. He flicked his wrist, indicating do it now.

But Zamam was babbling. "He has a place near the clan's winter pastures, where the Idel meets the Chulman. On this side of the Great Mother. You'll think you see a Russian hut, but look closely and you will find the spirit banner. If he is there."

The Idel and the Chulman, which the Russians called the Volga and the Kama. A huge area to cover, even if restricted to the near side of the Idel.

"You have to do better than that," he told Zamam. "We'll still be searching for her at Ramadan. Have you seen the place?"

Zamam stared at his feet until prodded. "Yes."

"Then you're coming with us. To show us the way."

"I can't, Sultan. Your brother will kill me!"

Ogodai grabbed Zamam's chin, pressed his dagger against the man's throat, and stared straight into his prisoner's eyes. "And if you don't, I will kill you. I'm here. He's not. Choose."

A long pause. Ogodai felt his patience fraying. Thoughts of what Firuza might be enduring at this moment flooded his mind. He tightened his grip, pressed harder. Beads of blood dripped from Zamam's neck.

"Very well," Zamam stammered. "I will show you."

Ogodai released him, stood, and addressed his warriors. "Feed him. Allow him to rest and relieve himself. But don't take your eyes off him. Bring him—and the eagle—here, bound, at first light."

They left, dragging Zamam in their midst, and Ogodai turned his attention to Rafik. "You and your men get some rest. We set out at dawn. And ready your fastest horses. My brother has far too much of a head start."

Buoyed by that small success, Ogodai went to fulfill his obligations to the council. Hands tucked in his sleeves for warmth, he moved into the camp. Grasses, not yet trampled by the herds, brushed against his boots. Moonlight, silence. To one side, the bey's tent glowed softly, indicating that Diliara, perhaps, remained in attendance.

As Firuza should be. He would find her tomorrow.

He skirted the women's tent and approached the men's. Here, too, he saw the glow of lanterns. The hum of voices broke the quiet. He pushed aside the embroidered flap and entered. Roars of approval and raised flasks greeted him.

He stopped, startled. Had the camp accepted him, then? That was a pleasant surprise. He searched the crowd for malcontents but saw at most a few sullen faces.

Three of the four clan leaders sat together in a corner. As Ogodai made his way to their small circle, he saw no sight of Ildar Shirin. "There are matters we must discuss, Beys. Will you not join me? And where is the honored Ildar?"

"He retired to his own tent." Kazbek Argyn rose to his feet. "Claimed fatigue from the journey and asked us to handle the matter for him."

Highly suspicious, that. As if Shirin had learned in advance of his favored candidate's plans—or perhaps had no desire to censure Tulpar, even in the face of this outrage against the bey's daughter. Either way, Ogodai decided, he applauded Shirin's withdrawal. An old hand like Shirin wouldn't confess to guilty knowledge if he had it, and the other beys were much more likely to accept Ogodai's way of thinking.

"Shall we move to my tent, then," he asked them, "where it is quieter?"

They didn't object, and soon the four of them had gathered in Ogodai's small tent. In his absence, Vafa had set out cushions to the right of the hearth fire and placed a tray in the center. Ogodai murmured approval as he passed. The servant retreated to a space near the door, and Ogodai encouraged his guests to sit.

Once the beys had settled themselves in a rough circle, he dipped his fingers in the cup of koumiss he held and flicked mare's milk into the flames to nourish the grandmothers. As he walked to the men's tent and back, he had been debating how much gossip had spread throughout the camp, how much Kazbek would already have told them. Having no way to know, he decided to start with the most important point.

"My brother has ridden off with Lady Firuza," he said bluntly. "He seeks to overturn your decision by means of brute force. I leave at dawn to retrieve my betrothed. I will return as soon as possible. Did you find my brother's slaves?"

Kazbek answered. "We did. They followed his orders, no more. When he and two warriors killed the guards, that shocked and frightened the slaves. When he left with Lady Firuza, he told them the same tale his driver later told the boy. His warriors, the driver—those three have run away. But the slaves didn't know enough to run. They stayed and did their duty."

"We shouldn't punish them, then," Ogodai said. "Rafik and I will go after Tulpar, as I told you. Meanwhile, I want you to continue the investigations into the attack on Jahangir Bey and the murder of his father."

"That we will do." Kipchak, too, flicked milk into the fire before tossing back his drink and depositing the cup on the rug with unnecessary force. "And what of your brother?"

Ogodai signaled to Vafa to refill the cup. "I will do what I must to convince him that he has lost."

"It won't be easy." Baryn studied the leaping flames, as if they carried a message from the ancestors. Perhaps they did. "Tulpar perceives defeat as a temporary setback. Most men would have backed down when Bahadur Bey turned against them. Are you prepared, Sultan, to do *whatever* is necessary?"

To kill Tulpar, he meant. Ogodai himself wondered how he would answer that question, if fate gave him no other choice.

279

But he knew better than to show reluctance before these warriors. "*Whatever* is necessary." Ogodai pulled his dagger from its sheath and pointed the tip to the sky. "My brother has pushed this rivalry beyond the point where compromise is possible. To secure my wife and the khanate, to avenge the death of Bahadur Bey, no price is too high. Do I have your backing?"

"The strongest khan has our backing," Baryn said. "I respect you, Sultan, and your father even more so. I hope to see you succeed in this struggle."

"I still have to prove myself," Ogodai replied, acknowledging Baryn's unspoken reservations. "That isn't *why* I leave to hunt for my brother, but I won't disappoint you." He placed the dagger on the rug and raised his cup to the flames. "With the grandmothers' blessing, I will engage him and defeat him. You will have your strong khan."

They roared their approbation. But long after the elders left, Ogodai lay awake, facing more clearly than ever before the reality of power on the steppe. If he won, they would follow him. If he lost, they would—perhaps with regret, perhaps not—hand Firuza over to the victor and install his brother as khan.

He couldn't afford to lose.

Firuza squinted at the planks above her. Planks—cut to size, neatly laid side to side, rising toward the center, where a great roof beam ran in a line that spanned her shoulders.

What was this? No smoke hole, no felt, no familiar domed tent.

Yet there must be a hearth fire somewhere, for the room had a comforting warmth. The pile of furs on which she lay supported her in soft luxury. And from somewhere, golden light poured into the space.

The back of her head hurt. She twisted her face to the right, but the pressure on her cheek reminded her of Tulpar's blow and the bruise it had caused. Better to try the left side: the right revealed nothing but wooden planks, anyway. Had her enemy brought her to a Russian hut?

Because Tulpar was her enemy. Stealing her from her home and her future husband—his actions had destroyed her last illusions about him.

Her head had cleared from the opium he had forced down her throat, although her tongue felt thick and fuzzy and bruises made it awkward to move her head and neck. The pain in her right foot had subsided to a vague discomfort, but she suspected that would change fast if she tried to put weight on it.

She pushed herself upright and looked around. The wooden building did resemble a Russian peasant cottage, although equipped in a style no peasant could afford. A single, one-story room, not large, with mica-paned windows set into two of the walls. A clay stove, shaped like an elongated tent, provided the heat. The trappings wouldn't look out of place in a khan's residence: velvet and sable, rich brocades in various colors and patterns, blue-on-white ceramics, brass jugs, exquisite lacquered boxes. In one corner, she saw piles of food: breads of various kinds, dried meat, bags of the sort used for preserved fruits, mushrooms, or nuts. Herbs hung from hooks in the ceiling amid strings of onions.

The lair of a tiger. And there, against the opposite wall, lay the tiger himself, sleeping as if he hadn't a care in the world. A bandage wrapped his right wrist.

How dare he lie there, heedless, after the way he treated me?

Firuza reached for her knife. He was well within range. Too bad she couldn't ride, but with so much food, she could survive here until her foot healed. Then she'd find out where Tulpar had brought her. His horse would take her home. To Ogodai.

Her hand came up empty. Tulpar had wrenched the knife away from her, there in the bey's tent. The wound on his wrist had come from her.

Leaving her with no way to defend herself. Firuza pulled up her left knee and rested her forehead on it, pondering her options—none of them good.

Ogodai might come after her, if he could find out where Tulpar had brought her. She had spent almost the whole ride unconscious, so she had no idea how much time she had lost. The light filtering through the panes indicated day, but morning or afternoon? Morning would mean the next day. If afternoon, her betrothed might still think her safe in the bey's tent. No, she couldn't count on Ogodai to help her escape.

Someone had stocked the cabin with food, brought in the rugs and the brocades, constructed the mattresses that supported her and Tulpar on benches at opposite sides of the room. A servant employed by Tulpar, who might have orders not to return. Foolish to place her hopes on a dependent.

She would have to stall for time until she healed—and ensure that Tulpar did not take advantage of her. He had talked about luring Ogodai here but also about keeping her for himself. Perhaps he hadn't meant that, but he wouldn't be the first khan to secure a bride by force of arms. And after the way he'd overpowered her today, it seemed likely that he could do with her as he wished.

A shiver ran through her. Two nights in Ogodai's arms had made the demands of marriage both real and appealing, but she didn't want to do those things with Tulpar. That meant she needed more than time. She needed a weapon. The kitchen area must have a knife.

A few feet, no more than ten. Her injured foot protested when she stood, balancing herself against the wall, and lowered it to the ground. But Tulpar did not stir, and the foot hurt less than before. If she placed it flat on the floor and relied on the other leg, she could manage.

With excruciating slowness, Firuza, using the wall as her crutch, limped toward the corner containing the food.

The horde's winter pastures still lay several days away, in the low hills beyond Alatyr. But Tulpar's outrageous behavior had one positive consequence: it freed Ogodai of the need to travel at the speed of wagons and feet. Mounted on Firuza's beautiful Kubelek, his own chestnut ready to relieve the mare as needed, he felt like Zamam's eagle as he galloped past the Sura's snake-like tail, careful to keep it on his left. They would soon pass the river's source, here in the foothills. The grasslands were already blending into terrain more similar to Kasimov, where Ogodai had spent the last two years: river bounded by forested hills.

Rafik rode close behind, his dapple-gray gelding not quite a match for Firuza's gorgeous horse. The rest of their combined troop, with Zamam bound in their center and the eagle caged and attached to one of the sturdier horses, rode at a more respectable canter in their rear.

He would slow the mare soon. She had far to go, from what Zamam had told them, and it wouldn't do to tire her prematurely. Even at a more sedate pace, Ogodai and his troop could reach the Volga by the fourth sunrise—sooner if they also took advantage of the moonlight.

The sky shone a clear, light blue under a brilliant late fall sun. Winged horses frolicked across the cerulean steppe, matching

the mad dash of their earthly counterparts. One even looked
as if it might have Bahadur Bey on its back. Ogodai tilted his
head back and howled a welcome.

Rafik pulled up alongside him, and together they rode for
the northeast.

It wasn't much of a knife, but it would do. A blade blunt from
hacking at dried meat, about as long as Firuza's index finger,
with a hilt of blackened wood, it had the advantage that she
could slip it into her sash until she needed it. This Firuza proceeded to do.

After so much effort to reach the kitchen area, she had
no intention of leaving until she had satisfied her hunger and
thirst. But another need, more urgent still, caused her to push
aside the hut's single door. She made it through without much
difficulty, although the more she used her injured foot, the
more the band of pain across her arch intensified. She couldn't
keep walking for long.

Once outside, she stopped, almost as stunned as she had
felt from Tulpar's blow. From the angle of the sun, she saw
that dawn had broken not long before. Rocky ground covered
in mossy grass sloped away from the cottage for a space about
twice the length of its walls before dropping from sight. Great
trees surrounded the hut and all the surrounding land, but
what amazed her most was the water. Water to the right, water
to the left, water curving off in a path more or less straight in
front of her: rivers wider than any Firuza had ever seen and no
grasslands in view.

Now she could guess where Tulpar had brought her. Her
people never came this far, but she had heard of it. The place
where the mighty Chulman flowed into the even mightier Idel
and divided, one half plunging toward the southern sea of silks

and spices while the other meandered northwest, eventually reaching the Russian lands. On the far side of the rivers, the ancient capital of the Bulgars had lain in ruins, so the bards said, since the grandson of Genghis Khan razed it.

People had lived here since time immmemorial. She should have had no trouble finding willing helpers. Instead, she saw no one at all. Nothing but trees and water.

She relieved herself as best she could—one project aided by the lack of an audience—and limped back inside. There she discovered a barrel of water, a bowl to clean her hands, and a rough cloth to dry them. One brass jug proved to contain cherry juice, which removed the last of the fuzziness from her mouth.

Food posed a bigger problem. Her purloined knife should stay where it was, so no dried meat. The onions, mushrooms, and beans required cooking. She settled for a handful of berries, a chunk of cheese, and a torn-off hunk of bread, which she tucked into her sleeve before hopping back to her mattress.

She had made as little noise as possible, but it still surprised her that Tulpar didn't wake. Under other circumstances, she would have investigated. She had stabbed him: the wound might have become infected. Or maybe the long ride had exhausted him.

After the way he'd behaved, though, she couldn't bring herself to care. The longer he slept, the more time she had to prepare herself for the encounter to come. Her earlier hope that Ogodai would look for her faded. She had traveled a great distance; many days must have passed since her capture. Even if Ogodai pursued her, he would not find her here, hidden in the woods so far from the horde's winter pastures. He would search for a while, then give up. It happened—often enough that she had heard the tales. Men captured the wives of other men, and the bereft husbands sought new brides and let the old ones go. She should accept her fate. So Diliara would counsel—not to mention Roxelana, that reed ever ready to bend to the prevailing wind.

Yet some stubborn part of Firuza's soul refused to surrender. Ogodai had enjoyed their time together. He had challenged Tulpar for her, sworn to protect her, listened to her when she talked of her dream, defended her to Jahangir. Ogodai would not abandon her.

So where was he?

No servant appeared. No chores presented themselves, even ones beyond the abilities of a bruised and damaged lady. At first, the silence seemed restful, but after hours with nothing to do, utter boredom set in. For a while, she worked on her poem for Ogodai, but the absence of writing materials eventually robbed that pastime, too, of its appeal. Her fear and distress gave way to irritation.

Tulpar had put her in this untenable position. She fingered the knife in her sash, tempted to toss it at him. She could have hit him with her own dagger, but not this one. A miss would wake him without incapacitating him, destroying her one means of self-defense.

Another immeasurable period passed as she imagined limping over to him and slicing a blood vessel in his neck. But that option seemed too gruesome for words. Defending herself was one thing; committing cold-blooded murder on a sleeping man a deed of quite a different order. She couldn't bring herself to take that step.

The sun glowed high through the mica panes before Firuza saw Tulpar stretch and flip onto his back. He rolled onto his side and scowled at her. "So you're awake. A lot of trouble you've caused me, Lady."

Of all the world's impossible billy goats, he was the worst. "I've caused *you* trouble? What have you done to my brother?

What did you do to my father? And what about me? Don't pretend you want me. I've seen how you look at Roxelana. Why couldn't you run off with her and leave me with my intended husband?"

"Spitfire." He swung his legs to the floor and sat up. "Want you or not, I will keep you in my power long enough for my well-behaved little brother to either present himself here or give up on you. Once he's out of the way, back we go to the horde, where you will convince the council to change its mind and the luscious Roxelana will be waiting."

He walked toward her. Firuza braced herself.

"No fear, my sweet." He sounded like a parent cajoling a child. "I won't hurt you. I'm good at this. You'll enjoy it. And once I get an heir on you, I'll leave you alone. You can manage the horde as you've always done. What difference does it make, in the end, who bears the title of khan?"

She felt the blood rise and fall in her cheeks. If she didn't defend herself right here, right now, Tulpar would force himself on her. Then Ogodai would never take her back.

Death would be preferable. Tulpar's or hers, she didn't care.

She let him cross three-quarters of the distance between them before she pulled the knife from her sash. "One step closer, and I'll plunge this blade into your heart."

His eyes flicked to her hand, then back to her face. He lifted a foot, and she tightened her grip, holding the blade at the ready.

He laughed. "By the ancestors, you're an enterprising girl! How did you get hold of that? But you've miscalculated, sweetheart. That miserable excuse for a knife wouldn't pierce a melon, never mind my heart."

He was probably right. "Maybe so, but I can slash an artery. You'll be just as dead." She twisted the blade suggestively, as if judging which artery to slash.

She saw him clench and release his hands, move a foot and withdraw it, tip his head to one side, then the other. He was too far away to slap her as he had before: she had chosen the distance for her challenge with that memory in mind. For one sickening moment, she thought he meant to dash forward and grab the knife from her, but instead he retreated to his side of the room and resumed his seat on the bed.

"Well, sweetheart," he said. "You're a perfect font of surprises. Never mind, I can wait. Stalemate, isn't it?"

And there they sat until the thrumming of horses' hooves, traveling at speed, set the benches vibrating against the walls.

Chapter 19

Volga–Kama Basin, 11 Rabi el-Thani 941 A.H./20 October 1534

As OGODAI'S TROOP MOVED INTO THE FORESTED HILLS OF the northeast, the value of Zamam's guidance became ever more obvious. On the second day, they passed the horde's traditional winter pastures and continued on, drawing steadily closer to the Great Mother River. Unlike Rafik and the other men of the steppe, Ogodai and his warriors had traveled these paths before. But the distances were great, the trees many, the number of isolated cottages in the woods higher still. Without Zamam, Tulpar's hideaway would have disappeared amid the greenery.

The chase consumed an inordinate amount of time. So much that Ogodai and Rafik debated whether Zamam was guiding them aright or deliberately leading them astray. Ogodai had hoped to catch up with his brother and retrieve his bride within a day, but two dawns without sight of the fugitive raised his doubts of Zamam's honesty to the skies. Renewed threats to the lives of man and eagle produced a change of direction, and by the next noon, the Great Mother appeared on the eastern horizon, exactly where Ogodai expected to see her. He rewarded their reluctant guide and his bird with their first meal in twenty-four hours and pressed on.

When not riding herd on Zamam, Ogodai had little to occupy his mind on the journey except for his mounting rage at his brother, interspersed with flashes of anxiety for his bride. So it should have surprised no one that when the troop halted before a nondescript peasant hut and Tulpar came dashing out, Ogodai swung his leg over his mount's back, jumped down, and greeted his half-brother with a punch to the jaw.

Tulpar smacked onto the ground with a thud. For a few blissful seconds, Ogodai thought he had knocked out his opponent. But before he had time to celebrate, Tulpar leaped to his feet and grabbed Ogodai by the ankle. He kneed Tulpar with his free leg. Tulpar jerked the ankle he held, and Ogodai's head hit the rocky soil. He saw stars, then a steadier gleam. Acting on instinct, he rolled sideways and grabbed his brother's wrist just in time to divert Tulpar's dagger. Then they were fighting in deadly earnest, Ogodai twisting and rolling until he could gain enough purchase to plant a knee on his adversary's chest. He slammed Tulpar's knife hand hard against the ground, over and over, while his brother writhed like a serpent to free himself.

"Damn you," Ogodai said in a series of breathy pants. "You steal my bride, you kill her father, you attack the new bey—who *supports* you. Will you stop at nothing to become khan?"

With one mighty heave, Tulpar threw him off. Ogodai braced himself to avert the next blow, but Tulpar didn't swing. Instead he settled cross-legged on the ground, hands draped over his thighs, palms open. "What the hell are you talking about? I didn't attack Jahangir. Let alone Bahadur."

He sounded sincere—no, astonished, as if the idea of committing murder had never occurred to him. Had Ogodai and Firuza misjudged him after all?

Firuza, who had suffered four days as this man's captive. Well, no one could say Ogodai had misjudged his brother over that. "Where is she?"

"Here."

Her voice sounded from behind his right shoulder. Ogodai whirled. Sure enough, Firuza stood near the door of the hut, supporting herself with a hand on the jamb. Her stance reminded him of a frightened bird, yearning but hesitant.

His smile felt as if it would split his face. He ran to sweep her off her feet. Her arms wrapped around his neck, and her lips parted eagerly for his kiss.

"How touching," Tulpar drawled. "The love birds are reunited." Ogodai steadied his bride with his left arm, leaving his right free, and shifted direction to find Tulpar surveying the troops. His eyes focused on Zamam, bound to his horse, a warrior on either side, one of whom had the horse's rein attached to his pommel.

"So that's how you found me," Tulpar said. "Very clever, *ené*." He strolled forward and tapped Zamam's knee. "If you're wise, you'll stay out of my sight from now on. I have no use for traitors. Got it?"

Zamam nodded, shamefaced. Without so much as a glance at Ogodai, Tulpar made a run for Ogodai's abandoned chestnut, mounted, and sent the horse at a full gallop out of the clearing.

"After him," Ogodai shouted. "And hold on to Zamam!"

Rafik waved his cap in acknowledgment and took off in pursuit of Tulpar. The Argyn men, in rough formation, dashed after them into the forest.

Ogodai's own warriors clustered around Zamam. His eagle screamed its distress to the heavens, startling the man transporting it. His hat flew into the bushes, and he clambered after it.

The head of Ogodai's personal guard edged his horse forward. "Should we follow, Sultan?"

Ogodai glanced at his bride. Bruises ringed her throat, marred her cheek. He stroked them, as if his touch had the power to heal. "He hurt you, beloved."

"Bruises, yes. I fought him. But he didn't violate me." She pulled a knife from her sash and held it up. Ogodai felt his eyes widen. "I didn't permit it."

She looked solemn, yet at the same time so determined that the desire to kiss her again almost overwhelmed him. But the guardsman awaited his answer. Ogodai tightened his arm around Firuza's waist and returned his attention to his troops.

"Stay here," he said. "Rafik will be back soon. The only horse that can catch that chestnut is Kubelek, and we need her to carry our future khatun to safety in Kazan. Then we will return and settle scores with my brother."

Firuza didn't object when Ogodai insisted on carrying her into the hut. Hobbling had not become more comfortable over the course of the day, and although she had seldom felt less helpless, she found Ogodai's concern for her profoundly reassuring. Any hidden fear that he might reject her had vanished with his smile. It felt good to rest her head on his shoulder, allow his strong arms to support her, let someone take care of her for a change. She didn't understand why, with the danger over, she had to fight back tears. She knew only that stepping through the hut door and finding her husband battling his brother, then standing back while the two men settled their conflict, had taken more out of her than she would have believed possible.

Tulpar had escaped—alive, unharmed except for the stab wound she herself had inflicted on him and whatever injury Ogodai had dealt to his pride. Which meant, surely, that the conflict remained unsettled and that Ogodai, manlike, intended to leave her in Kazan while he put an end to Tulpar. Or— horrible thought—while Tulpar triumphed, making Firuza a widow before she had a chance to become a wife.

She challenged Ogodai with this plan as soon as he restored her to the bench where she had already spent so many tedious hours. He kissed her forehead. "Yes, more or less, beloved. But if you wish to argue with me, can it not wait? I just spent four anxious days tracking you. My men and Rafik's are tired and hungry."

"Four days?" His need shamed her, the housewife and hostess, but shock overrode her stepmother's training. "You tracked me for four days? But how did you find me? And how did your brother keep me unconscious for four days? I awoke only this morning." No wonder her foot had begun to heal. Memory caused her cheeks to flush. "The poppy juice. I should have realized."

Ogodai's face darkened as he brushed his fingers across her throat. "Not only the poppy juice. There is more than one layer of bruises here, sweetheart. He seems to have throttled you to keep you quiet. He will pay for that."

"You came after me." Firuza clasped her hands behind his neck as the truth sank in. "You didn't give up, although you must have thought he dishonored me."

Ogodai sighed, then kissed her. "He can't dishonor you, only himself. You belong to me. Tulpar will answer for what he did to you." He stepped back, pulled a small scroll from his sash, and handed it to her. "If you prefer him, I will stand aside, however reluctantly. But finding this convinced me that you didn't."

Even before she had completely unrolled the scroll, she recognized its jagged edge. "My poem!" Her throat closed up. Joy, embarrassment, love—no, joy again—fought for supremacy.

Joy won. "It isn't finished. My first attempt." She rerolled the scroll, tied it with a spare ribbon stashed in her sleeve, and handed it back to him. "I meant it as a birthday gift. I didn't expect you to have to travel so far to receive it from my hands."

His eyes lit with the gold flecks she loved, and he caressed her cheek. But their moment of privacy had ended. His men poured into the cabin, eager to break their fast.

"The horses?" Ogodai asked.

"Fed and watered," the troop leader said. "I have two men rubbing them down. We will watch over them tonight."

"Good work. Yes, guard them well. I don't want to spend the rest of my life in this 'palace' of my brother's. Watch Zamam and his eagle, too. I have a feeling he has more to tell us, if we can convince him to talk." Ogodai turned back to her. "We will eat and rest here tonight, then move on. Does that meet your needs, my lady?"

Firuza strove for a lightness she didn't feel. "And Kazan?"

Ogodai rewarded her with a sympathetic smile. "My sister is there. Nasan. You will be safe with her. Also my brother— my true brother, my *qarïndash*—Daniil. I go to ask for his help. Together we will finish Tulpar."

They left the next morning—rested, resupplied with food from Tulpar's hut, and restored to their full complement with the return of Rafik and his men, abashed to report that Tulpar had escaped them in the forest. Ogodai dismissed their concerns. He had hoped they might succeed, but Tulpar's familiarity with the terrain, coupled with his possession of the faster horse, had always made that outcome unlikely.

He and Daniil would track Tulpar. Assuming Daniil agreed to leave his post for such a reason. But Ogodai had difficulty imagining his adventure-loving brother-in-law choosing his diplomatic responsibilities over an opportunity to test his mettle against a troublemaker like Tulpar. Time enough to consider alternatives if Daniil refused.

His more immediate problem was how to get Firuza to Kazan. Although she didn't complain, he saw no evidence that her sprained foot had healed enough for her to control her spirited mare. At some point along the way, they had to cross the river, and a boat would serve her better than a horse. But the Idel was notorious for its river pirates, and the closest port lay some distance away, so Ogodai preferred to keep to the woodland trails until he reached the outskirts of Kazan. That meant taking Firuza up in front of him on her own horse, which he could control while she minimized the effect of the jogging gait on her injured foot.

The extra weight would slow them down, but that couldn't be helped. Indeed, Ogodai rather looked forward to the next stage of the journey.

The squat wooden towers of the Kazan fortress loomed over Firuza like angry forest guardians. Long lines of planks extended to each side, joining each menacing sentry to its neighbor and penning in a mass of graceless peasant huts that strained at their bonds like frisky goats.

She shivered. Two more days on the road had not prepared her for this sight. Her recent passage across the Idel atop a wooden platform, dependent on a piece of billowing cloth to transport her instead of reliable, reassuring horseflesh, had already tested her powers of endurance. It didn't help that Ogodai had taken the boat in stride—nor that he appeared untroubled by the monstrous scene that greeted them when they reached the other shore. He was her only support in this strange and horrible place.

A pair of armored guards stood at the entrance, holding their horsetail-decorated spears crossed at the tips to bar entry. That image, at least, she recognized. They waved Firuza and her party through in response to Ogodai's murmured explanation, opening a door onto a world beyond her imagining.

A flurry of smells assailed her nostrils. Spices and perfumes mingled with refuse and animal droppings, the scent of the river, the acrid tang of urine rising from the house corners, the musty aroma of damp, dead wood.

Kubelek had swum beside the boat like the other horses, but here she tossed her head and sidled at the strange sights and smells. And the noise! The steppe was never silent, but the soft sounds of nature and animals bore no resemblance to the cacophony created by thousands of people in a confined space: the ringing calls to prayer, the rustling of garments, the cries of shopkeepers hawking various wares—uncaring, it seemed, of the muezzins' demands for their attention. Or so she thought, until she heard prayer rugs unrolling around her and knees hitting the ground.

Ogodai jumped from the horse and lifted her down. His captain had already unrolled a prayer rug in front of them. When her betrothed tugged at her skirt, she knelt beside him. She hadn't said the prayers in so long that the Arabic words lurched in misformed shapes from her tongue, so she concentrated on trying to remember the sequence of gestures, dreading the many services she must yet perform. It hadn't occurred to her, when Ogodai proposed their journey to Kazan, that the Tatars there were Muslims in fact—not only in name, like her own horde. Otherwise, she would have prepared herself better.

The midday prayers ended, and their party rode up the hill. The one-room wooden cottages gave way to elaborate multistory buildings covered in cream-colored stucco. Red tile roofs and painted, grilled windows hinted at more welcoming vistas behind the white stone walls, yet pointed towers shaped like minarets repelled those outside the gates. How would her ancestors locate her in this strange town of too many people, filled with alien sounds and scents and houses rooted in the earth?

The people, too, troubled Firuza, especially as she and her party climbed higher. Close to the gates, she hadn't noticed much difference between her own clothing and the dress of the Kazan natives. But the streets nearer the center of town teemed with men in silken turbans that put Tulpar's efforts to shame, embroidered coats, and leather boots. Women were few and far between, but those Firuza saw sported long veils trailing from conical jeweled hats trimmed with fur and layers of loose robes in bright colors and rich fabrics. The traveling dress of a nomadic bey's daughter appeared in comparison no more impressive than a herder's sheepskin jacket. From time to time, she glanced at Ogodai's face as they rode to see what he thought of these beautifully garbed ladies, but his expression gave nothing away.

The horses drew to a halt at the grandest entrance they had encountered yet. White stone walls topped with tile gave way to a stone version of the gates below, guarded by another pair of warriors with crossed spears. Beyond the gate, Firuza dimly perceived manicured greenery. Her stomach tightened; her knees felt weak. She wasn't ready to meet the khan of Kazan. What would they think of her, the exalted residents of this fairytale palace?

Her distress intensified as they passed the second checkpoint. The formal gardens—so symmetrical, so elegant, so precise—with their tumbling flowers and mirrored ponds and playful, gushing fountains looked nothing like the glorious wildness of the steppe. The buildings that had shown stern backs toward the town opened their hearts to the courtyard:

terraced balconies and open windows greeted the thin rays of the autumn sun.

Here Firuza discovered the women and girls missing from the streets. A few, obviously servants from their dress, moved amid the throng engaged in something she recognized as work. The vast majority flitted in gauzy draperies across the grass or perched like exotic birds in the patterned-glass pavilions placed here and there amid the shrubbery. One exquisitely beautiful young woman—a standout even in this gallery of lovelies— occupied a center seat in the farthest pavilion. Two dozen other ladies surrounded her, like bees swarming around their queen.

Ogodai dismounted as soon as their horse passed the gates. While the men who had accompanied them turned left and stopped, Rafik at their head, Ogodai led Kubelek to one side and regarded Firuza with a slight frown.

"The khatun will not permit me to take this horse into her presence," he said. "If I support you, can you walk?"

Firuza fought the urge to cling to her mare and not let go. "I must." Her voice sounded as tight as her throat felt.

Ogodai's strong hands closed on her waist, and he flashed his rare smile. "It's overwhelming, beloved, I know. I remember the first time I came here. But you'll do fine. I have faith in you. And Nasan will help."

Firuza nodded without conviction. She remembered Nasan, a ragtag pixie with a limited appreciation for society's demands and even less interest in meeting them. As a tutor in the ways of this alien environment, Nasan seemed an unlikely choice. But it would be rude to point that out to Nasan's older brother, now lowering her to the ground.

Besides, Nasan might have changed. Eight years had passed since she left Bahadur's camp, and she had married in that time. Perhaps they would have more to say to each other these days.

Firuza hoped so. Her acceptance into the world of the courtyard rested on Ogodai's tempestuous sister.

Which was not, in the least, a comfortable thought.

Ogodai scanned the clumps of women who ran and played and sang within the perfumed garden. Most likely, he would find his sister among the group clustered around Aslanbika in the far pavilion—although Nasan, being Nasan, would probably spot him first. And when she did, Nasan being Nasan, the entire court would find out at once. So he didn't bother to scan every clump they passed with equal care. The women looked interchangeable in their bright robes and fluttering veils as they dashed hither and yon, eager to soak up the last sunny rays before the flagged paths vanished from view until spring. The snows were late this year, but it still surprised him that Aslanbika didn't freeze in her pretty pavilion.

He tightened his grip on Firuza's waist, half-lifting her to take the weight off her injured foot. She would have to hobble on her own soon enough.

She shot him a frightened glance, and he murmured reassurance. He could guess how the palace must unnerve her. For himself, he looked forward to a bath, a good meal, and conversation with Nasan and her husband—more or less in that order, although he couldn't avoid first greeting his uncle Jan-Ali.

Jan-Ali had a prickly sense of what his honor required. Ogodai hoped that the goods they had confiscated from Tulpar's hideaway would be considered sufficiently fine gifts— or that Jan-Ali would accept the exigencies of their journey as an excuse, if not. Otherwise, the next few days promised to be long and awkward.

"Ogodai!" The call split the air, as he'd anticipated, as they reached the halfway point of their passage across the garden. "Auntie, look! My older brother is here!"

He had just enough time to settle Firuza on a nearby bench before one bundle of draperies separated itself from the rest and hurtled toward him at a speed that Firuza's Kubelek would have envied. Ogodai laughed and caught his sister in a hug before the force of her arrival could knock him off his feet.

A flood of Tatar enveloped him. Nasan had news—the main news being that she was glad to see him.

He set her down, nuzzled her cheek, and waited for the deluge of words to slow. "I'm delighted to see you, too, *sengel*," he said when it did. "Come and meet my bride."

Nasan bit back the thousand questions that pounded against her tongue. Not so much because experience had taught her that Ogodai would answer no more than one in ten, or even because of the vast number of listening ears in the garden, but because the girl sitting on the bench looked so nervous and unhappy. Nasan remembered Firuza as quick and competent, a favorite with the grownups who had often disapproved of Nasan's own exuberance yet at the same time a rider who commanded respect. The young woman who huddled on the bench didn't much resemble the girl in Nasan's memory. Yet Ogodai had said, "my bride," as if no other introduction were needed.

The woman on the bench raised her head as Nasan approached. Her chin, lifted in challenge, and the beautiful dark eyes—yes, those belonged to Firuza.

Her robes had the old-fashioned, almost barbaric—although Nasan hated that word, which her Russian sister-in-law too often used on her—beauty characteristic of a nomadic bey's daughter: quilted wool decorated with hand-woven trim and looping swirls of embroidery in many different shades. In place of the veils that swept out from behind so many hats here, she wore a fur-brimmed jeweled cap with a gold spike extending from the crown. Long turquoise earrings dangled to her collar bones, and a matching necklace circled her throat. Her hair swept back to fall in a single long braid down her back, and on either side, just below the cap, an exquisite winged horse made of turquoise and gold glittered against the glossy dark tresses.

Nasan wrinkled her nose. Alas, like most of the nomads, her new sister had little access to water. Nasan's happy fantasies of nomadic life always omitted that detail.

Never mind. A session in the *hammam* would work wonders. In every other respect, Firuza was quite presentable.

And quite nervous, obviously, about her reception here. Nasan recalled her own unwanted delivery to Moscow four months ago. The least she could do was ease Firuza's fears. It felt good to be the one on the inside, for a change. The one who knew what to do, how to fit in.

She held out both hands, a bit surprised when Firuza didn't rise to greet her. "Greetings, sister. I am Nasan. It is many years since we met, but you are welcome here. Permit me to present you to Aslanbika Khatun."

"Thank you." Firuza clasped Nasan's right hand with her own and used the other to push herself into a standing position.

"You are injured!" Nasan said.

"My foot." Firuza produced a wan smile. Nasan reached to support her, but Ogodai blocked her path. He slipped his arm around Firuza's waist.

"Lead the way, *sengel*," he said. "The khatun will never forgive me if I don't pay my respects before I go. She may be five years younger than I am, but she's still my aunt."

Chapter 20

OGODAI BREATHED A SIGH OF RELIEF AS HE ESCAPED THE garden. He really shouldn't leave Firuza to cope with that bevy of twittering females, but since she had stood her ground with Aslanbika, the others wouldn't give her much trouble. He hoped.

And Nasan would help. His hoydenish younger sister had demonstrated previously unsuspected social graces when she greeted Firuza. Incredible as it seemed, Nasan was growing up. The salutary effects of marriage? Or something else?

Ogodai hadn't spent a lot of time in Kazan, but he had attended his uncle Jan-Ali's installation as khan and last year's wedding—each of which had involved celebrations lasting the better part of a week. Plenty of time to learn the general layout of the palace, including the suite set aside for ambassadorial meetings. He expected to find Daniil there, which wouldn't do him much good if his brother-in-law were, as Nasan had implied in a hurried aside, stuck in the back while those of greater prestige conducted negotiations. In that case, Ogodai would have to return later, but he could station a servant to warn him when the session broke up. Meanwhile, he would make himself presentable. Aslanbika Khatun had pulled her skirts aside when he came close, and even without her reaction, he recognized his own unsuitability for a royal audience. He'd better fix that before approaching the khan—or even the Russian nobles, except for Daniil.

In fact, as Ogodai discovered when he reached the appropriate courtyard, the khan had chosen to meet with the ambassador one on one. No interruptions would be tolerated, the snooty lord of the chamber announced, and no exceptions made—certainly not for a second-tier nephew who hadn't authorized his arrival in advance. More relieved than annoyed, Ogodai retreated in search of his friend.

A series of tips led him to the training grounds, then to the stables, where he ran Daniil to earth at the stall of Firuza's palomino mare. The Russian, his fingers entwined in the mare's mane, was crooning to the horse as a mother croons to her infant.

Ogodai grinned. "Her name is Kubelek," he said. "Gorgeous, isn't she?"

Daniil dropped his hands and spun to face him. "Ogodai! What brings you here?"

He looked pleased but wary. His narrowed eyes evoked an image of the last time Ogodai had seen Daniil, surrounded by Russian soldiers and yelling at the sky.

Because Ogodai had turned him over to them. He'd had good reasons at the time—and had arranged for Daniil's release, to boot. He'd hoped the two deeds canceled each other out, that Daniil understood the necessity, that their friendship would somehow endure. In his month among the often hostile strangers of Bahadur's horde, Ogodai had recalled only his sense of Daniil as a brother. He'd assumed Daniil felt the same way.

Maybe not. In which case, this trip to Kazan had been in vain.

No, not in vain. He had ensured Firuza's safety. Whatever happened, Nasan and Daniil would escort his wife to Kasimov, where the might of the Russian state and Bulat's sword would protect her.

"Apologies," Ogodai said. "Are you still sore about the Kasimov business?"

"Wouldn't you be?" Daniil, frowning, leaned his back against the horse stall. Kubelek nibbled his ear, and he jerked upright. She nudged his shoulder with her nose, and Daniil's ready sense of the ridiculous surfaced. He burst out laughing and stroked the horse's glossy ears. "All right, all right," he said to her in Russian. "I'll forgive him. Just for you, Lady Butterfly."

But when he returned his gaze to Ogodai, he was still frowning. "I'm not mad about Kasimov. I can guess what happened there. You were protecting your sister."

When Ogodai nodded, Daniil went on. "But you *still* don't trust me. Nasan tells me you're fooling around with some horde on the steppe. With a half-brother who was supposed to have died. Yet you didn't say a word to either of us. Why?"

One question he could answer. "Because I had no warning. *Ata* threw me into the midst of a hornets' nest, and I've spent the last month trying not to get stung. That's why I'm here: to ask for your help. Was I wrong?" After weeks of treading with care, even with Firuza—because what did a woman know about military life?—it felt good to speak his mind.

"No." Daniil strode forward.

They hugged, cheeks touching—right, then left. Ogodai inhaled his friend's familiar scent, here blended with the frothy smell of a recently ridden horse.

Daniil clapped him on the shoulder as he drew back. "I'm glad you're here. This place is enough to drive a warrior mad: intrigues and backstabbing and people who never say what they mean or mean what they say. And that's on all sides. We'll go someplace in the open air and talk, you and I." Kubelek nudged him again, and he patted her neck without glancing at her. "But first, tell me about Lady Butterfly. I didn't see her yesterday when I visited the stables. Did she arrive with you?"

He'd called the horse that earlier, and Ogodai hadn't paid attention. He raised his eyebrows. "Well, well," he said, "you *have* been practicing, if you know that *kubelek* means butterfly."

"Day and night," Daniil said. "Not much to do besides learn the language. Although I still need your sister to help me follow what's going on. Have you seen her yet, by the way?"

"Yes. I sought her out. I brought my bride here. Firuza. Kubelek is her horse. I left her with Nasan—Firuza, not the horse. Then I came to find you."

Daniil tapped the side of his head, as if he couldn't believe what he was hearing. "Bride? You got married? And you didn't tell us *that* either?"

"It hasn't happened yet."

Daniil groaned. Ogodai grabbed his sworn brother's arm and led him from the stable. "It's a long story," he said. "We may as well get started."

Firuza had never imagined a situation so unprecedented that she would need to depend on Nasan to get her through it. Yet here amid the beauties of the harem, Nasan stood out as someone who remembered with pleasure her time among the nomads.

Within the confines of the nomadic camp, life divided neatly into familiar things, handled with ease, and not yet familiar things certain to yield their secrets as Firuza learned more about them. But no past experience had prepared her for the *hammam*. The rooms themselves astonished her: architectural marvels of marble and tile, arches and columns, platforms draped with somnolent women, copper basins and spigots, braziers for warmth and soft lighting, steam rising from a large shallow pool. There was the water itself—so much of it, warm and clear and free-flowing, as if it were not a substance more precious than gold. And the women, who on instructions from the haughty Aslanbika had converged on Firuza and bustled her off, supporting her on either side in deference to her injured foot. Here in this improbable set of connecting rooms they clustered around her, removing her cap and her robes, wrapping her in a diaphanous garment, unbraiding her hair, and chattering about her as if she had neither wit nor words to speak for herself.

"Her hair is good," one woman said. "Long and lustrous and darker than a sable's fur."

"But her skin!" another said. "Leather is softer than her cheeks." This woman, whom Firuza pegged as a Russian slave because of her braid, the color of feather grass in autumn, shuddered and called to a third woman, even more obviously a servant. "Send for Habiba and her ointments. She has work to do." The third woman tittered and withdrew, hand over her mouth.

Nasan stripped off her own clothes and accepted one of the diaphanous robes. "You can talk *to* her, Nuria. My sister's name is Firuza. She's not a doll for you to bathe and dress." She patted Firuza's hand, which rested against the marble bench where they had lowered her. "Let them do their worst. They mean well, and Ogodai will like it. Trust me. He's probably in the men's baths as we speak."

"Yes," Firuza said. She could have objected, but the luxury and strangeness of Kazan knocked her off-balance. Aslanbika's moue of distaste and rapid dismissal stung, too. Firuza felt hideously out of place. She didn't want to disgrace or disappoint Ogodai. "You will stay with me?"

"Every step of the way," Nasan assured her. "And since it will take most of the afternoon, you will have plenty of time to tell me what's happening with you and my brother." She squeezed Firuza's hand again and looked from one chattering woman to the next, around the room. "We are eager to hear."

No doubt. Firuza accepted the warning, but she had never had any intention of spilling secrets in such a crowd. Years spent under the lash of Roxelana's tongue had taught her well, and she had much she could share without venturing into forbidden territory. So she allowed Nuria and the others to remove her robe, arrange her on her back on the bench, and wash every part of her with soap. The water warmed and relaxed her taut muscles. To fend off the soporific effect of the bath, she turned to Nasan. "It began," she said, "the night my father died."

Ogodai cast more than one sideways glance at his betrothed as he lifted a mutton kebab from the platters arrayed on the tablecloth around which he, Firuza, Nasan, and Daniil formed a small square. Rafik should have joined them, but they had persuaded him to stay with the men in return for a planning session later. Otherwise people would wonder why Ogodai and his Russian brother had not banished their women to the harem.

The four of them sat in the middle of the room, on the floor with cushions at their backs; once the servants withdrew and left them to their meal, they would be able to talk with minimal fear of being overheard.

He needed to concentrate, but he could hardly take his eyes off Firuza. His winged horses gleamed in hair as rich as the night sky over the steppe, piled high on her elegant head and revealing skin of the same flawless ivory as his sister's. Her robe—soft silk in a palette that ranged from pale blue to the deep green of the taiga—hinted at curves that usually remained hidden. A white tunic encased her arms and shimmered as the full skirts of her outer robe shifted with her movement. A gauzy veil fell halfway down her back from the clasp that held the piled hair. He wished his sister and her husband elsewhere. Firuza had always been pretty, but the *hammam* had left her with a radiant glow. The effect was stunning.

Desire must wait, of course. He had ridden a week to reach Kazan, with no more than an overnight halt at Tulpar's hidden cabin, in pursuit of this opportunity to discuss with his sister and brother-in-law the situation he faced. He had an obligation to himself, to Firuza, and to Bahadur's horde to resolve this squabble with Tulpar as soon as possible.

The servants departed. Ogodai swallowed the delectably tender piece of mutton he had been chewing and spoke to Daniil. "Can you get leave?"

Daniil dipped a piece of bread into the bowl of goat stew he held. "Oh, I think so. Alexander Makhmetovich appreciates my true value on this mission—which is next to none, despite my efforts to make myself useful. He's been gracious about tolerating my ineptitude and helping me master the language and the diplomatic protocol, but in return I can offer only a few observations that the locals might not have shared if they'd seen anyone more competent than myself in the vicinity. I suspect he won't miss me."

"You add to the body count." Ogodai grinned, to show he meant it as a joke.

Daniil ate his piece of soaked bread before replying. "Underlining the grand princess's prestige, you mean. Yes. But the point has been made, surely. Alexander Makhmetovich is no fool. I'm sure he realizes I can advance the Russian cause more by helping you than by staying here. This horde of yours may be small, but if we secure it, we can head off a broader campaign to subvert the nomads."

"And Kazan," Ogodai said. "When I finally got in to greet our uncle, I heard of the attempt on his life. That can only have come from Sahib-Girei of Crimea—hoping, no doubt, to reinstall his nephew as khan here in Kazan."

"Yes," Daniil said. "So we assume."

"Gazim Shirin supported them," Nasan said, "as did Queen Gulnara. They have been punished."

She handed Firuza a bowl of noodles. Firuza stared at the bowl, a bewildered expression on her face. Ogodai took it from her and passed her a basket of meat turnovers instead. "Try one," he suggested. "You can eat it by hand."

She smiled her thanks and picked up a small pie, while he succumbed to momentary distraction again.

"You have Shirins, too," Nasan said. "You must. Every horde and khanate does."

Firuza still looked bewildered. Belatedly, Ogodai realized that she couldn't follow the conversation, so far conducted mostly in Russian. He gave her a quick summary.

"Yes," Firuza said. "Ildar and his sons. They supported my father. They transferred that allegiance to my brother, but they favor your half-brother over my husband-to-be."

"Ildar openly declares his support for Tulpar," Ogodai added. "The Mangyt bey, Jahangir—Firuza's twin—also favors my half-brother. The other council members don't. Two are generally well inclined toward me but will probably switch sides if I fail. The fifth—Kazbek Argyn, whose son Rafik accompanied me—backs me with a whole heart. Not coincidentally, he is also the bey most inclined to challenge Ildar's leadership and the one most likely to recall our father with fondness. He sent his son to warn us right after the bey's death." He lifted Firuza's hand and brushed his lips across its back. "Carrying a message from my lady."

"The bey's death," Nasan said. She must have noticed their exchange, because she switched to Tatar. "Bahadur Bey? I have been wondering about that. Firuza said it came without warning."

"It did," Ogodai said. "And Bahadur himself twice called it murder in visions. He even accused the council of wanting to deliver the camp into the hands of his killer. A vision sent through the shaman. He meant Tulpar, I suppose, although Tulpar denies the charge."

"He would, wouldn't he?" Daniil said. Mention of the shaman made him nervous, Ogodai saw. Yet Russians, too, believed in visions sent by holy men and women. Why should this be different?

"True," Ogodai agreed. "Although he sounded sincere. Surprised that I could imagine such a thing. Still, Firuza and I both see the circumstances as suspicious, but we can't figure out how it was done."

"It strikes me as odd," Daniil said, "that this Ildar Shirin of yours supports a young man who may have killed his former ruler."

"Not if Bahadur opposed Shirin's plans." Ogodai sipped cherry juice, considering. "Whatever those might have been."

Nasan leaned forward, her face intent. "Yes, of course. But let's talk about the death, shall we? If we know how, maybe we can deduce who and why. Firuza named it as the starting point, but she couldn't say more in the presence of the women. What happened?"

Ogodai stared at her, startled by her intensity, only to shake his head. Stupid of him to forget. Nasan had shown an interest in healing from a young age, an interest she must have pursued here in Kazan. He saw a pile of medical texts on the small table to her right, and from what his uncle Jan-Ali had said earlier, she had been the one to identify the spider that poisoned him. Why would she *not* take an interest in Bahadur's death?

Firuza was describing the night it happened. Her voice broke at spots, and Ogodai ached to comfort her.

Nasan reached for one of the books and flipped through it. Her teeth bit into her upper lip; her beautiful brows creased in an uncharacteristic frown. "Where is it?" she muttered. "I know I saw it. Cold in a warm room—well, that's just approaching death. But trouble seeing? Pulse too fast? Shortness of breath?"

Holding her place with a finger, she returned her attention to Firuza. "What did you think at the time? You must have suspected poison, even if you had no idea what kind or how it got into your father. A healthy man doesn't keel over and die within twelve hours. Unless his heart seizes up or he suffers an apoplexy, and you couldn't mistake those for anything else."

Firuza lifted a shoulder, her face the picture of distress. "We thought the shaman had mistaken her dose. But she insisted she had made no mistake."

"Dose?" Nasan quivered like a hunting dog scenting prey. "What dose?"

"For arthritis. My father had trouble with his hands, and increasingly with his knees. It made riding painful."

"Arthritis." Nasan returned the book to its table, where it teetered atop the pile before sliding to the floor. "That gives me an idea. Daniil, pass me that other book, next to you, with the green cover. If you please. And Firuza, do you trust your shaman? Was she telling the truth?"

"She ran away," Firuza said. "That made me wonder, but until then, yes, I trusted her. She had cured many ills. It's not hard to make a mistake, though."

"No." Nasan took the book that Daniil had extracted from a companion pile and riffled through it. "Tell me again what your father ate for dinner."

Firuza's shoulders slumped. "So long ago."

"But an important night." Nasan didn't sound at all like Ogodai's madcap little sister. More like their mother, set on solving some kitchen mystery. "Try."

Firuza, Ogodai could see, was trying. "You mentioned to me," he said, to help her, "that your father brought down a deer the day before."

"Yes," she said slowly. "We had venison stew, with carrots and wild greens. It was the fifth of Muharram, and the steppe was in full flower. There was koumiss. And wine from Crimea. Jahangir drank a lot. That irritated *Ata*—that Jahangir drank himself senseless. He shouted at me to fetch the shaman."

"To see to your brother?" Nasan had found whatever she sought. Ogodai saw that in the way she gripped the page.

"No. Himself. He stood up and almost fell." Firuza sounded distant, as if she had entered a trance that carried her back into the past.

"Did he drink wine?" Daniil asked.

"Some. Not a lot. He didn't sound drunk when he talked, although he may have been, I suppose."

"And all this happened *before* he took the potion?" Ogodai said, surprised. He hadn't heard this part of the story before.

"Yes, before." Firuza's voice strengthened with excitement. "He was already unsteady on his feet. From the dinner, before the potion. But no one else fell sick. So maybe he was drunk, even though he didn't seem to be."

"And he ate nothing but venison stew?" Nasan asked. "It would be difficult to poison one portion of that."

"There were cheese curds," Firuza said. "And oh! We had quail. I didn't eat any, but the men did. *Ata* had two. He loved roast quail."

"Quail," Nasan said, an odd note of satisfaction in her voice. She opened the book and held up the page of Arabic script, exquisite as art. "Someone has been very clever. Indeed, I wonder who among the nomads has quite that level of knowledge. When we learn the answer to that question, we will know who killed your father. But I can tell you how Bahadur Bey died."

A small hubbub broke out. Nasan waited for it to die down, the book resting in her lap as she held it open with her left hand. When they quieted, she explained. Ogodai had the impression she was enjoying herself.

"The arthritis is key," she said. "Doctors use hemlock to treat it. You have to be careful, because too much will kill. And in excess it produces just the symptoms you described: blurred vision, cold, inability to breathe. Shooting pain, too; your father might not have confessed to that."

"The shaman warned him," Firuza said. "He demanded more potion, and she refused. She said it could kill him."

"A conscientious woman—and courageous, if she was willing to defy her bey. She seems a poor choice for the murderer, even by mistake." Nasan waited for Firuza to acknowledge that, then went on. "The arthritis medicine could have been too strong—except that your father felt unsteady before he consumed it. So there has to be something else. That's where the quail come in."

"I don't understand." Ogodai and Daniil spoke in unison. Firuza watched, a fingertip to her chin.

"You could poison a quail," she said. "They're so small. A man wouldn't share one."

"Exactly," Nasan said. "You could poison a quail and make certain that it ended up in the right person's stomach. But quail are special. They love hemlock, and it doesn't affect them. If you feed it to the ones you want, they will poison themselves. And if the person who eats them then takes more hemlock for his arthritis…"

She left the sentence unfinished. Ogodai regarded her openmouthed. Daniil and Firuza looked equally stunned.

"How long would you have to wait before you killed the quail?" Firuza blurted out after a while. "Or before you served it? A week?"

"Less, I would think," Nasan said. "I don't know for sure. Why?"

"Because Tulpar left a week before *Ata* died. *Ata* threw him out, in fact, for arguing with him. That was what made us suspicious."

Nasan scrunched up her face, obviously thinking. "Tulpar is a sultan," she said after a while. "He wouldn't kill birds with his own hands. He wouldn't even feed them. But he could order it done. And if he ordered it done while he was away, no one would suspect him."

Ogodai caught Firuza's wrist before she could slap her own forehead, marring that perfect skin.

"He could have," she said. "His woman stayed behind. And Roxelana, who doesn't hide her desire for him. And, oh, Zamam!"

"Zamam?" Nasan and Daniil chorused. "Who is Zamam?"

Firuza explained about Zamam—his arrival with Tulpar, his decision to stay. "Our fletcher, Almas, accused Zamam of killing his dog. A beautiful coursing hound in the prime of its life. They squabbled for months, and eventually Almas brought the case before the bey, seeking justice." She waved her turnover at Ogodai. "It was the day you arrived. The last case of the day. The problem was that Almas had no proof. He had seen Zamam leaving the enclosure where he kept the dog, but Zamam insisted he went to see it because he loves animals."

"He does love animals," Ogodai said, reluctant to defend Zamam even to this small degree. "We persuaded him to cooperate by threatening his eagle. Would he harm a dog?"

"I don't know." Firuza crinkled her nose. "He might. Dogs are unclean, not as valuable as eagles. But it's still not proof. Almas didn't see Zamam feeding his dog, but it did sicken and die. Suppose someone gave it hemlock-ridden quail? As a test. Zamam, or another—Timur's mother, Roxelana, even Timur if he thought he was giving the dog a treat. But Zamam was the one Almas reported seeing."

"It's worth investigating, I agree," Ogodai said. "It's a bit too much of a coincidence that Bahadur kicks out Tulpar, Tulpar's man Zamam stays in the camp, a dog dies and the owner accuses Zamam of killing it, then Bahadur dies within the week. The dog did die first?"

"Oh, yes." Firuza stared at the wall as if transfixed by visions of the past. "There was a huge hubbub. It happened just after Tulpar left."

"That does point to Zamam. Although one should never rule out Roxelana, I suppose." Ogodai raised an eyebrow at Daniil. "Wait till you meet her, brother. She is trouble incarnate."

Daniil raised an eyebrow of his own, and Ogodai turned his attention to Nasan. "Could poisoned quail kill a dog?"

"I don't see why not," she said. "A coursing hound is smaller than a man. But we would have to test it ourselves, and I'm not inclined to murder a dog."

Daniil had maintained an uncharacteristic silence through most of the discussion of Bahadur's death, conducted in Tatar for Firuza's sake. Now he spoke. "Where do we start, then?"

"The council is already investigating both Bahadur's death and the attack on my wife's brother—the work of the same person, I assume. We should head back, you and I, before Tulpar has a chance to convince them that he has defeated me. On the way, we can question Zamam," Ogodai said. "I brought him—and his eagle—with me to Kazan. Let's talk to Rafik first, though."

"Yes." Daniil flicked Nasan's cheek with one finger. "You amaze me, wife of mine. Good work."

Nasan blushed, quite charmingly, at the compliment. For a split second, she resembled any demure harem beauty, even though she had just demonstrated yet again the qualities that made her nothing of the sort.

Ogodai suppressed his laughter. His sister seldom failed to amaze him, too.

Chapter 21

FIRUZA ALLOWED OGODAI TO LIFT HER ONTO KUBELEK'S back. She had urged him to take the mare with him, but he insisted that Daniil's borrowed mount would suit him just fine, that he wanted the reassurance of imagining her and her horse together on the road to Kasimov. It would ease his journey, knowing that she and the mare were safe.

She wanted to shout at him that *her* safety was not in question. The escort supplied by Daniil would ensure that she and Nasan reached Kasimov without incident. Once there, not much could go wrong unless her soon-to-be mother-in-law disliked her, whereas she might lose Ogodai altogether if his forthcoming battle with Tulpar went against him.

Firuza didn't say those things. Her parents had taught her that men went to war, and women shouldn't weaken them with pleading and remonstrations. She sensed anxiety in Ogodai, but mostly on her behalf. For himself, he seemed to greet the coming challenge with a certain anticipation—excitement, even. No doubt he told the truth when he said that he needed reassurance of her safety before he could focus his energies on the struggle to come. That was a gift she could offer with an open heart. She swallowed and leaned forward, caressing her betrothed's sun-browned cheek with her palm. "Fight well, beloved. Defeat Tulpar if you can, but come back to me."

A tear she couldn't suppress dripped onto his fur collar, pulled high against the approaching snows. Her ankle, much improved during their week in Kazan, throbbed with the cold but not so badly as to make riding uncomfortable. She dashed the tears away and straightened in her saddle. The ache in her heart far outweighed any lingering pain in her foot.

"Look after her, Kubelek." Ogodai's voice had a husky edge that belied his surface calm. "Don't worry, my sweet. With Daniil at my back, I am more than a match for Tulpar."

Nasan, who had been murmuring to her husband this whole time, came to sniff her brother's cheek. "You can trust me, *aby*. I will present her to *Ana* before the end of the week."

"Tell her not to send for *Ata*," he told her—not for the first time. "I need to finish this myself."

Nasan laughed as she walked around Kubelek to mount her own horse. As Daniil lifted her onto the saddle, she said, "*Ata* can't interfere. He's stuck in Lithuania. *Ana* is the one likely to ride to your rescue! But I will try to dissuade her."

His face crinkled in response. "Yes, do your best."

He patted Kubelek's flank, and the horse stepped out, keeping pace with Nasan's. The image of his smile remained in Firuza's mind. She couldn't help wondering whether she had seen his gold-flecked eyes for the last time.

Four days later, Ogodai reined in the roan gelding he had borrowed from Daniil. Through the thinning trees, he could already detect the outlines of round felt tents. The sounds of sheep, goats, and cows reached him on a snow-laden breeze. From this distance, the camp looked serene, untroubled, protected from the onrush of winter by the windbreak supplied by the hills and the coniferous forest. Only the presence of a half-dozen armed sentries indicated the possibility of anything amiss.

Daniil drew up beside him. As expected, Alexander Makhmetovich had raised no objections to the reassignment of his youngest and least capable aide. The ride had given Ogodai plenty of time to acquaint Daniil with the situation in the Tatar camp.

"Should we dump him?" Daniil jerked his head toward Zamam, still riding bound and sullen among them. "He's more a liability than a help."

Indeed, during their time on the road Zamam had failed to yield the information Ogodai sought. The man had stiffened his spine during their stay in Kazan—or perhaps he had learned enough about Ogodai to guess that the threats to harm the eagle, however firmly delivered, were hollow. The night before, Rafik, frustrated beyond belief by Zamam's refusal to cooperate, had freed the bird from its restraints. It circled for a while, then flew away, closing off even that less than satisfactory option.

"I'd love to," Ogodai said. "The man's a complete nuisance. But Tulpar threatened to kill him on sight. I'm hoping that will loosen his tongue, since nothing else seems to."

"Lovely family you have," Daniil said with a grin.

Ogodai shrugged. "Needs must."

"So what's next? Everything out there looks quiet enough. Do we know we have the right camp?"

Rather than answer, Ogodai beckoned to Rafik, who abandoned his conversation with the head of Ogodai's troops and urged his horse forward to join them. "Yes?"

"These are your people?" Ogodai waved at the tents visible through the trunks of the white birches and oaks, obscured by the conifers.

"Looks like them." Rafik advanced toward the edge of the forest, then returned. Snow muffled his horse's hooves. "Yes. I recognize the nearest sentry."

"Did you see signs of trouble as you got closer?" Daniil asked. "Other than the sentries—or are those normal?"

"At this time of year," Rafik said. "The horde has controlled these grazing lands for as long as anyone can remember, but hungry horsemen don't quibble about stealing a sheep or a goat. We station men and dogs at the boundaries, especially to the south, just in case approaching raiders need a reminder of whose cattle these are." He kneed his horse, and the beast danced sideways. "Should I go first? I can reconnoiter and report back if I see aught that strikes me as strange."

A reasonable suggestion but not, perhaps, well thought through. "Too risky," Ogodai said. "Suppose Tulpar has already inveigled his way in with some story to the council?"

"They're my people." Rafik looked incredulous.

Daniil shook his head. He didn't speak, but Ogodai guessed that his brother-in-law could predict what he would say. They had discussed their options yesterday evening.

"If your father has a say," Ogodai explained, "I'm sure he can prevent Tulpar from attacking you. But Tulpar knows who supports whom on the council as well as we do. He will have undercut your father if possible. If you arrive alone, he could accuse you of siding with the enemy—me. Better we approach as a group."

Rafik turned his horse, aligning himself at Ogodai's left shoulder. Daniil already occupied the space at his right. Ogodai stared forward, through the thinning trees. A light snow drifted down from a sky the color of an Arctic wolf's pelt. Were it not for his half-brother—ensconced, perhaps, amid the tents—he would look forward to the prospect of food and shelter.

Behind him, the massed warriors of his small troop had halted their mounts when their leader did and patiently awaited their orders.

This was it. The final confrontation with Tulpar, or just another day. No way to tell which from out here. Brooding over the possibilities wouldn't solve the problem either.

He glanced at Rafik, then at Daniil. They nodded when his head turned their way. Ogodai braced himself mentally, raised a hand, and brought his arm down, pointing at the silent camp. Three abreast, they moved forward, abandoning the protective forest for the open steppe.

The journey to Kasimov proceeded slowly, since the horses could travel no faster than the supply wagons that followed. Nasan, ebullient with the unexpected acquisition of a nomadic sister, kept up a steady flow of chatter, leaving Firuza with little time to worry about her reception in her husband's home— although she couldn't entirely escape the flutters caused by the prospect of meeting Sumbeka once more. A mother-in-law loomed larger in a young woman's life even than a husband, and Diliara's gentle if thorough rearing had ill prepared her stepdaughter for dealing with the woman of decision who so often appeared in Nasan's anecdotes.

Nasan dismissed such concerns with a wave of her hand. "You must be joking," she said. "*Ana* will love you. Even *my* mother-in-law would sell her soul for a bride like you— although in truth she's a decent sort even if she does wish to put me in a box and make me behave. And you will have no beastly sister-in-law to torment you, lucky thing." She laughed when she said that, and Firuza couldn't help smiling back.

When not envisioning rejection by Sumbeka, Firuza battled a constant stream of anxieties about Ogodai. Had he reached the camp? Had he challenged Tulpar already? Would he survive, whole and uninjured, to return to her?

She kept her worries to herself, lest she cause the misfortune she feared by speaking her thoughts aloud. But when, on one glorious wintry afternoon four days or so after they had set out, Nasan pointed to one hilltop fortress and said, "Kasimov!" Firuza's anxieties again flared into life like the embers from last night's hearth fire.

To calm herself, she studied the town where her husband had lived for two years. Kasimov looked compact and plain after the glories of Kazan. Its neat wooden palisades were well maintained. Earthen ramparts raised up the fortress and provided an additional ring of protection outside the town. The square gatehouses with their pointed roofs conveyed a comforting stolidity. Within the walls, minarets punctuated the skyline.

Nasan pointed to a white stone structure to the right of the gatehouse, within the fortress walls. As in Kazan, semi-cylinders of red clay overlapped to form its roof, and iron grilles half-obscured the windows. "The palace," she said. "*Ana* will be there, waiting for us."

She beckoned to their escort. A young man with the light brown hair and hazel eyes that seemed so much more common among the people of the northern khanates than among the nomads edged his horse forward through the throng. "Ride ahead," Nasan ordered. "Inform the khatun of our arrival."

He acknowledged her command with a wave of his spear and set his horse galloping toward the gatehouse. Nasan turned to Firuza. "Shall we follow? No need to tarry when we are so close."

Gallop into the presence of her mother-in-law, who would be setting eyes on her for the first time in six years?

"A little slower, perhaps," Firuza said. "A nice trot? It's fine for you; she's your mother. But she will hardly be impressed if I show up wind-blown and sweating."

Nasan shook her head, laughing again. "I told you: she'll love you on sight. I'll hardly dare show my face here once she realizes you are the woman she has always wanted me to become. But if it will make you feel better, we'll trot."

And so they did, right up to the palace courtyard, Nasan pointing out landmarks as they passed. As Firuza had guessed from the exterior, Kasimov was much smaller than Kazan, more approachable to one who still regarded an encampment of a hundred tents as a massive gathering. Many of the dwellings, in fact, *were* tents: the same round felt-covered homes that she had known her entire life. Even the mosque and palace, although grander than the humble residences of the poor, were simple rectangles adorned with white stucco walls and tiled window frames.

Firuza felt the tension in her shoulders ease. She would rather be in her own camp, with Ogodai. She still worried that Sumbeka might not approve of her. But Kasimov looked like a place she could adjust to, given time.

As they entered the palace courtyard, Nasan slid from her mare's back and tossed her reins to the nearest person, a man in servant's dress who received them with a startled expression that split into a broad grin as he watched Nasan dash across the courtyard, skirts raised in one hand. "It's the khan's daughter," he cried, unleashing a flurry of exclamations and movement that Nasan ignored. She ran straight into the arms of an older woman, middle-aged but still beautiful, who so resembled Nasan herself that she could only be Sumbeka. The khatun was crying and laughing at the same time, and the fierce affection with which she embraced Nasan brought a lump to Firuza's throat.

There was nothing for it but to dismount, favoring her tender ankle. She handed her reins to the servant holding Sorkhokhtani. He appraised her as he took them. She could imagine him wondering who she was, but she saw no reason to enlighten him. Instead, she walked toward Nasan and Sumbeka—slowly, to control her limp.

Ogodai ordered his men to stash Zamam, bound, in the nearest animal shelter. Even with winter closing in, here in the early afternoon all but the youngest beasts were outside the camp, grazing whatever they could dig from under the snow. Convenient for keeping a traveling companion out of sight long enough to stop him from being prematurely dispatched by a half-brother and rival.

"I suggest you keep your mouth shut," Ogodai told his prisoner. "You'll neither starve nor freeze here. We'll return for you eventually, but I wouldn't bet on your chances if Tulpar finds you first."

Zamam huddled against the frame of the unfurnished tent. The straw bed on which the troops had dumped him had no doubt looked better before sheep pulled stray bits off it, and the air was cold enough to show a frosty mist before every man's face. Freezing and starving looked like distinct possibilities, but Ogodai refused to let that thought deter him. He owed Zamam nothing except the courtesy due to any fellow human being. And he could serve that obligation best by bringing his contest with his brother to a successful conclusion. Without a backward glance, he strode from the shelter and rejoined Daniil.

Alas, his plans to conceal Zamam appeared doomed from the start. His party's arrival in the camp had not gone unnoticed. Timur darted from the audience tent at the far end of the camp, clapped his hand over his mouth, and ran back inside. Mounted sentries soon surrounded Ogodai, Daniil, and their combined troop of a hundred mounted warriors. Dogs raced to confront the intruders, skidded to a halt when Rafik yelled out their names, then approached more cautiously, snouts sniffing the air.

Ogodai had expected the sentries, like the dogs, to withdraw as soon as they recognized him—or, if not him, Rafik. Instead, the leading sentry doffed his fur-trimmed cap and bowed. "We have orders, Sultan, to take you to the khan."

Khan? Had matters deteriorated so far, so fast? Ogodai raised his eyebrows at Daniil, who responded in kind. On his left side, Rafik visibly quivered with rage.

"You have no need to escort me," Ogodai told the sentry. "I have much to discuss with the *khan*. He is in the audience tent?" It seemed like a reasonable assumption, based on Timur's behavior.

The sentry shook his head. "I must escort you, Sultan. Those were my orders."

"Let us go then." Ogodai kept his voice calm, but his mind raced. How had Tulpar suborned the council to declare him khan, when less than two weeks ago they had confirmed Ogodai in that post? How could he win back their support?

The struggle between him and Tulpar would end before nightfall. He sensed the ancestors gathering, waiting to see which of their descendants would join them today. Bahadur Bey, proud astride his winged stallion, watched with them.

Ogodai seldom prayed to the grandmothers. Although he respected the ancient spirits, he placed his faith in the One God, merciful and compassionate. Every warrior knew that the outcome of a battle—life or death—depended on a fate written into the stars before he was born. A man could survive the flight of a thousand arrows and die in a tumble from a weary horse.

So Ogodai didn't fear death. But he did want to live—to build a home with Firuza, have children with her, rule her horde. The words formed in his mind before he had a chance to censor them.

Help me, Grandmothers—Bey—to defeat Tulpar.

A clap of Sumbeka's hands summoned a bevy of maids and concubines, who swirled into the room and embraced Nasan. Firuza watched bemused as a faded, middle-aged blonde with high Slavic cheekbones and a kindly face reminiscent of Diliara bustled in.

"Tanya!" Nasan pushed through the crowd and hugged the newcomer. "How I have missed you."

"And I you, Khanim. I hope your young lord treats you well—and his family, too."

Firuza, hearing the slight accent in the woman's words, strove to place it. Tanya was a Russian name, surely? A slave, then. Nasan's personal servant, perhaps—but then why had she remained in Kasimov when Nasan married?

She hung back, not wanting to interfere in Nasan's reunion with the women of her father's harem. But Sumbeka caught her hand and pulled her into the throng, introducing her before dismissing most of the women with a few imperious words.

"Off with you," she said. "You'll have a chance to chat with the girls later. Tanya, bring us some food."

The concubines departed, fluttering and chattering like the exotic birds portrayed on the vases and embroideries that adorned the palace. Tanya signaled to a pair of maids, who rushed off and returned loaded with trays. Sumbeka ushered

Firuza and Nasan into a room decorated in warm patterns of orange and green picked out against a cream background. Iron braziers blazed in the center, but when Firuza took her seat on one of the cushioned sofas, she realized that the seats themselves gave off heat. She touched the cover, wondering.

"Pipes," Nasan said. "Amazing, isn't it? They carry heat from the kitchens and disperse it throughout the palace."

"Very different from our tents," Firuza agreed. "I don't recall them from Kazan."

"They have them. In the walls more than the benches." Nasan laughed. "It is one thing I don't miss from the steppe— the cold. And the dirt. Two things, then."

Sumbeka sat between them, taking one of their hands in each of hers. "We will eat and talk. Then rest well, my dear ones, for tomorrow we head east."

"East?" Firuza couldn't hide her surprise.

Nasan took the declaration in stride. "Ogodai asked us to wait. Not to tell *Ata*, especially. He wants to settle this quarrel himself."

Sumbeka's face assumed, if anything, a more determined expression. "Quarrel? Which Ogodai wants kept secret from your father?" She squeezed their hands, then released them. "My dears, you do have a story to tell, don't you?"

She lifted a platter of golden-brown turnovers, like the basket Ogodai had offered in Kazan, and held it out to Firuza. "Welcome, daughter. It has been long since we met. Tell me your story, because indeed we start east tomorrow, whatever my son wants or doesn't want. He should have fulfilled his betrothal to you years ago, as I told him—and my husband— many times. We will no longer wait for them. The petty squabbles of men do not concern me. Diliara and I have a wedding to plan." Her rather stern expression evaporated into pure mischief, highlighting her resemblance to Nasan. "Nor am I yet so antiquated that I have forgotten the delights of travel on horseback."

Firuza allowed a servant to pour warm water over her hands, catching it in a small bowl, before she accepted first a towel, then a turnover. The familiar actions gave her a chance to compose herself. Nasan was already chattering at full tilt, telling Sumbeka about her time in Kazan, what she had learned about Ogodai and Tulpar and the nomads, the plot against Jan-Ali, her suspicions of Aslanbika, and Firuza's unexpected arrival.

Firuza didn't interrupt. Her earlier fears had fled in response to Sumbeka's kindness, but anxiety for Ogodai expanded to fill the empty space. The petty squabbles of men? But this contest he faced was no trifle. He must confront Tulpar. And from the fight she had witnessed at the cabin, it seemed certain that they would not stop until one killed the other. What point in planning a wedding when the groom might not live to attend it?

Yet Firuza had no desire to stay here, safe but ignorant. By agreeing to travel to Kasimov, she had freed Ogodai to pursue his quarrel without worrying about her. Now she welcomed the opportunity to find out for herself. Ogodai couldn't be too angry that she and Nasan had failed to rein Sumbeka in— could he?

Besides, better an angry Ogodai than a dead one.

"Whatever happens, I will not marry Tulpar," she said, to leave no doubt where she stood.

They stared at her as if they'd forgotten her presence. "Of course not," Nasan said, although she sounded less than certain. Women had little choice in whom they married.

Sumbeka patted her hand. "It won't come to that. Arrogance was always Tulpar's besetting sin, and it is easy to underestimate Ogodai, even with Daniil at his side. They will prevail, I'm sure." The mischievous look returned to her eyes. "Especially with us to help things along."

If they got there in time. But Firuza kept that thought, too, to herself. She was getting quite good, she decided, at knowing when, where, and what to confide.

Chapter 22

TULPAR OCCUPIED THE CENTRAL PLATFORM, AS OGODAI had expected. Spine straight, legs crossed under him, hands on his knees, palms up—Tulpar had certainly mastered the presentation of himself as khan. The sultry lounging of Roxelana on the cushions beside him only added to his luster. Her obvious adoration also explained Jahangir's grim expression, the determined way he faced front, not exchanging glances with Tulpar even though the new, self-proclaimed ruler sat directly to his left.

Ogodai assessed his half-brother for evidence of the emotions that lay behind that stalwart presentation. Anger— the stiff shoulders and grim mouth pointed in that direction. Surprise? None visible. If Tulpar had expected his younger brother to yield without a fight, he had had sufficient time to hide any chagrin at his mistake. But confusion, definitely: the eyes that darted between himself and Daniil suggested that Tulpar wondered about the identity of this Russian and how the introduction of a foreigner might affect his own plans. And that the self-appointed khan might have less faith in his own strength than he wanted those present to believe.

Good. Keeping Tulpar off-balance benefited Ogodai and his allies—who needed, he concluded as he surveyed the rest of the crowd, as much assistance as they could get. He saw Ildar Shirin, unsurprisingly triumphant. Kipchak and Baryn, wriggling on their mats, unable to meet Ogodai's eyes.

Still, he allowed himself a flash of hope. If Roxelana had switched sides and caused a split between Jahangir and Tulpar, that gave him a tool that he could use to separate them. Shirin was a lost cause, but the others looked persuadable.

Although he had been right, it seemed, to fear for the safety of Kazbek Argyn. An empty place next to Jahangir signaled the absence of Ogodai's staunchest supporter.

"Where's my father?" Rafik demanded before Ogodai could ask the question himself.

Tulpar raised both eyebrows. "Greetings, Argyn *mirza*. Your honored father no longer feels capable of attending our council sessions."

"Is he ill?" Rafik took a hasty step forward.

"I would say, rather, incapacitated." Tulpar signaled to a guard, who approached Rafik, waving his spear in a threatening manner.

Ogodai shot a glance at Daniil. Together, they moved to block the guard. "You overstep your bounds, *aby*," Ogodai said.

"Do I?" Tulpar waved the guard back to his place. "A khan has no bounds." Roxelana collapsed in giggles, and he patted her head. "I know, dearest; the mere idea amuses. My little brother has much to learn." His insolent gaze returned to Ogodai. "Where did you abandon my beautiful bride, *ené*?"

Roxelana's giggles vanished. She sat up, glowering. Jahangir smiled.

"Firuza is safe." Ogodai kept his voice level, refusing to let his brother get under his skin. He spoke to Kipchak and Baryn, watching Jahangir out of the corner of his eye. "I hope you can say the same for Kazbek Argyn. The great lords of

Bahadur Bey's council deserve a better reward for their decades of service than incarceration at your pleasure."

"He told us he had killed you," Kipchak blurted.

Tulpar snorted, but Baryn chimed in. "It is true. We supported you. But once he killed you, what choice did we have? He, too, is Bulat's son."

"You told them I was dead?" Ogodai spoke directly to the man whom he had once regarded as family, who so obviously was not.

Tulpar shrugged, but he couldn't quite keep the embarrassment from his face. "It was worth a try. If you did show up, they would learn the truth. If you didn't..." He left the sentence unfinished.

It was difficult, but Ogodai forced his jaw not to drop. His brother's effrontery stunned him, but he needed to stay on his feet if he hoped to recover. "As you see," he said to the council, "my brother lied."

"Yes." Kipchak glanced at Baryn, than at Jahangir. "He deceived us. But it is difficult to know how best to proceed."

Daniil snorted and stepped forward, his shoulder touching Ogodai's in a clear statement of support. "You might reconsider," Ogodai suggested. "Even today, the hordes of the steppe value honesty above all. Will you submit yourselves to a khan who lies?"

The junior beys studied the carpet as if it were a map. In their discomfort, Ogodai read their uncertainty. Without Kazbek to lead them, they saw little advantage to opposing Shirin and Jahangir, more powerful than themselves. But if he could force a confrontation with Tulpar and emerge victorious, he might yet secure their support.

"And my father?" Rafik asked, with less aggression this time. Ogodai welcomed the question. Kazbek's situation had supreme relevance here.

"You need not fret, Argyn *mirza.*" Ildar Shirin said smoothly. "Your father has suffered no harm. He has merely discovered that he can't leave his tent, especially to attend council meetings. Once he accepts the inevitability of our choice, the khan will restore him to his former station."

"Let us hope that the khan sees fit to release Kazbek Argyn from captivity soon," Ogodai said, his tone biting. "In the meantime, permit me to present to you my brother-in-law and *qarïndash*, Daniil Nikolaevich Kolychev." He touched Daniil's elbow, and the Russian bowed. Ogodai then named each council member in turn, greeting them as Daniil echoed the formal phrases in Tatar.

The council members responded in kind. Roxelana stiffened, drawing closer to Tulpar as if seeking reassurance. Seeing the frightened glances she cast from one man to the next, Ogodai felt a certain pity for her. For all her sensual appeal, she had less control over her fate even than Firuza. He had secured his wife-to-be's safety, but who would guarantee Roxelana's? She had alienated Jahangir, and Tulpar might die in the struggle to come. She must know that Ogodai would dismiss her if he won the present battle. Yet that outcome, too, lay outside her control—although he wouldn't put it past her to intervene in the contest if she saw an opportunity to promote her own interests. She had as much stake in the results as any of them.

Indeed, were those not sheep's eyes she was making at Daniil? A sideways glance revealed his brother-in-law's lips twitching, but Daniil stared straight ahead, ignoring Roxelana's provocation. Fortunately for her, Tulpar couldn't see what she was doing.

Ever the opportunist. Ogodai made a mental note not to underestimate Roxelana, then turned his attention to the men. The tension in the tent caused his nerves to hum, like the strings of a *dombra*.

As the introductions wound down, he addressed the council. "After I beat my older brother in a fight and he escaped," he said, choosing each word with care, "I knew he might choose to return here. But your lady—*my* lady—had suffered enough at his hands. I value her safety even above rulership of your horde. I took her to Kazan, to my sister and her husband." He indicated Daniil. "You remember my sister Nasan; she lived among you as a girl. And you remember my mother, who has taken Firuza into her care. As soon as I saw her safely on her way to Kasimov, I came back to fulfill my promise to you. To lead you toward a prosperous and independent future."

"With Russians in tow," Tulpar said. He turned his head toward Kipchak and Baryn. "Is that what you foresee as best for your people? To serve the Russians?"

Kipchak shrugged. "I see only one Russian, and a kinsman at that."

"And a sworn brother," Baryn affirmed. "Brothers fight together," he added, as if rebuking Tulpar.

Both comments reassured Ogodai that he had read them correctly. He might yet pull this blazing ember from the fire.

"No doubt they have others in tow," Tulpar retorted.

"Do they?" Jahangir had, so far, maintained an uncharacteristic silence. His languid tone here seemed designed to annoy. "How many Russians did you see, Timur?"

Ogodai had almost forgotten the boy, who emerged from behind the platform in response to this summons. "Just that one, Bey." He pointed at Daniil. "The rest look like our own people."

It was true. They did. Jan-Ali and Alexander Makhmetovich had sent Tatar warriors—some in service to Russia, others to Kazan—to reassure the people of Bahadur's horde that they were not facing a Russian invasion. A sound move that Ogodai appreciated even more at this moment than he had when Daniil first proposed it.

The answer further unsettled Tulpar, Ogodai saw. Once more, he surveyed the council. Despite the various declarations, it appeared increasingly unlikely that the horde had formally acclaimed Tulpar as khan. Kipchak and Baryn were already wavering. But with Kazbek imprisoned, the council would remain divided even if both junior beys changed their allegiance once more.

Shirin had invested too much to withdraw, and only a naif would expect Tulpar to stand down on his own. But Jahangir was clearly unhappy with Tulpar's appropriation of Roxelana. Jahangir had asked a question that undercut Tulpar's argument. And Jahangir, despite his callous and incomprehensible disregard for his twin sister's welfare, might yet cast the deciding vote if Ogodai made it easy for him to switch sides.

With that goal in mind, he took two steps forward and focused his full attention on Jahangir. "No Russians," he said. "No Gireis. I told you before. I intend to rule *this* horde, not to subordinate its interests to those of any other khan or prince. To rule you as Bahadur Bey did, with Bahadur's son at my side and as my equal. You need only say the word. The alternative is to choose a khan ready to lie and cheat for his own gain."

Jahangir bit his lip, swallowed, and looked to his left, where Roxelana stared at Tulpar, then Daniil. Occasionally her eyes even drifted in Jahangir's direction, as if calculating her options.

Does Jahangir want her badly enough that she will sway him, despite her recent betrayal, despite Tulpar's proven dishonesty?

Ogodai waited, not speaking. He was a weak reed, Jahangir, and he faced a tough decision. The possibility of self-indulgence versus the promise of equal responsibility, boyhood versus manhood. Which would he choose?

A vision of giant scales, like those used to weigh tribute, hung before Ogodai's eyes. The very air congealed, pressing on his chest until he could scarcely breathe.

Tulpar left his platform in a rush. "Worthless hound! You dare have second thoughts? You swore to follow me!" He backhanded Jahangir across the jaw and continued his stalk toward Ogodai. "You have caused me nothing but trouble, *ené*, from the moment you entered this camp. We settle this now—you and me, one on one, winner takes all. These fools have already declared their intent to follow the stronger man. Enough words! Let us show them who deserves their support."

Ogodai responded with the terse nod such a challenge deserved. He looked at Daniil, who glared at Tulpar like a mountain demon surprised by an intruder. "Whatever happens, you will watch over my bride?"

Daniil clasped his shoulder. "Of course."

Tulpar emitted a sound close to a growl at the word "bride." Ogodai didn't care. Instead, he concentrated his mind on the battle to come. Fight his best. Fate would decide who won.

"Clear the tent," he told his brother. "Let's get this over with."

Think of it as a wrestling match. Ogodai checked his mail shirt, his helmet, the dagger in his belt, his sword. Tulpar retained—as he had that first day—the advantages of age and experience. But that was the point of wrestling: size mattered less than skill, and skill meant the ability to exploit an opponent's weaknesses, which in Tulpar's case included overconfidence. He, Ogodai, had used that arrogance against his half-brother in their earlier contest. He could do so again.

Of course, it would have been better not to engage in hand-to-hand combat, but he didn't have that choice. At least he could count on Daniil and Rafik to ensure a fair fight. In the hour that had passed since Tulpar issued his challenge, the two of them had disputed every suggestion put forth by the opposing side, checked every detail. They would continue to watch as the battle progressed. Rafik's father had joined them, released from whatever restraints Tulpar had placed on him and looking far from happy. Jahangir, Baryn, and Kipchak had proven less than steadfast in the past, but as Tulpar had noted, they would support whoever won. They had nothing to gain from undermining the fight.

Most of the hangers-on had left. Daniil, Rafik, Kazbek, Jahangir, Ildar Shirin, and the junior beys sat around the edges, leaving the central area free. Charcoal braziers positioned at the four cardinal points, although dangerous if the combatants came too close, provided enough heat to make Ogodai glad that no one had insisted they fight outside. The hearth fire had remained unlit since morning, so he needn't worry about that obstacle. Servants had rolled up the rugs and moved the chests and the khan's platform. The dirt floor gave his boots good purchase. He could do this. He could win.

He forced himself not to feed the fears that pressed on his mind. Visions of Firuza abandoned, wed to his half-brother against her will. Of his family grieving, himself dispatched to live among the ancestors before attaining the pleasures and responsibilities of adulthood. Whatever happened, he vowed not to become an angry ghost, not to haunt his family. And not to yield to his brother. A man's destiny may be written in the stars, but he meant to fight as long and as hard as he could. With the determination that had served him well on the battlefield, he cleared his thoughts of emotion.

A few feet away, Tulpar rocked gently on the balls of his feet. The light that streamed through the smoke hole showed off the gold filigree decorating his pointed steel helmet, the nose guard that bifurcated his face. He wore a brass breastplate, not Ogodai's serviceable mail. Tulpar's sword, too, was showy—its hilt chased, its blade etched with wavy lines—but Ogodai had no doubt it would cleave his skull if he misjudged its arc.

With a roar, Tulpar dashed forward, holding his sword in both hands. Ogodai met the charge in mid-run. The blades clashed and disengaged, clashed again. Ogodai twisted, taking advantage of his lighter weight, lighter armor, lighter sword to sweep past his brother's guard. A memory—more image than words—of teaching his sister Nasan this very move presented itself and slid away. His blade sliced a hole in Tulpar's fine sleeve and drew blood. Behind Ogodai, someone cheered. In Russian. Daniil.

Tulpar let out another yell and shoved Ogodai with his free hand. Blood dripped onto the ground, Tulpar's trousers, Ogodai's tunic, his mail shirt. Ogodai skipped sideways, frustrating the attempt to topple him. Tulpar kicked out, hooking his brother behind the knees with a foot while swinging his sword over his head. A killing blow if it had connected, but Ogodai rolled over and onto his feet, pulling his dagger from his belt and slashing at Tulpar's thigh. More blood, but at the cost of intercepting a blow from the flat of Tulpar's sword that upended him once more. He landed on his back. His sword flew from his right hand, his dagger from his left. Puffs of dirt rose around him, causing him to sneeze.

His vision cleared to reveal Tulpar again striding toward him, sword raised. He had to finish this, and quickly—but how?

Another image rose in his mind: Firuza, seated on Kubelek, begging him to return to her, tears running down her face.

Rather than go straight to standing, Ogodai rolled toward his brother, grabbed Tulpar's ankle with both hands, and pulled with every ounce of strength he could muster. Tulpar kicked out once more, but this time Ogodai forestalled him, throwing up his feet to lock around the kicking leg while he tugged on the standing foot. The sword blade hummed perilously close to his head, but he hung on, increasing the pressure by rolling in the other direction.

Tulpar fell. As soon as Ogodai felt his brother's footing slip, he released the ankle he held and grabbed the descending sword. The blade slashed his palm, but he barely noticed. In an instant, he sprang to his feet, reversed the sword. The hilt felt solid in his right hand, the tip pointed at Tulpar's throat. He planted a foot on his brother's chest. One stab with the sword, and the contest was over.

Tulpar stared up at him, shock visible on his face. For the first time, Ogodai saw fear in his brother's eyes. Fear and a touch of respect. They were both breathing hard.

"So," Tulpar drawled. "You win, *ené*. Are you going to kill me, as our father would no doubt recommend?"

He didn't sound in the least respectful, or even afraid, yet Ogodai had heard the catch that preceded the word "kill."

And Tulpar had asked a good question. Bulat *would* recommend death, Ogodai suspected. Tulpar, alive, would require continual watching. Unless…

"That depends on you." He saw Tulpar's eyes widen. He wasn't as indifferent to death as he wanted Ogodai to believe. "Will you swear to me on the Koran that you will leave this place and not return, that you will make no other attempt to steal my wife or to challenge me for the leadership of this horde?" He pressed the tip of the sword against Tulpar's neck, emphasizing that he could drive the blow home if he chose.

A murmuring started up around the circle, reminding Ogodai that he and his brother weren't the only ones present. He couldn't tell whether those watching approved or disapproved. But he sensed a certainty in himself that he had made the right choice. The details of the incident that had led to the breach between Tulpar and Bulat were known only to them. His brother's resentment arose from a sense of mistreatment that might be justified. If Tulpar refused to yield, Ogodai would drive that blade home whether he regretted the necessity or not, but fairness required that he give his brother a chance.

Tulpar hadn't responded. He turned his head slightly to the right, stopped. The tip of the blade drew a thin line of blood that beaded on his neck. The Adam's apple jumped in his neck as he swallowed. Ogodai pressed harder. "I'm waiting. Will you swear?"

"Damn it," Tulpar said. "Yes, *ené*, you win. I'll swear."

Ogodai pulled back the sword, removed his foot from Tulpar's chest, and extended a hand. Tulpar grabbed the hand and pulled himself to a standing position, cursing as he examined his wounds. "May demons fly off with you, Ogodai. I'm covered in bruises and bleeding like a hell-sent Russian pig."

Face saving. Ogodai ignored his brother's complaints and spoke to the circle instead. "Someone fetch a Koran. You'll find one in my saddlebags, if there are none to hand. And bind that wound. We can't have him dripping blood on the holy book. Let's administer the oath before my brother forgets."

"Oh, I won't forget," Tulpar said.

A servant, hastily summoned by Rafik, ran in and handed Kazbek Argyn a Koran that Ogodai recognized as his own. He passed it to a glum-faced Ildar Shirin, who held out the small book. A second servant tied a rough cloth around Tulpar's upper arm, then dabbed at the wetness on his sleeve. Tulpar placed his right hand on the Koran.

"I hope you know what you're doing," Daniil said. He grabbed a spare cloth from the servant and handed it to Ogodai, who wrapped it around his gashed palm.

"Me too," Ogodai replied. "Swear," he told Tulpar and raised the sword he still held.

His brother grimaced, then complied. "I vow by Allah and my ancestors to leave this horde today. I will not again attempt to steal Lady Firuza, nor will I challenge you for the position of khan." His fist clenched around the Koran.

"And what of Bahadur Bey?" In the heat of the fight, Bahadur's fate had slipped from view, yet the question leaped into Ogodai's mind as he realized he might not have another chance to ask it. "Before you leave, I want to know what happened. Did you cause his death, as the shaman said in her dream?"

The resignation in Tulpar's face yielded to astonishment. "Of course not. When she pointed at me, she meant I was the beneficiary of the scheme, not the assassin. Zamam poisoned the bey in response to orders from Islam-Girei, then attacked you for the same reason. But the fool got Jahangir by mistake."

Ogodai, stunned, could only stare at his brother. "You knew this and said nothing?"

"Why should I? I don't owe you allegiance." Tulpar shrugged. "Besides, it's supposition. If you want to be sure, ask Zamam. Or did you let him go?"

"We will ask him," Ogodai said. "You can be sure of that. At the moment I don't believe a word of it. You can't deny that you benefited more than anyone from Bahadur's death."

"I don't deny that." Tulpar raised the Koran. "But I swear on this holy book that I did not kill Bahadur, nor did I order him dead. In the years since our father cast me out, Bahadur and Shirin Bey kept me alive. I owe them both a debt I can never repay."

"You argued with him, though. He ordered you to leave the horde." Ogodai, struggling with this new picture—not just of Bahadur's death but of his older brother—focused on details, hoping that if he mastered enough of them, he could fit the disparate pieces into place.

"He ordered me to leave, on average, once a year," Tulpar said. "But he always welcomed me back. Yes, we argued. Often. I called him an old stick-in-the-mud. He called me an arrogant scoundrel. He disapproved of my service to Islam-Girei. Wanted me to give full allegiance to this horde. But Islam-Girei, too, provided help when I needed it. I couldn't turn my back on him. At heart Bahadur understood that."

He paused. When Ogodai didn't respond, he added, "Shirin had no reason to murder Bahadur either. Old friends don't kill each other because they disagree over which of two candidates would make a better khan. Islam-Girei, preparing for another rebellion against his uncle, was the one with a motive. He's desperate for troops. But I had no need to hasten Bahadur's death. I assumed I could defeat you when the time came." He gave a rueful chuckle. "Guess I was wrong."

He sounded sincere, as he had that day at the cabin. And when Ogodai considered the points his brother had raised, he had to admit that the story made sense. Islam-Girei *did* need all the support he could muster if he hoped to succeed in this latest attempt to unseat his uncle Sahib, and it didn't take an oracle to predict that Tulpar, who had long served Islam-Girei's cause, was a better bet for delivering such support than Ogodai, whose father loyally served the Russian crown—or even Bahadur, a known quantity dedicated to preserving his horde's neutrality in the Crimean and other conflicts.

Another opportunist, Islam-Girei. Ogodai glanced at Daniil, Rafik, Kazbek, wondering what they made of Tulpar's explanation. Their grim expressions gave no hint.

Daniil gripped Ogodai's shoulder. "Even if he's telling the truth, he'll remain a thorn in your side, brother. I hope you don't rue the day you decided to spare him."

Indeed, Tulpar glared at Ogodai, as if blaming the victor for the results of his victory.

"I know," Ogodai said. "I gave you a chance," he told Tulpar. "Don't make me regret it. Stay out of my sight from now on, if you know what's good for you."

For a long moment, Tulpar stared at him. "I'll leave at once. My sword?"

He must be joking. "I'll keep it."

Tulpar shrugged. "And Roxelana?"

"If she'll go with you, take her." The two of them were well matched. Ogodai glanced at Jahangir. The bey gazed at the ceiling, his expression unreadable, but he voiced no protest.

"Have I your allegiance?" Ogodai asked him. His gaze swept around the room, addressing Baryn and Kipchak as well.

"Yes," Jahangir mumbled, looking almost relieved. Maybe the burden of his father's death had weighed heavy on him, even though he'd done nothing to uncover the truth.

"Yes," the others shouted, leaping to their feet and punching the air. From his post next to Shirin, Kazbek Argyn inclined his head, a smile on his lips. Rafik grinned from the other side. Shirin gave a terse nod.

Timur poked his head around the tent flap, no doubt anxious to discover the results of the fight. Another loose end to tie. "But leave your son here," Ogodai told Tulpar. "I'll watch out for him."

"Better than Roxelana would, I'm sure." Tulpar's mouth quirked in something between a sneer and a smile. "Don't worry, Ogodai. I'll hunt elsewhere in the future." He sounded bitter, defeated.

"Good," Ogodai said. "Keep out of my way, and I'll keep out of yours."

Chapter 23

TULPAR SPUN ON HIS HEEL AND LIMPED TOWARD THE door. Although his arm was bandaged, blood dripped from his thigh, leaving a trail like ink blots behind him. The trickle from his neck had dried to a line of beads, but his halting gait revealed the effect of unseen bruises. Feeling his own aches and pains, the stinging in his palm, for the first time, Ogodai could imagine what damage a long ride would inflict. And the wounds had not been cleaned.

He cursed under his breath. He couldn't let Tulpar go in this state. Might as well have killed him outright.

"Stop," he said. He heard the reluctance in his own voice, but so what? Tulpar wouldn't believe a sudden change of heart, even if Ogodai had any desire to fake one.

His brother hadn't yet crossed half the space separating their makeshift arena from the tent door. He turned, that infuriating eyebrow raised.

"Sit." Ogodai gestured at the place for honored guests, asserting his own authority while signaling that he no longer considered Tulpar a rival. "The shaman should bind those wounds before you go."

Tulpar hesitated. "It wouldn't hurt," he said, sounding as grudging as Ogodai felt.

Ogodai waited, unmoving. After a while, Tulpar turned toward Rafik. "Tell Roxelana to prepare herself. We leave as soon as the witch finishes with her potions."

Rafik stared at Ogodai, neither acknowledging the order nor moving to obey.

"If you wouldn't mind, Rafik," Ogodai said, "please fetch the shaman. Perhaps you could alert Roxelana on your way."

"Yes, Khan." Rafik went off in search of the shaman. Daniil, his stance vaguely threatening, moved between Tulpar and the door. Tulpar waved him off with an irritable air, as if plagued by an over-eager dog, and limped back to the seat Ogodai had indicated.

No need to waste time, Ogodai decided. And since his brother had a salutary effect on Zamam, the delay might even serve a purpose. "Daniil," he asked, "would you summon the troops we brought from Kazan, and have them bring Zamam in as well?"

Daniil lifted a hand in response and left. While waiting for the others to return, Ogodai turned over his half-formed thought in his mind. Tulpar had named Zamam as Bahadur's murderer, but Zamam had yet to confirm any part of the charges against him. In fact, he had resisted every attempt at interrogation. And Ogodai, despite having defeated his brother and won the council's acclaim, had as yet a passing acquaintance with the members of his new horde, and they with him. It would take more than supposition to convince them that their new khan had right on his side, never mind that he had uncovered a conspiracy aimed at diverting their support to Crimea. Zamam might not be a long-time resident of the camp like Tulpar, but he had spent many more months here than Ogodai. As a result, a clear admission of guilt would be more likely to win the horde's trust than unsupported supposition. With Zamam's confession in hand, Ogodai, Jahangir, and the council could hope to resolve the situation by presenting their judgment against Zamam, whatever it proved to be, as necessary compensation for the death of their old leader and the attempted murder of his son. Without it, suspicions would swirl about the new khan and his council, feeding on any future cause for discontent that presented itself.

Could he use Tulpar to force a confession out of Zamam? Zamam feared Tulpar far more than he did Ogodai or Daniil. And Tulpar had a reason to cooperate, if only to clear himself before the council—and protect his son.

Ogodai studied his older brother. Could he trust Tulpar, even to this small extent? Should he?

He thought of what his half-brother had said about his debt to Bahadur and Ildar, about his continued allegiance to Islam-Girei in defiance of complaints—because they had helped him when he needed help. Perhaps Tulpar wasn't as much of an opportunist as Ogodai had believed. Although it still seemed unfair that his half-brother had extended his feud with Bulat to include the rest of the family, Ogodai had to admit that Tulpar had grounds for grievance against their father. If asked for help, Tulpar might agree or he might refuse, but the only way to find out was to try.

With these thoughts in mind, Ogodai moved to sit next to his half-brother, murmuring in his ear. After a while, Tulpar nodded reluctant assent.

The tent door opened, and Daniil came through. A pair of soldiers dragged in Zamam, followed by Rafik and the shaman. The shaman tended wounds with swift and silent efficiency. Ogodai submitted with a good grace to having his palm treated, then pushed her toward his brother.

Before the shaman reached him, Tulpar rose to his feet. He strolled toward Zamam, who shrank into himself as a rabbit does on the plains when the hawks fly by. Daniil looked a question at Ogodai, then stepped to one side to let Tulpar pass.

Ogodai crossed his arms and straightened, projecting the image of a khan in judgment. The pose felt unnatural, but he did his best to imagine himself as Bulat, stern and self-contained, hearing petitions and complaints. With any luck, he wouldn't make a complete ass of himself this afternoon.

He signaled to the shaman, who beat her drum and circled the room, muttering prayers as she sprinkled the company with milk from her ladle. Servants lit the hearth fire, augmenting the heat produced by the charcoal braziers.

As the shaman retreated behind the khan's platform, Tulpar took Zamam's chin in his hand and squeezed it. "I warned you to stay well clear of me, did I not?"

Zamam shivered, shrinking into his own skin. He didn't reply.

"Wise," Tulpar noted, his tone almost conversational despite the implicit threat of his pose. "You *should* fear me. And not only me. You have a lot to answer for, Zamam. Explain to me why I shouldn't kill you here, where you stand." He glanced at Ogodai, his sardonic grin well in evidence. "As a gift to my younger brother, the khan."

His fingertips showed white as he tightened his grip on Zamam's chin. "You stayed behind. To serve Bahadur, you said at the time, but that wasn't true. Instead, you carried out the schemes of Islam-Girei. You told everyone you served me, when in fact you served him, so that these men"—he swept a hand, indicating the council—"believed me guilty of murder. You attacked Jahangir. Can you deny it?"

When Zamam cringed, Ogodai joined Tulpar. Daniil, expressing silent support, followed him. The three of them loomed over the much smaller Zamam, who wriggled like a speared snake.

Ogodai pulled his dagger from his belt and touched the tip to Zamam's temple. "Let's start with Jahangir Bey. We can work our way up, so to speak."

Zamam swallowed. "An accident."

"Some accident." Jahangir touched his breastbone, as if recalling the thrust of the blade. Even weeks after the attack, the bey appeared pale. Sweat beaded along his upper lip, as if he had to fight to remain upright.

"It was," Zamam insisted. "You were not the target, Bey, I promise you. An error in the dark."

Kazbek spoke. "So much we guessed almost from the beginning, lords. Why would Zamam attack Jahangir Bey, who at that time supported Tulpar? Tell us the truth, Zamam. Who ordered the murder of Ogodai Sultan?"

"Tulpar Sultan." Zamam spat on the floor, where the hearth fire would normally blaze.

Tulpar smacked him, then bent double, clutching his wounded arm. Kazbek rose to his feet, hands clenched, and the other council members rose with him. Daniil and Rafik exchanged glances and aligned themselves on either side of Tulpar. With their help, he straightened. His face looked ashen under its surface brown, and sweat beaded on his brow.

For a moment, tension hung like an invisible curtain between council and defeated candidate. Then Tulpar laughed, a harsh sound that grated on the ear. "He lies. I did steal my brother's beautiful bride. I did not order his murder—or Jahangir's, or Bahadur's. Nor did I plan the destruction of the horde I wished to rule." His mouth twisted, and he gripped Zamam's chin in his left hand. "Lies won't save you, especially lies aimed at me. What possessed you to scatter the herds?"

"I didn't scatter the herds." Zamam again spat on the ground, narrowly missing Jahangir's boots.

Jahangir swore. "Then who did, pray tell?"

"Look at the arrow," Zamam said. "It was the fletcher."

"Bring the fletcher," Ogodai ordered. "Almas."

Ildar Shirin interrupted before anyone had a chance to obey. "Don't bother." He jerked his chin at Zamam. "He's still lying. Zamam hates the fletcher, and Almas hates him. Because of the cursed dog. I'm sure Zamam shot the arrows himself, so he could blame Almas, without orders from Islam-Girei or anyone else. He's an outsider, a townsman. Where do you think he met Tulpar, if not in the fleshpots of Crimea, during Islam-Girei's last reconciliation with his uncle? Carrying an eagle doesn't make you a nomad. It didn't occur to Zamam that he would condemn the camp to starvation. None of us would make such a mistake. You scatter the herds of an enemy, never your own."

He spoke the truth, Ogodai thought. Only a town dweller would so disregard the safety of herd animals—and those who depended on them.

"Good point," he told Ildar before turning back to Zamam. "You stand accused of murder and attempted murder. Ildar speaks of a dog. This is Almas's dog, the one you used to test the potency of the hemlock-ridden quail?" A swift survey of the council members' faces revealed shock and bewilderment. Ogodai summarized the murder as constructed by Nasan in Kazan.

The laying out of his scheme stripped Zamam of the last of his bravado. He slumped in his captors' hold, his face gray as a man already dead.

"Is that how it happened?" Ogodai asked.

Zamam cringed, a shell of his former self. "Yes. I killed Bahadur with hemlock in the quail. Islam-Girei's shaman gave me the idea, even before I came here. That Bahadur took the potion for his arthritis just simplified matters. But I intended no harm to Jahangir Bey. He simply got in the way. My orders were to ensure Tulpar Sultan's victory at all costs."

"Your orders from whom?" Ogodai asked. He already knew the answer—not least from Zamam's mention of the shaman—but for the sake of the council he wanted it clearly stated.

Zamam took a deep breath, then straightened, as if in what he could probably predict were his last moments of life he had determined to present himself in a manner worthy of a warrior. "As Tulpar Sultan and Shirin Bey said, Khan, from Islam-Girei. He wanted this horde to support him in the current rebellion, and he knew the only way to ensure that was for it to pass, as quickly as possible, into the hands of Tulpar Sultan."

The council emitted a collective gasp of fury and stepped forward as one. Zamam flinched in response, then pulled himself into a military stance once more. "I have committed murder," he said. "I deserve to die, although I don't regret serving the interests of my lord. I request only that I be allowed to die with honor."

In this moment of defeat, he radiated a strange, compelling dignity. "That isn't my choice," Ogodai told him. The law of Islam was clear on this point. He held out a hand to Jahangir. "You killed his father. He has the right to decide whether to seek compensation or execution." Jahangir straightened in his seat, surprise visible in his face, as if he hadn't expected Ogodai to observe the law.

Or hadn't known it. The understanding of the law in this camp left much to be desired. "I will abide by your decision," Ogodai told Jahangir. "But think well on it. He caused your father's death. He attacked you and endangered the entire horde through his scattering of the herds. He sought to blame my brother for his crimes. That he obeyed one who remains out of our reach doesn't excuse him. If the choice were mine, I would not pardon him. He has confessed before witnesses, and he admits to feeling no remorse."

Jahangir fixed his gaze on Ogodai, his expression unreadable, then turned away to survey Zamam, Tulpar, Rafik and Daniil, the council, the Tatar troops that ringed the tent. At last, he returned his eyes to Zamam, who stood, defiant, between his guards.

"You know what you have done," Jahangir said. "I cannot choose compensation, even if you did no more than implement the plans of Islam-Girei Sultan. You have destroyed our trust. As for your request to die with honor, those who slay in the dark and through treachery have no right to claim a warrior's death." With a flick of his wrist, he indicated Ogodai. "I will let the khan decide the method of your execution."

The council members turned their attention to Ogodai, their faces expectant. From the far side of the tent, Tulpar lifted a hand in salute, as if saying, "You wanted this job. Now it's yours." Daniil and Rafik, truer brothers than Tulpar would ever be, produced encouraging smiles. Zamam let his head slump into his shoulders.

No one ever said it was easy to be khan. Ogodai knew what the camp expected of him, and in this case he agreed. He returned to the platform and raised his right hand. The guards pushed Zamam to his knees. Unbidden, he bent over until his forehead touched the ground.

Ogodai stood straight and tall, the platform firm under his boots, and let the spirit of his mentor strengthen his voice. "This criminal administered the poison that killed Bahadur Bey. He attacked Bahadur's son, Jahangir, in an attempt on my life. And he threatened the safety of the herds and, with them, the survival of this horde. Take him outside and hang him, so that all will know that we do not tolerate such evil among us."

A long sigh went around the tent. The soldiers holding Zamam hauled him to his feet and half-dragged, half-carried him toward the door. They had no sooner passed through than the shaman scurried over to Tulpar to finish bandaging his wounds. This time he accepted her ministrations without complaint.

Meanwhile, Ogodai left to supervise the hanging outside.

Zamam thrashed a good deal, but he died swiftly. More swiftly than he deserved, no doubt. With him disposed of, Ogodai could turn his attention to governing his new horde—especially to establishing a relationship with Jahangir, who showed signs of becoming a reluctant supporter rather than a truculent opponent and who could not, under any circumstances, be ignored.

But first, Tulpar. His half-brother stood to one side, his son in his arms. The dispersing crowd eddied around them, a stream of humanity parting as it flowed past. Ogodai went to join them.

"Thank you for your help," he said, feeling stiff and awkward.

Tulpar bent his head over his son's, inhaling the scent from the child's scalp lock, then passed Timur to Ogodai. "Take care of him and his mother. I don't know when I will pass this way again."

"You may visit him if you like." Ogodai spoke without thinking, only to wish he had held his tongue. The last thing he wanted was Tulpar hanging around the camp.

Yet this wasn't politics but family: the welfare of a child, a broken bond between brothers, a father's love for his son— and perhaps, despite Roxelana's allure, for the woman who had borne that son.

His ambivalence must have shown on his face, for Tulpar laughed. Not the harsh laughter of the interrogation but genuine humor that lit his eyes and made him, for an instant, the hero of Ogodai's boyhood. "So long as I don't cross you," he said. "I understand, Ogodai. I don't blame you for guarding what is yours."

One of Tulpar's soldiers arrived with his horse, saddled and bridled. Tulpar, already on the horse's left side, swung onto the saddle and bent to brush his son's cheek. "Be a good boy," he said, "and listen to your uncle and aunt. I'll come back for you when you're older."

Timur nodded, his face scrunched as if to prevent tears. "I'll look after him," Ogodai said. "You know that. May the white road open before you, and the ancestors guard you on your journey."

Timur's mother emerged from her tent and sprinkled the grass before Tulpar's horse with mare's milk, creating the white road just mentioned. As Ogodai watched his brother prepare to depart, he had an odd thought: might he and Tulpar become allies one day?

He dismissed the question as too unlikely for consideration. Tulpar glanced over his shoulder, and Roxelana, dressed and veiled for travel, cantered up on a small white mare. Behind her, a stolid servant straddled a heavily laden horse.

The surprises would never end. The woman could ride after all.

"You're ready," Tulpar said. "Good. Let's set off." With a muttered *chu*, he loosed his horse's reins. Roxelana waved her whip and set off after him, his warriors thundering behind her. Timur's mother watched them go, her face set, implacable.

Ogodai placed Timur in her arms. "The boy will remain in your care. Lady Firuza and I will assist you as necessary, since his father will not soon return. Call on us for whatever you need." When she buried her face in the child's neck, Ogodai touched her shoulder in sympathy. "I'll send for Timur shortly. First I need to talk with Jahangir Bey."

Not only Jahangir, as it turned out. The council had gathered the horde along the central path, and howls of "Khan, Khan!" greeted Ogodai as he made his way through the camp. It was acceptance, at last, and Ogodai reveled in it. White banners embroidered in gold with the winged horse, Bahadur's symbol, flew on poles before every tent, ribbons streaming above them. The setting sun cast its glow against the distant hills that sheltered the camp from the icy winds of the east. Even so, the cold air chapped his cheeks, and he wasn't sorry to duck again into the tent where he had spent this portentous afternoon. Servants must have entered during his absence, for not only did the fire blaze brightly but someone had relaid the carpets over the dirt floor. Trays of food sat on low tables, and steam rose from a long-spouted brass jug. Vafa knelt beside it, ready to serve.

Jahangir entered, alone. He still looked pale, his face taut, his body too thin, but his steps were steady and his limbs didn't tremble.

Ogodai greeted him. "Sit and eat. We have much to discuss." To show his readiness to treat Jahangir as an equal, he sat cross-legged on the carpet and waited for Vafa to present them with water and a towel.

Jahangir sat across from him. Only after Vafa passed him a bowl of mutton stew did the bey cradle it in his hands and speak. "I was wrong about you."

Unexpected but welcome. Ogodai waited for clarification. When it didn't come, he said, "We were friends once. Can we not be friends again?"

"We were." Jahangir studied the steam rising from his stew. "It seems a long time ago. I let Tulpar convince me that you were your father's pet—a weakling propped up by an indulgent parent, unable to stand on your own. And I was jealous, because my father never indulged me. Whatever I did, he demanded more. He *did* more. Never, until that last day, do I remember him ill or unsure."

"He was like a rock," Ogodai said, struck by an understanding of what might have driven Jahangir to drink. "It must have been hard to live up to his standards." He sipped mutton broth, then grinned as a thought occurred to him. "But honestly, Jahangir, you spent two years with Bulat. You can't have believed him easy to please. Two strips off the same tent frame were Bulat and Bahadur."

"He was kind to me, your father," Jahangir mumbled. "Kinder than my own. Before I left, I didn't notice, but when I came back … oh, in the end I gave up, I suppose."

"*Ata* making his peace with Allah, probably," Ogodai said. "Your father was kinder to me, too, than my own. Or to you, no doubt. But I will admit that my father is less daunting than yours. And my mother doesn't hesitate to tell him when she thinks he's making a mistake, for all that she loves him." He speared a piece of stew with his knife. "It's what I like about your sister. She has the same kind of strength."

Jahangir nodded. "You're well matched. I didn't realize how much until you went after her that way." His shoulders hunched, and he stared at his food without eating it, as if it admonished him for his neglect. "I owe her an apology, too. I resented her for being so competent, our father's favorite."

"Yes," Ogodai said. "I'm glad to hear you admit it. She genuinely cares for you."

"I know." At last, Jahangir lifted the bowl to his mouth and sipped.

Silence fell. "Will you miss Roxelana?" Ogodai asked after a while.

"A bit," Jahangir admitted. "I'd already lost her, though. She always hitches her horse to the wagon of the most powerful male. You rejected her, but as soon as Tulpar put himself forward, she switched her attentions to him. And in case *he* lost, she was already lining up that Russian friend of yours—or didn't you notice?"

"I noticed." Who could have missed Roxelana making sheep's eyes at Daniil? "He's happily married, too. I don't think he would have fallen for her tricks. And if he did, well, God help him if my sister found out."

Jahangir laughed at that. "I remember your sister. She clouted me over the head with her sword more than once. Is she still a wild woman?"

"She's calmed down some," Ogodai said. "But I wouldn't push her too far. And callous as it sounds, I suspect you're well rid of Roxelana."

"You're probably right. Beautiful women are nothing but trouble."

They ate stew for a while, having exhausted that topic, until Ogodai exchanged his empty bowl for a cup of Vafa's tea and a plate of dried melon.

"We need to work together," he told Jahangir. "Your sister says you fight well."

"I like action. The petitions and the politicking of the council bore me to tears."

And to the bottle. "Then do what suits you best. Organize raids. Defend the camp. It's an important responsibility. Firuza and I will look after the day-to-day administration. I have my own troops, and I'll expand their ranks as needed. They will stay with me. But you may direct the other men of the camp— in consultation with me and with the council, of course."

"Of course. You don't plan to follow my sister's hare-brained advice about horse trading, then?"

"It's not harebrained advice." Did Jahangir really not see the wisdom of Firuza's vision? "The horde needs more than raids to ensure its survival. But we can't build a fortune in horses overnight. And when we do, we'll need an effective defense even more. Unless we want to see our carefully nurtured beasts enriching camps other than our own."

Jahangir raised his bowl in tribute. "You have a good head on your shoulders, Ogodai." His smile was rueful. "I was wrong to doubt you," he said again.

"For this we need a toast," Ogodai said. "Vafa, fetch koumiss. Ask the council to join us. And send messages to my parents. It's time to celebrate."

Chapter 24

BULAT ARRIVED SO SOON AFTER THE MESSENGERS HAD SET out that Ogodai suspected his father had encountered them en route. Less than a week after the fight with Tulpar, a familiar roar interrupted Ogodai's consultation with Jahangir about the allocation of the horde's forces. The two young men leaped to their feet as the tent door flew open to admit one scowling father.

"Out," Bulat said to Jahangir, who scuttled from the tent. Whatever discourtesy lay implicit in Bulat's flat statement—and barking orders at the bey of another horde certainly crossed the bounds of acceptable behavior—Jahangir obviously feared challenging so formidable and wrathful a visitor. He ducked out the door without so much as a backward glance.

Ogodai quelled a craven desire to run after him. He and Jahangir had a considerable distance yet to travel before again becoming friends, but they could agree on the advisability of avoiding an enraged Bulat.

He stiffened his spine as he rose to his feet. Khans didn't have to account for themselves to other khans, even angry parental ones. He pressed his palms together and bowed his head. "Greetings, *Ata*, and welcome. I hope the ancestors eased your journey."

Bulat waved this courtesy away with one hand. "Is it true that you let your brother live? I haven't been in the camp long enough to down a cup of koumiss, and the rumors are already flying!"

"Yes, it's true." The suddenness of the attack caught Ogodai off-guard. And raised his hackles. He clenched his fists and returned glare for glare.

"Have you learned nothing from me?" Bulat snarled. "Serpents don't lose their fangs. You will have to finish Tulpar one day. Why not today?"

"Because I didn't choose to," Ogodai said. "If you want him dead, arrange it. I'm not your sword arm."

"Since when? I made you, boy. Taught you everything you know. And I can unmake you, just as I did your brother. Don't think I won't."

"Is that why you pretended he was dead? Why you didn't tell me he was living in this camp?" It was the question that had haunted Ogodai since the moment he discovered his brother's existence. Would he at last get an answer?

In a sense, yes. Bulat grunted. "My scouts said he'd left the area. Besides, you have to stand on your own feet sometime."

Outrage flooded Ogodai. "Well, I did, didn't I? I won this seat myself, Father. I didn'ot send for your help." As a reminder, he dug the winged horse from his sash and showed the medallion's face to his father. "I solved the question of Bahadur's death, as you commanded. I claimed my bride, as you also commanded. I gained the support of the council, twice. I fought my brother—of whose presence here *you* failed to warn me—and beat him, fair and square. And when I had him at the point of my sword, I made the decision that seemed right to me. I take full responsibility for the consequences."

Even if those consequences included his father casting him out? Was he prepared to follow Tulpar into exile?

Yes. Because what was the alternative? To give in now and bow to his father's wishes, his father's wisdom, as he had since childhood—no khan, no man, no husband could yield to another in that way and retain his self-respect. Ogodai hardened his mouth, crossed his arms, and stared his father down.

When had Bulat become so short, so stooped?

"The responsibility, yes. That is yours," Bulat said. "But not the consequences. Your precious brother will plague the life out of us, and all because *you* couldn't drive the blade home when required."

"Will you cast me off, then, as you did him? Because I won't back down. Tulpar may plague you, as you say. Then again, he may not. If he does, I will fight at your side—if it seems to me you're in the right. But I make my own decisions from now on. You taught me that, too."

A long silence ensued. Ogodai continued to stare at his father, who glared back. Bulat rocked slightly on his heels. He thrust his hands into his sash. His mouth worked, as if words struggled to exit. In nineteen years, Ogodai had never stated his case in such blunt terms. Some child part of him urged him to give in, to apologize, but he pushed it down and stood firm. He was right. Sooner or later, his father would acknowledge that. He kept his eyes riveted on Bulat's face.

"If I tell you to go, you will go?" Bulat asked at last.

Ogodai heard the hint of uncertainty—or was it disbelief? "No. This horde has chosen me as khan. But if you don't wish to associate with me, I won't ask you to stay. Even to attend my acclamation and my wedding."

He ignored the lump in his throat and resumed the seat he had occupied when his father stormed in. "It's your choice, *Ata*. But I meant what I said. You are welcome here."

Another long moment passed. Ogodai waited for Bulat to stride from the tent, their breach unresolvable, as the breach with Tulpar had remained unhealed for a decade. For a lifetime.

His father stood, irresolute, throughout that interminable pause, then dropped onto the cushion vacated by Jahangir. "Let's not act like two bulls in the same pasture, son. I made a mistake with your brother. I don't want to repeat it with you. I'd rather discuss how to keep him in check."

It was a recognition of sorts—the best he could hope for, Ogodai suspected, knowing his father. He responded in kind. "If you don't mind, I will ask Daniil and Jahangir to join us. The problem concerns them, too."

Bulat regarded him sternly. Ogodai kept his gaze steady. Improbably, his father's face creased into a rueful smile. He shook his head. "Young ox. You're as stubborn as I am. Go ahead, invite whom you like. You might consider adding Kazbek Argyn, though. I haven't spoken to the man in an age. And while we're waiting, tell me what happened to my *qarïndash*."

"Yes," Ogodai said. "I think that's an excellent suggestion. In fact, let's summon the council. I'm sure they look forward to making—or renewing—your acquaintance. As for Bahadur…"

Firuza reined Kubelek in until she felt certain that the white felt rounds nestled in the foothills could belong to no one but her own people. Even then, she restrained the horse long enough to stand in her stirrups and assess the scene before her.

"What do you think?" she asked Nasan, who had pulled up beside her. Sumbeka, who had trailed them throughout the morning by a few lengths, caught up with them as Nasan, too, stood to peer at the still-distant line of tents.

Nasan pointed at a tall standard, nine white horse tails dangling from a central spear, the crowned dragon boat of Kasimov gleaming copper against a bright-blue background. "*Ata*'s banner," she said. "Otherwise I see only winged horses."

"My father's standard," Firuza said. "But where is Ogodai?"

Sumbeka interjected with her usual calm patience, "Ogodai does not yet have his own banner. He flew his father's, as sons in service do. But if he is here, and khan, he will adopt the winged horse, will he not?"

"I suppose," Firuza said. "Only what if Tulpar won?"

"If Tulpar won," Sumbeka said dryly, "then my husband is no doubt fit to be tied. Let's not panic, girls. When we get there, we will learn the truth."

"I can't wait." Nasan grabbed Firuza's reins. "Come, sister. That beautiful butterfly of yours is desperate to spread her wings."

Sorkhokhtani leaped forward as her mistress touched knees to sides. Firuza, not to be outdone, loosened her grip on Kubelek's reins. They raced neck and neck across the last of the open grasslands. "Girls, girls," Sumbeka shouted after them, but Kubelek scented home, and Firuza couldn't have slowed the mare if she tried.

She didn't try. The wind knocked the cap onto her shoulders, where it dangled from its strap. Her earrings slapped against her neck. Her cheeks stung, and her lips. With luck, she would see Ogodai in less time than it took for a pot of water to boil on the hearth. How could she wait?

"Ah, those wretched girls," Sumbeka cried. But pounding hoofbeats told Firuza that her mother-in-law had joined the chase.

Ogodai raced from the audience tent, grabbing his sword as he passed the stand set aside to hold weapons and buckling it around his waist as he reached the opening. A flash of memory catapulted him back to the day of Tulpar's arrival. The thrumming of hooves, the jingle of harness—the sounds shocked him with their familiarity. Had his half-brother returned already?

Men piled out from one tent after another. Voices rose and fell, many of them asking the same questions, no one answering. Jahangir emerged from the khan's tent behind Ogodai and joined him. On his other side, Bulat stood on tiptoe, peering, unable to see above the feathered turbans.

A childish shriek split the air: Timur, escaped from his mother, swaying on the rails of the pen that held lambs and kids too weak to forage in the wintry air. "Our lady!" the child cried. "Our lady! I see her!"

"Our lady," to Timur, could mean only one person. Indeed, as the child's shrieks rose in volume, an unmistakable palomino mare appeared at the end of the row of tents. Nasan's Sorkhokhtani galloped at the palomino's side.

Kubelek. Ogodai ran to intercept the horses. On every side, weapons clanged against the ground and cheers broke out. "Nasan is here," he told his father. "And your new daughter."

And then he didn't need to say anything. Firuza tumbled from her saddle into his arms, sobbing, "You're safe, dearest. You're safe."

"Quite safe, beloved," he murmured into her hair.

It didn't end there, of course. Nasan came off Sorkhokhtani while the horse had barely slowed to a walk, and his mother arrived even before that round of embraces and exclamations had ended. Bulat pressed forward to greet his womenfolk, Daniil his wife, and Jahangir his sister. Timur required an introduction and explanations. Diliara had to welcome her beloved daughter home, greet her dear friend of long ago, and marvel at Nasan's manifest grown-upness. Then the crowd poured in, raising Firuza on its shoulders and ferrying her toward the khan's tent. Somewhere in the press of bodies, Ogodai grabbed hold of Rafik and sent him to secure and tend to the horses.

An evening of feasting, talking, and joyous celebration followed. With assistance from the gifts that filled Sumbeka's saddle bags, Diliara managed to put together a banquet that exceeded any of the nomads' previous efforts. To celebrate the horde's settling in its winter camp, the election of a new leader, and the arrival of Ogodai's family, both men and women attended this feast. As Ogodai shared tidbits of food and conversation with Firuza, military details with his father, and family news with his mother, he allowed himself time to survey his people, knowing that his position among them was secure.

Timur barely left Sumbeka's lap. "She's enjoying her first grandchild," Ogodai whispered to Firuza.

"*Is* he hers?" She peered past him to the cushioned sofa where Sumbeka alternated between pressing morsels of roast venison on Timur and teaching him a counting game with the pieces of meat. The boy's mother sat to Sumbeka's left. "I thought Tulpar was your half-brother."

"Oh, he is." Ogodai rubbed his thumb against her palm. Could he spend the night with her? Probably not, with mothers bent on a wedding in the vicinity. "But *Ana* raised him. His mother left *Ata*'s camp not long after I was born." He dipped his head to murmur in Firuza's ear. "Still, *Ana* won't mind having a grandchild who is entirely her own." She blushed adorably and asked no more questions.

The next morning brought the formal ceremony of acclamation. Ogodai—dressed in his very best cloth-of-gold robe, a crimson sash and sable hat, his jeweled dagger prominently displayed—stood on a white felt mat laid in the center of a viewing stand constructed overnight at the edge of the camp. Every warrior present, arrayed in full and gleaming armor, found his place by rank between the stand and the Sura River. The women squeezed around the edges. Children pushed and shoved, were reprimanded, and pushed some more, seeking the best vantage point. The council and honored guests—the men and women of his family, the military commanders, the Tatar troops brought from Kazan—arranged themselves on the stand itself, forming an open circle. Eight sturdy warriors took up positions at the corners and midpoints of the mat.

Once sure that the people of the horde had found their assigned spots, Jahangir Bey, with Kazbek Argyn to his left and Bulat to his right, stepped forward. Spread across his outstretched arms, Jahangir carried the mighty sword of Bahadur Bey. Bulat bore the standard of Kasimov, and Kazbek the winged horse banner of the horde.

Jahangir raised the sword, still in its jewel-encrusted gold sheath, in his right hand. "Do you swear to defend the honor of this horde, to serve us and protect us with your life?"

"I do." Ogodai smiled—at his former friend, at his father beaming with pride, at his loyal supporters Kazbek and Rafik Argyn, at his sworn brother Daniil, and most of all at Firuza, standing to one side. He had never felt more adult, more responsible, more sure of his own abilities and the course he must take.

"Ogodai Khan," Jahangir yelled, waving the sword as if cutting the air above his head. "Ogodai Khan!"

With one voice the assembled horde returned the call. Jahangir lowered the sword, returned it to lie across his arms, and held out the weapon to Ogodai. He took the sword, feeling the heft of it, remembering a time when he couldn't have lifted it, never mind swung it. In his mind's eye he saw an image of the kindly bey, his tutor and mentor, who had initiated the series of events that led to this moment. It seemed as if Bahadur himself—mounted on the real Winged Horse, steed of the Sky God—shimmered in the clouds above the river. Ogodai sent him a silent thanks, a promise not to betray the trust laid on him.

He faced the massed warriors and waved the sword in turn. "To glory!"

"To glory!" They shouted back.

"To honor!"

"To honor!"

"And for our ancestors!"

Again the cry echoed across the plains.

Ogodai sat in the center of the white felt mat and laid Bahadur's sword across his knees. The eight sturdy warriors grabbed the mat and raised him, three times, to signal the horde's acceptance of him as ruler. As they did, the crowd called his name, over and over.

He had fulfilled his mission. He was home. And this afternoon, he would take Firuza formally to wife. His mother and Diliara had already completed the arrangements. Bulat's warriors had raised a tent mosque, and the imam who had accompanied the women from Kasimov would bless him and Firuza. Then the feasting could begin.

He sought her out with his eyes as the men returned his mat to earth for the third time. His khatun. Their journey together was just beginning.

Seated on Tulpar, the winged stallion of legend, Bahadur Bey watched his plans reach fruition at last. He could retreat to his tent among the ancestors, knowing he had done everything in his power to ensure the continuation of his line and the safety of his people—even, perhaps, the moral salvation of his son.

As Tulpar leaped for the heavens, a pair of swans rose from the Sura, circled the horse as if in greeting, then headed north.

North. Why north? At this time of year, any sensible bird flew south, to shelter near the Great Inland Sea until the sun chose to warm the world once more.

But these swans stubbornly flew north. Wondering, Bahadur watched them until the snow-laden clouds hid them from view.

Historical Note

HISTORICAL ACCURACY IN A NOVEL IS A CURIOUS THING. As Ian Mortimer, who writes fiction under the pen name James Forrester, has noted, historical novels are inaccurate by definition. Novelists often use historical events and personages as backdrop or as characters, but as soon as we put words in mouths or thoughts in heads, as soon as we imagine how it would feel to live through such an experience, we deviate from what the historical record can support. Otherwise, we are writing history, not fiction. Here, too, I have taken liberties with history—adding characters who never existed, repurposing figures who did, and pulling out of the range of possibilities and scholarly arguments those that best serve the needs of my story. I strive for authenticity, not for accuracy. As in *The Golden Lynx*, I have done my best to ensure that the details match what we know of the culture. The rest is a combination of fact and imagination.

Many of the political events mentioned as occurring in the background of this novel did take place. The khanate of Crimea did suffer periods of civil war from 1523 to 1537, including in 1534/35. The khans of Crimea did nurture ambitions to control the entire area once governed by the descendants of Juchi, the eldest son of Genghis Khan— the lands most commonly, if inaccurately, known as the

Golden Horde. Safa-Girei, nephew of Sahib-Girei, had been khan in Kazan until 1532 and would return after the assassination of Jan-Ali, the Russian candidate, in September 1535. The Shirins in Kazan were credited or blamed, depending on one's point of view, for supporting the coup against Jan-Ali, nineteen years old at his death. Although the Crimean khans seem to have largely broken the power of the Shirins and the other tribal elders by 1534, the old system of khan and council retained its authority elsewhere. Yet much of the sequence of events—and even the structure of the various khanates—remains uncertain due to the absence of documentation, although research based on the diplomatic archives of various countries is ongoing.

Specifically, scholars know that between 1400 and 1560 the descendants of Genghis Khan (Chingissids), whose charismatic authority had previously been absolute, lost their appeal for many of the nomadic hordes who made up the loosely organized Nogai Confederation. What we don't know is exactly when this transition took place in different hordes. Under the new system, the Mangyt clan, descendants of the legendary founder of the Nogai Confederation, ruled as beys without the assistance of Chingissid khans. Individual Chingissids might hang around a horde in search of wives or military alliances, but they couldn't expect to establish an independent power base there. Under the new system, too, Islam became an increasingly important source of legitimacy and identity for the Nogai. The older forms of worship did not disappear completely, any more than they did from Christianity, but they became folded into popular understandings of religion, where they remain to this day.

I have postulated, based on my reading, that this transition occurred at different rates in different hordes—more rapidly among groups with greater exposure to outside influence and less rapidly where a horde lay off the beaten track. Bahadur is a holdout, an anachronism in both the political and the religious sense, and his son Jahangir speaks for the newer method of horde governance, although he can't quite convince his council of the need for change. By the 1550s, the tale I tell of warring Chingissids would be highly unlikely; in 1534, it is not yet off-the-charts implausible.

Another issue involves my use of terminology. The correct title for a Chingissid in Muscovite service is either *tsar* or *tsarevich*, the Russian equivalents of khan and sultan (the son of a khan). Throughout this series, I use khan, sultan, khatun (wife of a khan), and khanim (khan's daughter)—the Russian variants of which are, respectively, *tsar, tsarevich, tsaritsa*, and *tsarevna*. Firuza and Diliara bear the formal title of *begum* (wife or daughter of a bey); I used the rough equivalent "lady" to avoid introducing yet another unfamiliar mode of address. For the sake of clarity, too, I refer to my characters as "Tatars" even though they would have identified themselves either generically as "Muslims" or by their affiliation with clan, place, or horde—Mangyts, Shirins, Kazanis, Krym, members of Bahadur's horde, and so on.

All the characters in this novel are fictional. Even those with real-life counterparts—Gulnara, Gazim Shirin, Aslanbika and her father, and Jan-Ali—have either had their names changed or their personalities reconstructed to meet the needs of the story. Islam-Girei Sultan, although a real Crimean Tatar in periodic rebellion against his powerful uncle, could not, of course, bear any responsibility for manipulating the politics of a nonexistent nomadic horde. There is no evidence of an assassination attempt against Jan-Ali in October 1534. Nor is there any reason to believe that Jan-Ali was homosexual, although it is true that his wife (the historical Söyëmbike), a noted beauty, did write to her father a few months after their wedding complaining that Jan-Ali didn't love her. If in fact his distaste for his wife was more than personal, the rather casual reaction to his preferences portrayed here is typical of Tatar courts at the time, as is the relaxed attitude my Muslim characters display toward the consumption of alcoholic beverages (on both points, see, e.g., the *Baburnama*—the memoirs of Babur, the Mughal conqueror of India, originally a Tatar khan of Central Asia). And yes, the Crimean Tatars, despite professing Islam, apparently did grow grapes and make wine from them—although I can't say for certain that the winemakers were Muslim; Crimea had a mixed-ethnicity population that included Greeks, Jews, and Armenians.

The political systems of the Tatar khanates depended on male kinship ties, both real and fictive. Rulers referred to one another as fathers and sons or as brothers, including sworn brothers (*qarïndashlar* in Turkic, *anda* in Mongolian), depending on their relative power and prestige. For a full discussion of this system, see Craig Gayen Kennedy, "The Juchids of Muscovy: A Study of Personal Ties between Émigré Tatar Dynasts and the Muscovite Grand Princes in the Fifteenth and Sixteenth Centuries" (Ph.D. diss., Harvard University, 1994), which unfortunately seems destined to remain unpublished. The Tatar terms used here—*ata* (father), *ana* (mother), *aby* (older brother, uncle), *ené* (younger brother), and *sengel* (younger sister; the *ng* is pronounced as in song)—are perhaps not exactly the forms used in the 1530s, but they are close.

The sources I consulted are too numerous to list, especially in a novel, but I owe a special debt to Devin deWeese for *Islamization and Native Religion in the Golden Horde: Baba Tükles and Conversion to Islam in Historical and Epic Tradition;* Jack Weatherford for *Genghis Khan and the Making of the Modern World* and *The Secret History of the Mongol Queens*, where I discovered Manduhai the Wise; Dariusz Kołodziejczyk for his monumental

The Crimean Khanate and Poland-Lithuania: International Diplomacy on the European Periphery (15th–18th Century). A Study of Peace Treaties, Followed by Annotated Documents; and Alma Kunanbay and Wayne Eastep for their gorgeously photographed *The Soul of Kazakhstan*. Brian Davies, Alexander Filjushkin, Edward L. Keenan, Anatoly Khazanov, Michael Khodarkovsky, Janet Martin, Donald Ostrowski, Vadim Trepavlov, and the late Cherie Woodworth are also among the authors whose books and articles I consulted. Ann Kleimola graciously answered my panicked questions about dogs and willingly shared with me her extensive knowledge of sixteenth-century Russian history, society, and governance. I extend my particular appreciation also to Charles Halperin—for his scholarship, for his contributions to the dog discussion, and for fact-checking this novel and its predecessor. Although I know that the author always bears final responsibility for the work she produces, I think it especially important under present circumstances to mention that none of these fine scholars should be faulted for my fictional use of their research.

The Islamic dates come from the online conversion calendar at www.oriold.uzh.ch/static/hegira.html, and the poisons from Serita Deborah Stevens with Anne Klarner, *Deadly Doses: A Writer's Guide to Poisons*—a reference book for which I am especially grateful, since the local police department tends to wonder if a writer calls up asking about deadly substances.

To find out more about the history behind the novels, follow my posts at blog.cplesley.com.

Cast of Characters

(in alphabetical order)

Alexander Makhmetovich: Head of the Russian delegation sent by Grand Princess Elena Glinskaya to Kazan in October 1534, a Tatar sultan converted to Orthodoxy and in Russian service.

Almas: The fletcher of the nomadic horde run by Bahadur, then by his son Jahangir.

Aslanbika: Wife to Jan-Ali of Kazan, based on the historical Söyëmbike.

Bahadur Bey: Ruler of his own small nomadic horde, father to Jahangir and Firuza, former mentor to Ogodai, and sworn brother of Bulat.

Bulat Khan: Tatar khan in Russian service; temporarily charged with ruling Kasimov, a Russian town traditionally assigned to Tatars and an important element in Russia's attempt to conquer Kazan; fictional older half-brother of the historical Jan-Ali and father of Nasan, Ogodai, and Tulpar.

Daniil Kolychev: Bulat's son-in-law, a Russian nobleman; husband of Nasan and, here, junior envoy to Kazan.

Diliara: Bahadur's chief wife and stepmother to Jahangir and Firuza.

Elena Glinskaya: Grand princess of Russia, ruling on behalf of her son Ivan IV (1530–84), later known as Ivan the Terrible;

widow of Grand Prince Vasily III, whose death in 1533 led to uncertainty and aggression at home and abroad; a historical character about whom only general details are known.

Firuza: Bahadur's oldest daughter, betrothed to Ogodai since they were twelve.

Gazim Shirin: Chief adviser to Gulnara; based on the historical Bulat Shirin.

Gulnara: Here called the queen of Kazan to avoid confusion with Aslanbika, although they hold the same rank; based on the historical Gawharshat, who was either the widow or the sister of Muhammad-Amin Khan of Kazan; she sees herself as the power behind the throne and Gazim Shirin as her minion, which roughly matches the relationship of Gawharshat and Bulat Shirin.

Ildar Shirin Bey: Another member of the powerful Shirin clan, which dominates most of the Tatar khanates and hordes. Ildar, an elder statesman who dislikes Bulat, represents this clan in Bahadur's horde.

Islam-Girei Sultan of Crimea: Nephew, rival, and heir of Sahib-Girei and his predecessor; Tulpar's chosen overlord since his exile in 1524. After more than a year of cooperation, Islam-Girei rebelled against his uncle in the summer of 1534.

Jahangir Bey: The eldest son and successor of Bahadur; twin brother to Firuza.

Jan-Ali Khan: Ruler of Kasimov 1519–32, then of Kazan until his deposition and assassination in September 1535; preceded and succeeded by Safa-Girei; a historical figure about whom little is known.

Kazbek Argyn Bey: Old friend of Bahadur and senior member of Bahadur's council; rival of Ildar Shirin.

Nasan Khanim: Ogodai's younger sister; wife of Daniil, baptized before her wedding as Irina but at best a reluctant convert; heroine of *The Golden Lynx.*

Ogodai Sultan: Eighteen-year-old heir of Bulat, betrothed to Firuza since childhood, just finding his feet as a leader at the beginning of this story (sultan, in Tatar usage, refers to the son of a khan, not to a supreme ruler as in the Ottoman empire).

Oraz: A young man sent to accompany a delegation of Crimean envoys to Jan-Ali.

Rafik Argyn: Son of Kazbek Argyn, a friend of Ogodai's from their days under Bahadur's tutelage.

Roxelana: Bahadur's favorite concubine, then Jahangir's, originally a Christian slave from the area that is now northwest Afghanistan, intent on using her considerable female charms to secure the best deal possible in this male-dominated world.

Safa-Girei Khan: Former and future khan of Kazan, nephew to Sahib-Girei of Crimea; an enemy of Bulat's family.

Sahib-Girei Khan: Khan of Crimea, 1532–51, despite the periodic attempts of his nephew Islam-Girei to unseat him. The Girei dynasty ruled Crimea for centuries; the name is often spelled Giray.

Sumbeka: Bulat's chief wife and mother of Nasan and Ogodai.

Timur: Tulpar's son, therefore Ogodai's nephew.

Tulpar: Bulat's eldest son and Ogodai's older half-brother; cast out by Bulat after a disagreement when Tulpar was sixteen and Ogodai eight; thereafter declared dead to the family and to their ancestors. Tulpar is also the name of the winged horse (Pegasus) of Turkic legend and appears in that light in this book—the two Tulpars are connected only by their name.

Vafa: Ogodai's personal servant.

Zamam: A soldier who meets Tulpar at Islam-Girei's court in Crimea, a year before Islam-Girei rebels against his uncle in the summer of 1534, and who switches his allegiance when Tulpar departs Bahadur's camp under a cloud.

Acknowledgments

In addition to the scholars mentioned in the Historical Note, I tip my hat here to my invaluable writers' group, now entering its seventh year: Ariadne Apostolou and Courtney J. Hall, who are also founding members of Five Directions Press. Each of them has read *The Winged Horse* at least three times, and it would not exist in its present form without their input. I would also like to thank Irina and Pamela, who read the entire book in draft form, and Diana Holquist, a fellow author, for friendship, emotional support, and advice delivered regularly over lunch at our favorite deli.

To my husband and son—and, of course, the cats, who purred encouragingly at all the right moments—words cannot express my gratitude. And to those who read the earlier books, my thanks. I hope *The Winged Horse* has lived up to your expectations.

The Author

As a child, C. P. Lesley thought everyone told themselves stories to help themselves fall asleep. It never occurred to her that anyone would pay her for them, and for a long time, she was right—no one would. But after years of producing horrible prose, reading books about novel writing, and pestering hapless fellow-writers and friends to read her drafts, some of the advice stuck, and she finished *The Not Exactly Scarlet Pimpernel*, then *The Golden Lynx* and its first sequel, *The Winged Horse*.

She is currently working on the next book in the series, *The Swan Princess* (Legends of the Five Directions 3: North).

When not thinking up new ways to torture her characters, she edits other people's manuscripts, reads voraciously, maintains her website, and takes classes in classical ballet. You can find out more about her and her books at www.cplesley. com.

ALSO FROM FIVE DIRECTIONS PRESS

The Swan Princess

LEGENDS OF THE FIVE DIRECTIONS 3

Moscow, April 1536

"IMPOSSIBLE." NATALYA KOLYCHEVA SWAYED, AS IF PUSHED off-balance by her daughter-in-law's request. Pearls quivered on her embroidered headdress; sunlight cast a glow on her layered silk robes. "Go riding in the city? After what happened last year?"

Nasan flinched. No one regretted the effects of last year's fall more than she. "I'm not with child now, Mama-in-law," she said. "How could I be, with my husband away these nine months?"

"There is too much work." Natalya gestured at the servants humming around them.

Too much work, indeed. Enough to keep a person busy from dawn to dusk. In winter, Nasan did not mind. Better to occupy her mind than to sit by the stove worrying about Daniil, her warrior husband, last seen limned against a hazy July sky. Since his departure, Nasan had given her mother-in-law no reason to complain about insufficient diligence.

Not that good behavior sufficed. Natalya had a knack for identifying others' shortcomings, even ones Nasan did not consider flaws. Like the urge to ride around Moscow on a fine spring morning.

For winter had passed into memory. Despite the snow that lay packed at the base of the fences, sunshine and crisp breezes called her forth.

"Just once around the outer walls?" she begged. How many times had she fallen during her days on the steppe? A dozen? A hundred? And every time she'd been told to haul herself up and get back on the horse. No excuses!

Natalya shook her head. "Your husband entrusted me with your safety. Would you risk another curse from an envious eye? It might prevent you from ever conceiving."

Nasan shivered and muttered a prayer—in Arabic, out of habit—provoking another rebuke for un-Christian behavior. "Lord Jesus Christ, protect me from the work of the Enemy," she added. Natalya responded with a curt nod. Nasan touched the amulet that hung from her neck beside her golden lynx pendant, concealed under her robes to keep Natalya from fussing about its "heathen" embroidery, and sent a silent plea for protection to her ancestral clan spirits, the grandmothers. "But Mama-in-law, I bear talismans against the evil eye."

"I won't permit it. Wives belong inside the house, not roaming the streets like loose women. Why do you think God punished you with that fall?"

So now God was responsible, and not the evil eye? "I did penance, Mama-in-law," Nasan reminded her. In truth, leaving church early for three months had disturbed her not a whit; her membership in this Christian community still felt artificial, even forced. Her reprieve should have lasted a year, but her mother-in-law had paid to reduce the term. Nasan had had no choice but to acquiesce. In the absence of her husband and son, Natalya ruled the Kolychev household, whether Nasan liked it or not.

Natalya grunted an acknowledgment. "Finish your tasks, then, and you may ride in the courtyard, among our own people."

The courtyard. Nasan glanced around the courtyard, which lacked enough free space to spin a top, let alone gallop a horse. Perhaps by evening she could *walk* her mare several times around the fences.

She thought of pointing out that more envious eyes existed within the household than without. But most likely, that would result in a complete ban on riding. *Natalya* had not learned to ride before she could walk; she did not understand the need to maintain one's skills.

"Very well." Nasan tucked her hands in her long sleeves and bowed to the inevitable. A ride around the courtyard was better than nothing.

Natalya did not answer.

Odd. Natalya placed great value on courtesy. Nasan raised her head and looked her mother-in-law in the eye.

And looked again. Lines of fatigue marked the older woman's face, and fine lines of red fanned out across her normally pale skin. As Nasan watched, a dry cough wracked Natalya's ample frame. What evil humor afflicted her?

"Mama-in-law, are you ill?" Nasan constructed a mental list, testing the results against the medical books she studied whenever the demands of household supervision and religious observance abated. Weakness, cough, a web of red across the skin—classic signs of a disordered temperament, but where did the imbalance lie?

"It's nothing," Natalya said. "I slept poorly." She touched Nasan's cheek. "When Daniil returns, he will ride with you. Until he does, you remain within these walls."

Nasan added sleeplessness to her list of symptoms. "When my husband returns," she said, avoiding his name as a respectful wife should. "Will that ever happen? This war drags on and on."

More important, did he want to return? They had parted on bad terms—she guilt-ridden, he cold and withdrawn. In his time away, he had not sent a single note addressed to her alone; only the rare message to the family confirmed that he still lived. He did not read or write, of course, but even a Russian warrior could find a clerk once in a while and dictate, "I miss you," to his wife. Daniil had forgotten her, it seemed.

"Patience, my dear." Natalya produced a rueful smile. "One day, the envoys will run out of excuses and make peace. Then, perhaps, you will give me a grandchild."

"May God so ordain." Nasan winced again—she couldn't help it. How old had her son been when the *albasti* stole his soul from her womb? Four months? Five? Before birth, a woman could not be sure, especially her first time. But the sight of his tiny body haunted her dreams: covered in blood and hair soft as a cat's fur, fingers and toes perfect, no longer than her hand but clearly identifiable as the desired male heir. He had not drawn a single breath; she had not once felt him kick. And when she had pleaded with the women to send men to the duck pond with sticks to stir up the water and force the *albasti* to return the unwashed soul before it could be eaten, they had soothed her as one soothes a madwoman. Daniil had not spent the night with her since. This was God's will?

The priests preached submission. The imams and mullahs, too. Nasan tried, but submission did not come easily to her.

Ana understood: even as she wrote of resignation, she had sent a wise woman with herbs to protect and heal her daughter. But Natalya had not allowed the shaman to cross her threshold, summoning Father Job to banish the woman with his cross. Nasan had slipped out the back and reached the healer in time to prevent her from cursing the household, had sneaked her into the stables overnight and paid for her journey home, but the ties that bound her to this Russian family had frayed under the strain. Trust no one here, the spirits whispered. Not even Daniil, in time of need.

Grim and distant memories better left for lonely evenings. She returned her attention to Natalya. "I'm sorry, Mama-in-law. What do you wish me to do?"

Natalya waved at a distant fence. "Supervise the preparation of the herb garden. See that the servants plant what we need for medicines and for cooking. Herbs do more good than those foreign books you love to study."

Books. Always books. What's wrong with books?

As if she'd spoken the question aloud, Natalya answered it. "I've told you before. Books are for priests. A wife should occupy her mind with household tasks and with pleasing God and her husband."

Advice that Nasan had heard many times since entering the Kolychev house as a bride. "The books tell me what to plant, Mama-in-law. Perhaps we can find something to help you sleep."

She fought an urge to run for the stables, leap on her mare's unsaddled back, and ride until she reached the steppe. Eighteen, a woman grown, a wife, a mother but for that fateful day—she could not run away like a petulant child. But with each day that passed, her yearning for freedom grew.

"Valerian will help me sleep," Natalya said. "You don't need a book to tell you that. We grow it by the bushel basket already."

"Yes, Mama-in-law. I'll prepare some for you." Using the recipe in her books, which prescribed valerian, too. And while she did, she could check for other cures. Doctors healed the sick, and so would she—whatever Natalya thought of books.

Dismissed with a nod, Nasan took a few steps toward the herb garden.

A harsh cry brought her up short. She twisted her head right, then left. An injured child? A servant come to grief? She saw no evidence of an accident. Work in the courtyard proceeded as before.

A second cry, a third—each timber slightly different—gave way to a flurry of calls, loud and raucous, as if designed to catch her attention.

And they had. She knew the sound. Where had she heard it before?

Of course! Nasan tipped her head back, searching the sky. Outlined against the pale blue of the April morning, a large flock of swans spread its wings. They flew in a ragged line, a leader followed by groups of two or three, feathered bellies barely clearing the church spires.

They had just taken off, then. She imagined them feeding in the Moscow River, tails raised as they upended themselves in search of a tasty sedge. Perhaps they had nested there overnight, and something had startled them into flight. If permitted her morning's ride, she might have seen them: webbed feet kicking the water, fat bodies ungainly until the magical moment when their powerful wings lifted them into the air and they soared among the clouds like spirits of air, blessing all who beheld them.

Awed by their beauty, she could not take her eyes off them—haloed by the morning sun, white against the clear blue sky, yellow beaks with their distinctive black rims the only indication that they were birds, not disembodied angels. As they flew higher, the leader slowed and the pairs and trios sped up, forming by some unwritten rule the familiar arc of an unstrung bow.

O, to fly with the swans and leave behind household duties, uncaring husbands, and sick mothers-in-law!

Someone prodded Nasan in the upper arm. "The garden," Natalya said—oblivious, it seemed, to the beauty of swans.

And why was that a surprise?

Nasan cast one last, long glance at the flock, then set off once more, only to jump aside as a manservant raced in from the kitchens. Eyes glued to the sky, bow in one hand and quiver slung over the opposite shoulder, he would have collided with her if she had not leaped away from him.

As a result, he had no defense when she hauled the weapon from his grasp. "Stop!"

Arrows spilled from his quiver and clattered against the edge of the duck pond—the same one where the *albasti* had completed its evil deed. The impromptu shower scattered the ducks and raised a storm of quacking. She quelled the man's instinctive protest with her best haughty stare. "To shoot a swan offends the spirits," she told him. "Will you bring bad fortune upon us all?"

"Spirits?" Natalya stepped forward, frowning. "Nonsense. Try again, Vanka. A pair of those birds would make a lovely dinner."

Dinner? Nasan choked down the bile that rose to her throat. Her hands twitched as Vanka raised his bow. Could she snatch it from him again? Trip him as he took aim?

Grandmothers, deflect his arrow. Save them!

She inched forward and extended a slippered foot, only to feel Natalya's hand close on her elbow.

Nasan tugged free, ignoring her mother-in-law's stagger. She could not let these fools curse themselves. For better or worse, they were her family. Their fates and hers were intertwined.

Vanka dodged her, repositioned himself, then lowered his bow before she reached him. Hearing him swear under his breath, she glanced at the sky and realized that her diversion had worked. The swans had flown out of range.

Thank you, Grandmothers. A soft breeze touched her cheek, a spiritual caress.

Alas, Natalya would be furious. What were the chances of heading for the herb garden and avoiding a confrontation?

Next to none, Nasan decided. Any attempt to avoid the expected apology would lead to yet another scolding.

With reluctance, she turned, ready to get it over with. But before she had a chance to speak, a third voice, high and clear, entered the conversation. "Spirits," it scoffed. "Who but a pagan thinks that killing a swan brings misfortune?"

"Exactly," Natalya said. Her toe tapped the packed earth of the courtyard, and her mouth was pinched. "*Quite* un-Christian."

No acceptable answer came to mind, so Nasan switched her attention to the newcomer: Maria—the widow of Daniil's brother, Boris. A year older than Nasan but not a day wiser, kinder, or more responsible. Such a creature *would* see a swan as nothing but food on the wing. And responding to Maria was easier. They were equals within the family, as Natalya was not.

"How am I more pagan than you?" Nasan asked. "You appease the *domovoi*. You fear it will curdle the milk and make mischief among the servants. Are house imps more worthy than swans? At least *my* ancestors had the sense to revere something beautiful."

"*Your* ancestors," Maria retorted, "were barbarians and killers."

"I come from the line of Genghis Khan!"

"The greatest barbarian of the lot!" Maria stamped an emphatic foot.

Unbelievable. Nasan clamped her hands on her hips and tried to stare her sister-in-law down. "As if your father wouldn't jump at the chance to marry you off to one of my cousins. Not that they'd have you!"

"Ugh! Who wants a Tatar husband? But when my father gives me to a good *Orthodox* Russian, I'll be sure to invite you to the wedding, so you can watch me serve swan." Maria plucked an imaginary piece of meat from the air and pretended to chew it. "Mmm. Delicious."

She must *want* to bring the wrath of Heaven down on their heads. Nasan, muttering a plea to the spirits to excuse her sister-in-law's stupidity, had no words left to explain to Maria the enormity of what she intended. Nasan's palm burned as it hit her sister-in-law's cheek, and Maria's howl of outrage drowned the cries of the distant flock. Nasan ducked as nails long as a hawk's talons reached for her face, but not before she felt her headdress drag at her hair. Maria grabbed it and pulled. Nasan let out a shriek of her own as the pins securing her braids dug into her skull.

"Girls, girls." Natalya caught the combatants by the arm and shoved them apart. "Behave yourselves, both of you. No insults, no slapping, no hair pulling. The Bible teaches us to turn the other cheek when we are provoked." She shook her finger in Nasan's face. "That applies especially to you, young lady. And Maria, what brings you here? I sent you to take charge of the laundry."

"I heard the noise and came to investigate," Maria said, simpering. "In case someone was hurt. Those cries—I thought a child must have fallen."

"Yes, of course," Natalya said. "Such a hubbub over a flock of birds." She frowned at Nasan. "Tearing weapons from the servants' hands, slapping your sister—I'm of a mind to send you off to confess your sins to Father Job. Fifty prostrations and no dinner should straighten you out. Especially fitting since you robbed the family of its feast."

Nasan lowered her eyes. Her cheeks burned. Every time she thought she had conquered her temper, something happened to prove her wrong. But really, Maria had asked for it. She should thank the stars that she didn't find itching powder in her sheets or a potion slipped in her food to rid her of that devil-spawn hair. And Maria had fought back. Why was Natalya not threatening to punish them both?

But how humiliating to be sent off to bed without her supper like a disobedient child, or even to fulfill whatever penance Natalya forced Father Job to impose. Nasan gritted her teeth and said, "I'm sorry, Mama-in-law. Please give me leave to tend to the herb garden as you ordered."

"Apologize to your sister," Natalya said, her voice steely.

Maria smirked and looked demure, like a person who would not think of skipping her assigned tasks or ripping Nasan's headdress from her head.

The unfairness, when she had tried to save these reckless women from themselves!

But there was no mistaking the determination in Natalya's face. Nasan crossed her arms and bowed to Maria. "I apologize, sister, for my unruly temper."

"Very well," Natalya said. "I forgive you. Your turn, Maria. Irina's lack of control does not excuse yours."

Irina. Nasan gave an involuntary shudder at the sound of her Russian name, which Natalya insisted on using, as if bent on obliterating her unsatisfactory daughter-in-law's very self. Two years of marriage, and Nasan had yet to adjust to the loss of her past. To Daniil's credit, no matter how angry with her he became, he used her Russian name only with others, never when they were alone.

Maria could not contain her moue of distaste, but she straightened her face and stepped forward. "I am sorry, dear sister, for responding in kind to your unprovoked attack." She pressed her powdered cheek against Nasan's in a pseudo-embrace.

Nasan bit her tongue. *That* qualified as an apology? But Natalya was nodding in approbation, as if Maria had done what she asked.

I must go, before I say something unpardonable.

The herb garden beckoned, a refuge. Nasan bowed once more in farewell. But as she straightened, her mother-in-law hunched over. Another fit of coughing wracked Natalya's sturdy form. She pressed a hand to her mouth. For the second time that day, she swayed.

Nasan reacted on instinct. Her arm circled Natalya's waist, steadying her. "Mama-in-law, you are ill. Sit, please. Maria and I will tend to the household while you rest."

"Speak for yourself, *sister*," Maria snapped. "I have my hands full."

Nasan glared at her. "Standing there doing nothing? Don't be ridiculous."

"I'm overseeing the laundry—or was, until you caused a commotion." Maria looked so prim and proper that Nasan longed to slap her again.

Natalya patted Nasan's shoulder. "That's thoughtful of you, child. I'll stop if I must. But we have baking loaves to oversee, and I should tell the steward to order more hops before we run out of ale. I gave you a task. Supervise the planting."

"I can do those things, too," Nasan said, pitching her voice in the dulcet range Natalya preferred. "Unless you'd rather entrust them to Maria." Maria's smug expression evaporated in a snort, and Nasan suppressed a smile.

"I'd sooner rely on the butcher's dog," Natalya muttered.

Nasan stared at her. Had Mama-in-law *said* that? Natalya crossed herself and mumbled a prayer, her cheeks red despite the general pallor of her countenance.

Off to one side, Maria glowered. For a wild moment, Nasan wondered if Natalya saw through Maria after all.

Or does she mean me?

Probably. It was the last straw. "I'll get started then," she said.

Natalya waved her off, and Nasan went—as quickly as decorum allowed. She had had quite enough of the Kolychev women for one morning.

http://www.fivedirectionspress.com/the-swan-princess

This book was typeset using Garamond, a body font dating from the early days of printing, with headings in Tangerine, chosen for its Arabic lines, evocative of Tatar script. The ornaments come from Type Embellishments One LET.

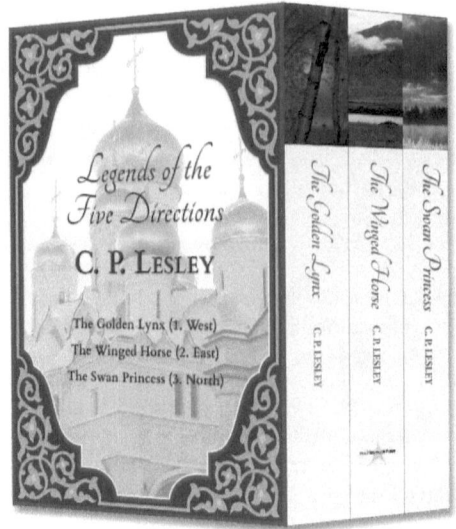

WHO IS THE GOLDEN LYNX?

This question drives the first book in Legends of the Five Directions, a series that will sweep you to the distant world of sixteenth-century Russia, amid the descendants of Genghis Khan and courts that could teach the Borgias a thing or two about political ambition, assassination, and chicanery. Follow Nasan and her kinsfolk as they struggle for power, honor, identity, and love across the steppe and through the vast forests of the Russian North.

"A richly depicted, exciting adventure set amongst the Tatars of 16th-century Central Russia. Fans of historical romance will find this a delight."
— Yangsze Choo, author of the acclaimed novel *The Ghost Bride*

http://www.fivedirectionspress.com/boxsets